Resounding Praise for the Novels of
New York Times Bestselling Author
LISA KLEYPAS

"DELIGHTFUL!"
Jill Barnett

"A DELICIOUS TREAT
FOR ROMANCE READERS."
Mary Jo Putney

"MS. KLEYPAS DOESN'T LET
TRUE ROMANTICS DOWN."
Cincinnati Enquirer

"WONDERFUL . . .
GRATIFYING AND DELIGHTFUL."
Denver Rocky Mountain News

"BRISK PACING, WITTY REPARTEE AND
MEMORABLE PROTAGONISTS."
Publishers Weekly

Avon Books by
Lisa Kleypas

LISA KLEYPAS

ONLY WITH YOUR LOVE

AVON BOOKS

An Imprint of HarperCollinsPublishers

This is a work of fiction. Names, characters, places, and incidents are products of the author's imagination or are used fictitiously and are not to be construed as real. Any resemblance to actual events, locales, organizations, or persons, living or dead, is entirely coincidental.

AVON BOOKS
An Imprint of HarperCollins*Publishers*
10 East 53rd Street
New York, New York 10022-5299

Copyright © 1992 by Lisa Kleypas
ISBN: 0-380-76151-3
www.avonromance.com

First Avon Books paperback printing: October 1992

Avon Trademark Reg. U.S. Pat. Off. and in Other Countries, Marca Registrada, Hecho en U.S.A.
HarperCollins® is a trademark of HarperCollins Publishers Inc.

Printed in the U.S.A.

10

To Pamela Bergeron with love . . .
Carpe Diem!

ONLY WITH YOUR LOVE

Prologue

The Gulf of Mexico
April, 1817

Together they lay in the tumbled bed, listening to the creaking of the ship. Celia rested quietly against her husband's chest, looking around the elegantly fitted cabin with a touch of wistfulness. In the long days since they had set sail from France the cabin had become a safe cocoon to her, a place she did not want to leave. A different world awaited her in New Orleans, one she was not at all certain she was prepared for.

"We are in the Gulf now," Philippe said, easing her from his chest and sitting up. The muscled surface of his back rippled as he stretched. "The journey is almost over, Celia. We should be home this very night."

"Home," she repeated with a forced smile.

Sensitive to the lack of enthusiasm in her voice, Philippe turned and looked down at her, bracing his hands on either side of her slight body. Modestly she rearranged the ruffled neckline of her nightgown and pulled the sheet higher over her breasts.

"Celia," he said tenderly, "there is nothing to

1

be afraid of. You are going to love New Orleans. You are going to love my family."

"If only I could be certain they were going to love me!"

Philippe's family was one of the most renowned in New Orleans. His father, Maximilien Vallerand, was a powerful man, a Creole aristocrat with vast wealth and political influence. In addition to his plantation he owned a small but profitable shipping business. In fact, the vessel they were on, the *Golden Star*, was a Vallerand merchant ship.

"They already love you," Philippe said with a smile. "They know all about you. After I finished my studies in France and returned to New Orleans, I could talk about nothing but you. And I read your letters aloud—"

"Philippe!" she exclaimed, a horrified blush flooding her cheeks. Emotions had always been difficult for her to express. To think of her private feelings being aired in front of Philippe's family—

"Carefully *edited* versions of your letters," Philippe said, and grinned at her affectionately. "Certain parts I reserved for only myself."

Celia stared up at him, entranced as always by his coaxing smile. He was the only man who had ever been able to reach beyond her shyness. Gentle and patient, he made allowances for her that no one else did. In the past men had been attracted by her looks but were always discouraged by her withdrawn manner. They had no way of knowing it was fear, not indifference, that made her so awkward and quiet. But for Philippe it was unimportant that she was not flirtatious or seductive.

"Did you tell your family I was a . . . an old maid?" she asked.

Philippe laughed. "Twenty-four isn't old, *chérie*."

"*Oui*, for a woman it is!"

"You could have been married long ago had you wanted it." He bent over and nuzzled into the soft curve of her neck. "You are a beautiful woman, Celia. You have no excuse for being so shy."

"I'm not beautiful," she said gruffly.

"Yes, you are. Extraordinarily beautiful." He smoothed her long hair, which glinted with the silvery-gold of moonlight, and stared into her soft brown eyes. He brushed a kiss over her lips. "And even if you weren't, I would still adore you."

Celia was filled with happiness as she looked up at him. Sometimes it was difficult to believe he was really hers. He was so handsome, with his thick black hair and blue eyes. She had never thought a man could be at once as strong and tender as he was.

"*Je t'aime*," she said, her voice soft and loving.

"No, no," he remonstrated with a smile. "English from now on. In the Vallerand household it is used at least as much as French."

Celia gave him a mock scowl and replied in her faulty English, "But . . . it sound better in French."

"Yes, it does," Philippe agreed with a smile. Carefully he pulled the sheet from her hands and eased it down to her hips. She stiffened and he laughed softly, his hand skimming over her meagerly clad body. "Still shy with me? . . . I won't allow it, *chérie*. You know me well enough by now to be certain I would never hurt you."

"I-I know you through letters, and chaperoned visits," she said breathlessly, doing nothing to stop the exploration of that warm, gentle hand. "But we have not spent much time alone together, Philippe, and . . ." Her words trailed away as he fondled her breast through the folds of her nightgown.

"And?" he whispered, staring into her eyes.

Trembling, she slid her arms around his neck, forgetting what she had been about to say.

His lips curved with a smile. "It is only because I love you so much that I've been patient with you. I want you, Celia. It has been torture, sleeping in the same bed with you and not making you my wife in truth. The vows have been said, and you belong to me till death do us part. But you asked me to wait, and I agreed because I didn't want you to be afraid of me—or of the intimacies we'll share." He kissed her forehead gently. "We've waited long enough, *ma chère.*"

"I . . . I feel the same, but—"

"Do you?" he murmured. "I don't think so. You'll have to show me." He lowered his mouth to hers and kissed her.

She protested feebly, understanding that Philippe's patience had finally run out. "Philippe, you have been so kind—"

"I don't want to be kind anymore. I want my wife." His hands swept over her body, cupping her breasts, pulling at the twisted fabric of her gown. "Show me, Celia," he whispered against her neck. She shivered at the scratch of his unshaven jaw, and turned her mouth to his.

Suddenly there was a loud rapping on the cabin portal.

"Monsieur Vallerand! Monsieur!" a young midshipman called out, his fist hammering on the mahogany paneling. There was no mistaking the terror in his voice. Celia stiffened in alarm as Philippe leaped from the bed. Not bothering to put on his breeches or even a robe, Philippe opened the door a few inches. "What is it?" he asked tersely.

"Captain Tierney sent me to warn you . . ." the boy said, gulping for air. "American-made schooner in distress . . . We went to assist . . . They just hoisted the Cartagena flag."

Before Philippe could utter a word the boy disappeared, shouting hoarsely. Beyond the door there was an explosion of noise and movement. "Boardaway!" someone was calling. "Boarders on the starboard bow!" Celia could hear the sound of gunfire and the clash of swords coming from the deck. The ship was under attack!

Startled, she lifted a hand to her throat, feeling her pulse thrash underneath her skin.

"Pirates," she managed to say.

Philippe did not deny it.

Thoughts whirled through Celia's mind. She had heard of the privateers who sailed against Spain with letters of marque from Cartagena. They prowled the waters of the Gulf, the Bahama Channel, and the Caribbean. She had heard the stories of their robbery and cruelty, how they tortured their victims, the horrible things they did to women. Fear rose in her throat, and she swallowed hard to keep it down. No, it can't be real, she thought. It is just a nightmare . . . oh, let it be a nightmare!

Philippe was yanking on his breeches and boots and shrugging into a white shirt. "Get dressed," he said shortly, and fumbled in a built-in rosewood cabinet for a brace of pistols.

Teeth chattering, Celia hopped from the bed to the floor, abandoning her modesty in favor of haste. Feverishly she searched through the trunk where some of her clothes were kept and found a blue damask gown. She nearly ripped her nightgown as she pulled it off, then yanked the damask over her body, not bothering with undergarments. Her pale silken hair flew in wild locks, falling over her face and neck, trailing down to her waist. While she searched for a ribbon to tie it back with, she heard bloodcurdling yells from above, and she quivered violently.

"How could this happen?" she heard herself asking. "How could Captain Tierney not know they were pirates? Why aren't we firing any of the cannon? Why—"

"Too late for cannon fire. Apparently they've already boarded the ship."

Philippe strode to her and took her hand, and Celia looked down as she felt the cold press of metal in her palm. He had given her a dueling pistol, a flintlock made of blackened iron! Slowly she raised her eyes to his.

There was a strange look on his face . . . alert, urgent, fearful. She supposed she must have appeared dazed, because he shook her gently, as if to bring her to attention. "Celia, listen to me. The gun will fire only once. If they come in here . . . you understand what you're to do with it?"

She gave a slight nod, her breath rattling in her throat.

"Good girl," Philippe murmured, and took her head in his hands, kissing her hard. She accepted the pressure of his lips docilely, still numbed by the realization that it was all really happening. It was too fast—there was no time to think.

"T-tell me it will be all right," she stammered, clinging to the front of his shirt. "Philippe—"

He wrapped his arms around her, holding her to him. "Of course it will," he said against her hair. "Don't be afraid, Celia. I—" He stopped abruptly, giving her a crushing hug before releasing her. Stepping back, he turned to leave the cabin.

Silently his name formed on Celia's lips. *Philippe.* As he walked away from her, the shadows in the companionway enveloped him in darkness. He did not look back. She was seized by a horrible premonition. "*Mon Dieu*, I'll never see you again," she whispered, and she felt her knees begin to wobble. Stumbling to the door, she bolted it with shaking hands, then backed into the corner of the room, the pistol cradled against her breast.

Chapter 1

Before ten minutes had passed the sounds of combat died away and hundreds of footsteps seemed to pound the deck. Celia remained in the cabin, longing to open the door and see what had happened. But all she could do was wait with terrified anticipation.

She stiffened with alarm as heavy feet walked the length of the companionway and the door rattled. "Locked," a voice growled. Celia jumped as a blunt object crashed against the other side of the door, splintering the fine paneling. Swiftly she readied the gun to fire. Another sharp blow, and the hinges creaked in protest.

Celia used her palm to wipe at the cold sweat on her face. She raised the barrel of the pistol, pressing it to her temple. At the touch of the metal to her skin, thoughts raced through her mind. If Philippe had died, she would not want to live. And if she did not use the gun on herself now, she would face a horrifying fate at the hands of the sea bandits. But something inside rebelled at the thought of pulling the trigger. She took a deep breath and steadied her hands.

The door crashed open. Frozen, she stared at the two men who stood there, both swarthy and unkempt, their matted hair held back with kerchiefs, their faces sunburned and stubbled. The shorter of the two held a cutlass in his hand, while the other clasped a bloodstained boarding pike.

Dropping his cutlass, the small but sturdily built man stepped over the sill at the bottom of the doorway. He licked his lips and watched her with keen eyes. "Put it down," he muttered in a thick American accent, gesturing to the gun.

Celia couldn't utter a word. *Now*, her mind insisted, *end it now* . . . But her arm lowered to her side. In a flash of self-hatred, she realized she was too much of a coward to take her own life.

"I'll stake me share of th'spoils now," one pirate said to the other. His mouth split in a yellow-toothed grin as he walked toward her.

Automatically Celia raised the gun and squeezed the trigger, feeling as if some force outside herself was guiding her actions. The bullet that should have ended her own life buried itself in the man's chest. A crimson flood spread over his unwashed shirt. Blood spattered everywhere, and Celia heard herself scream as the body crumpled at her feet.

"Little bitch!" Enraged, the other pirate grabbed her and threw her against the wall. The pistol fell from her hand and clattered to the floor. Her head hit the hard surface, and she half-fainted, sinking into a world filled with gray mist. She moaned as she was dragged through the companionway and up to the main deck, where she was dropped to the yellow planking. The ship rang with the sound of voices, and barrels and boxes being moved across the deck. There was a strange smell mingling with the scents of salt water and sea air.

Blinking hard and pushing herself up to a sit-

ting position, Celia saw one of the pirates drop a
crate of chickens, some of the live cargo taken
aboard to allow the crew of the *Golden Star* occa-
sional rations of fresh meat. The crate broke open
and the frightened birds scuttled in every direction, causing an outbreak of laughter and swearing. As she looked at the scene around her, Celia
put a hand to her mouth, afraid she was going to
be sick.

There were bodies everywhere, with gaping
holes, partially severed limbs, and glassy stares.
The deck was coated with blood. She recognized
some of the lifeless faces . . . the ship's cooper,
always so cheerfully busy with his hoops and
staves; the sailmaker; the cook; the boy who had
served as tailor and cobbler; some of the officers
with whom she and Philippe had shared meals.
Philippe . . . Frantically she crawled toward the
bodies, desperate to find her husband.

A booted foot shoved her back to the deck. She
cried out in pain as a hand tangled in her hair
and jerked her head back. Motionless, she stared
into the cruelest eyes she had ever seen. The man
was smooth-shaven and darkly tanned, his jaw
thin, his nose a decisive point in a sharp-featured
face. His hair was dark reddish-brown, pulled
back in a neat braided queue. Unlike the others
of the boarding party, he wore well-made clothes
that had been tailored to fit his wiry body.

"You cost me a good man," he said in a crisp
voice. "For that you'll make amends." He in-
spected her slim-hipped, small-breasted body
with an asexual glance. She tried to push down
the hem of her gown, which had ridden up to
expose her bare feet and calves. He smiled, revealing a jagged line of teeth. "Yes. You'll serve
as entertainment for my brother André." His

hand tightened in her hair, bringing tears of pain to her eyes. "André needs a steady supply of women. Unfortunately they never last long with him."

One of the pirates approached them. He was a stocky young man with heavily developed arms and chest. "Captain Legare, the best of the cargo should take well nigh an hour to unload. Not much gold, sir, but some fine dry goods, cinnamon, brandy, oil in jars—"

"Good. As for the remainder of their crew, lock them in the hold. We'll set fire to the ship when we put away for the island." Legare shoved Celia at the young man. "Bind the wench and put her in with the spoils. We're taking her with us. And tell the men not to touch her. She's for André."

At the mention of the *Star's* crew, Celia had begun to struggle. "There are some still alive?" she gasped.

The young man dragged her away, seeming not to hear her.

"*S'il vous plaît, aidez-moi,*" she begged, writhing in his grasp. Realizing he could not understand her, she switched to English. "Please help me. My husband is maybe still alive . . . He . . . he will make you rich if you help us. He is a Vallerand, Philippe Vallerand—"

"If he's alive, it won't be for long," the pirate replied coolly. "Legare leaves no one behind. He's very thorough. Haven't you heard of the Legare brothers? They own the Gulf. Only a fool would try to cross—"

He was interrupted by her cry of horror. "Philippe!" She struggled so frantically, clawing and biting, that he let go of her with a curse. Celia scrambled to a body slumped over the railing. "Oh God, *Philippe!*" The shirt over her husband's back was soaked with blood that seeped from a pike wound. His eyes were closed, his mouth frozen in a deathlike grimace. Sobbing, she searched for a pulse in his throat. There was no sign of life. As she tried to ease his body to the deck, the pirate seized her again.

"This is your husband?" he asked contemptuously. "Fine ransom I'd get for a dead man." With one efficient shove, he sent Philippe's body hurtling down to the ocean, where it splashed and floated among the other corpses.

Celia could not breathe. A wave of blackness seemed to rise up from the deck and smother her. Helplessly she collapsed in the pirate's arms, letting the darkness cover everything.

Locked in the belly of the ship with the booty taken from the *Golden Star*, Celia awakened slowly. Her hands and feet were tied. Groaning faintly, she sat up and squinted through the darkness. She could see nothing. Exploring cautiously with her feet, she gathered she had been set among a pile of crates, barrels, and casks. The rise and fall of the ship betrayed the fact that the pirates' schooner was making considerable headway. Captain Legare had said something about an island. She wondered dully how long it would take before the ship came to anchor there.

Her head snapped from right to left as she heard a tiny scrabbling sound. Her breath stopped. Drawing her knees up, she waited tensely, wondering if she might have imagined the noise. Suddenly there was an investigative nibble at her toe. She gave a shrill scream and kicked out with her feet. Mice? Rats? Oh God, how long was she going to be trapped down here with them? In the darkness there were more sounds, the pad of animal feet on the planking, a brief scuffle, a rodent squeaking.

Celia burst into tears, realizing that there was something else besides rodents in the hold. Should she scream for help? No one would bother to come to her aid. Her thoughts were interrupted by a quiet, steady purr somewhere nearby. She jerked in surprise as a warm, furry body brushed against her arm. A cat. Its long whiskers tickled as it rubbed the side of its face against her arm. She moved slightly, and her foot encountered the dead body of the mouse. With a shudder of disgust, she kicked it away.

One paw at a time, the cat crept into her lap. Celia did nothing to disturb it. She had always detested cats, thinking them sly, sneaking creatures, but this particular one she was willing to make friends with. "*Mon ami,* you've done more to protect me than anyone else today," she said in a watery voice, her head inclined toward the contented creature, who was kneading the fabric of her dress with its paws. The cat soon ventured off to investigate a noise, but later it returned to her lap.

Leaning her head against the side of a barrel, Celia murmured ceaseless prayers until she sank into an exhausted silence. Images floated before her, remembrances of childhood and her family, but most of all of Philippe. She remembered the first time they met. Her father, Dr. Robert Verité, had invited him to dinner. "Philippe Vallerand," her father announced, welcoming the young man into their small but cozy home. "An American, and one of my medical students . . . but well-mannered for all that." Good-naturedly they cleared a place for him at their long table. Be-

mused, Philippe stared at the enormous family.
"Eight children," Verité said with a hearty
chuckle. "Big, healthy brood. A man couldn't
ask for better. Here now, Claudette, change
places with your sister so she can sit by our
guest. You're already promised to a young man.
Let Celia have the chance to catch one!"

It was all Celia could do to keep from running
out of the room. Embarrassed and shy, she sat
stiff-backed in the vacant chair next to the handsome stranger.

The family began the meal in its usual noisy
way. The Verités all possessed dominating personalities. It had always been easier for Celia, the
oldest child, to fade into the background and let
the others attract the attention. Since their mother
had died ten years before, she had taken care of
them all, settling into a quiet domestic role. Men
had always found her company pleasant but far
from alluring. Long ago she had reconciled herself to becoming a spinster devoted to the service
of her family.

Celia watched as Philippe Vallerand adroitly
handled a barrage of questions, unintimidated by
the clamor surrounding him. His smile was natural and easy, his features clean and fine-edged,
his thick, close-cut hair a shade of brown so dark
it was almost black.

Mercifully he said nothing to her. It would have
terrified her to have to respond to even the most
mundane question. But every now and then he
would glance at her with those bright blue eyes,
and she had the feeling he could read her mind.
As the family laughed boisterously at her father's
humorous account of a surly patient, Celia felt
something slide from the pocket of her apron and
fall to the floor. It was a small book she had been

reading in her spare moments. Ducking to retrieve it, she nearly bumped heads with Philippe.

She curved her fingers around the book, and her heart stopped as Philippe's hand closed gently around her frail wrist.

"I-I have it," she managed to whisper. The family's chatter continued above them, but he kept holding her arm, while his other hand gently pried the book from her grasp.

"Rousseau," he remarked softly. "You like to read philosophy, mademoiselle?"

"S-sometimes."

"So do I. Would you allow me to borrow this?" The book looked absurdly small in his hand.

She thought briefly of refusing his request, since lending it to him would necessitate the ordeal of having him return it. But her fear of seeming rude outweighed her fear of the handsome stranger. "Yes, monsieur," she said timidly.

Still, he did not let go of her wrist. "Yes, Philippe," he prompted, a teasing light in his eyes.

She stared at him in astonishment. Surely he knew how improper it would be for her to call him by his first name.

Her father's voice resounded over the table. "Young Vallerand, may I ask what causes you to hide under the table with my daughter?"

Flushed and bewildered, Celia tugged at her wrist, but he would not let go. "Yes, Philippe," she said in a frantic whisper, and was rewarded with a slow smile as he released her.

He returned with the book a few days later, and in his quiet way insisted she take him outside to show him their garden. As they talked, she realized with some surprise that her usual shyness seemed to have disappeared. She confided in him more readily than she did in her own brothers and sisters. She was not afraid of him . . . not until he pulled her behind a wall of climbing roses and bent his head to kiss her.

"No," she said, twisting away from him, her heart racing.

"Untouchable," he murmured against her cheek, wrapping his arms tightly around her. "That's how everyone thinks of you, isn't it? You don't need anyone. You don't need anything but your books and your solitude." His lips were hot against her face, seeming to scorch her skin.

"Yes," she heard herself whisper. "That is what they think."

"I know it isn't true." His mouth played gently at the corner of her lips. "I understand you, Celia. You need to be loved. And you're going to be mine . . ."

In the dark, fetid ship's hold, Celia blotted her tears on her shoulder. It had taken her so long to realize that Philippe's love for her was real and lasting. He had gone back to New Orleans and stayed for three years until the American war with the British was over and international waters were declared safe once more. Three years of waiting and writing letters, three years of hope and frustration and doubt.

But Philippe had returned to France to make her his wife and take her back to New Orleans with him. Finally she had let herself believe that they would have a life together, and it had all been taken away in the space of few minutes. Now Philippe was dead. She felt ashamed of herself, for not only was she consumed with grief, she was also angry at him. It made no sense to blame Philippe—none of it had been his fault—but still she was angry that he had not been able to foresee the danger. She stared blindly into the stifling darkness while the drowsy cat rearranged itself on her lap. Now that Philippe was gone, she had no desire to live. She could only hope that death would come to her quickly, and that she would have the courage to face it with dignity.

He had several aliases, but his crew knew him as Captain Griffin. Like the mythical monster with the wings of an eagle and the body of a lion, he was swift, cunning, and lethal. Under his command a schooner could outsail any other vessel on the water. He sailed as he did everything else, by instinct. It was because of him that his men worked without the usual sloppiness of pirate crews, for he had made them understand that discipline and efficiency were the quickest means to the end they all desired.

Stretching out his long legs on the beach, Griffin settled his broad back against a grounded pirogue and lit a thin black cigar. After placing the cigar between his lips, he rubbed a hand over his shaggy beard and pushed back an unruly lock of hair that had fallen over his face. His blue eyes, as dark as the sea at midnight, sought and found his own ship *Vagabond* moored in the harbor.

For the past few days the schooner had been tucked in the safety of the harbor of Isle au Corneille, Crow's Island. More than a dozen other vessels were anchored there—brigantines, gunboats, and schooners of varying sizes, all armed to the teeth. Almost thirty warehouses—not to mention a village of palmetto-thatched huts, a brothel, and a few large slave corrals—had been built amid the thick groves of shrubs and twisted oak trees on the island.

While *Vagabond* was at anchor its crew had partaken of whores and spirits, both of which were cheap and plentiful here. Meanwhile at Griffin's orders the cargo had been appraised and unloaded into relay warehouses. As usual, the spoils of their recent plunders had been divided equally among the hundred men who comprised his crew.

Griffin drew again on the cigar and breathed out a puff of smoke. He was relaxed but still alert. Now that he had been declared an outlaw by the American government, he could never afford to let his guard down. A year ago, his ventures had been more or less legal. Armed with letters of marque from Cartagena, a seaport on the Caribbean coast of South America, he had preyed upon Spanish commerce and garnered a considerable fortune. But along the way it had been impossible to resist capturing a few fat-bellied merchant ships from other nations he had *not* been commissioned to attack . . . hence the upgrading of his status from privateer to full-fledged pirate. Griffin's only hard-and-fast rule was that his ship left American vessels unmolested. Everything else was fair game.

Feeling in need of a drink, Griffin stubbed out the cigar and rose to his feet in a lithe movement. He headed toward the crumbling fort, which contained the closest thing to a saloon the island possessed. It was a dismantled brig, set in the sand and converted into a tavern and dwelling place.

Brilliant with lamps and torchlight, the tavern, dubbed the Cat's-head, beckoned invitingly. It was filled with unruly seamen. Many of them were Legare's men, just in from a successful tour of the Gulf. Even in their drunken merriment the men took care to avoid Griffin as he crossed the threshold.

''Cap'n,'' a voice hailed from a table in the corner. Griffin threw a glance over his shoulder. It was John Risk, a black-haired Irishman with an able sword arm and a perpetually roguish grin. Risk was the second-in-command and the best cannoneer on Griffin's ship. He wore a black patch where one of his eyes used to be. The eye had been lost just last year, when he had saved Griffin's life during a hand-to-hand contest on the deck of a ship they were boarding. A hard-faced whore perched on Risk's lap, holding a half-empty bottle of rum.

"Cap'n, are we planning to up-anchor soon?" Risk asked carefully.

Griffin reached for the bottle, took a healthy swig, and wiped his mouth with the back of his hand. "Are you that eager to leave, Jack?"

"Aye, I've had a bellyful o' Legare's men boastin'. 'Twas six prizes they tuck on this trip . . . well now, didn't we do the same not three months ago? Next time out we'll show them rovers how to pack on sail! We'll come back towin' ten prize ships behind us! We'll—"

"We'll lay low for the time being," Griffin interrupted dryly. "After all the recent activity, the Gulf is crawling with gunboats fresh from New Orleans."

Risk scowled. "Aye, Cap'n. If that's what yer gut tells ye—"

"It is."

"Ye got the ship stocked heavy with supplies," Risk said reflectively. "P'raps we're finally settin' out to the middle passage?"

An ominous glint entered Griffin's dark blue eyes. "I don't run slaves, Jack."

"Aye, but the money to be made—"

"We make enough doing things my way."

Risk shrugged cheerfully. "Can't argue with

that, Cap'n. But the divvil knows Dominic Legare makes no scruple of it.'' He lifted the rum bottle to his lips, drank deeply, and shook his head. ''Six prizes,'' he muttered. ''Just look at that André Legare, fat bastard, with his bloody big grin, knowin' his brother Nicky's going to cut him a nice big slice of the spoils. For doing nothin' except anchoring his arse in a tavern while the rest of us—''

''Enough, Jack,'' Griffin said coolly, and Risk quieted.

Griffin looked in the direction Risk had pointed. André Legare was indeed wearing a grin. As usual, he was surrounded by platters of food and bottles of wine, his large belly overflowing onto his lap. His perspiring face was half-covered by a reddish beard clotted with scraps of meat and grease.

The differences between the Legare brothers were striking. Dominic was a cold, efficient shark, seeming to take pleasure in nothing except hunting and providing for his younger brother. A peculiarly self-contained man, he had never been seen with either women or boys, never drank, never acknowledged pain or required anything for his own comfort. He was excruciatingly meticulous in his dress and appearance. André, on the other hand, was a buffoon, a rotund, slovenly man with a bottomless appetite for food, drink, and women—in precisely that order.

''Dominic's brought a new woman for André,'' Risk commented. ''Heard the commotion when they took her off the *Vulture*—she's got a scream that'll make yer ears wither up and drop off. Poor wench. Do ye know what happened to the last one Dominic gave him? She was all—''

''Yes,'' Griffin said shortly, finding the subject

distasteful. Unfortunately, he'd once happened to see one of André Legare's victims as the body was being deposited on the shore. The girl had been tortured and mutilated by André's vicious sexual games. Those who knew of the younger Legare's treatment of women were repelled, but no one interfered. On Isle au Corneille a man's business was his own, unless it happened to interfere with yours.

Risk lightly jostled the prostitute on his lap. "Tell me now, darlin', why is it I never see André Legare with his paws on ye and yer erring sisters?"

"Dominic won't let 'im," she replied with a saucy pout. "We makes a good profit for the Legares."

Risk pretended dismay. "Then . . . in a roundabout way I've added to their pockets? And them already flush with money?" He pushed her off his knee, nearly causing her to land on the floor. "Shove off, darlin' . . . I've lost me yen for love tonight." As the whore scowled, he grinned and flipped her a gold piece. "An' do say somethin' nice about me to the other sisters. I'll be back again."

Catching the coin expertly, she slanted a smile at him and strolled away with swaying hips.

Griffin had retreated into the shadowy corner, paying little attention to Risk's antics. His attention was focused on Dominic Legare and his entourage, who had just entered the tavern and gathered at the opposite corner of the room. Bottles were passed around, brandy and rum splashing over the tables and floor. Carousing and singing drunkenly, they crowded around André while Dominic watched. A presentation was about to take place. When the last notes of the ribald sea chantey died away, Dominic snapped his fingers and gestured to someone behind him.

A roar of approval set the walls to trembling as a woman was dragged out of concealment and thrust in front of André. She was clad in a tattered, bloodstained gown, her legs and feet bare, her arms bound behind her. She should have been in hysterics, but she was silent and outwardly calm. Her gaze flickered around the room. Griffin realized with a touch of unwilling admiration that she was trying to assess her chances of escape.

"Lovely," Risk muttered. "A choice bit of goods, aye?"

Griffin agreed silently. She was obviously a woman of quality, with fair skin and delicate features. Her tangled blond hair glittered in the torchlight, pale and silvery and rare. He could not look away from her, could only stare while an unreasonable tide of wanting swept over him. She was too thin, breakably fragile. His taste was for robust women who would not be intimidated by a man his size. But he could not repress the thought of what it would be like to fit himself between her slender legs and crush her sweet mouth under his. The image caused a hot stirring in his loins.

Griffin folded his arms across his chest and leaned back against the wall, deciding that this was the first foolish move he had ever seen Dominic Legare make. Such a woman shouldn't be wasted on André.

"Why the hell are we nivver findin' women like that on *our* prize ships?" Risk wondered aloud.

After squealing in delight and wiping his greasy face on his sleeve, André caught the woman's slim hips and jerked her down to his lap. "By

God, Dominic, this is the best one yet!" His pudgy hands roamed over her. "So sweet, so soft . . . I'll make her scream for me tonight!"

"Yes, *mon frère*, do what you like with her," Dominic said. His tone was dry, but his lips were curved in a benevolent smile.

André rubbed his hands over her hair and smooth-skinned face. "I've never had a woman with this color hair. I'll have to make this one last."

Celia closed her eyes. His breath was rank enough to make her ill. The feel of his mouth on her face was more than she could endure. As he tried to kiss her, she jerked her head to the side and bit his ear, hard enough to taste blood. Screaming in sudden surprise and rage, André let go of her. Quickly she scrambled away and darted through the tavern.

Ignoring the stinging of her bare feet, Celia made her way toward the open door, her pulse racing in powerful surges. There was shouting and laughter behind her. The side of her hip bumped painfully into a chair. It was useless to run, but she didn't care. The will to live flooded through her, and every nerve screamed for her to escape.

Just before she reached the door a booted foot obstructed her path, and instantly her mad flight was over. She tripped and began to fall. The hard floor rose up swiftly to meet her. There was no way to save herself—her arms were tied behind her back. Suddenly she was caught and pulled upright by an unyielding arm. Gasping, she wondered how someone could have moved fast enough to stop her from hitting the floor. Her unseen rescuer steadied her by the shoulders, holding her facing away from him.

The owner of the foot that had tripped her stood up. "John Risk," the one-eyed pirate introduced himself with a devilish grin. "Where are ye running to, darlin'? Outside is no place for a lady. Ye'd be caught and ravished in a minute by the rovers on the beach."

"Help me," she said urgently, while Legare's men swarmed around them. For once her English was flawless. "I-I am a Vallerand. Take me to New Orleans. Maximilien Vallerand will reward you well for my safe return."

Risk's expression of insolent amusement vanished, and he looked up at the man behind her with a questioning frown.

Celia quivered as the man who held her bent to murmur in her ear. "By what claim are you a Vallerand?" His voice was deep and husky, and it sent chills down her spine. She tried to twist around to see him, but he would not let her.

"I am the w-wife of Dr. Philippe Vallerand," she stammered. "Our ship . . . the *Golden Star* . . . They killed my husband. It was yesterday, I think . . . perhaps the day before."

The fingers on her shoulders tightened, then tightened again, until she let out a cry of pain. The crushing hands relaxed their cruel grip.

"My God," Celia heard him say softly.

"You . . . you have heard of the Vallerands?" she asked.

Abruptly Dominic Legare was before her, shoving Risk aside. He looked well over her head at the man behind her, who must have been exceedingly tall.

"My thanks, Captain Griffin," Legare said. "Now you will allow me to take André's gift back to him."

Celia was shocked to feel the man's arm slide

around her, clasping her body just underneath her breasts. It was a gesture of ownership. The warmth of his hand burned through her dress. She looked down and saw a muscled forearm covered with black hair, revealed by a rolled-up shirtsleeve. The soft voice spoke again.

"Captain Legare, there is something we will discuss first."

Dominic lifted his thin brows.

The room became quiet, all eyes turning toward them. It was well known that Griffin was the only man on Isle au Corneille who did not fear Dominic Legare. Until this moment the two men had avoided all semblance of confrontation. They had spoken to each other only once before, concerning a minor dispute between two men from their respective crews. Although Legare's organization was larger and more powerful, Griffin's enmity was not something to be taken lightly.

"I have an interest in the wench," Griffin continued casually. "Are you open to an offer?"

Legare shook his head. "Now that André has seen her, I'm afraid that is impossible. I never disappoint my brother."

"Fifty thousand—in silver."

Risk's mouth dropped open as he stared at Griffin. Slowly he sat down as if his legs would no longer support him.

"No such paltry sum would interest me," Legare sneered. "I suppose you haven't heard of the successful run the *Vulture* has just made."

"A hundred thousand," Griffin said calmly.

Ripples of astonishment went through the room, punctuated by whistles and exclamations.

Celia quivered with fear. Why did this mysterious Captain Griffin want her enough to pay a fortune? And if Legare agreed, what did Griffin intend to do with her? The horrifying thought crossed her mind that she might be even worse off in this man's custody than in André's.

Legare was silent with surprise. His eyes narrowed. "What is it about the girl that interests you so?"

"One hundred fifty."

Legare sucked in his breath, then let it out slowly. His sharp eyes glittered with satisfaction at the prospect of refusing Griffin something he obviously wanted. He gave a jagged smile. "No."

André waddled forward through the crowd, his stomach jiggling. His round face was beet-red with excitement. "Yes, *yes!* Let 'im fight for her, Dominic! For years we've heard all the draff his men spout, boasting about their mighty captain . . . well, let's *see* him fight, *now!* Put 'im up against our best man."

Risk fumbled for the bottle of rum and downed a large swallow. "Sweet Jesus," he mumbled.

Dominic stared at Griffin consideringly. He addressed a question to André, while still looking at Griffin's expressionless face. "Would that really please you, *mon frère?* Enough to risk losing the woman I brought you?"

"Aye," came the ready answer. "We'll have 'im show us what he's made of, Dom!"

"Very well. This is the proposal, Griffin: you fight the man I choose. To the death, *naturellement.* If you succeed, you may have the girl for one hundred and fifty thousand, all in hard money. If my man wins, your ship and all the property you have stored in the relay warehouses belong to me."

Risk shot up angrily. "What the hell—"

"Aye," Griffin said in a businesslike manner.

The tavern burst into an uproar. Money began

to change hands, while loud wagers flew thick and fast. As the news was shouted to passersby, men began crowding inside frantically. Griffin scowled as he saw some of his crew squabbling with Legare's men. "Jack," he said to Risk, "spread the word among ours to keep their heads. We don't need—"

"Bloody hell, ye think they'll pay any heed?" Risk demanded incredulously. "Cap'n, ye know what ye've started! Things'll never be the same on the island. Ye've always told us to steer clear of any rivalry with Legare's men—"

"Yes, I know," Griffin interrupted, his expression grim.

"She's just a woman! She can't be worth this! Besides, the spoils in the warehouses weren't all yers t' gamble with. A share of the stake was *mine!*"

"Unfortunately," Griffin said, "I had no choice in the matter."

"Ye'd better win," Risk muttered.

Celia stood with downbent head, dazed and helpless. Some part of her mind understood what was happening, but her thoughts were strangely disoriented.

Suddenly André Legare approached her, tangling his fingers in her hair. She looked into his dark eyes, almost completely concealed by his heavy eyelids and puffy cheeks. His full-lipped mouth was stained at the corners. "I'll take her until the contest is through," André said to Griffin, pulling impatiently at the shining strands of golden hair.

Celia turned away from him and found herself pressed against Griffin's hard chest. There was an eerily familiar feeling about the way his arm felt around her, the heat of his skin through his shirt.

Although she was of more than average height
for a woman, the top of her head barely reached
his shoulder.

"Nay," she heard Griffin's voice over her head.
"I won't have damaged goods foisted on me after
going to the trouble of fighting for her."

Petulantly André looked for his older brother,
but Dominic was busy selecting a man to put up
against Griffin. "I won't damage her," he
whined, letting go of Celia's hair. "How do I
know *you* won't?"

John Risk stepped forward. "I 'spect Cap'n
Griffin's ideas of how to entertain a woman are a
wee bit different than yers, Legare. But if it sat-
isfies ye, *I'll* look after the sweet *cailin*. God knows
I'm not fool enough to try anything with her."

André stormed away, spewing loud com-
plaints.

Bracing his foot on the seat of a chair, Griffin
drew a knife from his boot to cut the bonds
around Celia's wrists. As she stood between his
thighs, she finally had the opportunity to look up
at his face. She couldn't hide her involuntary
shiver.

Chapter 2

The sight of Griffin threatened Celia in every way a woman could feel threatened. He was like a savage beast, with a wild mane of sable hair that fell past his shoulders. The line of his jaw was hidden by a thick beard. An open black shirt revealed sun-bronzed skin and a muscular hair-matted chest. He had a long straight nose, sharp cheekbones, and a bold look that proclaimed he would not recognize shame if he stood face to face with it. His eyes were such a fierce, stabbing blue that she flinched. She had never met anyone with eyes that color except for . . .

Griffin slashed the rope that bound her wrists, and all thought was driven away by excruciating pain as blood began to pump through her arms. The strained muscles of her shoulders exacerbated her agony. Celia swayed unsteadily, her ears buzzing.

Swearing at her, Griffin hooked an arm around her narrow waist. "Damn scrawny woman," he muttered, sliding the knife back into his boot. "Would you save your swooning for a more convenient time?"

"I-I'll try to restrain myself, Captain," she said.

Although her tone was meek, there was a thread of sarcasm in it.

Frowning, Griffin pushed her at Risk. "Take her, Jack. And don't make free with your hands, or I'll take your hide off in strips."

"Aye, sir," Risk said obediently, pulling Celia to the chair beside him. Folding his hands and resting them on the table, he gave her an angelic smile.

Griffin shrugged out of his sleeveless black jerkin and dropped it on the table. Fishing out a short length of rawhide from his pocket, he tied back his wild black hair. Celia watched him with wide eyes. She had never seen anyone like him before. His body was well-conditioned for battle, tall and rangy, but tough and muscled. His hands were huge and callused. Her father would call such a man "full of gristle". There was a frightening alertness in those shocking blue eyes.

"Wh-what do you want with me?" she whispered. Soft as the question was, he heard it clearly.

"Call it a debt I have to honor." He stood over her, settling his hands on the back of her chair. "And I always take care of my debts," he murmured, staring down at her. She shrank away, feeling she would shatter into pieces if he leaned one inch closer.

"I-if you take me to New Orleans," she said shakily, "the Vallerands will reward you for returning me un-unmolested—"

His eyes glinted with amusement. "If I do take you there, you'll be received the same whether you're molested or not."

"But the Vallerands would not want—"

"And you think I give a damn what the Vallerands want," he interrupted, his gaze traveling

over her body. She froze as she felt his fingertip
touch the tip of her ear and slide around the delicate curve. He tickled gently behind her earlobe,
as if she were a prickly-tempered cat. "Well, you
have nothing to fear from me, my little bag of
bones. When I lay with a woman, I like some
cushion to her."

Risk snickered, while Celia jerked her head back
to avoid that teasing fingertip. Although she
feared Griffin as much as she did the others, there
was something about him that provoked a far
deeper sense of outrage. Not even Dominic Legare seemed as casual in his cruelty as he did.

Griffin stared at the woman with new interest.
She had the translucent skin of a child, softly
rounded cheeks, a little snip of a nose. Her mouth
was formed with the fashionable rosebud pretti-
ness he usually had no taste for. Long, silky
lashes framed her luminous brown eyes. What
caught his notice, however, was something oddly
inappropriate for such a conventionally pretty
face, a mixture of intelligence and dignity that
gave her distinction.

Griffin looked over at his second-in-command.
"Has Legare chosen his man or not, Jack?"

Risk squinted at the other side of the room with
his one eye. " 'Tis hard to tell, with the pack we
have in here, all gathered 'round—ah, wait, looks
like Pounce. Big bear of a man—just might have
some reach on ye."

Griffin responded with a noncommittal grunt,
pulling his knife from his boot. The well-
sharpened blade gleamed brightly. Tossing it up
in the air, he caught it expertly by the hilt. "Pity
there's not room for the cutlass," he said. "So
much quicker that way."

"Show them a bit of fancy work," Risk urged,

excitement on his face. "Let Legare's men see
why we've followed ye to hell an' back, Cap'n."

"Nay, I'll do it without a show."

Without another word, Griffin turned and
walked to the center of the room, where the
crowd had cleared away a tight circle. The one
Risk had called Pounce, a tall, solidly built man
with a hideously slashed cheek, stepped forward.

The din of encouragements, threats, and excited cheers exploded into a frenzy. Terrified by
the noise and animosity that thickened the air,
Celia leaped to her feet, knocking over her chair.
Driven by instinct, she backed away from the fe-
rocious crowd, and felt an obstruction behind her
heels. Unceremoniously she fell into Risk's lap.
He had tripped her again.

"Big feet," he said, answering her glare with
an innocent smile. "Always in the way."

She tried to push herself off his knee, but he
kept his arm around her waist. Although he was
slim, there was a resilient steeliness in his limbs.
" 'Tis me duty to keep ye here," he remarked
pleasantly. "Don't fear I'll maul ye with these
scaly paws, darlin'. Ye're a sweet temptation, sure
. . . but I know too well that Griffin would start
in on me after finishing with Pounce."

And truthfully, his hold on her was far more
impersonal than any other man's so far. Celia
forced her muscles to unclench. "Poor mite," Risk
said, noticing the cracked surface of her lips.
"How long since ye last had water to drink?"

"I-I do not remember," she said in her uncertain English.

"We'll fix ye after the broil's over. *Vagabond*'s
got a first-rate cook, serves up grub that won't
sour in yer belly."

She did not even try to decipher what he had just said. "Your captain . . . will he lose maybe?"

"Oh, Griffin nivver loses. He's kin to the divvil an' fights twice as mean."

She looked at Risk curiously. His appearance was almost civilized compared to the others in the room. His hair was cropped short, completely unlike Griffin's wild locks. In spite of the ruined eye and the black patch, his clean-boned face was far from ugly. He was a young man, perhaps even her age. "Why does he do this?" she asked. "What does he want with me?"

"That's for the cap'n to say. But know this, ye'll be better off with Griffin than Legare."

She stared at him bitterly. For a moment she could not think of the right words in English, and then she formed a reply. "You cannot know for certainly."

"For certainly I do," Risk said, and laughed. He lifted her off his knee and stood up. "Come, darlin', let's have a look at the fight."

Celia didn't know how he could see anything with the room in such an uproar. They were all animals bellowing coarsely, with threatening fists and bloodlust on their faces. Occasionally there was a break in the crowd and she caught sight of the flashing of knives in the shifting circle. Risk did not bother to restrain a few vigorous shouts of his own. She strained away from him, but his arm was firm around her waist, and his guard did not slacken.

Pounce was a hulking giant, with a shaggy mane of dirty brown hair. Griffin ducked underneath the arc of a knife swing and aimed a kick at his midsection. As his opponent tumbled to the ground, Griffin launched himself forward. A booted foot caught him squarely in the chest, and he let out his breath as he hurtled over Pounce's head. Rolling as soon as he hit the ground, Griffin scrambled to his feet. They faced each other once more, breathing heavily, their clothes soaked with sweat.

"The great Captain Griffin," Pounce muttered. "When I finish with you, you'll be nothing but a smear on the floor."

Griffin did not reply, his blue eyes focused intently on the man's scarred, mocking face.

Pounce attacked with a series of knife thrusts, and Griffin leaped backward several times to avoid the bite of the blade. Shifting their weight with lightning speed, the opponents advanced and retreated in a fight that proved to be a game of balance. Griffin blocked one deep drive with his left arm, twisted in an unexpected move, and plunged his knife into Pounce's back with chilling precision. The other man died instantly, his large body crumpling to the floor.

There was a moment of astonished silence. Then the onlookers began to cheer and exclaim.

Laughing exultantly, Risk gave Celia a friendly jostle. "Now, darlin', ye know for certainly ye won't be ridden by André Legare tonight!"

Celia took a shuddering breath and looked away from him. Her face was stiff and drained of blood. She wrapped her arms around herself. From her point of view, Griffin's victory was hardly cause for rejoicing. There was no difference between him and the men who had killed Philippe. He was a cold-blooded murderer who would destroy anyone or anything that stood in the way of what he wanted. Perhaps his tortures would be more refined than André Legare's, but he was no less a monster.

Across the room, André Legare burst into a tantrum, his skin purple against his orange beard, his veins standing out in his puffy face. "I *will* have her. Dominic, I *will* . . . I *will!*"

Gently Dominic hushed his brother. "Of course, *mon frère*. You know I would not let him take away my gift to you."

André quieted. Dominic stepped over Pounce's bleeding body to Griffin, who had just extracted his knife and wiped the blade clean. "You proved yourself quite handy with the blade," Dominic remarked in a low voice, while the excited roar in the tavern refused to subside.

Griffin looked at him sardonically. "It was not my intention to prove anything."

"You did, however. And as we agreed, the woman will be yours. But tomorrow morning, not tonight."

Griffin was very still. "The woman is mine now."

"Unfortunately André will be inconsolable if he does not have one night with her."

A sneer twisted Griffin's lips. "She wouldn't survive one night with him. Your brother's practices with women are no secret, Legare. And she's as weak as water."

"I'll see to it that he is not overly rough with her."

"You misunderstand," Griffin said softly. "I'm not open to bargaining."

Suddenly John Risk interrupted them, having hoisted Celia in his arms and carried her through the crowd. "Here, Cap'n—a prize well-won!" He dumped her frail body into Griffin's arms.

Griffin looked down at the exhausted woman. Her gossamer hair spilled over his shoulder and chest. Strain had caused her skin to take on a brittle whiteness. The brown eyes were blank, as if

she had retreated to an inner world where no one
could reach her. It was obvious that the delicate
strength he had admired before was fading
quickly. He tried to assess how much more she
could take before the ordeal broke her.

Dominic Legare gave him a smile of malicious
amusement. "You'll have her at dawn, Griffin.
But tonight she will service André. And if you
care to begin a quarrel . . . so be it."

Griffin cursed inwardly. The crews of both
camps were already eager for an excuse to battle—
their small jealousies and rivalries had simmered
a long time. An argument between their two lead-
ers was all it would take to begin a war.

"Remember that my men outnumber yours,"
Legare pointed out. "And you would not risk the
deaths of a goodly part of your crew in order to
satisfy your desire for a mere woman, would you?
Your men would not forgive that—nor should
they. In short, Captain Griffin, you know as well
as I that you cannot afford the prize you have
won."

Risk's exuberance dissolved as he listened to
the short speech. "What the hell is this?" he demanded.

"Now, about the money—" Legare continued.

"Not a cent until she's in my hands for good,"
Griffin said slowly.

"*Bien sûr*, we'll settle it in the morning."

Risk gaped incredulously. "Cap'n, ye're not
going to let that drunken pig André have 'er for
the night! Ye know what he'll—"

"Quiet," Griffin said tersely.

"But . . ." Risk saw the warning look in his
eyes and fell silent.

Lowering Celia's feet to the floor, Griffin sent
her stumbling toward Legare with a careless

nudge. Dominic caught her by the shoulders. "Tell your brother to restrain himself with her," Griffin said coolly, "or I'll have his head."

Dominic's smugness vanished. "No one threatens André."

The bearded face was impassive. "I've just done André one hell of a favor."

Celia turned her head and looked at Griffin with wretched contempt. How was it that she could feel betrayed by him? She had not really believed he would take her to New Orleans, but some part of her had dared to hope there was a chance. His blue eyes had lost their snapping intensity, seeming cold and flat.

"*À demain*," he said in perfectly accented French.

Until tomorrow. She did not give a sign that she had heard. *Until tomorrow*, she thought bitterly, when he knew that for her there would be no tomorrow.

His gaze held hers for a chilling second, and then he looked away, seeming to lose interest. "Jack," he said, gesturing to Risk, and the pair walked away.

"Troublesome bitch," she heard Legare's quiet voice in her ear as he jerked her toward the waiting André. "I hope my brother rips you limb from limb."

Celia was sent stumbling into the room with a hard shove of André's foot. She fell to the floor, raised herself up on her forearms, and looked at the scarred Aubusson carpet beneath her with astonishment. It was not what she would have expected to see in the ruins of an ancient fort. The room was filled with gold and finery, elaborate mismatched furniture, baroque lamps, and luxury goods. Dust, rotting food, and liquor stains were everywhere. A ripe, sickly-sweet odor filled her nostrils, and she nearly gagged.

André bent over her with a leer. "Like what you see? All of it presents from Dominic. Like you."

"He . . . he takes care of you," Celia stammered, twisting and rising to her feet.

"Dominic? *Oui, toujours,* always. Since we were boys in Guadeloupe. Orphan boys."

She looked out of the corner of her eyes for some kind of weapon to use against him. "A-and he gives you all the women?" she asked, edging away from him. "He takes none for himself?"

André followed her every movement. "He gives all to me and takes none," he said thickly, and made a quick grab for her.

Celia gasped and stepped back, avoiding the heavy, grasping hand.

Laughing delightedly, he caught her tangled hair in his fist and dragged her to the disheveled mahogany bed. Celia screamed as she was thrown halfway across the mattress. In spite of his portly size, André had more than enough strength to force her to his will. The bedclothes were unwashed and foul. Before she could move, he had pulled her wrist to the bedpost and fastened it with a leather strap already hanging there. Breathing fast from excitement and exertion, he took hold of her other arm. Celia began to scream without stopping as he reached for the strap on the opposite side of the bed. She struggled violently, but she was too weak.

Having rendered her helpless, André took the top of her dress in his hands and ripped it open, exposing the pale beauty of her body. His huge belly pressed against hers as he leaned over her.

Baring his teeth, he lowered his mouth to her breast. Celia felt herself plummeting through endless depths of horror, and her mind began to turn inward, refusing to acknowledge what was happening.

Suddenly the crushing weight of his body was gone. Her screams faded into astonished silence as she saw a knife making a quick pass around his throat, a spurt of dark red blood. He dropped to the Aubusson rug, clutching his throat, making a peculiar gurgling noise. His body writhed and shuddered.

Griffin stood over him, casually wiping his knife on the wounded man's shirt. "I changed my mind," he said, smiling coldly into André's bulging eyes. "I couldn't wait for her until morning."

André clutched his throat harder, twitched once, twice, then closed his eyes. Slowly the pudgy hands relaxed.

Griffin sheathed the knife back in his boot and turned to the bed, ignoring André Legare's dead body. He stripped off his jerkin and began to unbutton the black shirt, while his searing blue eyes swept over the woman's still form. Dark bruises marred her skin. She needed fattening—she was slender enough that the points of her hipbones were sharply prominent.

But something about her awakened a primal urge that nearly undid him. Griffin was troubled enough by the momentary loss of self-control to waste precious seconds looking at her. Her breasts were small but perfectly curved, adorned by tiny pink nipples. He wanted to put his mouth on them. Slowly his gaze moved down her flat abdomen to the triangle of delicate golden curls. It would be so easy to climb on top of her, relieve the aching pressure that was rapidly building between his legs. He dropped his shirt on the bed and put his sleeveless jerkin back on. She watched with a vacant stare while he untied the leather straps around her wrists. Her skin felt downy and cool underneath his fingers.

"What is your name?" he asked in French, pulling her to a sitting position. She was pliant and motionless. He repeated the question more harshly, wondering if her mind had snapped.

"Celia," she whispered.

He was relieved by the fact that she was able to answer him. "We don't have much time, Celia." Deftly he stripped off the remains of her gown and pushed her arms through the sleeves of the discarded black shirt. She didn't move as he fastened it over her naked body. "You do everything I tell you. Understand?"

She looked at him with that blank stare. Cursing, he searched the room, found a half-empty bottle of rum, and brought it back to her. As he raised it to her lips, she recovered enough to protest and push it away. Griffin cupped his hand around the back of her head and brought the bottle close again. "Drink it, damn you, or I'll pinch your nose shut and pour it down your throat."

Trembling, she took a swallow of the sharp liquid and gasped as it burned through her innards. "Oh—"

"Again."

Obeying the stern voice and the uncompromising hands, she let him tip the bottle into her mouth once more. Another two gulps, and she felt as if she had been set on fire, inside and out. Color rushed over her white skin. She looked into

Griffin's bearded face, and then down at herself, as if just realizing what had happened.

"Better," he said quietly, seeing that the blank look had gone from her face. He set aside the bottle and helped her off the bed. As soon as her feet touched the floor, she tried to twist away from him. He pulled her against his body and pushed her head back, glaring into her terrified eyes. "Listen to me, you little fool. I'm your only chance in hell of getting off this island. And after what I've just done for you, there'll be a price on my head that even my own men will find tempting. You'll go where I tell you, and do exactly as I say, or I'll wring your neck."

There was no hint of softness in the sinewy body pressed against hers. He could kill her with a mere twist of his wrists. Shaking uncontrollably, she glanced at the floor, at the crumpled, bloodied mass that had once been André Legare. "Yes," Griffin said softly. "You understand what I'm capable of."

"Do not hurt me," she choked. "I'll do whatever you say."

"Good." He let go of her and pulled off the cord that held back his long black hair. Celia did not move. Gathering the folds of the gaping shirt together, he tied the cord around her waist. The garment hung on her slight frame like a tent, reaching to her knees.

"Wh-why did you come for me?" she asked.

"Because I fought for you and won. And no one takes what is mine."

"What do you want of me?"

He ignored the question. "Come." Taking hold of her wrist, he hauled her to the door, stopping abruptly as he sensed rather than saw her limp. "Dammit, what's the matter?"

"Nothing—it is just—" She fell silent as he knelt down and picked up one of her torn feet. The tender soles of her feet were accustomed to the protection of shoes. Going barefoot over rough surfaces had caused several painful scrapes and blisters. Every step felt as if she were walking on broken glass.

"Well, this should do a fine job of slowing us down."

"It was not my fault," she said mutinously.

Swiftly Griffin pulled out his long knife, and she covered her head with her arms, cowering against the door. Muttering something about idiotic females, he picked her up and hoisted her over his shoulder. He used one hand to hold her in place and grasped the knife with the other. Stepping through the doorway, he avoided the slumped-over body of one of Legare's men.

He carried her through the dark passageways of the aging fortress, moving with the grace of a lion, stealthy and sure. Celia dangled helplessly from his shoulder, dizzy and half-drunk. Miserably she wondered what would be in store for her at the end of this journey. Griffin seemed to know the maze of corridors well, ignoring fake entrances and blind alleys, cutting through empty rooms and bypassing the longer routes to an exit.

The sound of voices alerted him, and he ducked into an unlit passageway. He let Celia slide down his front until her feet were on the ground. The voices drew nearer until Celia could discern two different men and the sultry tones of a woman. Evidently she was taking them to a place where she would entertain them both. The conversation was vulgar and explicit. In spite of the danger of being discovered, Griffin smiled mockingly at Celia's bewildered expression. He concealed his knife in his belt so that no stray gleam from its surface would betray them.

"This way, hearties," the whore said in a sultry purr, and the seamen staggered after her with cheerful abandon.

"Make way, stan' on course, make way," one of the men called out, and the other guffawed.

Terrified, Celia pressed herself tighter against Griffin as the three figures passed by the entrance to the passage. His body was tough and hard. Although he made no move to comfort or hold her, she felt her fear lessen.

"Wait, wait I see . . . hard alee!" one of the rovers exclaimed, stopping and peering into the dark corridor. "Shift the rudder!"

Griffin tensed, fingering the hilt of his knife.

"What do y'see, darlin'?" the whore asked.

Celia knew the seaman had seen them and was going to call attention to them. Panic-stricken, she wondered what Griffin would do, if he might kill the three of them right before her eyes.

Griffin turned in an unexpected movement, pressing her back against the wall. Confused, she looked up at him, just as his long fingers sank through her hair and clamped around her scalp. His dark head bent, his bearded face swooping down to hers. There was the shock of his mouth on hers, a hard mouth that plundered hers ruthlessly. She made a small, frightened sound and caught at his wrists. As she gasped for air, his scent filled her nostrils, a salty, masculine smell. At first the kiss was nothing but brutal domination, but at the feel of her mouth under his, he angled his head and eased the crushing pressure. His tongue swept between her lips, exploring her mouth with savage hunger.

Weakly she pulled at his wrists, and he forced her hands over her head, pinning them to the wall. Quivering, she gulped in a deep breath, forgetting where they were. Everything faded away except the assault on her senses. Her lungs seemed to fill with fire, and she thrashed in vain to escape the scorching heat.

His knee pressed between hers, wedging them apart. Inexorably he pulled her forward until she straddled his sturdy thigh. Celia groaned in agony as she felt a terrible pleasure invading her body. It betrayed everything she was, everything she held dear, and still she could not hold it back. His hand covered her breast completely, his thumb rubbing gently over her nipple until it contracted to a point. Shivering, she arched her back, her body responding wantonly to his caresses. Somehow her arms were around his neck and her fingers were tangled in his thick hair . . . Somehow his hands were soothing her aching breasts, his thumbs stroking over the hard peaks, and her hips were pressing harder against his thigh in response to the gentle rhythm he had begun.

The whore peered at the outline of two writhing figures in the shadows, and she smiled knowingly. ''Why, it's nothin' but one o' the girls and some salty jack givin' it a turn.'' She ventured farther in the passageway, hand braced on her ample hip. '' 'Ey, me 'earty, care to join a merry crowd already half-seas over?''

Griffin lifted his head, taking care to keep his face out of the light. ''Begone with you,'' he said roughly. There was a dangerous note of warning in his voice.

Wisely the woman backed away to avoid the prospect of trouble. She motioned for her two companions to follow her. ''Leave 'em to their ruttin'," she said. "We got our own to do. You two jack-tars ever had a woman at th' same time?"

Eagerly the seamen followed her sashaying form down the corridor.

Celia watched until they had disappeared. Her breath rushed out in uneven bursts, ruffling through the crisp black curls on Griffin's chest. She could not look up at his face, not when she was suffused with humiliation. She was no better than the whore who had just passed by them. How could she have behaved in such a way? The feelings that had flamed inside her were unfamiliar and painfully confusing.

She knew there was such a thing as lust, a desire that had nothing to do with love, but until now she had thought herself incapable of such a thing. She loved Philippe so much that she couldn't bear the idea of life without him, and yet she had just been unfaithful to the ideals and the love they had shared. Her eyes stung sharply. It took all her strength to hold back her tears.

Slowly Griffin's knee withdrew from between hers, but his hand was still closed around her wrists. Neither of them moved until Celia forced herself to raise her chin. "Let me go," she whispered, her hatred easy to read.

His face was sheathed in darkness. She could see little but the glitter of his eyes. The silence deepened. He bent his head again.

"No," she whimpered, just before his mouth closed over hers. His muscular arms wrapped around her struggling body, one hand pushing her slim hips against the bulging ridge that strained against his breeches. Her lips were forced open by a devastating kiss, his tongue thrusting deeply inside her. Rage exploded in her chest. She fought him viciously, using her nails, her elbows, her knees. But he muffled her screams with his lips and slid his hand over her bottom in an insolent caress. Celia groaned and shivered, her resistance crushed by his strength, her senses careening.

He kissed her as Philippe never had, his mouth uncivilized, voluptuous, barbaric. The tip of his tongue slipped underneath her top lip, finding an excruciatingly sensitive nerve, teasing gently until she moaned in protest. He drew her trembling breath into his mouth, wet her inner cheeks with his tongue, traced the line of her teeth.

When he broke off the kiss and eased her away from his aroused body, she was too stunned to move. Gasping for air, she leaned her head back against the wall and closed her eyes.

His voice was mocking. ''I'm intrigued, Madame Vallerand. You look and speak like a lady, but you don't kiss like one.''

She quivered with fury, striking out blindly, her fists beating on his chest. Griffin laughed and picked her up, slinging her over his shoulder. ''Quiet, or I'll knock your head against the wall.''

As they emerged from a seldom-used entrance to the fort, more of a hole in the wall than an actual door, Griffin lowered Celia to the ground. Carefully he drew her to the corner of the building. The air was filled with merrymaking, fistfights, drunken quarrels, and the sounds of prostitutes entertaining their customers on the beach. There were pools of light shed by the torches, and a sea of shadows. Pushing aside a swath of Celia's hair, Griffin murmured into her ear.

"Do you see the row of three warehouses over there? A pirogue is waiting on the other side. If I tell you to run, move quickly and don't look back. All right?"

"All right," she echoed, her eyes fastened on the dark outline of the buildings.

He took her elbow firmly. "Come."

Celia was too anxious to notice the pain in her feet. Stealthily Griffin pulled her along the moss-covered wall of the fort and across a short stretch of sand to a group of worn boulders. Celia stopped with a gasp as she saw a scrawny figure propped up against one of the rocks. The man stirred and gave a contented snore, loosening his grip on the small jug of whiskey in his lap. Griffin sank to his haunches before the sleeping figure. Celia held her breath as she watched Griffin ease the jug away from the man's lax grip. Bewildered, she took the whiskey as Griffin stood and handed it to her.

Griffin's eyes swept the terrain. Seeing that the area was clear, he took Celia's free arm and propelled her toward the warehouses. Valiantly she tried to keep up with his long strides. As they rounded the corner of a building, a rough voice broke from the darkness.

"*Qui est-ce?*" The stalwart form of a man confronted them, one of Legare's men assigned to guard the warehouse. After one glance, he bellowed for help and rushed toward them with an upraised sword.

Celia froze like a frightened rabbit.

"Go!" Even the biting sound of Griffin's voice failed to jolt her from the paralysis. She started as she felt the stinging slap of his hand on her buttocks. Without thinking she began to run toward the open water.

Griffin hit the ground and rolled to the side, while the cutlass slashed into the sand. Before the attacker could extract the buried blade, Griffin pounced on him with a snarl, making short work of him with a deft thrust of his sword. Just as the man underneath him shuddered in a death throe, Griffin heard sand-muffled footsteps. Whirling around, he saw another of Legare's men, alerted to the emergency.

This time Griffin had no chance to avoid the swing of the blade. He swerved, feeling the bite of the sword on the side of his shoulder. Ignoring the searing pain, he reached up and caught hold of the pirate's arm, pulling the man down to the sand. Rolling over and over, they fought like dogs, snarling and gouging, until Griffin used a downward blow of his arm to break the man's neck.

Breathing heavily, he rose to his feet.

Celia stumbled across the beach, her lungs aching from her tortured gasps. There was a blurred shape before her eyes, a small craft on the water. She stopped as she saw the group of men gathered in and around the pirogue. Should she approach them? Was this the pirogue Griffin had intended her to reach, and if so, would the men help her or prove to be another set of cruel captors?

A large man with gleaming black skin strode toward her purposefully. A colored kerchief was wrapped around his head, and loose cotton garments covered his muscled body. His features were hawklike and expressionless. Celia's eyes widened at the sight of the brace of pistols hanging at his waist. Dropping the whiskey jug, she began to back away, then turned and ran in panic.

Her only thought was to find a place to hide. Darkness and danger whirled around her, and she no longer felt human, only a frightened animal hunted by a pack of wolves.

Chapter 3

Swift footsteps sounded behind Celia. Suddenly she was hauled off her feet and held in a pair of brutal arms. She screamed and tried to claw at her captor's face.

"Shut up, you little idiot," a familiar voice growled in her ear.

She put her arms around his neck, her groping hands finding the locks of thick black hair. It was Griffin. Without a word she buried her face in the crook of his shoulder and neck. She had no more thoughts of escaping him. He was her only chance of survival.

Griffin carried her to the water's edge, scooping up the discarded jug along the way. The black man Celia had seen before joined them.

"We've run into heavy weather, Aug," Griffin muttered.

"As usual, you understate, Captain." Aug regarded him gravely. "You are wounded."

"It's nothing. We'll see to it later. How goes it with Risk and the rest of the crew?"

"They and *Vagabond* are under way."

"Good. Not a man jack of us will be safe until we're far away from this bloody island."

A hint of a smile appeared on Aug's dark face.

"I think you chose the wrong Legare to kill, Captain."

"Aye," Griffin said ruefully, and shifted the weight of the small bundle in his arms. "I have a bit of goods to be smuggled into New Orleans." The journey would take at least twenty-four hours. "Let's shove off." He waded through the shallow water and lowered Celia into the pirogue, where a half-dozen of his most able-bodied men were seated with oars.

As he set Celia down, Griffin found it difficult to pry her arms from around his neck. "Let go," he said, but she refused to release her death-grip. "I said *let go*," he added in his most threatening tone. It was only when she still refused to move that he realized how afraid she was. He made his voice as soft as possible. "You're safe, *ma pauvre petite*," he said against her cheek. "No one will hurt you. Now be a good girl. Do as I say."

Her strangling clutch eased. Reluctantly she unwrapped her arms from around his warm neck and huddled alone on the wooden planking.

Griffin and Aug pushed the pirogue deeper into the water and hoisted themselves over the sides. In spite of Aug's protest Griffin took hold of an oar and contributed to the feverish rowing that took them away from shore. Finally the island disappeared from sight and they ventured into the sea marsh, a vast plain of water and marsh grasses dubbed the trembling prairie. It was a smuggling route they used regularly, and it took skill to navigate it without becoming hopelessly lost. His wounded shoulder aching, Griffin left off rowing and joined Celia at the front of the pirogue. The oarsmen settled into a slower, steadier pace that could be maintained for several hours. They worked silently, rhythmically, as if they were all part of some great machine.

"Here." Griffin dropped a heavy canteen of water into Celia's lap. "Drink it slowly."

She stared at the object dumbly, then realizing it was water, fumbled with the cap in a burst of energy. Dropping the cap to the floor of the pirogue, she gulped the water down greedily, reveling in the cool rush of liquid down her parched throat. Immediately the canteen was ripped away from her. She struggled to grab it back, her whole being concentrated on gaining more of the precious water.

Griffin held the canteen out of reach and pulled her onto his lap to restrain her. "*Slowly*," he said, half-annoyed, half-amused. "*Lentement*. Understand?"

"Oh, please," Celia begged hoarsely, "it has been so long since I—just a little more—"

"In a minute."

"But I need—"

"Hush. You don't want a bellyache, do you?"

Celia stopped straining to reach the canteen and stared at his bearded face suspiciously, deciding that he was being deliberately cruel. The small amount of water she'd managed to swallow revived her. She felt new strength coursing through her body. "C-Captain Griffin, why are you doing this? Why are you taking me to New Orleans?"

"Perhaps I wish to be in the good graces of your family. It's rare that a man finds himself in the position of being owed a favor by Maximilien Vallerand."

Celia stared into his midnight-blue eyes. "Please," she whispered. "Please. I-I have lost

everything. I have nothing left . . . no hope, no
husband, no future. You can at least tell me the
truth. Of what value was it to you, to take me
away from there? Why put yourself and your men
at risk? Wh-why did you want me enough to . . .
to kill . . .'' She would have continued, but something in those intense blue eyes made her feel as
if she were drowning. She had to look away in
order to catch her breath.

''Perhaps I decided you were worth it,'' he said
in a voice too low for the others to hear. ''Worth
dozens of lives. Worth any risk at all. It's been
years since I've even touched a woman like you
. . . a woman with soft white hands and the eyes
of a child. Aye, that's reason enough.''

Suddenly she was aware of how her breast was
pressed against him. She was naked underneath
his shirt, and he must have been able to feel the
shape of her body, the heat of her skin, through
the soft fabric. Uneasily Celia tried to move. He
would not permit it.

''There . . . there must be another reason,'' she
stammered.

''Even if there weren't, I'd still have taken you
from Legare.''

Mon Dieu, she thought, her heart beating wildly
as she realized he was not going to let her go
without demanding the use of her body as pay-
ment. She began to shake at the memory of his
insistent mouth, the length of his powerful body
crushing against her, the muscled thigh that had
parted hers with such ease. Even if he tried to be
gentle with her—and she doubted that he would—
how could he keep from killing her?

''You're trembling,'' he observed. ''Because
you know I want you. But when I take you, *ma
petite*, you'll want me just as much.''

Celia was stiff with fear. She wanted to escape the whisper that sent nervous chills over her skin. She wanted to climb out of his arms and run far away from that mesmerizing gaze and the reach of those hands that could be so gentle and so deadly. But she was trapped with him on the pirogue. And without him she would have no chance of reaching New Orleans.

"Selfish pig," she said unsteadily. "I do not want you, but you tell yourself that I do. It does not matter to you. It does not matter that I have just lost my husband."

"That matters more than you could guess. But since he *is* dead, Madame Vallerand, your wifely virtue is of no consequence to anyone." He handed her the canteen. She drank from it automatically, her thirst overpowering all other considerations. Once again he pulled it away from her after a few greedy gulps. "You have no sense of caution," he said, smiling slightly. "That's enough for now."

This last was spoken in English, and Celia answered in kind. "I do not think enough is yet," she said, her eyes on the canteen.

He did not answer, showed no intention of allowing her more, and she lapsed into a cowardly silence. Gradually the rhythm of the oars soothed her into a half-sleep. Twice her head bobbed against his good shoulder, and she jerked it back up, blinking rapidly. The third time she let it rest there, finding it too much of an effort to lift it again. Griffin offered no objections. "The other shoulder," she said groggily. "It is bad, *non?*"

"No, not bad."

With an incoherent murmur she settled against him, too exhausted to stay awake any longer.

* * *

The morning light awakened Celia from a dreamless sleep. Uncertain sunshine flickered through the trees overhead, illuminating a world unlike anything she had ever seen before. The pirogue was moving through a lush, gray-green swamp, curtained with long streamers of moss. The water was frosted with a delicate layer of vegetation upon which insects danced and scattered. Flowerlike ferns and clumps of cane lined the muddy banks. A heavy scent, green, fresh, and primitive, permeated the moist air.

There were cypress trees with staggeringly thick trunks that must have existed since the earth was created. Mudfish swam in between their half-submerged roots. Here in this mixture of woods and water, it was difficult to believe that somewhere there were paved streets and white-painted houses, drawing rooms with pianos, libraries filled with books and stately chairs. Civilization was another world away.

Slowly becoming aware that she was snuggled comfortably between Griffin's thighs, her ear pressed against his steady heartbeat, Celia tried to push herself away. There was stabbing pain in her back, neck, shoulders, legs—in fact, everywhere in her body. She couldn't suppress a moan of distress. One of Griffin's large hands settled on the back of her neck, his long fingers kneading gently.

"Don't," she said groggily, her natural sense of modesty rebelling against the prospect of being handled so familiarly, especially in front of others. Four oarsmen faced away from her, but Aug and two men at rest were seated in the stern of the craft. No detail escaped their notice.

Ignoring her protest, Griffin moved down to her

shoulders, massaging the tense, strained muscles. Celia closed her eyes in resignation. There was no use in objecting. And his hands were blissfully soothing, drawing out the aches and leaving her muscles tingling. His thumbs and the pads of his fingers worked in the hollows of her spine, back up her neck, then across her shoulders to her upper arms. Involuntarily she leaned into his hands, which seemed to know exactly how and where to touch her.

Griffin looked across the boat at Aug's impassive face. "What of the next relay?" he asked, kneading the soft muscles beneath Celia's prominent shoulder blades.

Aug replied in a dialect Celia could not quite follow. It was derived from French, but mingled with slurring words she didn't understand.

"That's good," Griffin said, moving Celia off his lap. "We should make as much distance as possible today. Otherwise Legare may catch up to us by nightfall."

Rather sorry that the massage had ended, Celia looked up at the man beside her. "How long will it take to reach New Orleans from here?"

"Hopefully before dawn tomorrow."

"How do you know Legare is—" she began to ask. She stopped as she saw his face in direct sunlight for the first time. Those intense sapphire eyes tinged with violet, framed with spiky black lashes. She felt herself turn pale.

"What is it?" Griffin asked sharply.

"Your eyes . . . they are the same as my . . . my husband's, and—"

His expression turned forbidding. She saw that she had displeased him to no small degree. "Many people have blue eyes," he said.

"But not like—"

"I've no patience for a woman's chattering," he interrupted, and moved to one of the idle oars. Wincing at the nagging pain in his wounded shoulder, he began to row. The muscles of his chest and arms bulged as he pulled at the oar. Celia continued to stare at him, wondering what he looked like without the long, shaggy hair and rough beard.

"Monsieur," she said timidly, having to repeat herself before he would look at her. "Monsieur. I am very much hungry."

Amusement flickered in Griffin's eyes at her faltering English. He nodded in the direction of a worn pouch a few feet away from her. "Look in there."

Spying the canteen next to the pouch, Celia reached for the water also. She darted a cautious glance at Griffin, her fingers tightening on the canteen. "And very much thirsty," she said.

"Then have at it," he said ingraciously.

Eagerly she rummaged through the pouch, finding it full of hard, crunchy biscuits and strips of dried meat. The first bite of biscuit crumbled in her mouth, chalky and flavorless. She washed it down with a swig of tepid water. Her small white teeth bore into the dried meat, which required several minutes of concentrated chewing.

When the panic had died away and her stomach was comfortably full, Celia placed the pouch and canteen back where she had found them. Now that her most pressing needs were satisfied, she twisted to look at the smarting soles of her feet. Her attention was diverted by Griffin's cutting voice. "I'll see to those soon. In the meanwhile do what you can to keep yourself covered."

Celia flushed, yanking down the hem of the

black shirt. Watching Griffin as he rowed, she wondered who he was and where he had come from. He looked like nothing more than a dirty backwoodsman, but his French was perfectly accented, spoken as if he were an aristocrat. He had the muscled torso of a laborer, a seaman, but his eyes contained keen intelligence, and she had the feeling that he had once known far better circumstances than these. He was a powerful man—a crew of pirates would not follow him unless he were greatly feared and respected—and yet he had risked his life for the sake of a helpless woman. *Why?*

The sun climbed higher, and the pirogue traveled farther down the quiet bayou to a place where it ended at a tiny island and branched off into several smaller courses. An ancient tree trunk bridge crossed one of the streams. Celia looked at the men in the pirogue closely, sensing anticipation in the atmosphere. They were all quiet as the vessel drifted toward the right bank.

The chittering whistle of a bird interrupted the silence. Celia frowned curiously as Griffin whistled back in a like manner. She was startled to see movement in the woods, swarthy faces appearing in the midst of the greenery, muskets and axes clutched in filthy hands. The men in the pirogue seemed to recognize them.

"Our next crew," Griffin said to Celia.

"They are friends of us?" she asked doubtfully, gazing at the motley bunch.

"Not exactly," he said dryly. "Rivermen owe their allegiance to no one. But I pay them to carry contraband and luxury items through the lakes to the river."

"Why cannot *this* crew row us?"

"It's just possible they are tired, *enfant.*"

One of the oarsmen looked up at her and grinned. "Tired, sure mebbe, but I'd row ye to China if ye wanted, ma'am!"

Not understanding but deciding the comment was friendly, Celia smiled faintly.

Aug leaped off the pirogue and secured it to a half-buried tree trunk on the bank. Groaning in relief, the men put down their oars and climbed off the vessel. Celia sat still, watching Griffin anxiously. He tied a small, flat leather pouch to his waist and hung a cutlass at his left side. "Hold that jug of whiskey," he said. She picked it up, cradling it in her lap. He slid his arms under her knees and back and lifted her easily into his arms.

As soon as they saw her long blond hair, the rivermen gave wolf calls and lusty shouts of appreciation. Celia clutched Griffin's neck in alarm while he carried her over the bank toward the tree trunk bridge. The men crowded around her. She flinched as rough hands brushed over her bare legs.

"This all the cargo ye brought, Cap'n sir?" one of the rivermen inquired.

"Finest little bit o' cargo I ever seen!" another exclaimed gleefully.

Someone yanked at a lock of her hair, and she squeaked in surprise. Griffin stopped suddenly, his cold blue gaze sweeping over the eager men. A thin smile appeared, nearly hidden by his wiry beard. "The woman is my property. If any man touches her again, I'll rip his privates off."

The group chuckled heartily, none of them seeming to take offense. The insulting hands withdrew. Celia hid her face against Griffin's hairy chest. "I think," she said in a muffled voice, "that without you here, they would—"

"Yes," Griffin said wryly. He set his foot on the creaking bridge. "Now, my charming bit of alligator bait, don't look down. And for God's sake don't throw me off balance or we'll both be up to our necks in mud."

Alligators? Philippe had entertained her with horrifying stories about the creatures, saying they were part dragon, part lizard. They had long tails, big jaws, sharp teeth. Her eyes squeezed shut. "Do not drop me," she whispered.

"After the trouble I've gone to getting you this far?" Griffin asked, and grinned. "Just don't drop the whiskey."

Celia didn't dare breathe as she felt him advance step by step along the felled tree trunk. The rivermen followed them expertly, giving a few more hoots and grunts at the sight of her pale legs silhouetted against the dark green of the bayou.

Jumping from the bridge to the ground, Griffin approached a collection of ramshackle huts in a clearing. "An old Indian camp," he said as Celia lifted her head and looked around curiously.

"What happened to them?" she asked.

"Driven away a long time ago. Too many traders and smugglers coming from the river." He lowered her to the ground beside the entrance to a crude hut. "Aug," he called out. "Step lively. We have only a few minutes."

"A few minutes?" Celia repeated. "What are you going to do?"

"Get inside." He pointed to the doorway. "And drink some of that whiskey."

Her heart began to thump unpleasantly fast. "Why? Why are you calling Aug? Why—"

"Must I repeat myself?" he asked, his tone laced with soft menace.

Blanching, she crept into the hut. A pallet was rotting in the corner. Large holes in the ceiling and a crumbling wall allowed a measure of light and air to filter inside. With trembling hands Celia uncorked the jug and lifted it to her lips. The liquor was vile, the sharp, strong taste of it burning down to her stomach. Seating herself gingerly on a corner of the pallet, she waited. A fat-bellied, furry-legged spider wandered by, and she watched its progress silently.

"I see you have a visitor," Griffin's voice came from the tiny doorway, and he ducked his head as he came inside. His booted foot sent the unlucky spider hurtling away. "I'd have expected you to scream."

Celia was tempted to tell him that at the moment she was far more afraid of two-legged creatures. "There were mice in the hold of Captain Legare's ship," she told him.

"Were there?" He knelt in front of her, ripping a ragged length of cloth in two. "Well, better to keep company with mice than service Legare's crew."

"Yes, that is true," she agreed fervently, then inched backward as he reached for her ankle.

"Be still." Griffin looked at the swollen underside of her foot, realizing how acutely painful it must be. She had not complained once. His gaze moved up to her face, while he felt a twinge of admiration. Given all the terror, grief, and abuse she had suffered during the past two days, and the fact that her husband had just been murdered, she was remarkably self-possessed. Many women would have collapsed under the strain. But it seemed there was iron beneath her vulnerable exterior.

Celia bit her lip as his thumb brushed lightly

over her blistered heel. "Poor little girl," he said, moistening the cloth with a splash of whiskey. His voice was gentle, caressing. She frowned in confusion, for all of a sudden he sounded like Philippe.

"What are you going to—" She yelped in pain as he probed at a sand-encrusted cut. "Ah, *mon Dieu*," she gasped, and covered her mouth with her hand to stifle another cry.

"Scream if you like," he said. "It won't bother anyone."

Her foot jerked out of his grasp as he touched the cloth to it again. She felt the pain spear through her body until even her teeth ached. "Please, it is not necessary—"

"You'll be a hell of an inconvenience if your feet start to fester. Hold still."

"I c-can't!" She tried to resist as he grasped her ankle again. Instead of applying the cloth, he searched the back of her heel with his thumb and forefinger. "What are you doing?" she asked in confusion. He pinched deeply into a cluster of nerves until her foot began to feel numb. Slowly she relaxed.

"Better?" he asked.

"Yes, better," she said with a sigh of relief. Although there was still discomfort, it was not nearly as bad as it had been. Deftly, Griffin continued to clean out the sand and tiny pebbles embedded in the tender sole. "How do you know how to do that?" she asked, giving him her other foot when he gestured for it. He applied the same pressure to the back of it.

"In my far-reaching travels I've learned a trick here and there," Griffin said, and grinned at her. "Later I'll show you some others."

"*Non, merci*, I would rather not . . ." Her voice

trailed into silence as Aug entered the hut carrying a folded cloth sack.

Impassively Aug knelt down beside them, sitting on his heels. He began to pull out a strange assortment of feathers, small stones, lumps of dried clay, bags containing powdered substances.

Griffin held his hand up in a staying gesture. "We don't have time for charms and fetishes, Aug. Dispense with the voodoo show. All I want is some of the green powder."

"What is this voodoo?" Celia asked warily.

"Voodoo? It's magic, medicine, superstition. They practiced it in Haiti, where Aug hails from."

"What is the green powder?"

"Something we're going to put on your feet. If, of course, Aug doesn't insist on some ritual burning of dirt, feathers, and nail cuttings first. Or slaughtering some poor fowl."

Celia stared at Aug, who was frowning at Griffin's irreverence. "Does Monsieur Aug worship the devil?" she asked suspiciously. If the answer was yes, she would not allow one particle of green powder near her feet!

Aug replied in the same patois as before, while Celia strained to decipher it.

"Not exactly," Griffin translated. "But he does believe that the spirits of the dead sometimes return to torment the living."

"Do *you* believe so?" Celia asked.

Griffin smiled. "Living people always seem to present more difficulty to me than dead ones."

Aug reached out to touch her foot, and Celia scuttled back in alarm. For the first time a smile twinkled in his black eyes. He murmured something to Griffin.

Griffin laughed huskily. "Aug wants you to

know he has no taste for skinny women. Now let him attend to your feet."

Solemnly she held still while Aug took her ankle in his broad hand and sprinkled an olive-green substance over her sole. He hummed a soft melody under his breath, winding strips of cloth over and around her foot. Meanwhile, Griffin swabbed his wounded shoulder with whiskey, cursing as the sting of the alcohol sank into the cut.

"Thank you," Celia murmured to Aug when he had finished bandaging both her feet. She turned her palms up and shrugged helplessly. "I wish . . . I wish I could repay you somehow."

Aug pointed to her hair and replied. Celia looked at Griffin questioningly.

"He says he could make some powerful charms if he had a lock of your hair," Griffin said. He shook his head. "No, Aug."

Hesitantly Celia reached out to Griffin's long leg and touched the top of his boot, where she remembered he kept his knife. He arched a winged black eyebrow but made no move to stop her. Her fingertips slid around the solid knife handle and extracted it gently. Trying to comb her hand through her hair, she was dismayed to feel the number of huge snarls and tangles in the golden mass. After she found a small lock near the back, she raised the knife and cut it quickly.

"Here," she said, handing the glinting skein to Aug, who thanked her with a nod. His blunt fingers moved with surprising delicacy as he wrapped the hair in a scrap of cloth.

"That wasn't necessary," Griffin said.

"It was," Celia replied, watching Aug as he left the hut. She touched one of her neatly wrapped feet. "I owe him a debt for helping me."

"And you feel obligated to pay your debts?"

"Yes."

"You owe me your life."

"Yes." She met his eyes without blinking.

"I look forward to being reimbursed," he said mockingly.

Something tightened inside her body, a knot of repulsion and anguish. Her loving husband was dead, and she was the prisoner of this dirty, hairy-faced stranger. He was nothing but a vagabond, a jackal who survived by stealing from others. For a moment her hatred of him outstripped her fear. She hated his rough beard and sullen-looking mouth, his insolence.

"I think," she said with every ounce of dignity she possessed, "that your pride would not allow you to force yourself on a woman who did not want you."

Easily reading her contempt for him, Griffin sneered. "There are many things I value over my pride, *petite*. Your body happens to be one of them."

As if a swift storm had appeared over an already choppy sea, his mood switched from unpleasant to cruel. When she timidly asked him where she could see to her private needs, he walked her into the woods where the others could not see them, and he mocked her embarrassment. Although he kept his back turned, Celia was mortified to the point of tears. The sound of her quiet sniffling as she rejoined him seemed to annoy him beyond reason.

"Stop sniveling, you little fool," he said in exasperation. "God knows why relieving yourself is a matter of such delicacy."

He snapped at her again when she didn't move fast enough to suit him. When the hem of the wrinkled black shirt had ridden up her thighs, he inquired sarcastically if she desired to be raped by every member of the crew, beginning with himself. At his bidding, she seated herself in the pirogue, staying as far away from him as possible. After exchanging a few parting words with Aug, Griffin clapped him on the back and boarded the vessel.

Employing oars and long poles, the new crew guided the pirogue along the sluggish bayou. In spite of their earlier insolence, the men quickly became accustomed to Celia's presence, and they made no overtures to her. She found her attention captured by the exotic scenery: dense foliage and clusters of amethyst irises, muddy water filled with turtles, thick-whiskered muskrat feeding on cattail roots. The insects seemed to plague her more than they did the others, and she slapped at the flies and mosquitoes irritably. By the end of the day, she decided she had never felt so grimy and uncomfortable.

Night brought coolness with it, and Celia began to blink sleepily, wondering if the journey would ever come to an end. The pirogue passed through the last humid stretch of the bayou and through its head, into a wide, cool lake. The light of a full moon glittered over the dark water.

Griffin was faced with a decision as the vessel surged across the rippled surface of the lake. If he pressed on through the night, he would have Celia at the Vallerand plantation in a matter of hours. They could cross the lake, travel by horseback to the Mississippi River, find someone to ferry them across, and make a short trip through the Bayou St. John. Legare was probably at their heels already. It would be best to deliver Celia to the Vallerands quickly, and then disappear into the night.

He looked at Celia. She sat a few feet away from him, huddled in a ball of misery, resting her head and arms in her lap. The disheveled cloud of hair obscured her face. Her neck was streaked with sweat and dirt. The black shirt was pulled closely over her body, but he knew that underneath it were bony knees and hips as slim as a boy's. Wryly he wondered how she could have inspired such lust earlier.

She sat up and looked straight ahead, clasping her hands in her lap like a prim little girl. Griffin was puzzled by the sight of her. She couldn't possibly be the same creature who wrapped herself around him like a second skin when he kissed her. Had he imagined the warm silken mouth, the seductive undulation of her body against his . . . Had he been so exhilarated by a mixture of bloodlust and danger that he had felt a response she hadn't given?

Celia rested her chin on her hands and closed her eyes. She was about to collapse from exhaustion. Scowling, Griffin decided they would rest for the night. The sleep would do them both good, and a few more hours would make little difference to his plans. As for the debt he had threatened to claim from Celia, he'd said that merely to torment her. She had been correct earlier. He would not force himself on a woman, certainly not one brittle enough to break in two if he touched her. She was in no danger from him.

At Griffin's command the crew pulled to shore following a route they knew well. Smuggling was their business, and no one was as familiar with the lakes and bayous near New Orleans as they. The pirogue touched ground. Two of the men clambered out to hold the vessel fast while its passengers disembarked. Celia opened her eyes and stared at Griffin blearily. She did not appear to understand his order to leave the vessel. He spoke to her sharply and took her upper arm, dragging her onto the marshy shore. Giving a short nod to the rivermen, he headed into the woods.

"Where are we going?" she asked, stumbling beside him.

"Keep pace with me," he said curtly.

Celia tried to hold her tongue, but after a minute of walking her resentful words burst forth. "How far must we go? Five miles? Ten? I am not wearing shoes! And you have boots, and long legs, and my feet are . . ." She fell silent with surprise as he pulled her into a small clearing that held a lean-to house and a paddock and stable.

With no attempt at subterfuge, Griffin strode to the dwelling and banged on the rickety door. "Nettle," he said gruffly. "Nettle, get out here and saddle a horse."

There was an apprehensive voice from inside. "Captain? Captain Griffin?"

"Aye, I'll take Lebrun tonight. Saddle him, and be quick about it."

A slim, mousy man with a balding head appeared. He looked first at Griffin and then at Celia. He was clearly shocked at the sight of a woman dressed in only a shirt.

"Nettle," Griffin said abruptly, "do you have another pair of breeches?"

"Of . . . of . . . yes, I do, Captain."

"My companion has need of some additional clothes. And bring food if you have any."

"Yes, sir."

Hurriedly Nettle darted into the house, emerged with a small sack, and handed it to Griffin, his gaze averted from Celia. Without a word he rushed to the stable. Griffin handed Celia a pair of worn but clean breeches.

"He works for you?" Celia murmured, yanking on the breeches gratefully.

"In a way."

"This is his horse you are taking?"

"It's my own horse," he said in a voice that forbade further questions.

In a remarkably short time Nettle led a magnificent chestnut horse with a white forehead over to them. The large horse, at least sixteen hands high, seemed nothing but a bundle of nervous energy.

"I'll return tomorrow," Griffin said to Nettle.

"Yes, sir."

Griffin took the horse's reins, inserted a foot in the stirrup, and swung himself into the saddle with ease. He stretched an arm down to Celia. "Take hold."

Gingerly she grasped his arm with both hands, and he caught her frail wrist, pulling her up to sit sideways in front of him. The chestnut pranced uneasily at the added weight. Celia grabbed for some means of support, her hands searching wildly over Griffin's thighs, waist, and arms.

His breath hissed through his teeth, and he clamped an arm around her, nearly cutting her in two. "Don't move," he said, sounding oddly strained. "Don't touch anything."

"I-is something wrong?"

Griffin considered telling her yes, something was very wrong, he was a hair's breadth away

from throwing her on the ground and falling on
her in a frenzy of lust. The feel of her against him
was agony. There was a demanding ache in his
loins. His hands itched to roam over her breasts,
down her waist, between her thighs. As his mind
searched for a subject to distract it from its present course, his gaze happened to fall on Nettle,
who was staring at them bemusedly.

"*Goodbye*, Nettle," Griffin said meaningfully.
Finding himself to be the recipient of an intimidating glare, Nettle wandered back to the house.

Celia felt an icy-hot shock as Griffin's hand
closed over her knee. Blushing violently, she allowed him to draw her leg over the saddle until
she was straddling the horse as a man would.
Aware of her trembling, he asked her brusquely
if she was afraid of horses.

"Yes," she lied. "A-a little, yes." She could
not tell him that the tremors running through her
body had nothing to do with the horse, and everything to do with the touch of his hand. She
didn't understand why it affected her so.

The forward lunge of the horse caused her to
fall back against Griffin's chest, and she stayed
there, held in place by his arm. They rode so
swiftly it seemed they were flying. Griffin
seemed to Celia to be well-acquainted with the
forest, since it was dark and he clearly had no
difficulty finding his way. Night birds flew from
their roosts in alarm as the horse passed by. The
foliage became dense, and Griffin was forced to
slow down.

"Are we going to travel all night?" Celia murmured.

"We're going somewhere to rest a few hours."

"Indian huts again?"

Griffin half-smiled. "A deserted woodcutter's

cottage. I use it now and then when I travel to New Orleans along this route.''

''What happened to the woodcutter?''

''He moved to a new place after I paid him for the property.'' He laughed softly. ''I suppose you think I did away with him.''

''Why should I not think that?''

''Why indeed,'' he said dryly.

''Captain Griffin, will you tell me why you are taking me to the Vallerands?''

''Not now.''

''But why—''

''At the moment I don't feel like explaining.''

For the thousandth time Celia wondered who he really was. ''Does everyone call you Captain Griffin?''

''I use other names, depending on the situation.''

''Your real name is French, *oui*?''

''Why do you say that?''

''Because of the way you speak. Your parents must have been French.''

''Creole,'' he said quietly. ''Would you like to know my first name?''

She nodded, her head still resting on his shoulder.

''Justin.''

''Justin,'' she repeated softly.

''Does it mean anything to you?''

''No.''

''I didn't expect it to,'' he said, a puzzling note of irony in his voice.

The woods opened up before them, displaying a view of a glistening lake. A small cottage nearby was half-concealed by pine trees. Griffin reined in the horse, dismounted, and reached up for Celia. She put her hands on his broad shoulders, feeling them flex as he lifted her from the saddle and lowered her to the ground. He let go of her immediately and strode to the cottage. The wooden door was swollen from the humid air, and it took a hard shove to open it.

"Here." He gave her the sack. "Go inside. Try to find some candles. I'll see to the horse."

Squinting in the darkness, Celia ventured into the cottage. The floor creaked underneath her feet. Seeing the outline of a window covered with heavy batten blinds, she crept toward it, her ears pricked for the sounds of rodents or any other creatures who might have taken refuge there. The blinds opened with a squeak, allowing a flood of moonlight into the room. Celia drew the curtain of coarse netting across the open window and turned to look at her surroundings. There was little furniture in the cottage, only a battered trunk, a tiny rope bed in the corner, a stove, and a table and two chairs.

Slowly she went to the trunk and lifted the lid, searching through its contents. There were a worn blanket, an ax, a mallet, tin cups, and various other articles. A breeze from the window stirred her hair, and she lifted her face appreciatively, relishing the cool air on her skin. It was quiet . . . so quiet.

Without warning, a strange coldness crept up inside her, a feeling that would not subside. Standing up, she wrapped her shaking arms around her middle. There was no reason to be afraid, she told herself. Only children were frightened of the dark. But the room was filled with a menace that hovered around her. It was the first time she'd been alone since she had been locked in the hold of the ship. Being alone in the darkness had suddenly become her greatest terror.

She was too afraid to move. The sack dropped from her nerveless hands.

Breathing hard, she forced herself to take a step toward the door. The shadows seemed to pull at her. *Griffin,* she tried to call out, but her voice was only a strangled whisper.

There was a movement outside the doorway. All at once she bolted out of the cottage in silent terror, feeling a hand catch at her elbow. "Celia—"

She wrenched her arm free and stumbled backward a few steps, her eyes wide. Griffin stood before her, his eyes narrowed. "What is it?" he asked. "Are you hurt? Did you see something?"

No, nothing so ordinary. Just a nameless, childish fear she could not control. "I-I'm all right," she said with difficulty, wondering if she had finally lost her wits. Griffin stepped forward, and she continued to back away. If he touched her, she thought hysterically, she would fall apart. She couldn't bear any more. She wanted it all to be over, now. She was so tired of being afraid, feeling lost. She wanted to be at home in Paris, in her own soft bed with its crisply ironed sheets, listening to her family's voices just outside the door. She wanted to go to sleep and never wake up.

"Celia." He spoke quietly, staring at her drawn face. "Celia, come here."

"No."

"We're going to the water."

"No—"

"Then do whatever the hell you want." He turned and walked away at a relaxed pace. After a few seconds of indecision she began to follow him.

He heard her footsteps behind him, and his frown eased. As he had expected, she was too exhausted to make decisions for herself. He was sorely troubled by his own reactions to her, which was why he was glad he would be rid of her on the morrow. Women were nothing but a momentary convenience, something to discard as soon as they sated his desires. This one was the first who had ever depended on him for anything, and he didn't like it. He didn't like the way he felt when that stricken look came into her eyes. He especially didn't like the damnable urge to comfort her that swept over him with increasing frequency. Softness was something he did not allow himself—ever.

He reached the water's edge and surveyed the area with expert eyes. "Take the bandages off your feet," he said shortly. "You may as well wash the powder off. By now it's done all the good it's going to."

Celia sat on the pebbled ground, stretching out her slim legs one at a time. It would be a relief to wash her feet, for they had been hot and suspiciously itchy all day. Leaning over her right foot, she pulled at the knotted cloth, loosening the bandage. The smell of the herbs, bitter and moldy, rose to her nostrils. Painstakingly she began to unwind a strip of cloth, finding that her fingers were unusually clumsy.

With a soft curse Griffin sank to his knees beside her, his thighs widespread. She stared at him, wondering what had irritated him. He unwrapped her foot efficiently and lowered it into the water. Celia closed her eyes at the feel of the cool water and the strong hands rubbing away the caked powder. Gently, his fingers slipped between her toes, over the ball of her foot, pressing deep into the arch. She responded with an involuntary sigh of bliss. He flexed her foot at the ankle, set it down, and reached for her other one. Celia was ashamed of the pleasure she received at his hands, but that did not stop her from relaxing and enjoying it.

All too soon the moment was over, and she opened her eyes as Griffin pulled off his boots. "Are you going to wash your feet also?" she asked.

He dropped his jerkin to the ground. "I'm going for a swim."

"But—but there may be alligators—"

"Not on this side of the lake." He smiled. "Not usually."

"But what will you do if one has decided to visit?"

"I'll tell him I've brought a Vallerand with me. That should frighten him away."

As he stripped off the last of his clothes, Celia turned her face with a gasp, covering her face with her hands.

"Very modest, for a married woman," his softly jeering voice fell to her scarlet ears. "Or did your husband bed you only in the dark? No, don't bother to answer. You're easy to read."

She glared at him through her fingers. Laughing, he plunged into the water. She watched him dive and disappear under the surface, then reappear. While he swam, Celia examined the soles of her feet in the moonlight, surprised to see how quickly they were healing. Scabs had formed where there had been deep blisters, and the swelling was completely gone. There was a line where the clean white of her feet met the grayish skin of her leg. Frowning, Celia looked out at the water, thinking of how wonderful it would feel to wash herself.

Griffin treaded water and faced her, seeming to read her thoughts. "I could have raped you many times over by now," he said bluntly. "Don't you trust me a little?"

Celia fingered the top button of the hateful black shirt indecisively, then unfastened it.

"On the other hand," his voice floated over to her, "I don't promise not to look."

Immediately she hugged her arms around her knees, abandoning the idea of swimming.

"For God's sake," he said in disgust, "I won't look." With that, he turned away and dove under the surface again.

Celia made up her mind to do it quickly. Feverishly she unbuttoned the shirt and slid out of the breeches. She waded in up to her hips, splashing and scooping up water with her hands. Once she submerged her head, scrubbing ferociously at her scalp, then flung her wet hair back and squeezed out the excess water. She didn't notice if Griffin watched her, and she didn't care. The lake was heavenly, and she felt clean and restored.

Making her way back to the lake shore, she wrapped her black shirt around her wet body and pushed her arms through the sleeves. She used a cuff to dry the beads of water from her face, and raked her fingers through the dripping skeins of her hair.

When Griffin came out of the water, Celia did not turn around. She was unbearably conscious of his naked body behind hers, the rustle of his clothes as he dressed again. Then there was no movement.

"I'm tired," she half-whispered, needing desperately to break the silence.

"*Allons*," Griffin replied, giving her a nudge toward the cottage. "Let's go. It's going to be a short night."

Chapter 4

Celia perched on the edge of the bed, nibbling a piece of hard yellow cheese and a crust of bread. The rough cotton ticking and the blanket beneath her were musty, but after the past few days the bed seemed luxurious. She looked at Griffin, whose dark form blended with the shadows on the other side of the room. He sat on the floor with his back braced against the trunk. The tip of his cigar glowed red as he drew on it slowly. The scent of tobacco was strangely comforting to Celia, reminding her of the after-dinner cigars her father enjoyed.

"Do others use this place?" she asked.

"Some of my crew on occasion."

Celia was compelled to ask more questions, even though she sensed how he disliked them. "Do you have a home somewhere?"

He took his time about replying, fitting the cigar to his lips and breathing out a puff of smoke. "I have my ship."

"Is there someone waiting for you? A wife, a family?"

"A family is one thing I've never wanted and will never have."

Celia believed him. She could not imagine him

78

with children, a wife, anyone at all. Several times she glanced at him as she ate. She could see nothing but the tip of the cigar. Then that was extinguished. Griffin was unnervingly quiet.

She longed to lie down on the bed and close her eyes, but she was afraid to. She might drift to sleep only to be awakened by his despoiling hands and his body smothering hers. If he were going to take her, he would do it now, tonight when she had no defense against him. She waited tensely, and jumped at the sound of his voice.

"If you're waiting for me to ravish you, you'll be disappointed. Go to sleep."

Relaxing a little, Celia lowered herself to the thin mattress and drew her knees up to her chest. She was tired, and it took only a few moments to drop into a deep slumber.

But when sleep came, it provided no peace. She felt herself moving, walking in and out of dreams, taking part in conversations that made no sense. An invisible force pulled her this way and that, slowing her when she tried to run, throwing her off-balance. Frightened, she covered her head with her arms and called for Philippe . . . She wanted him so much . . . She ached to have him hold her, protect her, love her. And suddenly he was there, his blue eyes smiling at her.

"Do you want me?" he asked tenderly. "I'll always be here when you call."

"Oh, Philippe, I thought you were dead. I th-thought you had left me—"

"No, I'm right here," he murmured. "Right here. Don't be afraid."

"But I am afraid . . . I am . . . don't leave me." *She tried to ask him what had happened to him, but her words were incoherent. As she babbled faster, he*

began to drift away from her. "No!" she cried, reaching out for him, trying to keep him with her.

Talonlike fingers closed over her shoulders, and she spun around in horror to confront Dominic Legare. "You'll do as a present for André," he said with a snarling smile. And he began pushing her toward a corpse, forcing her head down until she was staring into André's bloodied face. His eyes were open and frozen in an astonished expression.

Celia fought to escape Legare's hurtful grasp. She twisted away and screamed as she saw lifeless bodies everywhere. "Philippe, come back to me," she begged. "Come back!" She stumbled across the deck of the ship, searching for her husband, while Dominic Legare followed. If only she could find Philippe, he would protect her from Legare. She would find safety in Philippe's arms.

She came to the rail of the ship and stared into the water at the bodies floating face-down around the ship. Her husband was there. The water was dark with his blood. "Oh God, Philippe, no!" She reached her arms down toward him, and as if he had heard her, he began to flail at the water, slipping underneath the surface. He was drowning before her eyes. She screamed again and again for someone to help them, but Dominic Legare was behind her, choking off her cries with his hands . . .

Celia woke up fighting against the arms that confined her. "No! No—"

"Quiet," a low voice said above her head. "It's over now."

She shuddered convulsively, burying her wet face in her hands. "Philippe? Philippe—"

"No. You know who I am." Large hands smoothed over her head and back, and she lay folded up and gasping against a hard chest.

"Justin," she said weakly, not certain why his

real name sprang to her lips when she was more familiar with him as Griffin.

"You were having a bad dream, *petite*. Just a dream."

"I saw . . . Philippe . . . H-he was alive."

Griffin continued to stroke her back. "If he were, I would go back and find him. But Legare leaves no survivors."

She swallowed hard, beginning to regain her wits. "Why?"

"It was a practice he began years ago, when—"

"No," she interrupted. "Why would you care if Philippe were alive?"

There was a long, taut silence. "I'll tell you when we reach New Orleans."

"Why not now? Why does it have to be a mystery? What does it matter if I reach safety or not?" She began to cry brokenly. "You're no less guilty th-than the men who killed him," she said through her raw, angry sobbing. "You're no better than they! You've killed before, many times. His blood is on your hands as much as theirs!"

Even in her torment, she sensed she had somehow hurt Griffin. The arms around her withdrew, and he stood up from the bed, walking away. The shock of aloneness and encroaching darkness caused something inside her to shatter. She had to escape from the demons howling around her, run, find a place to hide. Wildly she sprang from the bed and stumbled to the door, tearing at it until it was open. But Griffin's arm came around her waist before she could slip outside. A panicked scream burst from her lips, and she clawed at him ferociously.

"Stop it, damn you!" He shook her slight frame. "Stop it!"

"No . . . let me go . . . *Philippe!*"

Griffin raised his hand to slap her, unable to think of any other way to stem her rising hysteria.

"No," she sobbed, collapsing against him.

Griffin's hand lowered. He stood there, breathing hard, looking down at her small, cowering figure. Her face was hot against his chest, her closed fists pressing hard on his shoulders. Bleakly he realized he would rather confront a shipboard battle than this frail slip of a woman—he could face danger, death, far more easily than he could deal with her tears. She needed comfort, kindness, things he was incapable of giving anyone.

Fear had made her spine grow rigid and her teeth chatter. The roots of her hair were wet, and her skin was clammy. He held her against his warm body, easily taking her weight. She felt like a child in his arms, small and slight. But she was no child, and he was uncomfortably aware of the texture and scent of her. The sight of her naked on André Legare's bed was still fresh in his memory. His pulse raced at the thought. He had fought for Celia Vallerand, claimed her. It was his right to take her. But some remaining shred of civilized feeling stirred within him, reminding him that she was a defenseless woman.

Celia wiped her nose on her sleeve. "I had a gun wh-when the ship was taken. I was going to kill myself before they . . . but I-I didn't. I was a coward. If I had another chance, it would be different. I wish I had died with Philippe."

"No," Griffin said, brushing at her wet cheeks with his thumbs.

"*I should have died,*" she whispered with scalding intensity, her eyes streaming with tears.

He bent down and picked her up, carrying her

to the bed. She clung to him and cried helplessly, giving vent to the sorrow and fear that had gathered inside her since Philippe's death. Silently Griffin set her down and leaned over her, his hand gliding over her hair, her shoulders, the back of her neck. Her body was light and delicate underneath his palm. Celia's crying finally dissolved into soft hiccups, and she wiped her face with a handful of the shirt, feeling drained.

"My head hurts," she said in a thin voice.

"Don't talk."

Surprised by the trace of kindness in his tone, Celia glanced up at him. He was so quiet, so self-controlled, it seemed impossible that he was the same man who had savagely killed André Legare right before her eyes.

"I did not mean what I said to you," she whispered. "About his blood on your hands—"

"You meant it. Don't be a coward."

Celia hesitated and nodded slightly. He was right; it was better to be truthful. She could not deny she was revolted by what he was—a thief, an outlaw, a murderer. "But you helped me," she said in confusion. "I do not understand why. You must want something from the Vallerands, or . . . perhaps you owe something to them. What is it?"

Her hand seemed to burn. Unconsciously she had placed it on his chest. She could feel the frighteningly strong thud of his heart, the heat that radiated from his skin. Pulling her hand away, she closed her fist, but her palm still tingled from his vital pulse.

Griffin flinched as if he had been touched by a branding iron. The feel of her in his arms was too much. He tried to call forth what little compassion and honor he still possessed, but he could not force himself to let her go. Never in his life had he wanted anything as much as he wanted her. "I'm in no one's debt," he said thickly. "But you owe *me* something."

There was no mistaking his meaning. Celia's heart gave a frightened leap. "When we r-reach New Orleans," she stammered, "Monsieur Vallerand will give you a reward for saving my life."

"I want it now." His voice was harsh and strained.

"I have no money—"

"It's not money I want."

She made a sudden bolt out of his lap, trying to crawl off the bed. His arms became bands of steel that locked around her chest and hips.

"*No*," she gasped.

The bristle of his beard scratched the back of her neck, the velvet heat of his mouth rubbed over the top of her spine. Celia gave a low cry. His hot breath roamed over her neck, and hair, sinking into her shirt.

"Please," she said wildly, "don't do this—"

He turned her to face him and grazed her mouth with a surprisingly soft kiss. She jerked her head back and struggled furiously, a short scream escaping her lips. His hands tangled in her hair, pushing her head down to the bed. A powerful thigh swung over her body, and he straddled her hips, crouching over her intently. She whimpered in fear, clawing at his face, his chest, but nothing would stop the ravenous mouth that wandered over her throat, cheeks, chin, and salty-wet lashes. Her cries were smothered as his lips forced hers open, his tongue plunging into the hollow of her mouth.

At first Griffin intended to take her without delay. It didn't matter if his desire was reciprocated or not—he had to bury himself inside her and satisfy his hunger. Roughly he pulled at the clothes that covered her.

Suddenly Celia went still. She turned her face away from him, closing her eyes, steeling herself to endure what would follow. Griffin stared at her naked body. She was slim and fragile, soft as silk, her skin translucent in the moonlight. He could see the delicate tracing of veins above her breasts, the pale satin points of her nipples, the glint of down that formed a line along her midriff.

Her lips were wet from his kisses. Slowly he bent over her, tasted those soft lips with a gentleness that was foreign to him. She clenched her teeth and held herself immobile while his mouth brushed over hers. He touched the side of her breast, traced the shallow curve underneath. A sweet scent clung to her, the natural fragrance that belonged to her alone. He pressed his mouth to a soft pink nipple until it formed a hard bud, brushed his beard against the aroused peak, then soothed it with his tongue.

Celia quivered in outrage. The way he touched her seemed like a mockery of what she and Philippe had shared. "Don't," she said hoarsely. "Just have done with it! Don't pretend I'm willing . . . don't pretend . . ."

He seemed not to hear her. His mouth left a trail of fire as it skimmed to her other breast. Strangling a moan, she rolled to her stomach, trying to douse the burning in the pit of her belly and between her thighs. Immediately he found the back of her neck and tormented the vulnerable spot with nibbling kisses. His warm fingers dipped into the hollows of her spine, pressing and kneading, working down to the smooth place where her buttocks began. Celia clenched her fists and turned her perspiring face into the cotton ticking. "I hate you," she gasped, her voice muffled. "*Nothing* could change that. Let me go!"

"I can't."

"I-it doesn't matter what you have done for me, I am not yours and you have no right—"

"You are mine. Until I give you to the Vallerands." He bent over her unwilling mouth once more, thinking that he'd never had to seduce a woman before, not when every corner of the world was filled with willing ones. For him, the act of mating had always been quick and intense. But now he wanted something different, wanted it enough to wait with unnatural patience.

He slid his large hand over her breast, covering it completely. Her heart beat wildly into his palm. "Don't be afraid," he said, stroking her breast in a calming movement. "I won't hurt you."

She gave a choking laugh at the incongruity of such words, when his muscular body was poised over hers so threateningly. She sensed the violence of the passion contained inside him, expected that at any moment he would tear open his breeches and fall on her like an animal. His mouth touched hers, and the unfamiliar laugh died away, melting beneath the scorching heat of his lips. The hammering rhythm of her heart seemed to drive the air from her lungs. Slowly he acquainted himself with the inside of her cheeks, the sensitive places under her tongue.

Celia felt herself slipping into a dreamlike trance. She no longer cared who she was, or what she was doing. All that mattered was that the feeling didn't stop. Her breasts ached, and she moaned as he circled them with gentle fingertips. The muscles of his arms tightened, and he pulled her upright until her nipples were buried in the mat of springy hair on his chest. His hand moved up the ridge of her spine, clutched the hair at the back of her neck. "Say my name," she heard him mutter against her throat. The feel of his rough beard against her skin sent a wave of shocking excitement through her.

"No—"

"Say it."

Celia sobbed in anguish, trying to conjure up Philippe's image, trying to recall herself to sanity. But Philippe's face had vanished, and there was nothing left but darkness and the tormenting caresses of a stranger. Tears slid down her face. "Justin," she said brokenly.

"Yes," he whispered, gripping her small head between his hands, lowering her to the bed.

"Justin . . ." She shuddered as his kisses swept over her face, harvesting the tears from her cheeks, chin, and jaw. The tip of his tongue ventured into the corners of her mouth, gained entrance to the moist softness beyond her lips. She had never been kissed like this before, with a slow thoroughness that sent her thoughts spinning into chaos.

Dimly she sensed the terrible guilt that awaited her if she allowed him to take her. If she put up enough of a struggle, there was a slim chance he might let her go. But to her everlasting shame, she found she had no more will to fight . . . her body was welcoming the drugging caresses that eased away all pain, all awareness of everything but rapture.

Unhurriedly Griffin stood up and removed the remainder of his clothes, his gaze never leaving her. The tiny bed creaked in protest as his weight lowered onto it once more. Celia gave a shivering moan as his hair-roughened leg intruded between hers. His lips covered hers while his fingers searched through the pale golden triangle at the juncture of her thighs. He found the tender line of closed inner lips, opened them with soft strokes. Weakly she tried to deny him, but he kept her legs apart with his knees and subdued her with a low murmur.

His palm coasted up the inside of her thighs, encountered the touch of wetness in the tangle of hair. Embarrassed and frightened, she turned on her side. He pulled her back, his hand gliding between her legs once more. Her inner muscles constricted as she felt his fingers probing the entrance to her body.

Celia tried to control her gasps, tried to ignore the maddening urge to push her hips up against that warm, knowing hand. One of his fingers slipped into her swollen passage, stroking the slick inner walls. "You're so tight," he murmured, the tip of his finger tracing a sensitive place inside her, causing her to jerk against him with a startled gasp. "Easy, *ma petite* . . . relax. I won't hurt you."

As Griffin whispered reassurances to her, he lost his ever-present awareness of the outside world, the keen alertness that had never left him before. He drew pleasure from her with single-minded concentration, as if thirstily drinking water from a spring. Celia's small hands touched his bearded face, his hair, his flexing back. Closer and closer her limbs moved to his, pressing against the unfamiliar hardness and rough texture of a man's body. He held her slim hips between his thighs, while the huge, taut length of his aroused flesh burned against her abdomen.

Griffin began to enter her, and paused at the

discovery that she was impossibly small. Celia
writhed under the exploration of his mouth and
hands, softly begging for release. Her fingers
curled into the back of his neck, and she pressed
her face against his shoulder, gasping with fear
and need. The gesture of surrender lured him on,
and he plunged into her softness with a single
thrust. It was then that Griffin's mind reeled from
shock as he heard a cry of pain, felt her awkward
attempts to accommodate him. The throbbing
flesh that surrounded him had never been
breached before.

Since attaining manhood Griffin had taken care
to avoid virgins. They were nothing but trouble,
and they held no attraction for him. The shock of
encountering his first virgin was not a pleasant
one. He should have recognized the signs—but
he had been too eager for her. And she had been,
after all, a married woman. Or had she? He seized
her face in his hands, glaring at her furiously.
"Who the hell are you?" he demanded. "Not
Philippe's wife, not *anyone's* wife. Tell me why,
damn you!"

She cringed away from him, unable to speak.
Her body was racked with agony . . . he was too
big, he was hurting her . . . his rage frightened
her. He moved slightly and she gave a cry of distress, tears sliding out from beneath her eyelids.

Breathing in harsh bursts, Griffin released his
grip on her face. "Dammit, answer me!"

She moaned and turned her head to the side,
trying to block out his anger.

Griffin wondered what the hell he was going to
do. For all his experience, the deflowering of in-
nocents was something of which he had no
knowledge. And he did not want to hurt her further. She pushed at his chest with her hands and

twisted beneath him. "Don't," he said, keeping her still. "Don't move." He lowered his mouth to the space between her eyebrows and kept his lips pressed against that small spot.

The warmth of his mouth there was strangely hypnotic, and she began to relax.

"You should have told me," he said. "I could have made it easier for you." He drew her wrists over her head. "Leave them there, *petite*. And be still."

Separating his mouth from her skin, he let his breath fall on her moistened forehead. Celia inhaled sharply as she felt him slide deeper inside her. The rough tips of his fingers traced over her lips, and then were replaced by his mouth. Leisurely he tasted, bit, and sucked at her lips, sometimes languid and light, sometimes hard and intense, until her mouth was warm and swollen and her entire body was tingling.

His hands brushed over her in long strokes, preparing the way for his gently questing mouth. Inch by inch he withdrew from her, and Celia gave a whimpering protest. She felt empty, restless, her body seeking more of the hard, masculine pressure. His lips coasted over the center of her chest, down her taut midriff to her navel. Delicately his tongue circled the tiny rim before dipping inside. Unable to bear the intimate wetness of his mouth there, she moaned beseechingly.

Griffin moved his body back over hers, teasing the feminine mound with strokes of his heavy shaft. She felt his hand slide under her back, and she arched willingly, allowing his probing fingers to find the base of her spine. Her breath caught as she felt pleasure spreading from her shoulders to the backs of her knees. He eased another few inches into her throbbing passage, stretching her until she clutched at his shoulders in a reflex of pain.

"Look at me, Celia," he said huskily.

She stared into his eyes, mesmerized by the depths of shadowed blue. The ache between her legs faded, and she made no protest as he pushed forward again, filling her completely. They exhaled together, both aware of a sense that time had stopped, leaving the two of them alone in a world without boundaries. Griffin plunged and withdrew slowly, luxuriating in her soft body.

Celia held on to him desperately, knowing she should have clawed and fought him until the bitter end. It was madness to want him. But he demanded her pleasure, forced it from her with unforgivably gentle lips and hands. She slid her fingers into his hair, kept his mouth on hers while his kisses ravaged and feasted without inhibition. Her hips strained toward his, and with a low grunt he grasped her buttocks, showing her a circular movement that intensified the fire between them.

The half-sweet, half-painful rapture exploded inside her with stunning force. Helplessly she arched up to his thrusting hips and gasped against his chest, her mind blank except for the thought that she must be dying. Griffin lunged inside her a final time, every muscle in his long body tautening into fine-tempered steel. His beard scratched the soft skin of her neck, while the heat of his breath singed her nerve endings.

The embers of pleasure glowed for a long time afterward, while he held her trembling body against his and drew her head onto his shoulder. Celia was too weak to move. She felt herself slowly drifting into an exhausted slumber. Then for a few moments she felt the deepest peace she had ever known, but it was soon eclipsed by shame. She could not deal with such feelings now though; she was too tired. She did not move from the warm circle of his arms, only rested more fully against him and let sleep overtake her.

Much later she was aware of a river of darkness that cradled and carried her in its slow current. Unable to decide if she was awake or lost in a dream, she abandoned herself to the sensation. Stealthy hands swept over her with devastating tenderness. A hard, expert mouth slid across hers. Her knees were parted easily, and she lay relaxed and drowsy as the force of him moved over and inside her.

Softly she moaned his name, unresisting as he pulled her legs up to his waist. Understanding her needs with terrifying accuracy, he adjusted his rhythm to accommodate her body, building and stoking the fire until her desire matched his. Later she would despise herself for letting it happen again, but for now there was only feeling, only sweet forgetfulness . . . and she craved it as she had craved nothing else in her life.

It was early in the morning, yet already the day was still and sultry. Celia crept outside cautiously, clasping the detested black shirt around her body. She kept quiet for fear of waking Griffin, who was still sleeping in the cottage. She had neither the strength nor the nerve to face him yet. As she made her way to the edge of the lake, she felt an unfamiliar soreness between her legs. The reminder of what had taken place last night caused her face to flame scarlet.

Nothing she had ever read, no gossip she had overheard, no religious doctrine, nor medical knowledge her father had imparted, *nothing* had prepared her for what she had experienced last night. There were many who believed that a decent woman should not feel pleasure even in union with her husband. Certainly there was no excuse for her to have responded to a stranger as she had. And not only was Griffin a stranger, he was a pirate, a scavenger who killed and stole and ravened the wealth of others. She felt sick with guilt. It was *incroyable* that she should sink to such depths, not three days after Philippe had been murdered. She had never imagined there might be a bestial side to her own nature, and she hated herself for it—even more than she hated Griffin.

Celia found it difficult not to cry as she dropped the black shirt at the lake's edge and scooped water on her bloodstained thighs. But she no longer had the right to tears—she would not allow herself that luxury anymore. She was responsible for what she had done last night, and she doubted that even a lifetime of remorseful prayer would ease her sin and shame.

Philippe, she thought in agony, *I am glad you never found out what kind of woman I really am.*

Unsteadily she washed herself, her remorse doubling with each scrape and bruise she discovered on her pale skin. Griffin had made those marks. Remembering the way she had pushed her body up at him and writhed underneath his hands, she bit her bottom lip.

There was a rustling sound behind her. She whirled around to see him standing there. He was clad only in his worn breeches, his hair-covered chest left bare and his long hair tied back at the nape of his neck. He looked at home in their primitive surroundings—far more at ease, she suspected, than he would be in more civilized circumstances.

His gaze wandered over her naked, glistening body, his interest undiminished even when she snatched up the discarded shirt and covered herself. "Don't go anywhere without me again," he said.

She stared at him with swollen, reproachful eyes. "I'll do what I wish," she dared to say.

"You'll obey me if you prize your neck. We're not in New Orleans yet."

The threatening softness in his tone sent a cowardly chill of fear through her. *"D'accord,"* she agreed, the word sticking in her throat. She inched away from the edge of the lake, holding the shirt tightly closed.

Griffin lowered himself on his haunches and scooped several handfuls of water over his face and chest. Droplets glittered like diamonds on his sun-darkened skin. He turned to glance at her through narrowed eyes. "Why were you still a virgin?" Tactfulness was a quality he had discarded long ago.

A searing blush covered Celia's body. Although she had been more intimate with him than with any other man in her life, she knew nothing about him. It was nearly impossible to confess such personal things to him. Still, if she did not reply willingly, she knew he would force her to. "Philippe was a gentleman. He . . . he said he would wait for me to feel comfortable with him before he required me to . . . to perform my duty as his wife."

" 'Perform your duty,' " he repeated mockingly. "No wonder he didn't press the issue, if that's how you regard it. And at your age—what is it, twenty-three, twenty-four . . . ?"

"Twenty-four," she muttered.

"In New Orleans you'd have been considered

a full-fledged spinster. At your age you should have welcomed Philippe into your bed with cries of gratitude. But you asked him to wait.''

''I wish I had not,'' she said under her breath, but he heard her clearly.

''So do I. God knows I never expected you to be a virgin.''

''If you had known, would you have left me alone?'' she asked bitterly.

He held her gaze for a long moment. ''No.''

No apologies, not even a pretense of concern for how she might feel this morning. Celia was torn between self-pity and outrage. He was nothing but an insensitive brute!

''You've lost nothing,'' he said, reading the anger in her eyes. ''No one will ever suspect it wasn't Philippe who bedded you.''

''My worry is not what I have *lost*,'' she said sharply.

Griffin looked at her questioningly.

Celia's forehead was wreathed in a frown. ''I am speaking of consequences, monsieur, something I am certain you never pause to consider. What if I conceive a child as a result of what happened between us?''

Although Griffin's face registered no emotion, inwardly he was startled. She was correct—he had never bothered to consider the possibility before. After all, the kind of women he visited all possessed remedies to prevent or take care of unwanted pregnancies. But a well-bred French Catholic girl would not be versed in such matters. ''It is a possibility,'' he said. ''Not a likely one. But if it does happen we'll deal with it then.''

''You will not know,'' Celia replied, her tone filled with hatred. ''You will not be there to find out.''

"I'll know," he said curtly.

"How? Do you know someone in New Orleans who would tell you such things?" When he did not answer, Celia felt a burst of rage inside. "Why must everything be a mystery? What am I to you, and what do you want from the Vallerand family? Are you really taking me to them, or do you plan to hold me for ransom?" At his continuing silence, she whirled away in disgust, turning her rigid back to him. "*Vraiment*, it does not matter to me anymore. I don't care where I go or what happens. I just want this all to end!" A mosquito settled on her arm, rubbing its tiny feelers in anticipation. She swatted it away angrily. "I hate insects, and I hate swamps! I wish to be as far away from you as possible! I want some real food, a-and a bath, and clean clothes. I want a soft bed to sleep in, and . . ." her voice rose plaintively, "most of all I want a hairbrush!"

Griffin's lips twitched in amusement. Her display of temper this morning was reassuring, a sign that her spirit hadn't been broken. He moved behind her, knowing from her intake of breath that she was aware of his nearness. He picked up a lock of tangled hair from her shoulder and looked at it appraisingly. "It could use a good brushing," he agreed.

She still faced away from him. "Do not make jest of me!"

"I'll buy you a shipload of hairbrushes."

"To atone for last night?"

He laughed softly. "Would that satisfy you?"

"There is nothing you could give me that would *begin* to atone for what you've done to me."

"Apparently you have no idea of what I have to offer."

"Shiploads of stolen bounty?" she asked. *"Merci, non."*

She stepped away from him, but he followed and turned her around, holding her shoulders in his hands. "That and a great deal more," he murmured. "I don't have to take you to the Vallerands. I could make other arrangements." His grip tightened as she tried to pull away. "Be still. I never have the opportunity to hold a lady of quality in my arms. I may as well enjoy it while I can. You're an intriguing woman, Celia. I wouldn't tire of you easily. And in spite of what you claim, the satisfaction wasn't *all* mine last night."

"What are you saying?" she demanded, squirming in his grasp.

"I'm pointing out that things could be quite pleasant between us. Instead of going to the Vallerand family, you could let me take care of you."

She went absolutely still. "What?"

He studied her with intent blue eyes, while a half-smile played on his lips. "I'd give you the choice of where we go. Anywhere in the world. There are more exotic and beautiful places than anyone could see in a lifetime. If you grew weary of traveling, I'd establish you in your own home, two or three if you like. You'd have money to spend on whatever you wish. The only thing I'd ask in return is that you never refuse me your bed."

"And endure more nights like the last?" she asked, feeling more degraded with every word he spoke.

"I can promise you far more agreeable experiences in the future."

"You are asking me to be your mistress," she said in a choked voice.

"I believe so," he said dryly.

She stared at him with wide eyes. "How could you *think* that would appeal to me? How could you suppose I would even consider it? All I have ever wanted is what all women want, a husband and children, and a quiet home—"

"Is that so? You wanted something else last night."

Horrified, Celia recognized the truth of his words. There *was* another side of her, one she would have to suppress and guard against for the rest of her days. He had made her see that.

"You disgust me," she said unsteadily.

He smiled as if her reaction was what he had expected.

"You took advantage of me," she continued. "I would *never* have behaved in such a way had I not been so distraught about my husband. You cannot *buy* me as if I were a prostitute, you . . . you insolent monster! You're dirty, unkempt, barbaric—and I find you *revolting!* I know exactly who you are and where you came from. You are a gutter rat, and you belong in the sewer!"

"I take it the answer is no?"

She was enraged to the point of speechlessness.

His smile remained a few seconds longer, and then his expression became serious. "Look at me."

Celia felt her heart stop as she heard those last three words, the same words he had spoken several hours ago in the heat of passion.

"I said look at me, Celia."

Unwillingly she raised her eyes to his.

"Your grief over your husband may have been the reason you gave in to me the first time. But not the second."

* * *

When Celia asked Griffin how much farther they would have to travel, she was startled to learn they were much closer to the Crescent City than she had thought.

"About three hours," he said, reining the horse back to a slow gallop when it tried to break to a canter. They were riding along a trail in the forest, nearly invisible until one stumbled directly onto it. "After crossing the river, it's a short ride to the plantation on the Bayou St. John."

"How do you know where the Vallerands live?"

"I'm . . . acquainted with them." They came to a stretch where many low-hanging tree branches forced Griffin to slow the horse to a walk and duck his head.

"That cannot be true," Celia said haughtily. "The Vallerands do not associate with thieves and pirates."

Griffin laughed. "The Vallerands *were* thieves and pirates until two generations ago. So were many other fine families of New Orleans."

"Are you not afraid of Monsieur Vallerand?"

"I'm not afraid of anyone."

Irked by his arrogant self-confidence, Celia tried to nettle him. "Monsieur Vallerand is very powerful and dangerous. Philippe told me that his father has the best sword arm in all of Louisiana. When he hears what happened to Philippe—"

"He already knows what happened to his son," Griffin said quietly. "Your ship was due in port two days ago. It was one in a string of attacks in the Gulf. They'll have no choice but to assume the worst."

A string of attacks? How many other ships had been overtaken? Celia gave a little shudder as she remembered all the slain men on board the Vallerand merchantman, the mutilated bodies, the blood-slick deck. She was not the only woman who had been bereaved. Many families would be mourning the losses of sons, husbands, fathers, and brothers. "I heard Legare give an order," she managed to say, her throat constricting, "to lock the men who were still alive in the hold . . . and . . . set fire to the ship. How could anyone . . . It is inhuman . . ."

"I agree," he said tersely.

"Do you? Or are you and Legare cut from the same cloth? After you capture a ship, perhaps you find it convenient to do just as he—"

"Nay, there is nothing to gain by the slaughter of innocent men. I take ships for profit, not out of bloodlust."

"But you have killed before. I have seen it with my own eyes. You killed at least three men while taking me away from the island."

"If I hadn't, you'd be dead. After being tortured for hours by André Legare."

"You and the others on that island . . . you are so different from the men I've known. Philippe was like my father. He had such kindness, such respect for life, and he would never hurt anyone. He would rather bear pain himself than see someone else suffer—"

"Much good his kindness did him," Griffin said coldly.

"He died without regrets."

"So will I, when the time comes."

Celia realized with awed uneasiness that it was probably true. Griffin was like an animal in the wilderness, never thinking of the past or future, only of how to satisfy his needs for the present. Regret, guilt, shame, repentance, all of those hu-

man qualities were something he could not afford
or perhaps even understand.

"When did you begin your pirating?" she
asked.

"I began as a privateer. All strictly legal. I captured ships from warring countries who gave me
commissions to do so and rewarded me well when
I delivered enemy goods to port. But on one or
two occasions I was tempted to help myself to the
wrong ship, and I was branded an outlaw."

"Which is what you are."

"True."

"If you are ever caught—"

"I'll hang."

"But you cannot continue being a pirate, because Captain Legare will be looking for you, and
he wishes to harm you, *non*?"

"I'll probably stay out of sight for a while."
Grim satisfaction colored his voice. "I wish I could
have seen his face when he found out his brother
was dead. Oh, I enjoyed sending André to hell."
He felt Celia tremble, and he frowned. "There's
no reason to be afraid of him. I'll keep you safe
from Legare."

"I am afraid of *you*," she said in a tense voice,
and after that there was nothing but silence between them.

They reached a secluded bank of the Mississippi River where two men in rough garb ferried
them across on a flatboat. The men were obviously part of an established smuggling network,
for they treated Griffin with great respect and
seemed to feel a sense of companionship with
him. At Griffin's request, one of them gave Celia
his hat. She stuffed her long hair under its wide
brim and pulled it low over her face. Because of
the looseness of her outlandish garments and her

less than amply endowed form, she gave the appearance of being a skinny boy.

While the men conversed in soft tones clearly meant to elude her, Celia rested her hands on the wooden railing of the flatboat and stared into the sluggish water. In one of his letters Philippe had described the muddy river to her. He had said that some claimed the silt-filled water was healthier to drink than clear. Viewing the amber depths skeptically, she decided it could not be true.

Clusters of woods and hardy trees reached up toward a deep turquoise sky rippled with hazy clouds. Turtles swam near the banks of the river, congregating around the exposed roots of a tree that grew half-in, half-out of the water. As she looked downriver she saw a smudge on the horizon that might be the distant city of New Orleans.

Vessels from all over the world would be crowded at the docks there, while the quay would undoubtedly be filled with the colorful and motley mixture of people Philippe had written about. Celia could hardly believe she had finally reached the place she had dreamed of for so long. But there was no feeling of anticipation, no excitement—only emptiness inside. She had broken with her past, and lost her future.

"It will be different from France," she heard a deep voice from behind her.

How was it that Griffin seemed to read her thoughts? "Yes, I know," she replied.

"The people here are rougher than those you left behind. Even the most refined Creoles have an earthiness—at times a wildness—you may find difficult to become accustomed to."

"*Cela ne fait rien,*" she said. "It does not matter. I will stay here as long as the Vallerands allow. I have no wish to return to France.'' She had no doubt her father and her family would welcome her back, but after all that had happened to her, she could not resume the life she had once led.

Griffin came to stand beside her, aware of the way she flinched at his nearness. ''You'll do well here,'' he said flatly.

''Why do you say that?''

''Once the proper mourning period is observed, you'll be the most desirable catch in New Orleans. An attractive French widow, relatively young, having inherited a considerable fortune— aye, you'll be targeted by every eligible man from the Vieux Carré to the American District.''

''I will never marry again.''

''Why not?''

''I was not meant to be anyone's wife.''

He shrugged lazily. ''Perhaps. I know I wasn't meant to be anyone's husband. I've always thought of marriage as an unnatural arrangement.''

''Unnatural?''

''No one can remain faithful to another for life. There isn't a woman alive I wouldn't grow tired of sooner or later.''

''Not all men feel as you do.''

''Even in the best of marriages one partner or the other is eventually tempted to stray.''

''You're wrong,'' she said coolly. ''No one on earth could have tempted Philippe to stray from me. And I would never have . . .'' Suddenly she stopped, her heart beginning to pound, her hands balling into fists as the truth hit her. She *had* betrayed Philippe. Last night all her principles of honor and fidelity had been forgotten. Agonizing shame welled up inside her. Although Philippe was dead, she felt no less an adulteress.

Griffin knew exactly what she was thinking. He was troubled by the sudden urge to take her in his arms and comfort her. It was good that he would soon be rid of her—he didn't like the side of himself that she seemed to bring out. "Don't blame yourself for last night," he said with callous lightness. "It was enjoyable, but hardly worth the significance you attach to it."

As the meaning of his words sank in, Celia's spine went rigid. Never had she hated another human being as she did him! "It was *not* enjoyable," she said, glaring at him from underneath the brim of her hat.

"No?" He smiled, finding an unexpected pleasure in provoking her. "What was it, then?"

Her face reddened, and she took several breaths in an effort to calm herself. Hot, insulting words rose to her lips. She wanted to tell him how revolting he was, how vile the memory of last night was. But as she looked at his mocking face, she could not speak. His eyes were such a pure, stabbing blue—deeper than the sky or sea. She remembered the gleam of them in the darkness, the sound of his low voice in her ear, the brush of his beard on her breasts. She remembered the muscled weight of his body on hers, and the way his hard flesh had filled her so intimately. Underneath the coarse shirt her nipples ached, and she bit her inner lip in horror. What had he done to her? How could she stop this wanton craving he had awakened?

Seeing her distress, Griffin willed himself to keep his hands at his sides, when all he wanted was to touch her, pull her hips to his, kiss her hungrily. It was then that he realized how dangerous she was. He had to keep his wits about him in New Orleans. There was a price on his head, and if anyone discovered he was there, it would mean certain death. The thought helped to clear his mind. Only a little longer until they reached the Vallerand plantation, and he would be able to wash his hands of her.

"You're a distracting wench," he observed, idly flicking the brim of her hat with his finger. "Dressed like a woman, you'd be a sight to behold . . . all perfumed and powdered, dressed in silk and ribbons. I'd like to see that."

There was a faintly teasing note in his voice that struck a chord of recognition in her. Bewildered, she continued to stare at him, wiping the sweat from her palms on the sleeves of her shirt. "I have just realized something, Captain Griffin," she said. She concentrated on his bearded face. "Not only are your eyes the same color as Philippe's, but your brows are the same shape. One is naturally arched a little higher than the other."

He was silent, watching her closely.

Celia shook her head, suspicions burgeoning in her mind. She could not ignore the fact that there were similarities, albeit superficial ones, between Griffin and Philippe. Was that purely coincidental? Could it be? If what she was thinking was true, then she was the greatest fool and he was the most heartless scoundrel that had ever lived. "You have admitted that you are acquainted with the Vallerands," she continued slowly. "Perhaps it is more than just an acquaintance . . . Perhaps it is some sort of . . . kinship?"

Still he did not reply. But those unfathomable blue eyes continued to rest on hers, and she felt her knees weaken. Had she not been so confused and frightened during the last two days, she might have guessed before now. "S-somehow you are related to Philippe," she whispered, swaying unsteadily. Immediately his arm was there to support her, and she accepted its strength without thought. "You are helping me because I am Philippe's widow, and you . . . are a Vallerand."

Chapter 5

When Celia had found her balance, Griffin let go of her and spoke very quietly. "I'm helping you at the risk of my own life. If you make any kind of a scene, or try to alert anyone between now and the time we reach the plantation, I'll have to kill you for the sake of my family and my own neck. Understand?"

She could not help but believe his threat. She had seen for herself that he was a ruthless cutthroat. Her fear of him, however, was outweighed by indignation and a sense of terrible injustice. "You must have known Philippe," she accused. "Why did you not tell me?"

"I didn't want you to blurt it out to the men on the island, or the relay crew."

"How could you have done what you did to me last night—especially if you *knew* Philippe?" she whispered angrily. "Are you a Vallerand? Or of some related family? Are you one of Philippe's cousins? *Mon Dieu*, why did you take me last night if—"

"Because I wanted you. Now keep still."

A temper she did not even know she had flared out of control. "I will not," she said, her voice rising. The two men working the oars glanced at her. "I will not be silent! I asked you a question, and I have the right to an answer! How can you have been so vile as to—"

She was cut off with astonishing quickness as his hand clamped over her mouth with a pressure so firm that she could not open her jaw enough to bite him. Eyes wide, face mottled with rage, she clawed at his hand as he snapped an order at one of the men. A sweat-stained kerchief was brought over, and Celia managed a half-scream before a wad of cloth was shoved in her mouth and Griffin tied a length of foul-tasting cotton over it. She struggled furiously as her hands were bound behind her with the cord from Griffin's hair. He turned her to face him, shaking her slightly. His long sable locks fell over his face and shoulders.

"I should have done this two days ago," he growled. "Now stop wiggling or you'll fall overboard. And if you do, I won't go in after you." Despite the harshness of his words, his grip on her arms was gentle as he pulled her to a wooden crate. "Sit down," he said. She stiffened her legs and stared at him challengingly. His eyes narrowed. "It wouldn't trouble me in the least to force you."

Slowly she eased down, her eyes fastened on the horizon, her chest burning with hatred. After experimenting with a few twists of her wrists, she realized Griffin had left no possibility of her untying the cord by herself. Oh, it had been wise of him to silence her! The way she felt right now, she would have no hesitation in shouting his identity at the top of her lungs. She wished there was some way she could have him sent to the Cabildo, the filthy Louisiana prison Philippe had described to her with such horror after he had

attended some sick inmates there. She wished she
could see Griffin hanging from the end of a rope!
Was he a Vallerand? Justin Vallerand . . . Feverishly she racked her brain. Philippe had told her
the name of his father Maximilien, stepmother
Lysette, cousins, and half-sisters. The name Justin was not in the least familiar.

The flatboat reached the bank, drifting into a
tiny cove framed by a dense growth of trees.
"Good work," she heard Griffin's voice rumble
softly, and he paid the men for their passage
across the water. He picked Celia up as easily as
if she were a doll, stepped from the craft, and
ventured into the copse. Celia tensed in his arms,
her velvet-brown eyes widening as she saw what
they were heading into. This swamp was darker
and more oppressive than the one they had traveled through before. Limbs of immense oak trees
blotted out every trace of sky, while vines and
gray moss streamers choked off all but a few
shafts of sunlight. Everything was dank and ominously still, permeated with a moist rotting smell.
Heaven knew what kinds of creatures seethed
underneath the stagnant water. The swamp was
a living being . . . she felt as if they were entering
the mouth of a monster and traveling down to its
belly.

Two small wooden boats equipped with oars
were tethered to the arched root of a half-
submerged tree. Carefully Griffin stood Celia on
a bit of firm ground. "Don't move," he said. "I
don't want you stepping on a snake or landing
yourself in a sinkhole. I'm going to see which pirogue is in better condition."

Don't move? Celia couldn't even blink. She
watched as Griffin poked around the tiny vessels.
It was the middle of the day, yet the swamp was

a tunnel of murky gloom. If they became lost, no one would ever find them. They had no provisions. How could Griffin possibly find his way through this endless maze of trees, water, and slime? She would almost rather take her chances back on Isle au Corneille than face this.

Griffin came back to retrieve her, sliding his arm around her narrow waist. He frowned as he felt the tremors running through her body. "I feel compelled to point out," he said casually, "that if you had agreed to become my mistress, you never would have had to set foot in a swamp again." When she gave no sign that she had heard him, he continued talking in that same light manner. "There's no danger here. I roved through this territory often when I was a boy." He paused, considering her hate-filled eyes thoughtfully. "I can't risk untying you. There's a chance we may pass someone on the bayou. With the price on my head, I have to keep you quiet."

He lowered her into the pirogue, settled in the seat facing hers, and used one of the oars to push them away from the sodden bank. "Sit still," he said, twisting to see what was behind them.

She huddled as low as possible, her nerves twitching. Gigantic frogs hopped away at their approach. A water moccasin moved sinuously through the water. She kept her eyes on the interior of the boat, stifling a distressed moan. Griffin rowed rhythmically and tirelessly, only slowing their pace when it was necessary to maneuver the boat past rushes and fallen logs. There were times when the water was only a foot deep, the soft mud underneath pulling at the oar.

As Griffin worked steadily, the muscles of his great arms flexed, and the flat surface of his stomach tensed. Occasionally mosquitoes and other tiny predators descended on his gleaming brown skin, but he seemed not to notice them. Celia's gaze was unwillingly drawn to him. He would frighten anyone with that savage body and wild beard and hair. Ironically she recalled the fairy tales she had pored over as a little girl, of princes and chivalrous knights rescuing young maidens from beastly ogres. Although Griffin had rescued her, he resembled an ogre, not a prince.

Closing her eyes, she thought with melancholy of Philippe's face, handsome and utterly masculine. His mouth had been pleasingly wide and expressive, one moment serious, the next curved with a teasing smile. His jaw, so strong and cleanly cut, his nose straight and perfect. She could almost feel his short, shiny dark hair sliding through her fingers, and the brush of his shaven cheek against hers. She could almost hear him whisper tenderly that he loved her. What a fool she had been not to have made love with Philippe. Now what should have belonged only to her husband had been taken by a brutal stranger who had no respect for her innocence or what it had meant to her.

Griffin seemed to catch sight of something in the distance. Celia followed his gaze and saw a flicker of movement in the quiet green bayou. Griffin turned back to her, his expression cold. "A flatboat coming this way," he said. "Keep your head down. And don't make a sound."

She met his gaze defiantly. She could make trouble for him, if only by causing enough of a disturbance that the passersby might decide to investigate. If they saw that she was bound and gagged, they might intervene. Surely they would be glad to collect a bounty for a notorious pirate captain.

"You little fool," Griffin muttered. "They wouldn't help you. And once they realized you're a woman . . . put your damn head down."

Slowly she obeyed, allowing the hat to shield her face from the view of others.

Griffin continued to row while the other boat passed them at a distance of close to thirty feet. There were two men aboard, obviously smugglers, operating a flatboat that was little more than a glorified raft. A coarse blanket covered a low stack of boxes. The men appeared to be unaware of Griffin, but he knew that was not the case. They were Kaintocks from up the river, rough backwoodsmen who transported both legal and contraband goods between New Orleans and Louisville. Although Kaintocks were usually uneducated, Griffin knew of no better riflemen. They had to be superb shots in order to protect themselves from bands of cunning river pirates who would rob and slaughter them without mercy.

Celia did not look up when she heard one of the smugglers send a greeting across the water. The language he used sounded vaguely like English, but it had a mangled, nasal quality that distorted the words beyond her comprehension. Griffin replied in a like manner, his voice emotionless. Nothing else was said, and each vessel continued on its way. Finally Celia dared to lift her head and breathe in relief.

Griffin was watching her keenly, his eyes like sapphires. "It won't be long," he said.

Not long . . . and the waking nightmare of the past days would come to an end. Celia wished her hands were free so she could rub her aching forehead. It was only now that she dared to allow herself to believe she would be delivered more or less safely to Philippe's family. The thought brought a treacherous pain to her throat. She longed to share her grief with decent, kind people who would mourn Philippe as she did. She wondered if she would ever feel secure again, if she would be able to find a quiet life that would afford her a measure of peace.

She watched Griffin, who devoted his full concentration to rowing. Her blond brows knitted together. If he *were* related to the Vallerands, she thought, it could not be closely. They were a wealthy family, and they would have provided one of their own with a fine upbringing and an education that would steer him toward some gentlemanly occupation. He was an intelligent man—he certainly would not have become a filthy brigand had there been another choice for him.

The warmth of sunlight heated the back of her shirt. Surprised, Celia looked up and saw that the dense overhang of trees had thinned out. The water had deepened into a channel with distinct banks, while the lush vegetation and debris of the swamp had obviously been cleared by human hands. The pirogue moved along the east bank of the bayou. Celia stared over the fringe of wild grasses and between the cypress and willow trees. Then her gaze was riveted on the outline of a cluster of buildings that could only be a plantation.

Griffin seemed to understand the wild curiosity behind her silence. "Five plantations front this stretch of the bayou," he murmured, pulling on the oars between words. "This is Bonheur. The next will be Garonnes. After that the Vallerands."

Her eyes stung, and despite her best efforts she felt herself begin to tremble. Griffin rowed more slowly now, his movements less fluid than before. There was a distant look in his eyes. The air around them was hot and oddly luminous, and Celia breathed deeply through her nose, feeling as if she would suffocate.

Griffin guided the pirogue to the bank and tied it to the root of a weathered oak. He took a moment to look up a steep incline toward the main house of the Vallerand plantation. "Five years," he said under his breath. The structure had changed not a whit. Cool and gracious, it was poised serenely against a backdrop of cypress trees and the blue Louisiana sky. The white stuccoed house was elegant in its simplicity, two stories high and ornamented with deep covered galleries and slender columns. The scent of the earth beneath his feet and the hints of poplar and magnolia in the air brought back the past as nothing else could have. Five years . . .

Boys' voices echoed in the woods.

Justin, attends! Wait for me!

Let's go downstream, Philippe, and look for pirates. Don't let Father find out . . .

Quickly Griffin glanced around, then relaxed as he realized the voices were remnants of long-buried memories. He lifted Celia out of the pirogue and steadied her against a tree. Carefully he removed her hat and smoothed her sweat-soaked hair. Her body was shaking with nervous tension.

"You're safe now," he said, untying the gag and fishing the wad of sodden cloth from her mouth. She made an incoherent sound and touched her tongue to her dry lips. His fingers moved to her wrists. "No reason to be afraid. They'll take care of you." He unwrapped the cord that bound her and used it to tie back his hair.

"Who are you?" she asked unsteadily.

"Not before I get you to the house." He looked up at the brilliant sky. "Broad daylight," he said, pulling her with him up the slope. "I must be insane."

Celia looked down in surprise as her thin fingers were engulfed in his large hand. It was the first time he had ever taken her hand in his.

They approached the back of the plantation house, pausing in the shadow of a grove of cypresses. Herbs growing in the kitchen garden spread a pungent scent through the warm air. Celia's gaze wandered from the tiny chapel building and the storehouses on the right to the orange trees and flowering bushes that marked the edge of an immaculate green lawn. She knew from Philippe's descriptions of the plantation that this was only a corner of the property. Farther on there would be more gardens, greenhouse, hen coop, mill and bell tower, bachelor house, overseer's house and stable, and slave cabins bordering extensive fields.

Wondering why Griffin had stopped, she took a step forward, only to be hauled back again. She followed his gaze and saw a dark-skinned boy carrying a pair of buckets toward the smokehouse. Although she had tried to prepare herself for this aspect of plantation life, the sight still startled her. What did Griffin think of this enslavement of others, when his friend and cohort Aug was a Negro?

Griffin glanced down at her, reading her thoughts. "Nearly half my crew are either former slaves or Negroes from Haiti," he said gruffly. "There are things I never questioned when I was a boy. Now I know one man was never meant to own another."

Careful to keep them from being observed, Griffin urged her toward the kitchen, which was attached to the house by a long porch. They passed the smokehouse, from which emanated the smell of smoking pork. Celia swallowed convulsively, her mouth suddenly drenched with saliva. A lazy orange cat reclined in the shade of the house, its tail flicking as it watched them approach.

Keeping Celia to the side, Griffin peered in the screened door of the kitchen, his eyes glinted with satisfaction. "As I'd hoped," he said, and pried the door open with the tips of his fingers. Celia stumbled beside him, following blindly as he pulled her inside.

The kitchen was large, possessing a fireplace with logs at least twelve feet long. There was an enormous iron cookstove, racks of pans and cranes from which pots and kettles hung. Three women, two Negro and one white, were putting up preserves. The air was thick with the aroma of boiling fruit and sugar. At the sound of the intruders, the women turned simultaneously and froze at the sight of the bearded giant who had entered their domain. No recognition was evident on their faces.

The woman at the stove, who had been stirring the contents of a boiling pot, stared at Griffin uncomprehendingly. Her hair, the most brilliant shade of red Celia had ever seen, was disheveled and curling from the steam. Her porcelain skin was flushed pink. A black dress and gray apron swathed her small but voluptuous form. She looked to be in her late twenties, her lush beauty fully developed and matured. Celia collected her scattered thoughts enough to decide that this must be Lysette Vallerand, Philippe's stepmother.

The plump, bosomy woman working at the

wooden table in the center of the room was the first to move. She lifted the small paring knife she had been using to slice strawberries, and brandished it threateningly.

Griffin smiled. *"Restes tranquille,"* he said. "Settle your feathers, Berté—I don't intend to steal anything today."

"Monsieur Justin," the cook exclaimed.

The red-haired woman dropped the spoon she was holding. "Justin," she breathed, her hazel eyes dilating. "Is it you? I cannot believe—" She broke off and turned to the lean, dignified woman with iron-gray hair. "Noeline, go find Max. Tell him to come quickly." Noeline departed with a murmured assent.

Celia shrank back into a corner, watching in confusion as Lysette descended on Griffin like a small storm, scolding tearfully and throwing her arms around him. "For so long we've wondered what happened, why you never . . . *Mon Dieu,* you don't look like yourself . . . you . . ." She stopped and peered into his dark face. "You know about Philippe—I can see it in your eyes."

"Yes, I know," Griffin said. Gently he extricated himself from Lysette's grasp. She was the only woman in the world he had any respect and affection for. Even so, he did not like to be touched. Not by anyone. Brusquely he gestured to Celia *"Belle-mère . . .* this is Philippe's wife."

His statement was met with shocked silence. "It can't be," Lysette said. "Philippe's wife was with him on the merchant ship, and—"

"She was taken to Crow's Island by the men who captured the ship. I happened to be there at the time."

"Justin, is there any chance Philippe—"

"No chance," he said huskily.

Lysette nodded sorrowfully and turned to study Celia's strained face. "My poor dear," she said with compassion. "I can only imagine what you must have gone through." When Celia did not speak, Lysette turned to Griffin questioningly.

"Use French," he said. "Her English isn't good."

Celia passed a trembling hand over her moist forehead. The hot, sweet air in the kitchen filled her nostrils. She felt dizzy as she stared at Griffin. "Why did you call her *belle-mère*?" she asked in a faltering voice.

Lysette threw Griffin a sharp look. "Justin," she said in French, "you didn't tell her who you are?"

He shrugged. "The less she knew the better."

"Of course," Lysette said with a scowl, and turned back to Celia. "He's made a lifelong habit of trusting no one, least of all women. The reason he calls me *belle-mère* is that I am his stepmother. Justin and Philippe are—were—brothers. Twins, in fact."

Celia shook her head dazedly. "No."

"Here, come sit down in this chair, you look pale—"

"No!" Celia fought off the gentle hands, feeling as if she had just been hit in the stomach. She leaned against the wall, staring at Griffin's implacable face. "Philippe did not have a brother. He never mentioned one, never—"

"It's safer—not to mention more convenient—for them to ignore my existence," Griffin said.

Lysette sputtered with indignation. "Perhaps if you did not disappear for six years at a time we would find it easier to include you in the family!"

"Five years," he corrected.

Celia continued to stare at Griffin. "If you were

truly Philippe's brother, you . . . you would not be
an outlaw. A *pirate.*" She gave the last word a loath-
ing emphasis. "And you are not Philippe's twin,
because he was only twenty-five, and you . . ."
Confused, she fell silent. She had assumed he was
at least in his thirties. Oh God, might he bear some
resemblance to Philippe underneath all that hair and
beard? The eyes were the same. She put her hand
over her mouth, feeling ill.

"I'm older than Philippe by about five minutes," Griffin said. "Or so I've been told."

"Eight," came a masculine voice from the
doorway. "I was there."

The voice belonged to the most imposing man
Celia had ever seen. There was no doubt it was
Maximilien Vallerand. He more than matched
Philippe's descriptions. His features were steely,
and his eyes were an oddly pale shade of brown
that looked like gold. A handsome man of forty-
five, he had the lean, long-limbed body of a
horseman and the dark elegance of a Creole aristocrat. He was dressed in black breeches and
boots, and a snowy white shirt open at the throat.
His hair was jet-black, touched with silver at the
temples. It was easy to see where Philippe had
gotten his looks.

Justin stepped forward and met his gaze steadily. "Father. I know what Philippe meant to you.
I'm sorry."

For a second the golden eyes glittered, and
Maximilien appeared to swallow back some painful emotion. It was only then that Celia noticed
the deep shadows that sleepless nights had left
under his eyes, and the harsh lines of grief on his
handsome face.

There was a brittle silence while the two men
assessed each other. Celia found it hard to believe

they were father and son. Aside from their similar
build and height, there was no likeness between
them. She was reminded of a sleek panther con-
fronting a shaggy swamp cat. Maximilien Valler-
and was polished and sophisticated. He had a
presence and authority that commanded the attention of everyone around him. But Justin was
unkempt, ragged. He had only the shrewd cunning of a scavenger. Years of association with the
lowest ranks of society had erased any cultivation
he might have once had.

"I know the man responsible for Philippe's
death," Justin said abruptly. "Dominic Legare.
He and his men took the ship, put the crew to
death, and kidnapped Philippe's wife." He indi-
cated Celia with an awkward gesture. "I brought
her to you. That's the only reason I'm here. I
swear I'll make Legare pay for what he's done."

"No," Maximilien said. "The commanding officer of the naval station has been supplied with
new gunboats and men to stop the attacks in the
Gulf. You will allow him to take care of it."

"No military man could ever get to Legare,"
Justin sneered. "I'm the only one capable of
tracking him down."

"I cannot lose another son," Maximilien said,
his voice scratchy. "We must talk, Justin. You
can't continue—"

"No time to talk," Justin interrupted. He
turned to the cook, who had been observing the
scene with rapt interest. "Food, Berté. Something
I can carry off with me. I have to get the hell away
from here before I'm caught. I'll take some of
those ash cakes in the hearth."

The woman waited until she received a con-
firming nod from Maximilien, then scurried to the
fireplace. The cakes, made from flour, buttermilk,

and shortening, steamed as they were removed from the hot ashes.

Justin turned his gaze on Celia, who was still wedged in the corner. He scowled and strode to a nearby chair, shoving it toward her with his booted foot. "Sit down," he said roughly. "You're about to faint."

She jerked away from him as he reached for her. "Don't touch me," she cried, reeling from the shock and humiliation of finding out that Griffin was Philippe's brother, his *twin*. He had taken and used her body, knowing she would have to face his family afterward, knowing she would be too ashamed ever to tell a soul about it. He had betrayed his brother's memory deliberately. By making her respond to him, he had placed half the responsibility on her shoulders. What contempt he must have for her . . . almost as much as she had for herself. She had never felt so helpless and outraged. She wished she could hurt him, strike at him, repay him for what he had done to her.

Lysette tried to soothe her. "Celia, we all understand that you have undergone terrible—"

"You understand *nothing*," Celia heard herself interrupt wildly. A vision of Philippe's blood-soaked back flashed before her. She clutched her tattered shirt and pulled it closer around her body, feeling as if she needed protection from their prying eyes. "How could you? How could you begin to understand?"

"You're right," Maximilien said, surprising them all by approaching Celia and taking hold of her shoulders. The calm authority of his voice broke through her agitation. She found herself held by his penetrating golden gaze. "The fact that you are here is a miracle, and one of the few

decent things my son has done in his life. I can
see you are exhausted, *petite bru*. You will allow
my wife to see to your welfare, *d'accord*? You are
part of my family now." He gave her shoulders
an encouraging squeeze and released her. "Everything will be all right. Go with Lysette."

The way Maximilien spoke was gentle and kind,
but somehow he left no possibility of refusal. Celia
nodded docilely and went toward Lysette's outstretched hand.

"Amazing," she heard Justin jeer. "For the last
three days I've had to threaten her every step of
the way. You do know how to handle women,
Father."

Celia stopped at the door, pausing to look at
him, her thin face white with hatred. "I pray to
God I will never see you again," she said stiffly.

"You won't," Justin replied, mockery glinting
in his eyes. "But you won't forget me."

As soon as Celia turned away, Justin's face was
wiped clean of emotion. He stared after her, not
accepting the wrapped bundle Berté handed him
until Lysette and Celia were completely out of
sight. "She's been through hell," he muttered.

Maximilien stroked his clean-shaven chin
thoughtfully. "How much of that was your
fault?"

Justin smiled. "You always did know the right
questions to ask, Father." He lifted the bundle of
ash cakes and sent the cook a grin. "*Adieu, Berté.
Et merci.*"

"Where are you going?" Maximilien demanded. "Stay here, dammit."

Justin shook his head. "You know I can't.
I . . ." He paused as Berté resumed her work at
the stove, her ears twitching.

"Berté, leave," Maximilien said. She obeyed

with a grumbled observation about the inconvenience of men in the kitchen.

"I have to keep moving," Justin said. "I killed Legare's brother André while taking Celia out of that hellhole. I'd have killed him too if only I'd had the chance. Now Legare won't rest until he's severed my head from my body. I'll have to get to him first. I've already endangered the family by being here."

"I can protect my family," Maximilien said grimly. "Including you."

Justin raised his brows, laughed shortly, and shook his head. "Even if you could handle Legare, you couldn't keep the authorities at bay. If they knew I was here, I'd find myself dangling from the end of a rope before the week is out. Too many people suspect who I really am. And a host of crimes I haven't committed have been laid at my feet. Not even your vaunted friendship with the governor could stay my speedy execution."

Maximilien swore with helpless anger. "Damn you for choosing this life for yourself. It didn't have to be this way."

"No? Since the day I was born it was common knowledge I was rotten to the core. I was obligated to prove everyone right."

"Stubborn fool," Maximilien said quietly. "I made unforgivable mistakes with you and Philippe. Mistakes you've had to pay for. The sins of the father . . . but even now it's not too late. Let me help you. You underestimate me in many ways, *mon fils*. I understand more than you think."

There was an iron grip on Justin's insides that would not let go. For too long his survival had depended on suppressing any softness in himself. He couldn't accept anything from his father, from anyone. He needed no one.

"Goodbye, Father," he said, not meeting Maximilien's eyes.

"Justin, wait—"

"God be with you." With that, he slipped outside, making his way back to the pirogue and the bayou.

Chapter 6

September, 1817

"*Regardes*, I have put on weight." Celia twisted to view her reflection. She hadn't looked closely at herself in a long while, only glanced in the mirror to neaten her hair or straighten her clothes. Some time during the past four months of living with the Vallerands, the frailty had gone from her arms and the hollows had left her face and neck. Even her breasts, which had been small and flat before, had developed a nicely rounded appearance.

Lysette smile, watching as a seamstress adjusted and pinned the hem of another black gown for Celia. "You were so dreadfully thin when you first came to us," she said. "I'm glad to see Berté's cooking has had such a good effect."

Celia twisted again, raising her eyebrows as she saw how the bombazine silk draped over her curving hips and buttocks. The gown was fashionably high-waisted and collarless, trimmed at the neckline and shoulders with black jet beads. The skirt flowed gently from her hips to the ground, concealing her ankles and feet. She took

an experimental breath, watching as the bodice of
the gown tightened over her breasts.

"Hold still, madame," the seamstress re-
quested.

Celia made a face. "Soon I won't be able to
wear any of my gowns."

"*That* will be a long time coming," Lysette said
dryly, and approached the standing mirror to ap-
praise her own reflection critically. "I, on the
other hand, must regain the figure I lost with Rafael." She beamed at the chubby red-haired infant on the floor, who was playing with swatches
of fabric. "You were worth every pound, darling.
Do not listen to Maman."

The seamstress, a pretty young Irish girl named
Briony, paused and spoke through the pins in her
mouth. "Monsieur Valleyrand wouldna change a
hair on yer head, madame."

Lysette laughed and shook her head. "Max is
not a fit judge of my figure. He loves me."

Celia smiled slightly, thinking to herself that
there was no need for Lysette to take off an ounce.
She was a petite Venus, voluptuous and perfectly
proportioned. With her red hair and vivacious nature, she was as vibrant as a flame. It was not
difficult to see why even a man as powerful and
aloof as Maximilien Vallerand was wrapped
around her finger.

"Max doesn't like to see me in black," Lysette
said with a sigh, returning to the brocaded settee
and picking up a tiny pair of pantalets she was
mending for one of her two young daughters.
"All last year we were in mourning because of
the passing of his mother Irénée. And now . . ."
A touch of melancholy entered her expression,
and Celia knew she was thinking of Philippe.

The mourning period would last for another

eight months, during which the adult members
of the Vallerand family would wear nothing but
black. And for a long time afterward, Celia would
not be able to dress in anything but somber
shades of lavender and gray. There were Creole
customs Celia had to observe strictly, or she
would face the censure of New Orleans. When
she wrote letters, the border of the paper was
black. She wore no jewelry except for a jet brooch,
and when she ventured out in public, her hair and
face were concealed behind a dark crepe veil. Even
the buttons on her clothes were small and dull-
surfaced. The social functions she was allowed to
attend were limited, and she had no interactions
with men.

Celia found the isolation no hardship. She welcomed the privacy she found on the plantation.
For her the days held a serenity she sorely
needed. Lately Lysette, a sociable creature with
many friends, both Creole and American, had
tried to persuade her out of her solitude. But Celia
didn't need anyone to gossip with or confide in,
and she didn't want to take part in family gath-
erings. All she needed was work with which to
occupy herself and time to reconcile herself to
Philippe's death.

There were countless chores Celia helped with
at the plantation, which was a small world in itself. The women made wine, butter, bread, preserves, and sausage; put up vegetables; and kept
detailed books of supplies to be purchased. Making soap and candles required a full day of labor
each month. There were always glassware, silver,
and china to be washed and polished, not to mention carpets to be cleaned and laundering to be
supervised. The one task that seemed endless was

needlework: stitching, darning, mending, quilting, and embroidering.

Celia became acquainted with many of the slave women as she shared in the housework, but she was too shy to imitate Lysette's familiar manner with them. She did not understand the complex relationship between slave and slaveowner, the sense of being part of the same family yet maintaining boundaries that were never crossed. Some of the plantation wives clearly regarded their servants as property, while others seemed to have genuine affection for them. One day the mistress of a neighboring plantation called on Lysette and broke down into sobs while telling of the death of an old family servant. "She was more of a mother to me than my own," the woman had cried, mopping her face with a lace handkerchief. Celia had been confused by her attitude. If the servant had truly been such a beloved friend, how could the woman have kept her in enslavement? Perhaps in time, Celia thought, she would come to understand this odd society.

Southerners were puzzling, Creoles in particular. But Celia was bewildered most of all by the Vallerands. They were a large family with innumerable cousins, and their past was filled with scandals and dark secrets that were hinted at but never revealed. Celia wished she could tell Philippe that he had not prepared her for them at all!

It was impossible to avoid hearing the rumors that circulated about all of the Vallerands, even Lysette. During one afternoon of calls and refreshments, Lysette's sister-in-law, Henriette, had sat next to Celia and told family secrets under her breath. An attractive woman with a fondness for gossip, Henriette was the wife of Maximilien's younger brother Alexandre.

"Bien sûr, how Maximilien has changed since their marriage ten years ago,'' Henriette whispered with relish. "Before then, he was the most cold-blooded, ruthless man alive. It was said that he did away with his first wife!"

"Pas vraiment," Celia murmured skeptically. Maximilien was an intimidating man, but one had only to see his gentleness with Lysette and his children to know he was incapable of such an act.

"Oh, *sans doute!* Of course, later the suspicion was proved untrue. But in those days everyone believed the worst of him, and with good reason."

"Why do you say that?" Celia asked.

"He was cruel to everyone. Even Lysette."

Celia shook her head decisively. *"Non,* Henriette, nothing will make me believe that."

"It's true, all too true. Although he is devoted to Lysette now, the only reason he married her was because he *ruined* her."

"Ruined?" Celia repeated, wondering if she had heard correctly.

"Oh, *oui!* Lysette was engaged to another man, but Maximilien seduced her and dueled with her fiancé. He was a heartless devil in those days. And his son turned out to be just like him—not your husband Philippe, of course, God rest his soul. I'm speaking of the *other.* The twin who ran off. Justin." She leaned closer and murmured confidentially, "He became a pirate. My husband Alexandre told me so."

"How disgraceful," Celia murmured, feeling herself turn pale.

"Yes, isn't it," Henriette said, looking pleased. "Didn't Philippe ever tell you? I'm not surprised—the Vallerands are all very strange about Justin. They never speak of him. I suppose they wish he'd never been born. His activities could cause terrible trouble for the family. Alexandre says Justin was always a rude, selfish boy." She sighed sadly. "And Philippe was such an angel, so dear and kind to everyone. Oh, I am not causing you distress, am I?"

"Not at all," Celia said calmly, while her insides jumped in agitation. No one but she, Maximilien, and Lysette knew the truth of how she had arrived in New Orleans. Maximilien had devised a story to explain her sudden appearance, claiming that a few intrepid sailors from the besieged merchant ship had survived the pirate attack and brought Celia back to safety.

"If Justin's involvement were known," Maximilien had said in private to Celia and Lysette, "it would be that much easier for the authorities to set a trap for him. Each time his name arises, there is a surfeit of interest in his whereabouts. The rise in pirate activity is bad for local businesses and certain political careers. I know of several highly placed men who would dearly love to make an example of Justin."

"I wish they would make an example of Dominic Legare," Celia said stiffly. "As you know, I have no liking for your son, Monsieur Vallerand. But he is not as cruel and evil as Legare."

"Of course not," Lysette interceded gently. "Deep inside there is goodness in Justin, or he would not have put himself in danger by bringing you here, *n'est-ce pas?*"

Celia was silent, her gaze falling to her lap. Lysette knew nothing of what had transpired between Celia and Justin, and Celia intended that she never find out. It was clear that Lysette wished to think well of her stepson, and furthermore, the Vallerands would probably be disgusted with Celia's part in what had happened. Goodness, Celia thought contemptuously, was not one of Justin's dominant qualities. Or hers either. She had not been able to tell the local priest of her horrendous sin during confession, and so she was in no way absolved of it. But how could she confess to another living being that she had slept with her dead husband's brother—and worse, had found carnal pleasure in the act?

Had the industrious life she led at the Vallerand plantation not been so pleasant, Celia might have considered joining the nuns at the Ursuline Convent. The idea of peace and solitude was very appealing, and she did not intend to marry ever again. Philippe had been her first and only love, and she had no desire to accept a lesser substitute. The Vallerands, however, had given her the privacy the convent would have offered, without the restrictions. And there were Lysette's red-haired children, Evelina, Angeline, and Rafe, to whom Celia was already becoming something of a *tante*. It was a Creole custom for widows and unmarried spinsters to serve as chaperones for their relatives' children. The two girls, ages eight and six, often came to visit Celia in the *garçonnière*, a small but charming residence built close to the main house.

Usually the *garçonnière* would have been occupied by the male bachelors and teenage boys of the family, but Lysette and Maximilien's son Rafael was only an infant, and there were no other Vallerand males living on the plantation. At Lysette's urging, Celia had redecorated and furnished the dark, masculine *garçonnière* for her own use. Maximilien encouraged her to look through the furniture and artwork that had been stored away in the main house. "Take what you like," he said. "Most of it hasn't been touched in years."

To her delight, Celia unearthed treasures that were moved immediately to the *garçonnière:* soft green and rose tapestries, crates of lovingly wrapped pink-flowered china, an Italian baroque clock adorned with tiny satyrs, a Louis XV chaise and side chairs, gilded and upholstered in lemon-shaded damask. Celia chose delicate patterned paper for the walls and fresh white paint for the woodwork and doors. Soon the *garçonnière* was changed into a comfortable cottage with light, airy rooms. Celia loved every inch of it, especially the parlor with its French glass doors and white marble mantel, and the unusual octagonal-shaped library with its Creole-made furniture.

"You have made this place so beautiful," Lysette exclaimed as she viewed the results of Celia's efforts. "You have a way with colors and arrangement, and . . . *qu'est-ce que c'est?*" She had opened a door to the smallest room in the house, one devoid of furniture except an old rectangular table, a stool, and an easel. No curtains framed the windows; no rugs covered the floor. There were blank canvases stacked against the wall. Sketchbooks, brushes, and paint were scattered over the table. Lysette stared at Celia with surprise. "Max told me you had asked him to bring some supplies from town, but I did not suspect you were an artist."

Celia's cheeks flooded with color. "Oh, I am not an artist, not at all. I merely . . . Well, I enjoy . . . Oh, please do not look at any of those. I would rather they remain private."

Lysette withdrew her hand from the closed sketchbook.

Afraid she had offended Lysette, Celia strug-

gled to explain, her face hot with embarrassment.
"No one has ever seen my drawings. They . . .
they are hen scratchings . . . merely an idle pas-
time. As a child I liked to paint and sketch, but
then my mother died and there was no longer
time for me to . . ." She cleared her throat uncomfortably. "I hope you do not mind that I converted this room. The work I do here is of no
merit, not good enough to be seen by anyone, but
I find it relaxing and . . . I could not do it at all if
I thought someone might see it. If Philippe were
alive I would never have taken it up. He would
have insisted on looking at my amateurish efforts,
and I could not bear that."

"Why, Celia . . ." Lysette's voice was gentle.
"There is no reason to be distressed. You may
use this room for any purpose you like. I am glad
you have such an interest. I would never do anything to interfere with it."

"Thank you," Celia replied almost inaudibly.

Lysette studied her downbent head. "You are
a quiet, undemanding person, *chère*, too much so.
At times you worry me."

"I have everything I need . . . there is no reason to worry." Celia began to back out of the
room before any more could be said. For Lysette,
it was natural to lavish affection on those around
her. But Celia had been close to only a few people
in her life: her father, her brothers and sisters,
and Philippe. Only with them had she been able
to risk sharing her private thoughts and feelings.

She had written to her father about Philippe's
death and the new life she had found here. Her
series of matter-of-fact letters had been answered
with sympathetic but equally prosaic replies from
her family. Perhaps outsiders would find their attitude odd. The Verités were an unemotional lot,

cool and practical, avoiding displays of sentiment. Her father believed that as long as physical health was maintained, all other concerns were minor. And of all Robert Verité's children, Celia knew herself to be the most deeply reserved. No one, not even Philippe, had reached the distant and remote part of her heart, the part that would always be locked away from others.

There were strong needs within her, longings impossible to put into words. She felt she would have been safe with Philippe, that he might have eventually come to understand the reckless emotions that were hidden inside her. It haunted her, the question of whether they could ever have found true intimacy together—not just of body, but of soul. Now she would never know.

Celia never allowed herself to think of Philippe in the hours just before bedtime. If she did, she was certain to have violent dreams in which she would see him drowning, reaching up to her, pleading with her to save him. She would awake drenched in sweat and tears, shaken with the feeling that Philippe was alive, when she knew he was not.

"No, Vesta." Celia nudged away the orange cat who was attempting to climb into her lap. Vesta had tired of watching the splashing water in the fountain and had placed a wet paw on her knee. Since Celia had moved into the *garçonniére* the cat had taken up residence with her. Reconciling herself to the uninvited guest, Celia had named her after the ancient Roman goddess of the hearth. The two of them sat in Celia's favorite corner of the Vallerand garden, a secluded spot bordered by a double row of lemon trees. Four paths made a rectangle, one side of which was a stone wall. An arched niche and a fountain of graduated basins was built into the wall.

It was a sunny day with a light breeze, the kind of day that was so common in France and so rare here. Celia pulled off her wide-brimmed black bonnet and tucked one of her feet beneath her contentedly. The pose lacked decorum, but no one was here to see her. She sketched the scene around her idly, letting her mind wander from one daydream to another.

Annoyed by Celia's refusal to hold her, Vesta jumped from the bench to Celia's feet and reclined on her side to clean a white and orange paw. Celia smiled and kicked off one of her slippers, using her toe to tickle the cat's furry stomach. A loud purr hummed through Vesta's body. The cat looked up at Celia through half-closed eyes.

The steady trickle of the water, soothing breeze, and gentle sunlight made Celia drowsy. She leaned back against the wall. Lysette had told her that Philippe had often frequented this place, reading books of philosophy and poetry. Celia tried to imagine him sitting here, the sunlight illuminating the chestnut brown in his dark hair, his body sprawled on the bench, long legs crossed.

On impulse she began to sketch his face, the lean jaw and high cheekbones, determined nose and heavy slanting brows. His head was set upon a strong neck, his hair brushed back except for the cowlick that caused a few heavy locks to fall over his forehead. The charcoal moved over the paper as if guided by a force other than her own. In a trance, she watched other details taking shape, wide, firm mouth, laugh lines around his eyes, shadows and indentations that had given his face that singular look of confidence and intensity.

Celia frowned as she surveyed the drawing. Something was wrong . . . The eyes . . . They were flat; the shape wasn't right. She slanted the outside corners upward, darkened the irises until they nearly blotted out the pupils, added heavy strokes to the brows. Chewing on her lower lip, she worked diligently. Finally she held up the sketch and squinted at it, shaking her head. Vesta mewed at her questioningly. "It's not right," Celia said aloud. "Not quite. Why can't I remember how Philippe . . ."

Suddenly the paper trembled in her hand. The eyes were more lifelike now . . . but they did not belong to Philippe. She felt cold sweat collect on her forehead and upper lip. A mocking glint had entered those eyes, and they seemed to stare at her knowingly.

Look at me, Celia . . .

Swallowing with difficulty, she forced herself to let go of the sketch, and it fluttered to the ground. Vesta pounced on it immediately, puncturing the rustling paper with her claws. Celia put a hand to her chest, feeling her heart racing out of control. *Don't be a fool,* she told herself fiercely. *He's not here, and you'll never see him again. How can you upset yourself so easily?* But the feeling remained. She closed her eyes.

Sometimes the memory was as vivid as if it had happened yesterday, the past months dissolving into nothing. She could still feel Justin's hands closing over her breasts, his thighs pushing hers apart, his hot breath striking her skin. As his body had filled hers he had looked into her eyes, drinking in her intense pleasure. He had made no concession to weakness or fragility—indeed, he had taken ruthless advantage of it. *I couldn't have stopped him had I wanted to*, she thought, and flushed with angry confusion. The point was, she *hadn't* wanted to stop him, and for that she would always despise herself.

Celia took the scraps of paper Vesta was toying with and crumpled them in her fist.

Feeling restless, she deposited her art materials in the *garçonnière* and went to the kitchen of the main house, which was buzzing with activity. The morning air was saturated with a yeasty smell. Tables were loaded with stone crocks that had been greased with lard and filled with rising bread dough. Women dexterously kneaded and shaped the dough before placing it in sheet-iron molds. Noeline, the Vallerands' housekeeper for many years, murmured a greeting to Celia as she brought in a tray of flour that had been sunned and aired.

Lysette was at the bread block in the corner, twisting bits of dough into rolls that would be eaten at dinner. Her daughter Evelina stood over the unbaked loaves, brushing the tops of them with a feather dipped in lard before they were placed in the ovens. Angeline sat at the table gnawing on a heel of crusty bread. Celia smiled as she saw how the daughters resembled their mother, all of them with cinnamon-red hair twisted at the napes of their necks.

"Tante Celia," Angeline cried, and hopped down from the table, wrapping her slim arms around Celia's waist. "We are helping Maman with the bread."

"Yes, I can see that," Celia replied, smoothing the child's hair.

"You are not helping," Evelina said to her younger sister. "You are only eating."

Angeline's face was wreathed in a scowl. "Maman said I could."

"Well," Celia interposed reasonably, "it is necessary for someone to make certain the taste is agreeable, *non?*" She took the slice of bread from Angeline's small hand and bit off the corner. "Mmm . . . What is it the Americans say? It is grand."

The little girls giggled and chimed in to correct her pronunciation. Lysette regarded them disapprovingly. "Do not be disrespectful, my girls."

"*Non*, I have asked them to help me," Celia said with a laugh. "Their English is much better than mine."

"It took me a long time to learn the language," Lysette confessed. "But in New Orleans it is necessary. There are so many Americans here, more and more every year. Of course, some Creoles would never condescend to speak a word of English. They will not even allow it to be spoken in their presence. Max insists that the children be able to speak both. He says it would put them at a disadvantage to be isolated from either culture."

"Philippe had an ear for languages," Celia said absently.

"So does Justin, but . . ." Lysette stopped in mid-sentence, looking uncomfortable as she saw the other woman flinch. "*Pardon*, Celia."

"It is all right," Celia murmured.

"I don't know why I mentioned him. For the past day or two I have thought about Justin several times. I even saw him in a dream." Lysette shrugged and smiled whimsically. "Noeline says it's a sign from a loa."

"A sign from what?"

"You'll have to ask Noeline to explain," Lysette said, and put her hands over Evelina's ears, mouthing the word *voodoo*.

Being from a Catholic family, Lysette had no belief in the African and Haitian gods that some slaves—immigrants from Santo Domingo—and some whites from New Orleans worshipped. She did not want to encourage superstition in her children. The voodoo cult had taken root in the city. Each year hundreds of believers gathered on Lake Ponchartrain or the Bayou St. John for a festival to worship their deities.

Celia hadn't suspected that Noeline placed credence in voodoo. Driven by curiosity, she ventured outside where the dignified housekeeper was picking up another tray of sun-warmed flour. "Noeline?"

The elderly black woman lifted her graying head. "*Oui*, madame?"

"Could you tell me what a loa is, *s'il te plaît?*"

"A loa," Noeline repeated, setting the tray back on a wide tree stump and straightening her lean form. Her lustrous black eyes twinkled with a smile. "Dere is many diff'rent kind, madame. A loa is a voodoo spirit. Dere is two parts in every loa, good an' bad. Now Legba keep watch at every crossroad . . . Legba is god of sin, make de blood run hot . . . *comprenez?*"

Celia nodded, flushing slightly.

"But Legba also good to take pity on man. Wid Legba's help, man can maybe 'scape from destiny. Now Erzulie and Damballa—"

"I understand," Celia interrupted, before Noeline went on to describe each and every loa she knew of. "Tell me . . . why did you tell Lysette that her dream about Justin may be a sign from a loa?"

"De loas work in dreams, madame." Noeline's

eyes sharpened. "You been havin' de dream too?"

"Not about Justin," Celia replied softly. "About my husband. I keep dreaming he is alive."

"Ah." Noeline tilted her head, regarding her with friendly sympathy. "Dat not from de loa, madame. When a man is gone, dere is emptiness . . . in de heart, in de bed, *c'est vrai?* But someday you find a new man to take away de emptiness, and dere will be no more dreams."

"I don't know," Celia said doubtfully. "I don't think I'll ever marry again."

Noeline smiled. "Ah'm an ole woman, madame, an' ah know what you say ain' gonna happen *always* happen."

That evening the Vallerands hosted a small "at home" for some of their family. A few elderly cousins came to visit, as well as Maximilien's brother Alexandre and his wife Henriette. They congregated in the parlor and talked uninhibitedly. While the conversation went on, they partook of strong black coffee and baba—a porous cake dipped in rum.

Celia was quiet, preferring to sit near the corner and listen to the lively exchanges of the family. Often her gaze would linger on Lysette and Maximilien, who sat on the settee. Usually their son would have been put to bed by now, but tonight Rafe was snuggled high against his father's chest, sleeping peacefully. Occasionally Maximilien would smooth a large hand over the baby's fuzzy red hair. Celia was touched by his tenderness with the child.

The guests remained until just past midnight, when the last crumb of cake had been eaten and the last drop of coffee consumed. After handing the baby to Lysette, Maximilien saw Alexandre and Henriette to the door. He turned to see if there were any more guests.

"All gone," Lysette said.

"Thank God." Max untied his black cravat and let it hang around his neck. He grinned at his wife, who was murmuring softly to the baby. Lysette looked up to meet Max's golden eyes, and his expression changed. The pair shared an intimate glance that warmed the room several degrees.

In a flash of discomfort Celia realized she was intruding on a private moment. She cleared her throat. "Er . . . *bonne nuit,* I will be leaving now," she said, conjuring a yawn and heading toward the back of the house. "It was a lovely evening."

"Wait," Max said, dragging his attention away from his wife. "I'll have Elias or Arnaud escort you to the *garçonnière.* It's too late for you to go alone."

"*Merci,* but it is not necessary," Celia said. "It is only a short distance from the house. I have walked there by myself many evenings."

"If you are certain—"

"Oh yes, yes," Celia interrupted hastily. "I have no need of company."

"Good night," Lysette said a touch dreamily, turning to carry the baby upstairs.

Celia left the house with the same restless feeling that had plagued her all day. There was no doubt of what was going to happen between Maximilien and Lysette when they retired to bed. How wonderful it would be to have the security of a husband, a family. Guiltily she tried to banish the envious thoughts from her mind, but she couldn't.

Celia stepped on the path that led to the *garçonnière*. She wondered what it would be like to have Philippe waiting there for her. Her eyes stung. She had never felt so lonely. Even in the years when she and Philippe had been apart, she had known he would come for her someday. Now there was no such comfort. She stared down at the ground while she walked, imagining he was still alive, waiting for her at the cottage door. *"I wanted you all evening,"* he might have said, wrapping his strong arms around her, brushing his lips over her hair. *"I want to take you beneath me . . . hold you . . . love you . . ."*

The image vanished abruptly, and she was left with nothing but the darkness. Crickets chirped, and the breeze rustled through the trees. The night was heavy and black around her. Her heart beat heavily, and she knew in a moment of panic that the cold fear was about to overtake her again, the fear of being alone in the dark that had plagued her ever since her escape from Isle au Corneille. It was something she could not seem to overcome.

Quickening her step, she focused on the dim outline of the *garçonnière*, her breath coming hard and fast.

Something reached around her. Her body jerked in terror. She opened her mouth to scream, but a hand covered her mouth, smothering the sound. She writhed hysterically, her eyes bulging, her body straining against the steely arms that held her immobile.

A not-quite-familiar voice was at her ear. "Easy, darlin', easy. Yer in no danger from me. It's yer old friend Jack Risk. 'Member me?"

She trembled violently, his words failing to penetrate the blanket of terror around her.

Risk continued speaking to her softly. "Ye have to help me, darlin'. That's why I waited for ye to come out. Come now, put some starch in yer knees. I need ye to do somethin' . . ."

He froze as he heard the click of a primed revolver and felt the press of cold metal against his temple. A steady voice cut through the silence. "Let go of her, you little bastard. *Now*."

"Jesus," Risk muttered. His hands eased away from Celia's waist and mouth. He held his arms well out from his sides.

Celia stumbled away, sobbing in anguish and relief. She whirled around to see Maximilien holding a gun to Risk's head.

The young pirate looked just as he had four months ago, a scarf knotted around his head, a black patch covering his damaged eye. Breeches, boots, and a tattered shirt covered his lean form. Celia's eyes widened as she saw that one side of his body was soaked with blood. *Bon Dieu*, had he been wounded?

"Old Vallerand himself?" Risk inquired gingerly.

Max ignored the question, his gaze flickering to Celia. "Did he hurt you, *petite bru?*"

She shook her head, unable to speak. Her throat had closed up permanently.

"All right," Max said calmly. "Go into the main house." When he saw her hesitate, he spoke more firmly. "Go on."

Step by step she edged toward the house.

"Before ye do anything," Risk said to Max, "ye might want to hear me out."

"If I don't kill you for trespassing on my land, I most certainly will for assaulting my daughter-in-law."

"It wasn't an *assault*, I was—"

"Who the hell are you?"

"A bloody fool, I am," Risk muttered, and winced as the gun prodded him lightly. "Th' name's Jack Risk."

"Why are you here?"

"I come about Cap'n Griffin," came the sullen reply.

Celia leaned against the outside wall of the house. The fear began to lessen its clutch on her throat, and she began to breathe easier. She watched intently as Maximilien allowed Risk to turn and face him.

". . . now I wish I'd dumped him in the stinkin' bayou and got it over quick," Risk was saying moodily, his posture relaxing into a comfortable slouch. "He's all shot up, looks like a sieve. Won't last long, but I thought ye could—"

"Where is he?" Max asked harshly.

Risk gestured toward the water. "Down there in th' pirogue."

"Anyone else there?"

"Nay, not a soul. I swear it on me mother's grave."

The two men started down the incline where the pirogue was moored, and Celia stared after them with wide eyes. Justin was wounded, perhaps dying. Had there been a confrontation with Legare? She wiped her slick palms on her dress and followed Max and Risk, compelled by curiosity and some emotion she dared not name. A twig snapped underneath the toe of her slipper, and Max glanced over his shoulder. Their gazes met, and she paused uncertainly. To her relief, he did not tell her to go back, only turned and continued down to the water's edge. The men reached the pirogue and stood over it. Max's shoulders tensed visibly.

Celia crept to the spot beside Max and caught her breath. Justin was there, his body covered in bloodstained clothes and bandages. He was unconscious, sprawled in an ungainly heap in the center of the tiny boat. His face was turned to the side, but she could see the bristly mass of his beard. One long hand rested palm-up on the wet planking, his fingers curled slightly. It was odd to see him, a man of such vitality and power, reduced to this helpless state. She looked up at Max, who had not said a word. His face could have been carved from marble.

"I couldn't carry him far," Risk commented. "Went through hell just to load him in th' pirogue."

Max placed the pistol in Celia's hand, arranging her fingers around it with care. "The trigger is delicate," he said gruffly.

She nodded, blanching as she remembered the last time she had held a gun.

Max threw Risk a sideways glance. "You're coming up to the house with us, Mr. Risk. I want to speak with you privately."

Risk began to protest. "Nay, I've done what I set out to do. There's a ship and crew awaitin' my return. Take yer son an' do what ye can for him. I can't keep him safe anymore—can't keep me own head above water! There's danger for me here, an' everywh—"

"I'm not offering you a choice."

Risk stared at the pistol, evidently unnerved by Celia's unsteady grip on it. "Darlin', there's no need to point that at me—"

"*Taisez-vous*," Max said curtly, silencing him.

Celia wondered if Justin was still alive. The heap in the boat was ominously still. Max waded into the water until it covered his ankles. He bent over the pirogue and hefted the slack body up and over his broad shoulder, exhaling with the effort. Laboriously he made his way toward the house, while Celia and Risk followed.

Celia kept the gun pointed at Risk as they walked. The sight of him, not to mention Justin, had brought back all the dark memories of Crow's Island. There was no reason for her to trust Risk any more now than she had then. Her mind was swarming with questions. "Was it Legare?" she asked in a low voice.

Risk answered readily. "Aye, Legare's been at us like a dog after a rat. His men are everywhere. No place for us to cool our heels. Legare attacked the *Vagabond* in the Gulf—near two weeks ago, it was. Griffin was caught in a cannon explosion, and he . . . was in a bad way. Me, Aug, and a couple of the others sneaked him to a place where he could lay low and heal up, a bottomland swamp where—" He broke off and cleared his throat. "Well, I'll be damned if Legare didn't root us out. He came along the overland route and launched a surprise attack." He shook his head, his tone laced with pride. "Our men fought like sons-of-bitches. Legare had to retreat." His boyish enthusiasm drained away as he added, "Course, by the time we got Griffin out of there, there warn't much left of him."

"You endangered yourself by bringing him here," Celia said quietly. "Why did you not abandon him and see to your own safety?"

"*Abandon* him?" Risk asked, sounding insulted. "Ye'd ask that even after what he done for ye! I'd go to hell for Griffin—gave me eye for him, I did, and he'd do the same for me or any jack-tar on his crew."

"What he did for me," Celia repeated bitterly.

Justin Vallerand . . . Captain Griffin . . . whoever
he was . . . was a cruel, selfish brute. Were he
not wounded so badly, she would have been
tempted to inflict further damage on him!

They entered the house through the French
doors in one of the back rooms, and Lysette flew
to meet them. Noeline appeared close behind.
Uncomprehendingly Lysette stared at the small
parade, her eyes lingering on the ungainly load
her husband carried. "Max—"

"Upstairs," her husband said, nearly out of
breath. He brought his son to the bedroom Justin
had occupied as a boy, pausing as Lysette scurried to light the lamps. The room was spartanly
furnished with simple mahogany pieces, including a high-post bed draped with scarlet damask.
Hastily Lysette stripped back the flat, heavy
counterpane, and Max lowered the wounded man
onto the white linen sheets.

For a moment there were no words spoken as
Lysette and Noeline bustled around the room.
The housekeeper piled towels and medical supplies on the bedside table. Lysette snatched up a
pair of scissors and began cutting away the tattered clothes and filthy bandages. Silently Celia
handed the pistol back to Max. She moved to the
side of the room, her fingers clenching together
as she saw the extent of Justin's injuries.

A bullet wound festered in his right shoulder,
another in his thigh. Deep rapier slashes scored
his midriff, while purple bruises marked the place
where his ribs had been broken. Crusted blood
formed trails from his nose and ear. His skin was
black with powder burns and covered with lac-
erations. There was a peculiar jagged wound on
his right side that might have been made by a

sword thrust. It had been clumsily stitched and
looked none too clean.

"We took th' bullets out, Aug and me," Risk
mumbled. "Don't think there's much use in trying to save him now."

Silently Celia agreed with the observation.

Lysette exclaimed softly as she pried away the
bandage that had covered the wounded man's
eyes.

"Blinded in the explosion," Risk said.

Automatically Celia stepped forward. Lysette
stayed her with a firm gesture. "Noeline and I
will see to him. Perhaps the rest of you should
leave the room."

"Should we not send for a doctor?" Celia
asked, surprised at the steadiness of her own
voice.

Max shook his head, dragging his bleak gaze
from his son. "Once it became known my son
was here, we would be overrun by local and fed-
eral authorities, not to mention bounty hunters. I
couldn't keep them from taking him no matter
what his condition."

"Aye," Risk agreed wisely. "For men like Griffin and meself, there's no safe harbor."

Max looked back at Justin. "We'll have to do
what we can for him and hope that—" He broke
off, his jaw clenching. When his emotions were
in check once more, he motioned Risk to precede
him out of the room. "I have questions for you."

Celia stayed behind, watching the two women
remove the remainder of Justin's clothes. The
sight of his nakedness was startling; clearly the
memory of that powerful body had not faded from
her mind. Having occasionally assisted her father
when he had attended his patients, she had
caught glimpses of other men—but none so ro-

bust and flagrantly masculine. In spite of the wounds, there was still an aura of danger around him, as if he were a sleeping lion who might awaken and lash out at any moment.

A housemaid appeared at the doorway with a basin of steaming water, and Celia took it from her with a nod of thanks. She set it by the bedside and picked up the rent garments Lysette had tossed to the floor. Noeline took them from her, wrinkling her nose at the rank odor of the clothes. "I get more clean rags," the housekeeper murmured. "An' burn dese."

"*Bonne idée,*" Celia said in approval, and dipped a rag in the hot water, wringing it out carefully. There was a strange, sick feeling in her stomach as she saw the bloodied surface of Justin's eyelids. She wondered how she could feel moved to pity when she hated him so much.

"I've never seen injuries quite like these," Lysette said under her breath, prying at a bandage that was sticking to Justin's upper arm. Celia saw with compassion that Lysette's small hands were trembling. Gently she took over the task, removing the bandage with efficiency, seeing without surprise that the open wound underneath was as infected as the others.

"I have," Celia said quietly, wadding the bandage and setting it aside. "When the Austrians and Prussians marched on Paris. The Emperor Napoleon had turned France into a nation of soldiers. A boy who had been wounded in the resistance . . ." She paused, fumbling for the right words in English. "*Depuis trois ans . . .* it was since three years—"

"Three years ago," Lysette corrected.

"Yes. This boy was brought to his home in Paris. My father was summoned, and I accom-

panied him. The boy had injuries much like
these." Celia pressed a hot rag against Justin's
ribs, and his body twitched. They would have to
reopen and clean his side. "My father told me the
wounds were typical of wartime."

"Did the boy die?" Lysette asked.

Celia nodded shortly, gathering the long mane
of Justin's brown-black hair and pulling it away
from his dirt-caked face and shoulders. "The danger is the infection. If we are able to bring him
through the infection and fever . . ."

"We must," Lysette said with quiet intensity.
"For Max's sake."

Celia was puzzled by the complex relationship
between father and son. Clearly they were at
odds, sharing a troubled past that cast a shadow
over their feelings for one another. But Maximilien's concern for Justin was undeniable. Celia
knew that it would cause him great pain to endure the loss of a second son only a few months
after Philippe's death. As she stared down at the
wounded man, she was troubled by a new
thought . . . if by some miracle Justin did survive,
he might be left permanently blind. The image of
his searing blue eyes flashed before her. She knew
enough to be certain that Justin would choose
death rather than face a lifetime of forced depen-
dence on others.

Putting aside such considerations, she began to
cut the stitches at his side.

"The plantation is stocked with herbs and dis-
tillations to draw out poison," Lysette remarked,
heading to the door. "I am certain Noeline is preparing some poultices. I'll return in a moment,
d'accord?"

"Certainly." And Celia was left alone with him.
She plunged the rag back into the hot water,

wrung it out, and laid it over the rankling wound. He must have felt the pain even through his oblivion, for he groaned and began to stir fretfully.

"I could easily take my revenge now, *mon ami*," she said softly. "*Bien sûr*, you never dreamed you would someday be at my mercy, did you?" Her brow creased as she concentrated on removing the decayed matter from the gash. As she worked, she saw his chest rise and fall with a broken gasp. "But try as I might, I cannot take pleasure in seeing you brought to this." She pressed a cloth firmly against the wound, staunching the flow of fresh blood. "You'll do well to be forbearing. There are many unpleasant hours ahead of us."

Mumbling incoherently, Justin managed to reach feebly toward his side. Celia pushed his hand away and continued talking in the same measured tones. "No, *mon ami*, do not move. You intend to make things difficult for me. I will not let you."

Using the corner of a moistened rag, she probed delicately around his swollen eyes, cleaning away the clotted soot and blood. She laid the length of one hand against his cheek as he tried to turn his face. Her touch seemed to calm him, and he quieted. "You are going to be well again," Celia said, dabbing the cloth against his skin. A mixture of bitterness and determination welled up inside her. "You will not die . . . You must get well so you can avenge Philippe's death. You said Legare would pay with his life, and I will hold you to your promise."

Chapter 7

"**H**ow is he?" Celia stood in the doorway of the bedchamber, having just come from the *garçonnière*. Last night she had slept poorly, absorbed in thoughts of Justin and how he might be faring. She knew that the Vallerands and Noeline were giving him the best of care. His welfare was their concern, not hers. All the same, she felt a compelling need to see him this morning even before she washed her face or had breakfast.

A sheet had been pulled up to Justin's waist, the linen snowy white against his skin. Celia remembered from what she had seen last night that he was the same dark bronze all over. She recalled the way he had plunged into the lake without out a shred of clothing on, free and pagan in his nakedness.

His eyes were bandaged, as were the rest of his wounds. He turned his head on the pillow and muttered in French.

Lysette sat in a bedside chair, her hair untidy, her face drawn. "The fever is running its course," she said.

"You are tired," Celia observed, but her gaze was still upon Justin.

"Max insisted on staying up with him all night—and I can never sleep when Max is not with me." Lysette changed the cloth on Justin's forehead. "He is with the children now, explaining that we have a guest who has taken ill."

"Will they try to see him?"

"No, I do not think so. And if they do, I doubt they'll suspect who he is. It has been five years since his last visit, and he was here for only a few minutes then."

"Philippe . . ." Justin moved until he had dislodged the pillow from beneath his head. His words were almost too slurred to understand. "My fault . . . don't punish . . . Philippe didn't . . ."

Lysette replaced the pillow and checked the bandage around his eyes. Celia forced herself to stay in the doorway, although every nerve in her body demanded that she go to him. *You've taken leave of your senses,* she told herself, but the feeling remained. Justin continued to mutter, his hands moving restlessly across the mattress as if searching for something to hold on to.

"He seems to be recalling incidents that took place when he and Philippe were boys," Lysette said, easing back in the chair. "Sometimes they would both be punished for trouble that only Justin caused. Philippe never complained, but I am certain Justin felt terribly guilty."

Celia could not imagine Justin feeling guilty for any reason. "*Alors,* there was rivalry between them?" she asked.

"Oh, yes." Sadly Lysette looked at Justin's bearded face. "I am afraid that throughout their childhood they were often ignored by their father. Max cared about nothing after his wife Corinne died. Aside from disciplining his sons he had little to do with them. Everyone in New Orleans considered Philippe to be the good brother and Justin the bad one. It was a burden for both of them.''

"I suppose Justin was jealous of Philippe."

"Oh, they were jealous of each other. Yet I am certain they would have defended each other to the death." Lysette stood up and put a hand to her back, obviously feeling the effects of many hours spent at the bedside.

"I will watch him now," Celia offered.

"Non, merci, I could not ask that of you. I will have Noeline attend to him."

"It would be no trouble," Celia said in a brisk tone. "Remember, my father was a doctor. I am no stranger to the sickroom."

Lysette threw a glance toward Justin's half-naked body. "But what must be done for him—"

"I am—was—a married woman," Celia said evenly. "I will not be shocked. And Noeline will be of more help to you in running the plantation, whereas I have nothing to do today." She gestured for Lysette to leave the room, as if the matter were settled.

Lysette paused, staring at her strangely. "I'm aware of your feelings about Justin, Celia. I know how distasteful it would be for you to take care of him."

"We Frenchwomen are practical. I will not allow my feelings to interfere with what must be done."

Lysette still stared at her, then shrugged. "Very well. Noeline and I will be attending to household tasks. If a problem arises, send Carrie or Lena to find one of us. Thank you, Celia."

"It is nothing." Celia sat in the chair. "Lysette, why did he run away when he was young?"

Lysette stopped at the door and considered the question for a long moment. "Part of it was the family, and part was Justin's nature. He resented authority of any kind. Especially his father's." She left with a sigh.

Celia could not explain why she was so determined to be with Justin at this moment. She only knew that she had to stay. She stared at him, remembering how that powerful body had covered hers, the savage force of him driving deep inside her. What should she feel for him? He had hurt and humiliated her, but he had also saved her life.

"You are a most unpleasant sight," she told him. "Fearsome monster, Griffin . . . the name suits you. I may be able to believe you are Philippe's brother, but not his twin. You have his eyes, but that is all the likeness you can boast of." She touched the bandage over his face. "And perhaps not even that, not anymore."

She let her fingers drift lightly over the bandage. He stopped moving his head, as if he sensed her touch. A low groan escaped his lips.

"I can well believe you were jealous of Philippe." Celia hesitated before touching the rumpled mane of his hair. It was barbaric for a man's hair to be so long, but it was thick and smooth against her fingertips. "Philippe was everything a man should be," she continued, "and you are everything he shouldn't. How could the two of you have been brothers? Philippe was so gentle, so civilized, but *you* . . . there is not a thimbleful of decency in you." Her gaze turned distant. "I know all about jealousy. I have younger sisters. They are pretty girls who have always charmed men without effort, while I . . ." She paused and smiled ruefully. "You already know about my lack of charm.'' Her smile disappeared. ''You wanted me because I was Philippe's wife, n'est-ce-pas? You think of me as an object to be stolen, then discarded at will. But Philippe desired me for myself. You will never understand that. You will never feel such a thing for a woman, and because of that you'll never know what it is like to be truly loved. Even for a little while it is worth—''

Abruptly Celia stopped, realizing she was smoothing Justin's hair. She snatched her hand away. What possessed her to behave so oddly with him? Troubled, she busied herself with the salves and bottles on the bedside table.

Demons were attacking him, tearing at his flesh with long black claws, gouging out his eyes. Bound and gagged, Justin could do nothing but writhe in torment, screams bottled in his throat. There was smoke and fire all around him, and he was drifting into the very pit of hell. Suddenly there was a cool touch on his face, and a presence that drove the fiends away. He gasped with relief. The demons waited a short distance away, ready to resume their torture. He could hear their cackling as they watched him.

There was a gentle sound, an angel-whisper that promised safety and peace. Fiercely he concentrated on the unseen protector, willing her to stay beside him. The demons were coming closer, reaching out for him once more. He could not face them alone.

Celia picked up a jar of pungent salve Noeline had prepared and began to smooth it over Justin's swollen face and cracked lips, and the places where his beard had been scorched. His lips moved, forming soundless words. ''Later I will change the bandage over your eyes,'' she said out loud. "I am not a doctor, *mon ami*, but I do believe you will see again. You are a fortunate man. Perhaps Noeline is right about the loas. There must be one on your side."

Celia set the jar of salve down and turned back to his still form. She froze, thunderstruck by the sensation that he was aware of her. He knew she was there.

Her gaze riveted on his expressionless face. "Justin?"

Suddenly he moved. Growling, he lifted his hand to his bandaged shoulder. Celia caught at his hand, afraid he might inflict damage on himself. Her slender forearm was gripped by punishing fingers that cut off her circulation. She drew in a pained breath.

"No, let go," she hissed, prying at his hand.

Before she could draw another breath, she forgot about her arm, forgot that he was hurting her. She began to tremble, feeling something open between them, a current of warmth like nothing she had ever experienced before. She stared at his face in astonishment. He was breathing raggedly. For a second Celia knew his emotions as if they were her own. He was afraid, alone, trapped in darkness, tormented by creatures with claws digging deep, ripping—

"No!" Frightened, Celia stumbled out of the chair, her heart thundering in her chest. She wrenched her arm from his grasp, rubbing at bruises that were already beginning to show. She turned to look at him. The fingers of his right hand were clenching and unclenching.

Unwillingly she turned back to the bed. Justin was not moving now, but she sensed his inward response to her nearness. Oh yes, he knew she was there. She passed a shaking hand over her face, pushing back the hair that had fallen over her forehead and eyes. What was happening? Surely her imagination was playing tricks on her. She wanted to escape from the room, from him. But she was strangely afraid to leave him alone.

"I have no reason to stay here with you," she said. "I owe you nothing, and I will not . . ." Her voice dissolved. Unable to help herself, she sat on the edge of the bed and took his hand, stroking the back of it. His fingers closed around hers again. "Justin? Can you hear me?" Celia watched him closely, but he was subsiding into a feverish sleep.

Her gaze fell to his hand. He had long, well-shaped fingers, tanned and powerful hands that were accustomed to hard work. The backs of his hands and the knuckles were sprinkled with dark hair.

Slowly Celia looked down the length of his body, noticing that the sheet had fallen low over his hips. Color climbed high in her cheeks as she contemplated the pattern of hair across his chest and groin, scars of long-ago wounds, and hard muscles of an active man. The skin on the back of his neck was pale where his long hair had shielded him from the sun.

He was the first man she had ever been able to scrutinize in such a way. She was at once fascinated and embarrassed. She wondered if other women had found Justin Vallerand attractive. Certainly he was strong and exceedingly masculine, but not handsome in the least. She was certain he possessed not a shred of vanity, or he would have made some effort to keep his beard and hair from being so long and ragged. He was coarse and primitive. Perhaps, she thought to herself, he cannot help the way he is. A man cannot change his own nature. "I wonder if you are capable of loving anyone at all," she mused out loud, unconsciously toying with his lax fingers. "*Non*, that would not be at all convenient for a pirate, would it?"

"It is Thursday morning and friends will be calling soon," Lysette said anxiously. "Should I turn them away? What should I tell them? We cannot keep Justin's presence a secret for long. Everyone on the plantation knows there is a stranger in the house. Soon the news will spread to town. Then there will be inquiries, and the police will take an interest, and—"

"I am aware of all that," Max said gruffly, pulling his petite wife to his lap. "For the time being we'll have to think of some convincing lies."

Lysette linked her arms around his neck and sighed in frustration. "I am a poor liar, Max. One lie always leads to another, and I can never keep them all straight."

Celia watched the pair from the corner of the library. She had just come from Justin's room, where she had spent yet another long night. For almost a week she had occupied the chair near his bed hour after hour, insisting in her own quietly stubborn way that she was more suited to the task than the others. After all, they had their own responsibilities—Lysette and Noeline for the running of the plantation, Maximilien for his shipping business.

Justin had not yet regained consciousness, but he mumbled in his sleep, sometimes mentioning his mother's name. Corinne had died when the twins were only five. Celia remembered that Philippe had spoken of his mother with sadness and regret, but Justin seemed to regard her with nothing but hostility. The only other name he would utter frequently was Philippe's, but Justin's feelings for his brother were far more difficult to decipher.

When compelled by exhaustion Celia would allow Noeline or one of the Vallerands to take her place for a few hours. But she always returned as soon as she was able. And when she was there, Justin rested more quietly, swallowed the broth she spooned between his lips, docilely accepted her ministrations when she cleaned his wounds and changed his bandages.

After stitching his wounds closed, they had sprinkled them with a styptic powder Noeline had provided. Celia recognized it with surprise as the green powder Aug had used on her feet. At her request Noeline showed her the herb it was made from, the dried and crushed roots of wild geranium plants that were abundant in the swamp. To cool Justin's fever they brewed a bitter concoction of Indian sage, pouring boiling water over the white flowers and hairy leaves, and letting it steep for hours. It was difficult to make him drink the foul liquid, but Celia coaxed and forced him to swallow. She alone could make him obey her.

No one quite understood the situation, least of all Celia. It was certain that the Vallerands speculated on her motives and on Justin's untoward reaction to her. Heaven only knew what they thought. "Celia," Lysette had said in a perplexed manner, "perhaps you feel you owe it to Philippe's memory to take care of his brother, but—"

"It has nothing to do with Philippe," Celia replied sincerely.

"But there is nothing you are doing for Justin

that cannot be undertaken by Noeline or me, or even—"

"He is better when I am there." Celia winced as she heard the defensiveness in her own voice, but she could not suppress it. "You know it is true. You have remarked on it more than once."

"Yes, I have," Lysette admitted. "But that does not mean you must exhaust yourself taking care of him."

Celia schooled her features into impassiveness. "Justin is your stepson. You have the right to say what must be done with him. If you wish me to stay away from him, that is what I will do."

"No, I am not talking about—" Lysette stopped and scowled mildly. Both of them were aware that they were on the brink of an argument. "I have no desire to bicker with you, Celia. All I am doing is trying to make you understand that you do not have to tire yourself nursing him, not when there are others capable of carrying the burden."

"I understand that."

"Good."

"*Bien.*"

They had exchanged a glance of annoyance, and Celia had returned to Justin's room, relieved that Lysette was not going to stop her. Day by day it was becoming more important that she stay with Justin and watch over him every minute. He seemed to know when she was there, seemed to recognize the sound of her voice.

Celia dragged her attention back to the present, listening to Lysette's conversation with Max. "What are we going to tell people, *bien-aimé?*" Lysette asked. "The minute they think we have something to hide, they will suspect it has to do with Justin."

"I have a plan," Max said slowly, "but it isn't

a good one. If we have to resort to it, there will be danger for all of us. And I doubt we'd have a chance in hell of pulling it off. I need time to think of something else."

Lysette and Celia exchanged a worried glance. Then Lysette turned back to her husband. "Time," she said, "is something we do not have, Max."

"*C'est vrai*," Celia agreed with a frown of worry. "Perhaps you should tell us about this plan you have conceived. Perhaps we should consider . . ."

She paused as an odd feeling shook her. Struggling through layers of darkness, an image rose up before her . . . it was Justin. Turning pale, she clenched a fold of her skirts in her hand and walked rapidly to the doorway. "Excuse me. I am going to look in on Justin," she said. She strode toward the wide double staircase and began to run, her feet flying up the steps.

Slowly Justin awakened, wondering where he was. What had happened to him? He was on a bed with sheets and pillows, a novel occurrence for him. He was surrounded by darkness. The air was scented with bitter herbs and freshly washed linen. Groaning faintly, he tried to open his eyes but couldn't. He lifted his hand, surprised at the weakness of his limbs. He was never weak.

Beginning to gasp with effort, Justin put his hand to his face and felt heavy bandages over his eyes. The realization panicked him. There had been a battle . . . gunshots . . . Legare's victorious face, a sword pushing into his side . . . Risk's anxious pleading . . . He had known he was dying. His body hurt, and he couldn't move his leg, couldn't even feel it. Had it been amputated? He fumbled with the bandages, needing to rip them away and see for himself what was wrong. Pain stabbed between his eyes, and his head began to swim.

"No, no." A soft, urgent voice fell on his ears. Suddenly there was a woman beside him. Her cool hands took hold of his, pulling them down to the mattress. He tried to push her away. "Let your eyes stay covered," she soothed. "They must heal. Rest now. *Doucement*, you are all right."

All at once he remembered the angel in his dreams. It was her voice, her light hand on his head, her presence beside him. "My leg," he managed to say hoarsely.

"It is healing," she murmured, blotting away the sweat that stood out on his forehead. "You will be able to walk on it again."

"Hurt . . ." He tried to tell her that his head felt as if a red-hot poker were being driven into it. She seemed to understand. A strong, slender arm slid underneath his neck, propping him up. The side of his face brushed against the tender resiliency of a woman's breast, and he was surrounded by a delicate flowerlike fragrance. The rim of a glass was pressed between his teeth. At first he choked on the acrid taste of willowbark that had been stirred into the water.

"No . . ."

"Just a little," she coaxed. "A swallow or two." Seeking to please her, he forced himself to drink. All too soon she lowered his head back to the pillow, and he was deprived of the comfort of her arms. He felt the last of his strength drain away. "Are you real?" he managed to ask.

"*Bien sûr*, of course I am real." She stroked his hair with light fingers.

After a moment he felt her moving away.

"Stay," he croaked. But she left, as if she had not heard him, and he could not say another word.

A full day passed, but Celia did not return to Justin's room after the fever had broken. His need for her was over. His wounds were free of infection and he would begin to recover his strength. If the Vallerands had been puzzled by her concern for him before, they were frankly dazed by what they saw as her sudden lack of interest now. In a matter of hours she had apparently gone from obsession to indifference, and they did not know what to make of her. "I am tired," she had explained, unable to tell them that she was afraid of facing Justin when he was fully conscious.

Celia was distraught over what had happened when he had awakened. She kept remembering the scene over and over, and the awful, aching tenderness that had possessed her. She remembered the heaviness of his head on her arm, the obedient way he had taken the medicine she had held to his lips, the scratchiness of his voice as he demanded that she stay. She had *wanted* to stay, to stroke and soothe and comfort him. It was impossible that she could feel such a thing for that filthy pirate, and she had to avoid him until she was able to control her emotions.

That evening she accidentally overhead Lysette and Maximilien discussing her abrupt change in attitude as they sat alone in the parlor. Celia was just coming in from a walk in the garden to have dinner with the family. Hearing her name, she stopped inside the front entrance hall, her ears pricking.

"It is not that I dislike her," Lysette was saying, "I just do not understand her. I can never be certain of how she truly feels."

There was the sound of Max's husky laugh. "It's not necessary for you to understand her, *petite*. And I would wager Celia herself doesn't know how she truly feels."

"She claims to hate Justin. But if that were true she would not have wanted to tend him during the fever."

"One thing is obvious," Max said thoughtfully. "Something transpired between them that they're both determined to keep secret."

Celia felt her cheeks turning red. Maximilien was a perceptive man, and he had a fair idea of what his son was capable of. Did he suspect they had been intimate, with or without her consent? Mortified, she slipped out the front door, intending to walk around the house to the *garçonnière*.

There was a carriage coming down the long drive to the plantation, elegant but modestly fitted. Celia paused to watch its approach. The passenger of the vehicle emerged without the help of the attending footman and strode up the front steps of the main house with the brisk precision of a military officer. He was an American. Although he was out of uniform, she recognized him from the memorial service they had had for Philippe. If she remembered correctly, the young man was Lieutenant Peter Benedict, the assistant to Commander Matthews, the master-commandant in charge of the naval station in New Orleans.

Benedict seemed surprised by her presence on the front porch. "Madame Vallerand." He took her bare hand in his gloved one and bowed his head over it politely. "A pleasure to see you. You may not remember me."

"*Oui*, I remember you, Lieutenant Benedict," she said, looking at his boyish face. It was the sensitive visage of a man of earnest disposition, one who paid strict attention to his duty and protocol. As she met his warm brown eyes, she recalled that Benedict and Commander Matthews had been appointed by the president to deter the pirates in the Gulf. Locating a stray pirate, especially one of Justin's reputation, would be a considerable feather in the lieutenant's cap. Had Benedict heard any of the rumors about their houseguest? Had he come to find out if it was Justin?

"I am here to call on Monsieur Vallerand," Benedict said, giving her a searching stare.

Celia did her best to look unconcerned. "This is a social call, Lieutenant?"

"I hope so, madame." He took a step toward the door, then stopped as she did not move.

Just then Noeline opened the front door and regarded the visitor impassively. "Welcome, monsieur," she said, her gaze darting from Benedict's serious face to Celia's anxious one.

"Lieutenant Benedict," the man introduced himself. "I am here to see Monsieur Vallerand."

Noeline appraised him, looking unimpressed. "Come inside, lieutenant, s'il vous plaît. I go see if Monsieur Vallerand have time for you."

"Tell him it would be in his interest to see me," Benedict said. "I am here on behalf of Commander Matthews."

They walked into the entrance hall, the mahogany paneling and benches gleaming from a recent polishing. Celia decided to leave the lieutenant by himself and find some way to warn the Vallerands of the danger. She followed Noeline toward one of the double parlors, pulling nervously on the long sleeves of her black gown.

Max emerged from the parlor, raising his eyebrow as he saw their somber faces.

Unconsciously Celia took hold of his arm. "Monsieur," she whispered frantically, her fingers digging into his wrist. "Your son is in danger. The visitor—he is from the naval station. He must have heard something. What should we tell him? What should—"

"Shhh." Max patted her hand lightly before prying it off of his arm. He looked over her head at the young naval officer who was straining indiscreetly to hear them. "I will take care of it," Max said to Celia. "Go to Lysette, hmm?"

"All right," Celia replied inaudibly, while Max stepped forward to greet Benedict with the handshake that Americans preferred in their social and business dealings.

Lysette was in the parlor giving instructions to Noeline. "Have Mary bring some *café*," she was saying. "Not as strong as usual—the Americans like it watery. And bring something to pass around, some cakes or *langues de chat*." She noticed Celia standing nearby and gave her a reassuring smile. "Do not wrinkle your forehead so, *chérie*. It makes you appear worried."

"I *am* worried."

"But why? Max will not let anything happen to Justin."

"I wish I could believe that."

"Celia, you must place your trust in us. *Maintenant*, whatever Max says, you must not contradict him. And try not to appear surprised, *d'accord?*"

"*D'accord.*" Celia peered at her closely. "Do you know what it is he plans to do?"

"I have my suspicions—" Lysette began, and

was forced to stop as the two men entered the room.

Lysette welcomed the lieutenant with a dazzling smile. He took her hand with reverence, seeming tongue-tied for the moment. Lysette was one of New Orleans' reigning beauties, and her effect on men young and old was always the same. She was lovely even clad in mourning, her crimson hair and white skin gleaming radiantly against the severe black of her clothes.

"Lieutenant, how very nice of you to call," Lysette said.

"I am sorry, madame, to disrupt your evening."

"*Non, non,* it has been far too long since we have spoken. How is Commander Matthews? All is well at the naval station, I hope? *Bien,* that is good to hear. With the skill and intelligence of men such as you and the commander, I feel certain the pirates will soon be driven from the Gulf."

"*Au contraire,*" Max interrupted brusquely, "Governor Villeré believes the pirate problem is worsening."

Benedict bristled. "Were we supplied with sufficient men and equipment, Monsieur Vallerand, our forces would be more effective against the brigands. But the people of New Orleans do all they can to encourage the pirate trade. Indeed, they welcome the contraband goods being smuggled into the city."

"The naval station seems to be adequately supplied—" Max started, and Lysette interrupted hastily, knowing her husband's enjoyment of political disputations.

"*Mon mari,* perhaps we should not begin to debate the matter at this time. Do be seated, every-

one. Mary will bring refreshments soon." She
settled gracefully on the settee, and they all followed suit. "Lieutenant," Lysette said lightly,
"do tell us what prompted this call."

"I came to inquire as to your family's welfare,"
Benedict replied.

"You did? How kind of you."

Benedict waited for some further comment but
encountered only silence. Three pairs of eyes were
focused on him. He cleared his throat and continued. "Commander Matthews has expressed a
similar concern, hence my visit. In the last few
days we have heard rumors . . ." His voice trailed
off, and he looked at them expectantly. No one
said a word. The lieutenant was forced to break
the silence again. "This morning, Monsieur Vallerand, I happened to encounter your brother Alexandre and his charming wife Henriette in
town—"

Henriette, Celia thought anxiously, the woman
who loved to gossip.

"—and she relayed some rather interesting information," Benedict said.

"I'm not surprised," Maximilien replied calmly.
"Henriette has often been known to do that."

"Yes, well, she told me that the rumor is true."

Max's fingers began an idle tapping on the arm
of his chair. "And this rumor is . . . ?"

"That you have a houseguest who is ailing. Not
just *any* houseguest."

Celia clenched her hands in her lap. She felt the
blood draining out of her face. After all the time
she had spent caring for Justin, he would be taken
away. The authorities would be cruel to him. He
was still weak, and it would not take much for his
wounds to reopen. The scene from this morning
flashed before her once again, his head cradled in

her arm, his trusting obedience, and husky voice asking, *Are you real?*

Max's voice broke through her thoughts. "Yes, it is true, Lieutenant."

Benedict regarded him with suspicion. "Who is it? A relative? Or a close friend?"

"A relative." Max met his eyes without flinching. "My son, in fact."

Benedict's color deepened with excitement. "Really," he said, obviously fighting to stay calm.

No! Celia wanted to cry out, unable to believe Max was betraying Justin. Telling Benedict that Justin was here was tantamount to signing his death warrant!

"He was brought here in the dead of night several days ago," Max continued, "suffering from severe wounds inflicted during his escape from a pirate island." He glanced at the two women nearby. Lysette was staring at him steadily, while Celia had turned parchment-white. Taking a deep breath, Max plunged headlong into the deception he had hoped would not be necessary. "It is indeed a miracle," Max said to the lieutenant, "that my Philippe has been returned to us."

There was a moment of frozen stillness. Celia could not even think.

"*Philippe,*" Benedict repeated, aghast.

Max nodded matter-of-factly. "Yes."

"But Philippe is dead!"

"We assumed the pirates had killed him," Max said. "But he managed to survive the attack and four subsequent months of captivity. You are the first to know the good news, Lieutenant. Philippe is alive."

Benedict switched his incredulous gaze to Celia. "Is this true, madame?" he demanded.

Celia nodded jerkily, too stunned to speak.

Somehow she had the wits to avert her face and hide her astonishment. Her mind was reeling. It was all some joke, some cruel joke. She wondered if Maximilien had gone mad. Did he think he could deceive anyone with this foolish lie? All the lieutenant had to do was go upstairs and look at Justin to know he was not Philippe. How much time did Max think he could buy with this ploy?

She felt Lysette's arm slide around her shoulders. "You can imagine the strain and shock this has been for Philippe's wife," Lysette said to Benedict. "As you can see, she is terribly distressed by his condition. He nearly died from his wounds. She has exhausted herself these past days in caring for him."

Benedict stood up, looking pale. "I would like to see him now."

"I'm afraid that is impossible," Max said, also standing up. He towered over the lieutenant. "Philippe is too ill to see anyone."

"It is necessary that I ascertain if—"

"Later," Max interrupted, a dangerous glint in his eyes. He looked so forbidding that the younger man instinctively took a step backward. "Perhaps in a few days. When he is stronger."

"I must see him now. There is information he may have concerning the pirate island and the men who captured him."

"Philippe is not able to speak with anyone. He has been in a delirium for several days. He has also been blinded. Whether or not the condition is permanent is still in question. He needs rest, and plenty of it."

"I will not pose any questions to him. But I insist on seeing for myself if—"

"This is my house, my property. You are in no position to insist on anything, Lieutenant. My son has been through enough without being made an exhibition of to satisfy your curiosity. I will not allow him to be seen by anyone in his present condition.''

"Monsieur Vallerand," Benedict said, "I know what honor means to you Creoles. Are you prepared to give me your word of honor that the man upstairs is Philippe Vallerand?"

Max stared at him coldly. "That you would dare ask it of me is an insult."

The lieutenant stiffened, apparently just realizing that he had affronted the most renowned and lethal duelist in Louisiana. Duels were frowned upon but still widely practiced here. For a hot-tempered Creole, there was no remedy for an insult except a contest of swords or pistols. "I did not intend it as an insult, monsieur, not in the least. Forgive me."

Max nodded shortly. "If you must have it, I give you my word of honor that the man upstairs is my son Philippe."

Benedict drew in a shaky breath. "It is unbelievable. Why have you not let it be known before now?"

Lysette replied, her arm still around Celia's back. Celia wanted to shake it off in irritation but did not dare, conscious of the lieutenant's prying stare. "Our only thought has been for Philippe," Lysette said. "We did not wish to contend with hordes of visitors—well-meaning though they might be—all crowding inside the house and demanding our attention and explanations."

"Has he been seen to by a doctor?" Benedict asked.

"He is being given the best of care," Lysette assured him.

Benedict looked from Lysette's pleasant face to

Max's implacable one, and lastly at Celia's down-bent head. "I must report this to Commander Matthews immediately," he said. "I have no doubt he will require that Philippe be questioned as soon as possible."

"Not until my son's health permits," Max replied.

"Excuse me, I must leave at once."

"I will see you to the door."

The two men left the room. Celia lifted her head and stared at Lysette.

Lysette withdrew her arm and folded her hands together. "I told you Max would think of something." She tried to sound confident, but the effort was not convincing.

Celia could not hold back a spurt of laughter edged with hysteria. She covered her mouth with her hand and continued to gasp with amusement. "Ah, *mon Dieu*," she finally said, wiping a tear or two from her cheeks, "I knew I had lost my mind, but until now I thought I was the only one. Did Max really say . . . no, I am dreaming. Oh, this is the strangest dream I have ever had!"

Max had just returned. "You're not dreaming," he said sardonically.

Lysette looked up at her husband, who had begun to pace around the room. "Max, what will happen now?"

"They will watch us closely. From now on they will be aware of all our comings and goings. They'll do everything in their power to prevent a suspected pirate from eluding them." He went to the fireplace and braced his arms on the mantel, staring into the empty hearth. "Justin isn't well enough to travel or defend himself. I could not spirit him away from here without being caught. And even if that were possible, there is no place

I could remove him to where I'd feel assured of his safety. I'd rather have him convalesce here. He'll masquerade as Philippe until I can come up with a more permanent plan." Max threw a glance over his shoulder, noting Celia's stillness. "It will not last long, Celia."

"*Masquerade as Philippe,*" Celia said in a voice so thick and sarcastic that she could hardly recognize it as her own. "Masquerade as my husband . . . a doctor . . . a gentleman? Justin would have a difficult time convincing people he is a *human being.* And how are you going to keep him hidden from all eyes? The most obvious flaw in this . . . this *foolish* plan is that twins or not, Justin does not look like Philippe!"

Max began to pace again. "Not at the moment, with that beard and absurdly long hair. But Justin and Philippe were identical twins."

"*Identical,*" Celia exclaimed, startled. She looked at Lysette, who nodded slightly. "*Alors,* you think he can be made to look like Philippe, but what about their voices, their mannerisms, their habits—"

"We'll keep Justin from being scrutinized too closely," Max replied.

"Everyone in New Orleans knew Philippe," Celia said. "He helped many people, had friends everywhere. You cannot really believe we will be able to fool them all."

"For a short time we can." Max came to the settee and sank to his haunches in front of her. Although his eyes were golden instead of blue, she was reminded of Philippe. Philippe had looked at people in such a way, as if he could see through all their fears and pretensions. "Celia," Max said quietly, "It will not work without your cooperation. People will not believe he is Philippe if you are not convincing as his wife."

"It would not work *with* my cooperation either," Celia said. "I could not behave as if he were my husband. I could not regard that . . . that loathsome beast with any sort of wifely affection, and furthermore—"

"Celia." Max took one of Celia's hands, holding it firmly. "I rarely ask anyone for anything." His voice was deep and mesmerizing. "I am not the kind of man who enjoys being obligated to others. But there is nothing I will not do to protect my family. Justin is my son every bit as much as Philippe was. In the past I made terrible mistakes that they both suffered for. As a boy Justin would never accept anyone's help even when he needed it desperately. I will not fail him now. If Philippe were alive, I know he would ask you to help his brother. I am asking you in Philippe's stead. Help Justin, not for his sake but mine."

Celia swallowed hard, tearing her gaze away from him. "I do not want to," she muttered.

"But you will?" Max prompted.

No wonder he was known as a persuasive man. He had a talent for putting things in a way that made it impossible to refuse. "Yes," Celia said reluctantly. "Because you and Lysette have been kind to me. I owe it to both of you, and to Philippe." She pulled away from him and stood up, finding that her knees were weak. "I am going back to the *garçonnière* to think in private," she said.

Lysette came up to her and hugged her. "Thank you, Celia."

Nodding briefly, Celia left the room.

Max came up behind Lysette and wrapped his arms around her, resting his chin on her small head. Lysette covered his arms with hers and snuggled back against his chest. *"Bien-aimé,"* she whispered, "do you think it will work?"

He sighed against her red hair. "My sweet, ask me anything but that."

An hour and a half later Celia came back into the house. The sounds of murmured conversation emanated from the dining room, and the scents of fish and cornmeal were in the air. She wondered how the Vallerands could sit down to dinner after what they had been through. Her own appetite was completely gone. Moodily she went to the double staircase and stood at the bottom, resting her hand on the balustrade.

She felt a pull from upstairs, a force that compelled her feet to move before she even realized she was climbing the stairs. She felt as if there were fine cords pulled taut inside her body. The palm of her hand was slick against the balustrade. Hot and cold shivers raced down her spine. Justin was waiting for her. He knew she was coming upstairs, she was certain of it.

She walked softly down the richly carpeted hallway, stopping at the open door of his room, her wide brown eyes focusing on the figure in the bed. Justin was sitting up, his bandaged face turned in her direction. She had not betrayed her presence by the slightest sound, but he was as aware of her as if he had seen her.

"Celia," he said huskily.

The way he said her name made her shiver. Quietly she went to him, stopping at the side of his bed.

Justin was very still, drinking in her presence. So it *was* she, the angel who had watched over him. Her cool hands, her soft voice. She had bathed and fed him, forced medicine down his throat, held his hand, assuming he would not remember anything. But he did remember at least some of it. And she had done it, all the while detesting him. Why in the hell had she taken care of him?

Suddenly he grinned, finding it very amusing. "Celia," he said with a low, piratical laugh. "My little wife."

Celia stiffened. There it was, that nasty, mocking grin she had expected. So Maximilien had explained the situation to him. "I am not your little wife!"

"To the rest of the world you are."

"It will be nothing but a . . ." She struggled for the right expression. "A *faux-semblant*—"

"False pretense."

"Yes, that! And I would not be helping you had your father not begged me to."

"Father begging? My God, I'd have liked to see that. Of course, I'd like to see *anything*." Justin reached out and snatched her arm with ease. Even in her irritation Celia was startled by his accuracy. Pulling her closer, he settled his hand on her hip. "You've been eating well," he observed. She jerked away with a sound of outrage. "I like you better this way," Justin said. "It's damn uncomfortable to bed down with a bony woman."

"You and I are *never* going to bed down," she said through her teeth. "That is one of the things I came up here to tell you. I will agree to help preserve your miserable life only if you submit to my rules." She pulled a folded piece of paper out of her pocket. "I have written them down, and I—"

"All right," he interrupted.

"But you have not heard—"

"I agree to your rules. Whatever the hell they are."

"I wish to read them to you."

"Read them to me later. I'll be bedridden and at your mercy for days."

Celia stayed a safe distance away from him, walking around the bed. His head turned as if he were watching her. Silently Celia observed that his color was excellent. He seemed to be recovering with astonishing speed.

"What are you thinking?" Justin asked. "I can't see your face."

"With that beard you look like a big goat."

He smiled, raising his hand to the wiry mass. "I'll have to shave it soon."

"Even then no one would ever mistake you for Philippe."

"Is that so?" Justin relaxed against the headboard, his smile turning into a sneer. "I'll fool even you, sweet wife."

"Do not call me that!"

He scratched his side, wincing at the pull on his broken ribs. "I would like a bath." A dark patch of hair flashed underneath his arm.

"Later."

"I want it now."

"Lysette or Noeline will see to it," she muttered.

"I knew you would be too much of a coward to do it—while I'm awake, that is. But you bathed me while I was unconscious, didn't you? Aye, I'll bet you became acquainted with every inch of my helpless body. You probably stared at me for hours."

"I did not, you . . . you conceited pig!"

"Didn't bathe me?"

"I did *not* enjoy giving you bed baths! I did it

because it was necessary. But I do not find you attractive, and I am not a coward merely because I have no desire to see you naked. And I will not bathe you again!''

"If you say so." He paused and pointed out, "A good wife would do it for her husband."

"You are not my husband. And one of my rules is that you will not take advantage of this masquerade by making ridiculous demands such as this!''

"Ridiculous? I hope that someday you'll discover how ridiculous it is to be unable to do a damn thing for yourself and be forced to beg someone to wash your stinking body! At least give me a cloth to wash the parts I can reach." He heard her walk away from the bedside. "Leaving?'' he taunted. Still no reply. There was the splash of water from a pitcher into a basin. He lay there expectantly, listening to her footsteps as she walked back to him. The sheet was stripped from his body with startling suddenness.

Celia was grateful for the bandages that covered his eyes. She never could have done this had Justin been able to watch. The sight of his nakedness had been jolting enough when he was unconscious, but now that he was awake and knew exactly what she was seeing, she felt a crimson blush cover her from head to toe.

Impersonally she tucked fresh lengths of toweling underneath him, dipped a sponge into the basin of water, and began to wash his neck and shoulder, taking care not to wet his bandages. Justin sighed quietly and relaxed, not bothering to hide his pleasure at the feel of the cool water on his skin. She pushed his beard aside as she scrubbed his chest.

"You're good at this," he muttered. She did

not reply. He moved his arm as she eased it away from his side. "Say something to me. It's been a long time since I've heard a woman's voice."

"What would you like for me to say?"

"Tell me how it has been for you the past few months."

"Your family has been good to me," she said. "My life here has been quiet and peaceful. Until you arrived."

He grinned. "Trouble seems to follow me like a flea-bitten dog."

"I hope that you leave soon and take it with you."

"God, so do I." Justin touched the bandage over his face. "When will this come off?"

"I do not know. The eyes are usually the quickest to heal."

His fingers moved experimentally over the cloth. "How bad are the injuries?" His voice took on a new edge. "How long does this thing have to stay on?"

"I am not a doctor."

"You know enough to guess."

She could not give him a guess, not when there was a chance he would never be able to see again. "You need time and rest," she said calmly. "That is all I can tell you."

Justin was unnaturally still, as if he could read her mind. "Have I lost one of my eyes? Both?"

"I do not know how much vision you will have. First we will have to wait and—"

"Then I'll find out for myself." He dug his fingers underneath the bandage and began to pull it off.

Celia stared at him in horror, then grasped his hand in hers. "Justin, stop it! Justin—"

He shook her off impatiently.

"No, it is too soon, you will hurt yourself!"
She flew back to him, chattering in French, trying
in vain to stop him from tugging off the white
linen strips. Even in his weakened condition he
was able to keep her at bay. The bandages fell to
the floor.

Justin tried to open his eyes and his head was
filled with a white-hot explosion. He gave a gar-
bled cry, shielding his face with his arms. Dimly
he heard Celia's voice over his vicious curses.

Panic-stricken, Celia rushed to his writhing
form. "Oh, you stubborn fool, of course it is too
soon for you to see anything! Stop it, you've hurt
yourself!"

He felt her touch his head and he shoved her
away, maddened by the pain. Undaunted, Celia
persisted in prying his hands from his face, and
she wrapped a towel over his eyes. Noeline entered the room, having heard the commotion as
she passed by. Her dark eyes took in the situation
in one glance. Celia looked at her wildly. "A sed-
ative," she said, somehow managing to sound
calm. "Quickly." Wordlessly Noeline went to the
dresser and poured fresh water into a glass. Justin
groaned, feeling as if his eyeballs had been ripped
out.

"Be still," Celia hissed into his ear, pulling his
head against her soft shoulder. It was the only
way to keep him from doing more damage. "You
deserve this—I told you not to take those bandages off! If you want to be able to see again,
you'll rest quietly and allow yourself time to
heal!"

"Get the hell away from me . . . unfeeling
bitch . . ." he gasped, but his shaking arm stole
around her waist as if she were his only refuge.
His breath burned through her dress like steam.

She grasped the edge of the sheet and yanked it over his naked body, feeling somehow protective of him. Ridiculous, considering that Noeline had known him since the day he'd been born.

Noeline brought the sleeping draft, and Celia took the glass in her free hand. "Justin, drink this."

"What is it?" he asked through clenched teeth.

"Something to help you." She forced it against his mouth until she heard the glass click against his teeth. Some of the liquid sloshed onto her breast.

He choked a little and swore helplessly. "No, goddamn—"

"Drink this now," she said, her voice soft but unyielding.

He downed the contents of the glass in a few gulps, some of the liquid trickling from his chin to her bodice. While Justin swallowed, Celia looked at Noeline despairingly. "Please bring some more of that balm you made for his eyes. And some clean strips of linen."

Noeline frowned at the pair on the bed as if such dramatic scenes were too much for her limited patience. "*Oui*, madame."

Celia set the glass aside and looked at the dark head cradled against her shoulder. Justin was quiet except for his rough breathing. She could only guess at his suffering. His head dropped heavily against her breast, then lifted as he tried to fight the oblivion stealing over him. Celia's aggravation was tempered by a new feeling of tenderness. He was like a big, bad-tempered animal that lashed out at those trying to help him. "Justin," she said gently, cradling his head. "It's all right. Rest now."

"I won't be blind," he mumbled. "I won't be . . . led around . . ."

"No, you will be fine," she crooned. "Quiet now. Quiet." She continued to murmur reassurances until he sighed deeply and slumped against her, his arm loosening from around her waist.

They kept Justin sedated the next day, deciding that it was the only way to keep him still and allow his wounds further time to mend. "He is not going to make things easy for us," Lysette said ruefully. "You may have had experience with difficult patients in the past, Celia, but I assure you Justin will prove to be the worst you've ever encountered." Justin was too groggy to resist as Lysette and Celia administered another small dose of laudanum.

Unfortunately, when Justin finally awakened he proved Lysette's prediction to be true. His mood was ugly, every word spoken in a tone of pure meanness. He was even insulting to Lysette, snapping at her irritably. "Bring me something decent to eat," he growled. "No more of this sickroom swill."

"You can't have regular food yet."

"Then don't bring me anything!" To punctuate the sentence, he lifted a small bowl of clear broth in his good hand and threw it across the room. Lysette left in a fury, sending up a frightened maid to clean the mess.

Justin clasped his hand over his aching ribs as he heard the housemaid scuttling around the corner of the room where the bowl had landed. His leg hurt. So did his shoulder and side and stomach. But worst of all was the knifing pain in his head, a pain that drove deeper with every throb of his pulse. When he had complained earlier, Noeline had offered to give him another sleeping draft, and he had cursed her out of the room. He didn't want to sleep any more. He wanted to be able to get out of bed and move around, he wanted his head to stop aching, and most of all he wanted to escape this relentless darkness.

"You," he barked at the housemaid. "Finish that and take a message to Madame Val—to Celia. Tell her she can't hide from me forever." He paused, thinking that the message might not be enough to get her up to his room. "And tell her the bandage on my side is slipping." It was a torturous ten minutes before he heard Celia's footsteps and smelled her sweet fragrance.

"You took your time," he sneered.

"All your roaring and growling has upset the household," she said coolly. "Noeline is muttering something about evil loas, Lysette is red in the face, and the children are convinced we are keeping a monster in the bedroom."

"Devil take you all!"

"What is this about your bandage?" She bent over him, pushed the sheet down enough to view his side. "It is not slipping." She noticed the deep lines on his forehead, and her voice softened. "Your head aches, doesn't it? After your tantrums I am not surprised. Here, I will change your pillow."

He grunted in assent. Gently she lifted his head, pulling away the flattened pillow and replacing it with a fresh one. She moved around the bed, straightening the sheets, then opened the window to allow a cooling breeze into the room. "Are you thirsty?"

"Thirsty? Not when someone's pouring some foul liquid down my gullet every—"

"Would you like me to read to you?" she interrupted.

"No." Justin raised a hand to his throbbing forehead, exasperated by the pain and tedium. She pushed his hand away and slid her fingers underneath his matted hair, stroking his temples and the sides of his skull. He was still with surprise, realizing how much he liked her hands on his brow, her fingers in his hair. And that was strange, considering his usual aversion to being touched.

"Is that better?" came her soft voice.

If he said yes, she would stop. If he said no, she would stop. "Maybe a little," he muttered. The light caress continued until he began to feel a bit drowsy. He sighed softly, and then her hands left him and she stood up. "Don't go," he commanded.

"There is nothing I can do for you."

"Read to me."

She went in search of a book and returned to his bedside, seating herself with a rustle of silk damask. His head turned in her direction as he listened to the sound of her voice. The novel was mundane, boring, but he didn't care. It soothed him to hear the turning of the pages and her low voice. Idly he tried to picture her face, but he couldn't remember it clearly. Only a tangle of pale blond hair, thin cheeks, dark brown eyes.

Over the past four months Justin had thought every day of Philippe, and of Celia. It was impossible to picture them together. He had tried, but he could not think of her as his brother's wife. He knew he should feel guilty for having taken her. But that had always been his downfall, not feeling guilty at the appropriate moments. He was not at all sorry for what had happened between them. How often did she think of that night? he wondered. Or did she choose to think of it at all? Beginning to doze, he imagined that the pillow underneath his head was her soft lap.

Chapter 8

Someone walked into the bedroom. Justin recognized the sound of Maximilien's heavy-booted feet immediately. At least once a day Max came to visit him, checking on his progress and bringing him news of New Orleans and the Gulf. Recently there had been a lull in pirate activity, but the naval commander was no less determined to bring the outlaws to justice.

"Lieutenant Benedict was here again," Max said without preamble. "I have held him off for a week, but I can't avoid his demands to see you any longer. He wants to question you about the pirate island and your supposed escape. And I am certain he'll try to trick you into admitting you're not Philippe. I told him your injuries had caused some loss of memory. That should help you to skirt around some of his questions."

"How long did Benedict and Philippe know each other?" Justin asked.

"Perhaps a year. The lieutenant's wife, Mary, suffered a miscarriage during a riding accident, and Philippe saved her life. Benedict said he would be indebted to him forever."

"That's good," Justin said. "That will make

Benedict more inclined to give me the benefit of the doubt.''

''Or that much more determined to prove that you are not Philippe.''

Justin's mouth twisted sardonically. ''It would be easier to play the part had Philippe not been such a blasted saint.''

''At least you'll look like him.'' Max surveyed him thoughtfully. ''You'll have to begin by shaving and cutting off that hair.''

''Aye,'' Justin said gloomily. ''Noeline's been sharpening the scissors for a week.''

Max chuckled. ''Ask Lysette to shave your beard. She became adept at it when I injured my arm last year.''

Justin tilted his head in an attitude of curiosity. ''How did you do that?''

''Doing some work around the plantation. Just a sprain, but it kept me from using my right arm for a week or two. I needed help with many things, most particularly shaving. After some practice Lysette became quite proficient, but the first few days . . . well, imagine having a nervous woman at your throat with a razor blade.''

Justin laughed. ''You're a braver man than I, Father.''

They talked for a few more minutes and then Max left. Justin fingered his long beard thoughtfully. It struck him that they had just had the kind of relaxed, amiable conversation Max and Philippe had always enjoyed. The kind he and his father had never been able to have before. He wondered why that was possible now, and why the brittle edge to their relationship seemed to have softened.

* * *

Lysette watched as Celia busied herself in the kitchen with Justin's supper tray. "Celia, it is not necessary for you to prepare his meals," Lysette said quietly. "Noeline is perfectly capable of that."

"It is no trouble." Celia folded and refolded a napkin. She knew why Lysette was concerned. For the past week Celia had allowed Justin to dominated her every waking moment. Whenever he wanted something she was the one he called for. His temper rarely flashed out with her as it did with the others, and her very presence seemed to ease his restlessness. He did not like the way anyone else changed his bandages or even arranged his pillows. The process of eating, especially, was something no one but Celia was allowed to witness. The blindness disadvantaged him in many ways, and he was infuriated by his loss of independence. Celia read to him, soothed his headaches, entertained him with stories of her childhood in France.

Just why he required her for these things and why she obliged him was something she could not explain even to herself. All she knew was that the few times she had ignored his demands and let one of the others see to his needs, she had felt a terrible nagging urge to go to him.

"Celia," Lysette said, her brow furrowed, "I am aware of the demands Justin has made of you. I want to make it clear that you are not responsible for him in any way. Perhaps he reminds you of Philippe and that is why you—"

Celia interrupted with a laugh. "*Bon Dieu*, he does not remind me of Philippe, not at all!"

Lysette did not return her smile. "I am trying to understand why you feel this obligation to care for him."

"There is nothing to understand," Celia said,

her amusement dying. "It has nothing to do with feelings. It is a matter of practicality. You have your husband, your children, and the plantation to care for. Noeline has many responsibilities. I have more time than anyone else, that is all."

"Very well." It was clear that Lysette did not believe her, but she was willing to let the matter drop.

Celia looked down at the tray, struggling with an urge to confide in her. She wished that Lysette were a few years older. If only there was some older, motherly woman Celia could talk to. She still grieved for Philippe, still cried when she thought of him. And she despised Justin's callousness. The death of his twin seemed to have made little impression on him. She did not think Justin really cared about anything except himself and his own comfort. It would not be wise to entertain illusions about him.

But why, then, did she feel this frightening connection to him? Why was she sometimes able to know what he was feeling so acutely? Was it because they had known each other intimately? She did not think so. Perhaps it was because he had saved her life. Perhaps that was why she felt a compulsion to take care of him.

"The food is getting cold," she murmured to Lysette. She left the kitchen and went into the house, carrying the tray upstairs to Justin's room.

Justin was silent as she crossed the threshold. Preoccupied with her thoughts, she glanced at him only briefly, noticing that he was sitting up in bed and wearing a blue robe. She was halfway across the room before she realized that something was different. Her fingers gripped the tray until the tips turned white.

Justin had taken the bandage off his face once again. There were smears of herbal salve underneath his eyes. His face was turned toward her, his blue eyes wide open. The dishes on the tray began to rattle, and she set it down on the floor before she dropped everything.

"Justin?" she asked. Step by step she made her way to the edge of the bed and sat. He continued to stare at her with those bloodshot, unblinking eyes. His chest was moving up and down rapidly, his breathing unsteady. "Justin, can you see me?"

Slowly he lifted his hand and touched the curve of her cheek, and watched the pink flush that had begun to rise from her neck. He withdrew his fingers, although he wanted to touch the shining blond hair drawn back so smoothly and pinned at her nape. Her dark eyes were as velvety brown and innocent as he had remembered. He wanted to cover the vulnerable curves of her lips with his own, to run his hands over her gleaming skin. Her body had filled out; her breasts were round, her waist small and neat.

"Can you see as well as you did before?" she asked.

"Aye," he said huskily. "I think so."

Celia swallowed back tears of relief. She had not known until this moment how afraid she had been that his sight might not come back. "Oh, I'm so glad . . . I thought . . . I was afraid . . ." She stopped in confusion, intensely aware of his riveting blue eyes.

He had not taken his gaze from her face. "You're more beautiful than I remembered."

Her heart began a heavy thudding rhythm. She should get up from the bed and put some distance between them. But she continued to sit

there, caught in the grip of a strange confusion.
She bent her head, her gaze falling on his large
hand as it rested close to her hip. He was not
touching her but she felt him staring at her.

"Y-your father told me that Lieutenant Benedict will see you tomorrow," she stammered.
"You will have to make him believe you are Philippe."

"You'll have to help me."

"I . . . I don't think it will be possible. I don't
think we will be able to convince anyone . . ."

Justin waited patiently for her to finish.

"I cannot pretend that you are my husband,"
she whispered.

Justin wanted to touch her, wanted to feel her
soft skin under hands, her small body next to his.
But it was not his right, and here in these civilized
surroundings his usual techniques of force and
conquest could not be used. Here he could not
take something—or someone—just because he
wanted to.

"I understand," he said slowly. He had never
been good at situations such as this. He had never
taken an interest in analyzing feelings, his own or
anyone else's. He judged others by their actions
and what his own instincts told him. "It's repel-
lent, isn't it," he continued, "to make a mockery
of Philippe's death this way. If I don't manage to
betray my identity, you'll have to discard your
black gowns. I've robbed you of the mourning
period you're entitled to. You'll have to lie to everyone you know and convince them of your joy
at having your husband returned to you. And
you'll have to pretend that the man you hate the
most is the man you love. You're wrong if you
think I'll get any enjoyment out of it. I'm aware
of all the offensive aspects of this charade. If it

weren't necessary to save my own skin I'd have refused to do it. God knows it won't be easy to play Philippe. I'm a proficient liar, but how to portray all that honesty and decency . . . *Bien sûr*, it taxes even my fertile imagination.''

"You mock Philippe for his goodness," she accused in a low voice.

"Not at all. When I was younger, yes." He smiled briefly. "It infuriated me, the way he could walk away from an insult or a challenge. I was never able to resist a fight even when I knew it was senseless."

She raised her luminous eyes to his. "Why did Philippe never mention you to me?"

Justin gave a sardonic laugh. "I'm hardly someone to boast of, *ma petite.*"

"Philippe should have told me. Having a pirate for a brother is not something that can be kept a secret for long!"

"Oh, Creoles can keep secrets for generations, unlike the French. Perhaps it's the Spanish influence. Spaniards are very good at intrigue. Philippe may have thought—and rightly so—that it would be years before you found out about me." He leaned back against the pillows and closed his eyes with a grimace. His face was lined with strain.

"You should sleep now," she said softly. "You must be well-rested for tomorrow."

"I'm nothing if not well-rested," he returned, his eyes still closed. "It's all I've done since I was brought here."

Celia stood up from the bed. "I will tell Maximilien and Lysette that you have recovered your sight. They will be very happy."

"More likely relieved."

"Yes, that too." She leaned over him to adjust

the pillows behind him, as she had hundreds of times before. But this time was different . . . this time his eyes flickered open to watch her, and the moment was startlingly intimate. She pulled back quickly. Everything was different now that he could see. The helplessness was gone. His wounds would heal, and he would be as he was before. And there was no question that he would leave as soon as he was able, never to be seen by his family again.

"You always smell like flowers," he murmured. "It's like . . . violets, or . . ."

"Lavender."

"Lavender," he repeated. He turned his head and fell asleep, clearly exhausted. Celia watched him for a long time. Why had Justin turned out so different than Philippe? She had tried to find out the answer, but no one would explain it to her. There had to be a reason; something had to account for one brother being the pride of the family and the other a disgrace. She wondered if Justin and Philippe had hated each other. Wouldn't Philippe have told her of the existence of his twin had he felt any sort of affection for Justin?

"Oh, Philippe," she whispered to herself, "would you have wanted me to help him? Or would you turn in your grave if you knew?"

Lysette smoothed her daughter's red hair, looking seriously into the small faces so like her own. Angeline was perched on her lap, while Evelina sat on the arm of her chair. "So you see, *mes anges*, it is like a game. We are going to pretend that he is Uncle Philippe, just for a little while. And we must not tell anyone about our game."

"*Oui*, Maman," both little girls said obediently.

Celia held Rafael's chubby form in her arms and watched Lysette apprehensively. She wished it had not been necessary to tell the children who Justin really was, but Lysette had been adamant.

"They are old enough to see that he is not Philippe," she had said. "And they would know we were lying to them. Telling them the truth will increase the danger for Justin, but I must think of my children first. They have never had reason to doubt anything Max and I have told them. They are good girls, and they will obey me if I tell them to be quiet."

Celia hoped fervently that Lysette was right. She smiled at the two girls as they left the room, and moved to give the baby to Lysette. Rafe, who had been fidgeting, settled contentedly on his mother's shoulder.

"They did not seem shocked by what you told them," Celia remarked.

"Oh, children take everything in stride," Lysette said with a soft laugh. "It is adults who have difficulty accepting the vagaries of life."

Celia paced to the window and back to her chair. "It has been very quiet upstairs."

"Yes," Lysette replied, "Justin seems to be making fewer protests with Noeline than he did with me. Of course, she is more accomplished with the scissors than I am with the razor."

In spite of her tension, Celia smiled, remembering the yelps and protests that had filled the whole upstairs while Lysette was shaving off Justin's beard. "Did you cut him very badly?" she asked.

"Two tiny nicks," Lysette boasted. "Not bad at all. And taking off the beard has made such a difference in his appearance. One could almost mistake him for a gentleman. Justin's poor face is remarkably untouched considering all the battles and hardships he has survived.'' She smiled whimsically. ''He looked at himself in the glass and complained that no one would think him a very fearsome pirate now.''

''Good,'' Celia said in a heartfelt tone.

''He'll feel bereft indeed after Noeline finishes shearing off all that hair.''

Celia nodded and took a deep breath, expelling it in a shaky sigh. ''I wish this morning were over,'' she said. ''I wish Lieutenant Benedict had already come and gone.''

Lysette regarded her with a perceptive stare. ''You are worried for Justin, aren't you?''

''Aren't you?'' Celia asked, flustered.

''*Oui, naturellement.* He is my stepson. I knew him when he was a boy, before he left home. And I do care about him. But . . . I learned long ago that he does not wish to form attachments to people or places. It is wise never to expect anything from him. I think that is why he chose the sea. On a ship he is constantly moving.''

''But why become a pirate?''

''Oh, I suppose it was the worst thing he could think of. It was the way he could finally prove that he was as wicked as everyone had always suspected. He had a boy's natural instinct to misbehave, always running away from home, going where he should not, stirring up trouble. But the gossips made more of his escapades than they should have. And the fact that his twin was so quiet and responsible only made Justin's behavior seem worse. I thought that much of his rebellion had to do with Max, that if Justin knew he had his father's love and approval—'' Lysette shrugged. ''Perhaps it came too late. Even after they came to an understanding, it wasn't enough for Justin. Max was only part of the puzzle. Justin still needed something no one was able to give him. I've come to believe that no one ever will.''

Their attention was caught by the sudden appearance of Noeline in the doorway. The kerchief on her head was askew, and there was a look of exasperation on her usually dignified features. ''Ah ain' never gonna have a go-roun' like dat again,'' she announced.

''It is finished?'' Lysette asked.

''*Oui*, madame.''

''Noeline, thank you. I know that Monsieur Justin has done his best to try your patience. Where is he now?''

''In de pahlor.''

''Downstairs? How did he come all that way?''

''He is walking wid de cane dat Monsieur Victor use to carry.'' Victor Vallerand had been Maximilien's father.

''His leg,'' Celia said in concern. ''He may have started the bleeding again. Oh, I knew he would push, I knew . . .'' She rushed out to the second of the double parlors that bordered the entrance hall.

She saw a tall figure standing with a cane by the window. He was dressed in a blue coat and buff-colored breeches. His thick, waving black hair was cut close to his head, and the face that turned toward her was clean and starkly handsome. Celia felt a sickening wave of dizziness. She drew closer to him, her legs trembling beneath her. His blue eyes smiled at her, and the corner of his mouth quirked disarmingly. She saw the hint of a dimple in his lean cheek. His deep voice

was tinged with amusement. "You're not going
to faint, are you?"

It could have been Philippe. The resemblance was
so perfect that she gave a wrenching cry. What she
most wanted, what she had ached for, was there in
front of her—and it was an illusion, an illusion she
couldn't bear. She turned to escape, but he snatched
her wrist before she moved out of reach. He kept
hold even though her frantic tugging pained him.
"Celia, no. Look at me!"

"I can't," she said, bursting into tears. "I can't
bear to see . . . Philippe's face . . ."

"Dammit, it's my face too!" Justin pulled her
closer, and she dropped her forehead on his
shoulder, crying weakly. He spoke against her
ear, sounding shaken. "It's my face too."

The feel of Celia weeping against him made his
heart beat in an anxious staccato. He wanted to
kiss her, wanted her to stop her broken sobbing.
Fumbling for a handkerchief, he found the neatly
folded one Noeline had tucked in his coat. Un-
used to drying anyone's tears, he pressed it
against her half-hidden face and dabbed clumsily
at her cheeks. Gasping, she took it from him and
blew her nose.

Justin did not notice Lysette and Noeline standing in the doorway. He rubbed Celia's spine and
kneaded the back of her neck while she fought to
control her emotions. "Help me to the sofa," he
said. "I'm about to lose my balance."

Lysette pulled Noeline away from the doorway,
and they exchanged a worried glance before deciding tacitly to let the pair settle the matter on
their own.

Sniffling, Celia helped Justin ease down into a
sitting position on the sofa. He pulled her beside

him, his hand wrapped firmly around her upper arm.

"Let me go," she whispered.

"Not until you look at me," he said roughly. "You should be able to see the differences between me and Philippe. Look and tell me you see them." When she did not move, he caressed the inside of her arm with his thumb. "Celia. Don't be afraid."

Slowly her gaze wandered up to his face. He was right. To strangers they would have been identical, but to those who knew them it was certainly possible to tell them apart. Justin's shocking blue eyes were different from Philippe's gentle ones. His nose was a shade longer, and his mouth was a little wider, his lower lip more deeply curved.

His body, too, was different. The clothes he was wearing would have fit Philippe perfectly, but Justin was leaner, toughened by years of scavenging and fighting. He had lost even the minimal amount of fat that most healthy, active men possessed. Unwillingly Celia remembered how he had been before his injuries, when he had rescued her from Isle au Corneille, the power and limitless strength that had flowed from him.

He had the same long black eyelashes as Philippe, the same cowlick, and the same dark handsomeness. "I see the difference," she croaked. "And the likeness."

Not a muscle in his face moved, but there was an odd play of concern and anger in his eyes. "I'm not Philippe."

"I know," she whispered sadly.

"Are you going to think of him every time you look at me?"

"I . . . I don't know." She winced as his grip on her arm tightened until it began to hurt. "Oh—"

Suddenly he let go of her. "This situation is obscene," he snarled. He couldn't stand the thought of her being reminded of Philippe, comparing him to Philippe, looking at him and wanting Philippe. It was insane for him to be jealous of a dead man. Of his own brother.

Both of them found relief from the tension by setting their tempers free.

"*Ce n'etait pas mon idée,*" she said heatedly, too upset to speak in English.

"It wasn't mine either! It was my father's idea, an idiotic one. Go find him—tell him we're not going to do it!"

"We have no choice!" she snapped. "It is too late now."

They glared at each other, and Justin raised a hand to his jaw, remembering too late that there was no beard to stroke. He cursed violently. "Dammit, I want my beard back!"

"It was a nasty beard," she said, continuing to glare at him as she blew her nose once more. "Philippe would never have allowed himself to look like a goat."

"Aye, there were a hell of a lot of things Philippe never allowed himself to do. But I'm not Philippe."

"It is not necessary to keep telling me that!"

"Then stop looking at me as if—"

"I see," Max said from the doorway, "that we have a marital squabble brewing."

Justin stared at him icily. "This isn't going to work."

"Yes it is," Celia said in determination, scrubbing the handkerchief over her moist face. "I have not made you well only to see you arrested and hanged. I *refuse* to have endured the past two dreadful weeks all for nothing!''

"No one asked you to do a damn thing," Justin sneered.

"Then who was it that shouted for me to run up the stairs, down the stairs, every time you wanted a drink of water or—"

"*Assez*," Max said sharply. "Enough. Perhaps the two of you have forgotten that the lieutenant will be arriving at any moment." His hard golden eyes moved from Celia's flushed face to Justin's inscrutable one. "The two of you do not exactly give the appearance of a loving husband and wife. Let me remind you that Justin's life depends on how convincing you are." He was interrupted before he could finish the lecture.

"Monsieur," Noeline came to inform him serenely, "de lieutenant is coming up de drive."

Celia started up from the sofa, but Justin pulled her back down. "Stay here," he said quietly. Wide-eyed, she watched as Maximilien strode out of the room to the entrance hall. The parlor was abruptly quiet except for the ticking of the figured bronze clock on the mantel. "Where is Lysette?" Justin asked.

Celia discovered that she was almost too nervous to speak. "Sh-she is going to stay with the children upstairs."

His large hand slid over her trembling one. "Relax," he muttered.

"I cannot pretend that you are Philippe," she said, jumping as she heard the sound of the front door opening.

Justin took her jaw in his hand, turning her face toward him. Suddenly all his own annoyance and jealousy disappeared in a surge of concern for her. It was unsettling. Completely unlike him. He didn't want to cause her pain, not even if it meant sacrificing his own neck. "Then don't," he whispered. "Not if it hurts you. It isn't worth it."

Her eyes were round with wonder as she saw that he meant it. "You're mad," she said faintly. "Of course your life is worth it. I will help you." She heard someone walking to the doorway of the parlor. Before Justin could say anything else, she lifted her hand to his newly shorn hair, smoothing the dark, silky strands back from his face. The gesture was tender and possessive, the gesture a wife might make to her husband. Justin caught his breath, color creeping up to his cheek-bones.

Lieutenant Benedict walked further into the room, staring at the pair in a transfixed manner. Justin looked up and smiled slightly, his blue eyes gleaming. He extended his hand in greeting. "Peter. It is good to see you again."

Benedict took the proffered hand, clasping it firmly. "Philippe?" He sounded slightly out of breath.

"Forgive me for not being available to you before now. As you've discovered, the Vallerands are quite protective of their own." Justin pulled Celia closer against his warm side and pressed a kiss to her temple. "Thanks to my wife's expert nursing, I expect to be fully recovered soon."

Celia smiled and gestured for the lieutenant to sit in a nearby chair, and he complied quickly.

"I heard you had been blinded," Benedict said, staring at Justin closely.

"We removed the bandages from his eyes last night," Celia answered for him. She gave a soft laugh. "Actually, Philippe took them off himself before we could stop him. The saying is true—

doctors do indeed make the worst patients." She
threw Justin a glance of wifely concern. "As you
can see from the redness, Lieutenant, his eyes are
still not completely healed. And he is prone to
headaches."

Benedict shook his head slowly. "My God, Philippe," he said, his voice changing. "The chances
of surviving a pirate attack . . . being captured
. . . the escape . . . The story is incredible."

"Yes, I know," Justin said ruefully. "It is incredible." A glint of mischief entered his gaze. "I
hear it has led you to entertain doubts about my
identity."

Benedict had the grace to look embarrassed. "I
must do my job, Philippe. And your brother is
known to be a dangerous outlaw. Until I saw you
for myself I could not be certain what was going
on."

"I don't know how dangerous my brother may
or may not be," Justin said with boyish frank-
ness, and smiled. "But it would be bad for my
practice, Peter, were people to suspect me of being a pirate. I am trained to wield a scalpel, not a
cutlass."

"Philippe, I must ask you some questions. I
hope you will be able to furnish the Navy Department with information about these brigands.
Is it true you were held captive on Crow's Island
for the past four months?"

"Yes." Justin frowned and rubbed his forehead.

"Were there any others taken beside you?"

"No, I was the only one."

"Can you tell me why they chose to spare
you?"

"I believe it was because of my medical knowledge. There are no doctors on Isle au Corneille."

"Obviously you were well-treated," Benedict remarked, regarding Justin skeptically. Celia had to admit that Justin did not look like a man who had been held captive for several months. In spite of a touch of sickroom pallor, his skin was still darkly tanned. Were it not for his wounds, his body would have been in superb condition. "Can you describe the island to me, and how it was fortified? And how you escaped, of course."

"There seem to be some gaps in my memory," Justin said, lacing his fingers with Celia's and drawing her hand to his thigh. "I will tell you all I can. I don't know how much of it will be useful."

Celia listened with admiration as Justin answered the questions with a minimum of detail, giving just enough information to make his story plausible. He told of being held on the island, described the fort and its maze of passageways both above and beneath the ground, related how he had bribed some of the pirates to help him, and discussed the battle that had ensued during his escape. Benedict required him to repeat several parts of the tale, obviously searching for inconsistencies, but Justin did not betray himself. After a half-hour had passed, Max interrupted the questioning by clearing his throat.

"Lieutenant Benedict," Max said, "It is obvious that my son is beginning to tire. I am certain you would not wish to deplete what little strength he has left."

"No, of course not," Benedict replied reluctantly.

Celia leaned over Justin worriedly. He was white underneath his tan, and there were dots of sweat on his forehead. The furrows between his thick eyebrows betrayed his pain. She blotted his forehead with the handkerchief. "Another head-ache?" she asked.

"No, it's all right, I can go on," he said. "I just need—"

"You need to rest." She slipped her palm over his shirt-covered torso, letting her hand linger on the bandage wrapped around his middle. "You shouldn't have come downstairs," she said, while Max and Benedict conferred behind her in quiet tones.

"I had to get out of that blasted room," Justin murmured.

"There was no need for you to put on clothes. You could have worn a robe."

He gave her a brief grin that was too mischie-vous to belong to Philippe. "In certain situations a man feels at a disadvantage without his clothes."

"Philippe," Lieutenant Benedict said, walking to the sofa, "I suppose this will have to do for now. But there is much more I would like to know—when you have recovered more of your strength, that is."

"Certainly," Justin returned, and struggled up with the use of his cane, ignoring Celia's protests. He draped an arm over her narrow shoulders to steady himself. "I hope your wife is in good health."

"Yes, she is," Benedict replied, looking at him speculatively. "When may I tell her you will be resuming your practice?"

Celia answered for Justin, slipping her arm around his waist. "I will insist that Philippe re-cover completely before contemplating a return to his work." She smiled at the lieutenant. "I've only just had my husband returned to me . . .

New Orleans will have to forgive me for wanting him all to myself for a little while.''

After bidding them farewell, Benedict left with a bemused expression. Justin let out a long sigh, his body aching from the exertions of the morning. Max gave him an oddly preoccupied glance. ''It went well, I think,'' he said shortly. ''I'm going to talk with Lysette now. She will want to hear about it.''

Celia kept her steadying arm around Justin's waist as they made their way to the stairs. ''Do you think the lieutenant was convinced?'' she asked.

''Not entirely,'' Justin replied with a brooding frown. ''But he could have made it much more difficult.'' He swore under his breath as he lifted his leg awkwardly on the first step. ''Maybe that will come later.''

''You were very . . . different in there,'' she said, bracing him with her slim body. ''So friendly and nice.''

''Like Philippe.''

''A little,'' she conceded. ''Philippe was open, trusting, in a way that you are not. He liked people, wanted to help them. They could see it in his face. That was why he—''

''Aye, I'm aware of all that,'' Justin said tersely.

''Why are you not more like Philippe?'' she couldn't help asking, and he laughed dryly.

''That, *petite*, is the question I was asked throughout my trouble-ridden youth. I wished to be like him. On occasion I tried. But there is bad blood in the Vallerand family. Almost every generation turns out at least one *âme damnée*. It seems that is to be my fate.''

Âme damnée . . . a damned spirit, a lost soul.

Celia shivered slightly, and she knew he had felt it.

They finally reached his room, and Justin lowered himself to the bed with a groan of relief, sweating profusely. Carefully Celia pulled off his shoes and helped him ease his arms out of the blue coat. Holding his hand to his side, he leaned back against the pillows. She unwrapped his necktie and unfastened the top button of his shirt, but he pushed her hand away. "No," he said. In spite of his pain and weariness, he wanted her. If she undressed him, he wouldn't be able to keep from yanking her to the bed and forcing himself on her.

"I wish to check your shoulder—"

"Later. It's all right."

Celia went to pull the drapes completely closed, then returned to his bedside. Their eyes met in the semi-darkness. "Thank you," he said gruffly, "for what you did for me this morning. I know it was difficult."

"I did it for Philippe," she murmured. "Not for you. I think Philippe would have wanted me to help his brother."

There was the flash of his jeering grin. "Do you? I'm not so certain. I think he wouldn't want his wife anywhere near me. If I were Philippe, I'd have come back from the dead to stop you from—" He stopped suddenly, his voice switching to a more impersonal tone. "Philippe, God rest him, wasn't fool enough to trust me around any woman he cared for."

"Justin," she asked softly, "has there ever been a woman you cared for?"

He gave her a taunting smirk. "Many."

"No, I did not mean that. I meant . . ." She paused and bit her lip.

"You're asking if I've ever been in love?" He snorted derisively. "Why do women have such fascination for matters of the heart? I suppose it's their way of—"

"Bah, do not answer me, then," she said in annoyance.

"The answer is no. I've enjoyed my share of women . . ." He paused, and in the short silence that followed they both thought of that night in the lakeside cabin. ". . . and had a liking for some. But I've never been in love." He yawned and settled himself more comfortably. "And I will never be. Love's a damn nuisance. Thank God I'm not susceptible."

"Perhaps someday—"

"Never. It's not in me." He closed his eyes, indicating the conversation was over.

Thoughtfully Celia wandered out of the room and shut the door behind her. She could not imagine Justin being in love, nor could she think of what kind of woman would inspire him to it. But she was certain that if he ever did succumb to love, it would be only once, and for him it would be a dangerous, destructive emotion.

The double parlors were filled with callers. One day a week was visiting day, when the ladies of New Orleans paid calls to one another, partook of refreshments, and exchanged news and gossip. This week it seemed that every girl, matron, and *tante* within traveling distance had found the Vallerand plantation the most inviting place to visit. The news of Philippe Vallerand's return had exploded throughout the city.

The horde of callers was doubly large because Lysette had cultivated many friendships with American women as well as Creoles. It seemed that only under her roof could the two groups mingle harmoniously. There were many reasons for the conflict between Creoles and Americans. In the last decade Americans had poured into the city and begun to take control of the city's wealth, business, and government. They were building a new section of the city uptown to compete with the Creoles' Vieux Carré. Creoles considered it indecent to squabble over pennies as the Americans did. They regarded the Americans as crude, unprincipled merchants, always in a hurry, bad-mannered. The Americans thought the Creoles were lazy and decadent, their men hot-tempered, their women too flirtatious.

The Vallerands, however, were oddly compatible with both cultures. Both Maximilien and Lysette had come from families with established names that no Creole could reproach. Their bloodlines were undeniably aristocratic. But Maximilien was respected by the Americans for the small but efficient shipping business he owned and managed. Moreover, he was a friend of the American governor. Lysette was a respected matron held up to Creole girls as an example of proper behavior, yet she was young and stylish. She spoke perfect English and counted many American women among her friends.

"What would you do," one of Max's Creole friends had asked him curiously, "if an American someday expresses the desire to court one of your daughters, Max? *Certainement* you would not allow such a thing! You see that this interaction with Americans can lead to no good!"

"I would judge the man by his own merits," Max had replied with shocking candor. "Being Creole would not automatically make a man deserving of my daughter's hand, just as being

American would not make him *un*deserving." It
was quite a liberal view, but then, Maximilien
had long been known as a man of unorthodox
beliefs.

Lysette's voice could be heard all the way upstairs as she sought to calm the excited chattering
and squabbles brewing among her guests. Her
usually soft voice had an edge that cut through
the noise as she invited them all to partake of refreshments. The scent of strong, heavily sugared
coffee rose to the upstairs rooms where Justin
prowled.

Justin did not dare show his face for fear of being beset by a crowd of eager women. As Lysette
had explained to him, Philippe had been the most
sought-after doctor in New Orleans. The combi-
nation of his medical skill, handsomeness, and
quiet charm had made him exceedingly popular,
and the news of his "return from the dead" had
been welcomed enthusiastically.

"*Bien sûr*, Philippe," Justin muttered wryly. "I
see now why you were so eager to take up the
medical profession."

He limped along the hallway with his cane, his
ears pricked for the sound of Celia's voice from
downstairs. Many questions were being asked of
her, but her replies were too quiet for him to
hear. As he passed by the door of Philippe's
room, closed as always, he heard a noise from
within. The hair stood up on his arms, and he felt
a small shock. How many thousands of times had
he burst into Philippe's room unannounced and
dragged him away from his books? Memories
flashed through his mind. He could almost believe he was a boy again, and that if he opened
the door right now he would find Philippe there.

With a hand that was not quite steady, he reached for the knob and turned it.

The door swung open, and Justin was confronted with the small upturned faces of Lysette's daughters. His half-sisters. They were sitting on the floor with a polished wooden box between them, and several small objects scattered about. Searching through Philippe's possessions, he thought. It was only natural for them to investigate.

Evelina and Angeline stared at him with round hazel eyes exactly like their mother's. They were both exquisite replicas of Lysette, with almost no trace of Vallerand in their features. So far they had avoided Justin, instinctively cautious of coming face to face with the stranger who had appeared so mysteriously and caused such an uproar. The girls knew without a doubt that he was not Philippe, the half-brother they had adored.

Justin looked at them curiously, having taken little interest in them until now. He had caught glimpses of them around the house and thought them pretty creatures, but felt no sense of kinship to them. "What do you have there?" Justin asked mildly, hobbling into the room.

Silently Evelina scooped up handfuls of the scattered objects and put them into the box as quickly as possible. Angeline seemed frozen, her gaze fastened on Justin's face. He smiled at her and levered himself into the chair with difficulty.

"Arrowheads," he said, peering down at the floor. "Philippe and I used to find them along the banks of the bayou. One time we even found a hatchet. Choctaw Indians used to live here a long time ago. I suppose we always hoped that if we looked hard enough we'd find one or two. Or maybe a pirate.''

Evelina spoke then with great dignity. *''You* are a pirate, *n'est-ce pas?''*

''Oh, not a bad one.''

''All pirates are wicked.''

Justin grinned at her. ''But I would *never* do anything to hurt little girls.'' He reached out for the box, and Evelina gave it to him, taking care not to touch him. Flipping open the lid, he stared at the numerous arrowheads Philippe had saved all those years ago. A reminiscent smile crossed his lips. Only Philippe would have retained such useless things for sentimental reasons. ''I remember roaming through the swamps with him in search of adventure,'' he said, more to himself than the girls. ''We had a little pirogue we would paddle back and forth. How Grand-mère would scold us when we returned covered in mud from head to toe!'' He laughed and turned his gaze to Evelina. ''Do you ever go down to the bayou, *enfant?''*

''Papa told us not to. *C'est dangereux.''*

''Ah.'' He nodded sagely. ''Papa once told me the same thing. It is wise to obey him.''

Angeline crept forward until her tiny hands rested on the arm of his chair. ''He is *your* papa *too?''* she asked in childish surprise.

''Angeline, *viens*, come with me,'' Evelina said sharply, pulling her younger sister back. ''Mama said we should stay in the nursery.''

Reluctantly Angeline followed her from the room, casting several glances back at Justin. He grinned at her and turned his attention back to the arrowheads. Picking one out, he set the box aside. He rubbed the polished surface between his thumb and forefinger, contemplating it in tently, remembering the day he had last seen Philippe, when they were sixteen . . .

"Justin, don't leave!" Philippe had stopped him just before he reached the pirogue. What few possessions Justin intended to take with him had already been stowed in the bottom of the tiny craft. It was midnight, but the clear white moonlight illuminated their young faces. "If you leave now I know it will be for good," Philippe said desperately. "You must stay. I need you here, Justin."

"None of you need me here, and you know it. I make trouble for everyone. I don't belong here. I . . . Dieu, you know all the reasons."

"Wait a little while longer, wait and think. If you only—"

"I've waited and I've thought." Justin smiled humorlessly. "The reason I tried to leave in the middle of the night, mon frère, is that I wanted to avoid a scene like this."

"But the trouble between you and Father is gone."

"Yes. But every time he looks at me he's reminded of the past, of . . . painful things. Of her. I see it in his face."

"Justin, you're nothing like our mother, you—"

"I'm exactly like her," Justin said coldly. "I don't want to be, but I can't change it. It's better for all of us if I leave."

"What will you do?"

"Don't worry. I'll do far better out there than I have here. I want to be free. I want to go where no one knows I'm a Vallerand. I've never pleased anyone here, and never will, so I may as well begin to please myself. You stay here and be the good son. Be the only son. I'll take the bad blood with me." He saw his brother's eyes glitter suspiciously. "Crying like a girl," Justin mocked, but Philippe continued to stare at him.

*And suddenly Justin realized that his own eyes were
stinging. He cursed and turned away, stepping into the
pirogue . . .*

Celia stood in the doorway, having left the visitors downstairs with the excuse that she wanted
to look in on the children. She had been on her
way to the girls' room when she saw that Philippe's door was ajar.

Justin was inside, sitting in a chair with his
knees spread, his head bent. One of his fists was
clenched around an unseen object. His expression
was closed. To look at him no one would guess
at his emotions, but Celia sensed his pain, the
grief he was fighting to suppress. And along with
her empathy came a feeling of wonder.

"So you did care for him," she said.

Justin looked up at her, startled. It took a moment for him to speak. "Get the hell out of here,"
he snarled.

Celia was unintimidated. "You speak about
Philippe so casually. I thought his death had
meant little to you. But it wasn't real to you until
now, was it? You could not let yourself believe
that he was gone."

His gaze dropped from her face.

Walking farther into the room, Celia studied his
averted profile. "You loved him, didn't you?" she
whispered. He didn't reply, and for her that was
answer enough. Slowly she knelt by the chair,
staring up at him.

"It was always the two of us," he said, looking
at his closed fist. "When we were boys we lived
like savages, roaming through the swamp, doing
as we pleased. For the most part we raised ourselves. Father didn't give a damn as long as we
caused him as little trouble as possible." He

smiled bitterly. "He was a cold bastard. All of New Orleans suspected him of murdering our mother. For years I believed it too."

"You . . . you . . ." she stuttered, wondering if she had heard him correctly.

"My mother was a heartless bitch who cared only for her own pleasure. She shamed my father by having affairs with other men. She had no maternal instincts whatsoever. Philippe and I were nothing to her but an inconvenience. After she died, my father could not look at either of us without being reminded of her." His eyes met Celia's. "To everyone else Philippe and I were objects of curiosity, suspicion, sometimes pity. Other boys would dare us to fight for our honor. While I was always ready to oblige, Philippe tried to play the peacemaker." He laughed quietly. "Although I'd provoke him at times, Philippe always came to my defense, even sharing the punishment for my misdeeds. And I protected him when I could. He was a dreamer, a sentimental idiot. I couldn't begin to understand where he got his damn naive innocence. He was . . . remarkable. He was all I had. Love him? God, yes, I—" He swallowed hard and tightened his fingers.

"Justin," she whispered. "What are you holding?"

He didn't seem to hear her.

Taking hold of his fist, she pried it open finger by finger. In his palm was a brown arrowhead. His hand lay open, unresisting as she picked up the small object. She recognized it from the box that had been on Philippe's dresser. Her eyes widened in concern as she saw the smear of blood on Justin's palm. The point of the arrowhead had pierced the tough skin.

"Justin," she gasped, and without thinking she pressed her lips to the welling drop of blood.

He sucked in his breath as he felt her soft mouth buried in his palm. Her blond head was bent over his hand, the tip of her tongue touching the puncture wound and collecting the salt-flavored droplet.

Celia froze as she realized what she was doing. She took her lips from his skin and stared at the large hand cradled in hers. Shocked by her own actions, she continued to kneel at his feet. Justin was still, and so was she, but she heard how his breathing had quickened. She wanted to look at his face, but she was terrified. What was happening to her? She wanted to pull that strong, warm hand to her throat and down to her breast. She wanted to crawl further into the lee of his thighs and feel his mouth on hers. Somehow the specter of Philippe's death had just been removed from between them, and she was afraid of Justin in a way she had never been before.

She raised her head jerkily and stared into his eyes. The dark blue depths contained a bewilderment that matched, perhaps even surpassed, her own. Celia was helpless to move or speak. Her face felt hot, and her heart thumped painfully in her chest. She knew that her stillness and silence was an invitation. Gradually his hand turned until both of hers were imprisoned. They stayed like that for what seemed to be minutes, hours, frozen in a timeless place where his awareness and hers grew in leaping surges.

They broke apart quickly, Celia springing to her feet with an incoherent excuse about looking for the children. "The girls . . . I must find them," she said hoarsely.

"Celia—"

But she was gone before he could say anything else. Justin stared at the empty doorway, then dropped his head and cursed viciously. He had to leave. His instincts told him that a silken net was closing around him. If he didn't escape soon, he would be entangled forever in its soft, tenacious bonds. But he couldn't leave—he didn't yet have the strength or the resources to evade Dominic Legare. This fragile masquerade was his only protection. The only question was, which threat was greater? The one posed by Dominic Legare . . . or the one posed by his own brother's wife.

Bored and restless, he could not resist seeking Celia out in the afternoon, wandering to the *garçonnière* where she disappeared for an hour or two every day. He was irritated with the limitations his wounds placed on him, his usually free stride reduced to a pained hobble, his side and shoulder aching. The plantation was quiet as everyone attended to his own tasks and took little notice of him. Impatiently he knocked on the small front door and scowled at the housemaid who answered it. "Where is Madame Vallerand?" he asked. The girl eyed him uneasily before running to tell Celia of the visitor.

Celia appeared, clad in a simple blue dress and a full-length white apron. Her hair had been gathered with a ribbon and left to fall down her back. She lifted her tawny brows. "What is it?" she asked without preamble. "*Ça va?*"

"Yes, I'm all right." Justin experienced the same mystifying reaction he always had when she was near, feeling soothed and comfortable. "What is the apron for?"

Celia hesitated before answering. "I am painting."

He looked at her in mild surprise. "I didn't know you painted. Let me in. I want to see your work."

"No," she said firmly. "No one sees it. It is not very good. I paint only for myself."

His interest piqued, he set about to cajole her. "I wouldn't criticize."

"Even if you did, your opinion means nothing to me."

"Then let me come in."

"No, I will not have you ruin my privacy merely because you have need of entertainment!"

"Then you won't let me in?"

She tried to stare him down, but a reluctant laugh escaped her. The flash of smiling beauty caused a strange constriction in Justin's chest. "All right," she said gruffly, and turned to walk down the small hallway that led to the room where she worked. Justin was at her heels immediately, the thump of his cane muffled by the carpet on the floor.

As they crossed the threshold of her studio, Celia was aware of a pang of nervousness. She wondered half-angrily what had prompted her to give him, of all people, the opportunity to ridicule her. Adopting a businesslike air, she went to the easel by the window and regarded the almost-finished watercolor with her arms folded. Justin followed and stopped behind her, leaning his weight on his good leg. He stared at the painting closely.

She had painted the bayou in dark greens, grays, and blues, capturing the shadows and thick trailing moss, the ancient trees with their limbs like outstretched arms. It looked gloomy and threatening; her fear of the place was evident in every brushstroke. Contemplating the picture, he said the first thing that came into his mind. "It's not always that sinister."

"It is to me."

"Sometimes it can be beautiful." Then he went off on his own, investigating the sketches scattered around the room and the canvases piled carelessly on top of one another. Her work was delicate and deft. Even in her more amateurish efforts her feelings showed through. He smiled at the sketch of a bored driver and footman leaning against a carriage as they waited outside the house. And there was a painting of Maximilien on a horse as he surveyed the plantation—Justin recognized the proud tilt of his father's head and the upright line of his back. Glancing at Celia over his shoulder, he smiled, and she seemed to relax. Perhaps his liking for her work wasn't based solely on its own merits. Perhaps it was influenced by his feelings for her. But he didn't give a damn why he liked it, he only knew that he did.

He came across a sketch that caused him to stare intently. It was of Lysette nursing her baby, her slender arms cradling his small body, her long curls falling in a curtain around the head at her breast. The scene was disarming in its intimacy and tenderness, a glimpse into the private feminine world men were seldom permitted to see.

"Please . . . you must put that away," Celia said in a low voice. Her cheeks were flushed. "It would embarrass her if she knew you had seen it."

Obligingly he set it aside and walked to her. "Have you done any of Philippe?" The question seemed to bring a brighter flush to her face.

Celia was still, her velvety brown eyes raised to his. For once Justin could not read her thoughts. Seeming to make a decision, she turned and went

to a nearby table, leafing through a book of
sketches. She brought one back to him, the parch-
ment trembling a little. He took it from her, anticipating the ache of recognition as he saw his
brother's face. But his eyes widened in surprise.
The sketch was not what he had expected. The
portrait was of a man with a derisive smile on his
lips, an insolent expression lurking in his gaze,
and features just a little too lean to be Philippe's.

"It's me," Justin said. He threw her a questioning glance.

"Yes," she said softly. "It seems to happen
whenever I try to draw Philippe. It is never just
right. The more I work on it the more it resembles
you."

They spoke in hushed tones, as if they were in
danger of being overheard.

"Why?" he asked.

"I . . . don't know."

"When was this done?"

"A few days ago. I was thinking of him."

"And of me."

"Yes," she whispered.

He was silent, staring at her, feeling his heart
beat heavily, feeling himself being dragged toward a discovery he did not want to make.

"Perhaps you should leave," Celia said with
an effort, taking the sketch from him. "Lysette
will be here soon. An Irish girl is bringing over
gowns from the dressmaker. We thought it
would be convenient to have the last fittings
done here."

Celia was both relieved and affronted as Justin
left almost immediately. She busied herself with
straightening her supplies, and gradually the inner turmoil caused by his visit subsided. Lysette
swept into the *garçconnière* with a cheerful smile,

followed by the Irish girl, Briony, and footmen burdened with towering stacks of boxes and supplies.

"You must tell Monsieur Deneux that we are very pleased with the gowns," Lysette said as Briony finished the last alterations for a lovely sea-green silk, high-waisted and cut very low across the bosom. The color was entrancing against her white skin and red hair, and Lysette took an obvious guilty pleasure in the new gown. "How wonderful it is to be out of mourning."

" 'Tis wonderful that Mr. Valleyrand is back home," Briony replied in a subdued voice.

Celia watched the seamstress adjust one of the short, full sleeves of the gown. They had ordered several ensembles from the dressmaker for both Celia and Lysette, beautiful gowns in rose, blue, green, and lavender. Privately Celia thought that she had never seen the Irish girl in such a distraught mood. Briony was usually cheerful and animated, her brown curls dancing, her small form never at rest. But now she looked pale, and her green eyes were feverishly bright in her white face. Had Briony and Lysette been involved in some kind of dispute? There was an obvious tension between the two in spite of their efforts to behave as usual.

"Well now, that's the last o' them," Briony said, unfastening the back of Lysette's gown. "I'll take them back to the shop an' we'll have them done by Thursday."

"Thank you." Lysette stepped out of the gown and handed it to her. "I will finish dressing here. Go to the main house and tell them to have the carriage brought around."

Celia stared at the Irish girl, then glanced at

Lysette. "She seems rather troubled about something, *n'est-ce pas?*"

Lysette shrugged a little too nonchalantly. "Ah, girls that age have such changeable moods. Celia, will you tell Noeline to have the maids take the gowns to the carriage? I believe she is in the kitchen with Berté."

"Certainly." Celia took the path from the *garçonnière* to the main house, enjoying the cool breeze that stirred the leaves and brought with it the scent of lemon trees. Dusk had settled over the plantation, the horizon tinged with the last traces of red from the sunset. She paused as she saw Briony disappear behind the hedge of the garden. Perplexed, she followed the girl, wondering why she had not gone directly to the main house.

Justin sat in the garden on the stone bench by the fountain. The rustle of light feet walking across the grass caught his attention, and he looked toward the sound. It was a girl he had never seen before, a pretty Irish girl with freckles and curly brown hair. Her small figure was clad in a modest blue gown of worsted fabric, and a long white apron. Bits of thread clung to her sleeves and bodice. She must have brought Celia's gowns from the dressmaker.

Justin's eyes narrowed inquiringly as she approached him. She was staring at him oddly, her eyes huge, her face stark white. With alarm he saw that tears were ready to fall down her softly rounded cheeks. *Bon Dieu*, he *hated* to be confronted with crying females! Why the hell was she crying, and why was she looking at him as if—

"Philippe," she whispered, sitting on the bench

beside him. Her small work-roughened hands came to his face, touching him tenderly. "Oh, Philippe, me love, when I heard ye weren't dead . . ."

Before Justin could say a word, she pressed her mouth to his in a sweet, searching kiss.

Chapter 9

$\sim\!\!\!\sim\!\!\!\sim\!\!\!\sim$

Astonished, Justin tried to take stock of the situation. Obviously the girl was a former lover of Philippe's. But Philippe had not been the kind to trifle with servants. He had not even taken a quadroon mistress when he'd come of age. Philippe had always been attracted to girls of frail gentility, not robust wenches such as this.

While one part of his mind speculated on how closely Philippe and this girl had been acquainted, the other part noted how surprising it was that she moved him so little. Usually he would have taken great pleasure in the advances of a comely wench, and immediately have begun to teach her a few things she didn't seem to know about kissing. But although her lips were soft and sweet, he took as little satisfaction from the kiss as if he were starving and had been offered merely a cup of weak tea. And it wasn't the girl's fault, it was his. There was only one woman he wanted.

"Puir darlin'," she said in a low, passionate voice, feeling the bandages through his shirt. "When they told me ye were dead part o' me died too. I know there's nothin' I can have o' ye now. Yer wife is a good woman. I wouldna seek to take ye from her. But I can still love ye, Philippe, an' I will fer the rest o' me life. I just wanted one moment fer meself, one last kiss. In me heart ye'll always be mine. I'll nivver give meself to another man. I'll wait forever, even if ye nivver want any part o' me. Whatever ye care to take I'll give gladly. 'Tis a sin to love another woman's husband, but I don't care. I canna tear me very heart out by denyin' what I feel.'' She kissed him again, but this time she sensed that something was wrong, and she pulled her head back to look at him. ''Philippe? What is it?''

Her tear-streaked face went blank, and her trembling fingers touched his lips, chin, and cheek, exploring gently. Then her hand fell away. ''Ye're not Philippe,'' she gasped. She swayed, and he took her by the shoulders. She regarded him with wide eyes. ''Ye're the brother. Justin.''

Justin was quiet, knowing there was no denial, no lie that would make her believe he was his brother.

Her throat worked as she tried to speak. She stared into his midnight-blue eyes and found her voice. ''Philippe talked of ye often.''

''He did?'' Justin questioned in surprise. He'd thought that Philippe had not spoken about him with anyone, not even Celia.

The girl's shoulders quivered in his hands. ''Where is Philippe?'' she asked, her voice breaking. ''He's . . . dead, isn't he?'' Justin nodded slightly. She gave a grief-stricken moan and bit her lip.

''What is your name?'' Justin asked bluntly, and she choked back her sobs.

''Briony. Miss Briony Doyle.''

''Miss Doyle,'' he repeated. ''Are you going to keep my secret?''

''Wh-why have ye taken his place?''

"There are men who seek to take my life. The same ones who killed Philippe. I can't force you to hold your silence. All I can do is trust that you will do it out of respect for Philippe. I think he would have asked you to help me."

Briony nodded slowly. "I'll help ye."

"Thank you," Justin said, wondering if she could be trusted.

"Philippe loved ye," she said softly. "He worried over ye every day of his life. I'll keep yer secret, Mr. Valleyrand—if ye'll keep mine."

"Aye." Justin let go of her, and she continued to sit there, her shoulders slumped. He pitied her, seeing that although she was just a girl, her grief was as deep as Celia's had been. Perhaps even deeper, for he knew without asking that Briony and Philippe had been lovers, and that Philippe had been the center of this girl's life.

"I lost him when he left fer France to marry Celia Verité," Briony confessed, her voice hollow. "I knew he loved me. I made him happy, but I'd nivver be worthy of him. He dreamed of marryin' a fine lady wi' soft hands, one who understood the poems an' such he liked. I nivver asked him fer anythin' . . . I knew he would leave me someday. I gave him all o' meself an' didna try to hold him to me. A Valleyrand an' an Irish lass." She shook her head with a wavering smile. " 'Twas a daft notion."

"Philippe was a fool," Justin said gently. "I think you must have been good for him."

Justin would have liked to have seen his brother with this impulsive girl, someone who would have jolted him from his dreams and his safe inner world. Someone who had loved him enough to follow her heart instead of conventions. Celia had loved Philippe, but she never would have challenged him.

"Puir Madame Valleyrand," Briony murmured as if following his thoughts.

"Don't worry about her. She's a strong woman," Justin said, and gestured for her to go to the house. "It's best that you leave before you're seen." He paused. "You won't tell anyone who I am?"

"No," she said. "I wouldna betray Philippe's brother." Stiffening her spine, she stood and walked away, rubbing her eyes with her sleeve.

Justin watched her thoughtfully, pondering the discovery that Philippe had been in love with two women, suffered doubt and indecision, and taken a girl's innocence because he had wanted her too much to heed the warnings of his conscience. *My God*, he thought, *we may have had more in common than I thought,* mon frère.

He felt a tingling on the back of his neck and turned to find Celia standing close by. She was glaring at him. Even in the gathering darkness he could see that she was flushed.

"Eavesdropping?" he asked. "How much did you hear?"

"Nothing. But I saw her kissing you," Celia said with suppressed rage. "I saw her hands wandering all over you, and the way you merely *sat* there, you randy goat!"

He gestured to his cane. "I could hardly jump up and run away."

"Do not offer me any ridiculous excuses! Do you think anyone is going to believe you are Philippe when you behave in such a manner? Philippe would never have dallied with a servant girl, and—don't you dare smirk at me!"

"My, my, how shrewish you are tonight," Justin said silkily. "Almost as if you were . . . ah, jealous?"

She looked as though she'd swallowed a bug. The struggle to control herself was plain on her face. Finally, in an icy voice she said, "I never suspected your conceit was so immense."

He had never been as pleased by anything as he was by her jealousy. "You didn't like to see her kissing me. Admit it."

"I admit to being surprised that you had the gall to try to seduce her when we are trying to convince everyone that you are Philippe."

"And Philippe would never flirt or dally with a poor Irish seamstress."

"No, he had more honor and decency in his little finger than you have in—"

"He had honor," Justin conceded. "He had decency. He also had an affair with the wench."

Celia's jaw dropped. *"What?"*

In spite of the seriousness of the situation, Justin felt a tigerish enjoyment in telling her. "An affair. I don't know when it began, but it lasted until the day he left for France to marry you. I was not trying to seduce her. She threw herself at me, thinking I was Philippe."

"I will not listen to such lies! Oh, how low and contemptible you are, you—"

"I overestimated Philippe," Justin mused. "It seems he wasn't a saint after all, but a red-blooded man with flaws like everyone else."

Celia wanted to reach out and throttle him. "You are wrong, *absolument!* Don't you think that if Philippe had done something like that Lysette and Maximilien would have known?"

"Aye, that's precisely what I think," Justin said, becoming more serious. "Which is why you and I are going to find Lysette right now."

"I will not go anywhere with you!"

"Then don't," he said indifferently. "If you're afraid of the truth . . ." Shrugging, he reached for his cane and pulled himself to his feet. "But I intend to have some answers."

Muttering in French, Celia followed him to the main house, her spine rigid with outrage. Fleetingly, the worry crossed her mind that she was every bit as upset over seeing Justin in an embrace with Briony as she was with the suspicion that Philippe had had an affair with her.

Celia had to be honest with herself. When she had seen the two dark heads together silhouetted against the violet sky, she had felt betrayed. No, it was wrong, she could not feel this way! She had no claim on Justin, nor did she want one. He was an outcast, an outlaw. In the past he had done things that were beneath contempt. If she allowed herself to feel anything for him, it could be nothing more than pity.

They reached the house, Celia noticing that Justin's uneven gait was becoming smoother with each day that passed. How quickly he healed. It would not be long before he was well enough to leave. And then what? Maximilien had refused to discuss any plans for Justin's departure from New Orleans, or what explanations they would give after he was gone. "It is enough that you concern yourself with the day-to-day worries of the present," he had said when Celia had persisted in questioning him. "Leave the future to me." There was no way of arguing against such arrogant self-confidence.

Brusquely Justin told Noeline to call Lysette to the parlor. He lowered himself onto the settee while Celia seated herself as far away from him as possible. Feeling his gaze on her, she glanced at him. Although he was not smiling, the dimple had appeared in his cheek, and there was a wicked glint in his eyes.

"Why do you look so pleased?" she burst out. "You are hoping my husband was unfaithful to me. You would like to see me humiliated by his indiscretions, and you—"

"*Attends,*" Justin drawled, holding up his hand in a silencing motion. "If Philippe did lay with the girl—and I'd bet my good leg that he did—it was before he married you. He wasn't your husband, and therefore he wasn't unfaithful to you."

"He made promises to me," Celia said in a low, intense voice. "I waited for three years for him to come for me."

He gave her a mocking smile. "And you expected him to be celibate all that time?"

"*Naturellement!* He loved me. He could have waited for me!"

"You know less about men than I thought," Justin said, shaking his head. "Philippe was a young man in his prime, not a priest. And for that matter, I would suppose that even priests have natural physical urges. A man—or woman—can't deny certain basic needs—"

"You are disgusting!"

"Basic needs," he continued, "that at times have little to do with love." He stared at her with direct blue eyes. "As you well know."

Celia was pinned to the chair by his stare. A crimson tide washed slowly over her face. Raising her trembling hand to her chest, she tried to calm the panicked rhythm of her heart. "Oh," she breathed. "How could you?"

"You'd like for me to pretend that night never happened," he said quietly. "But one thing I've never been is a hypocrite."

"No, just a thief, outlaw, despoiler of women—"

"*Pardon,*" Lysette's blithe voice came from the doorway. "I was in the nursery with Rafael. It took a minute or so for me to . . ." She frowned as she saw the wounded anger on Celia's face, and Justin's unreadable expression. "*Qu'est-ce que c'est?*"

"We have a small mystery to be solved," Justin replied, moving his gaze from Celia to his step-mother.

"Oh?" Lysette suddenly looked far, far too innocent. "Perhaps we should wait until Max returns home and then—"

"Nay, you'll do very well," Justin said. "You already know the answers to our mystery, don't you *Belle-mère?* You can begin by explaining why Miss Briony Doyle threw herself into my arms a few minutes ago."

"Briony? She . . . Oh dear!" Dismay crossed Lysette's delicate features. "I had asked Briony to keep her distance from you. I thought that what I told her would have kept her from . . . ah, *mon Dieu* . . . she knows, then?"

"She knows," Justin said flatly. "*Belle-mère,* tell me—and my charming wife—exactly what the relationship between Philippe and Miss Doyle was."

Lysette cast an apprehensive glance at Celia. "I do not think it is necessary to divulge something that should be kept private—"

"Yes, it *is* necessary," Celia said fiercely. "I am weary of all the secrets this family keeps! I wish to know what happened between Philippe and that girl. Did he love her? Did he make her his . . ." She found that she could not bring herself to say the words.

Lysette looked at their determined faces and her

brow wrinkled in concern. "Philippe would not have wanted you to know, Celia. He never intended for you to know—it had nothing to do with you. But he never could have anticipated these circumstances, or what you would be asked to do for the sake of the family. Before I explain you must understand that sometimes people cannot help the way they feel. Sometimes they find themselves in situations over which they have no control—"

"She understands all that," Justin interrupted. "Tell her."

Lysette nodded and took a deep breath. "Philippe and Briony were *amoureux* for more than a year," she blurted out. "He very nearly married her."

Celia stared at her blankly. "Philippe?" she asked in a tiny voice.

"He and Briony tried to ignore each other. For a long time they denied how they felt. But then . . ." Lysette cleared her throat awkwardly.

"But I was waiting for him," Celia half-whispered. She could not imagine Philippe in love with another woman. He had told her he loved her. He had written her long letters describing his feelings for her. A wave of hurt swept over her. "I-I thought I was the only one."

Lysette regarded her compassionately. "You were the one he married, *chérie*. It took him a long time to choose between the two of you. After much soul-searching, he decided you were the one he truly wanted."

Celia did not find that comforting. "But if he loved Miss Doyle, why did he not marry her?"

"Because he loved you too, dear, and he realized how much better suited you were to be his wife. You are educated and from a nice French family, a doctor's daughter—"

"I was the *safe* choice," Celia interrupted, her confusion changing to stormy anger.

Justin broke in. "Why are you upset? He chose you, didn't he? You got what you wanted. That's the only thing that matters."

"It is not! If Miss Doyle and I had been equal in name and position, I would have been the second choice!"

He scowled in impatience. "You don't know that." Looking at Lysette, he lifted his brows questioningly. "How many people knew about their . . . ah, liaison?"

"No one except the family. Philippe conferred with Max about what to do, and Max told him—"

"You mean he married me because of his *father's* advice?" Celia demanded, her voice rising with the fury of a scorned woman. "How long did it take him to make this decision? How much deliberation and *conferring* did it take before he finally came to France to marry me? I waited for three years! He wasn't waiting for the war to end, he was taking his time about deciding which woman to marry!"

Lysette winced and sent a look of appeal to Justin.

Justin nodded slightly, his gaze flickering to the doorway and back to her in a silent command for her to leave. "Thank you for explaining things, *Belle-mère.*"

"Do you think Briony will divulge what she knows?" Lysette asked.

"No."

"I pray that she will not." Lysette sighed and retired gratefully.

The two of them were left alone. "Now," Justin said. "Why this show of outrage?"

Celia jumped up and strode to the window, wrapping her arms around her middle. "Isn't it obvious? You know the reasons, you just want to gloat while I—"

"I'm not gloating. Come here and sit down."

"I will not—"

"Come here," he repeated firmly, "and sit down." For a moment he thought she was going to refuse.

Reluctantly Celia sat a foot or two away from him. "What do you wish to say?" she asked sullenly.

"That Philippe cared for you. Enough to marry you. The fact that he had to make a difficult choice shouldn't bruise your vanity. You should find it flattering that you were the one he finally chose."

"My relationship with Philippe wasn't what I thought it was. I thought he loved me completely, that there wasn't room for another woman. There shouldn't have been a choice. He shouldn't have had to ask anyone for *advice*." She said the word as if it were a profanity. "He should have known without question that the one he wanted was me." Suddenly realizing how demanding and selfish she sounded, she hung her head, her hands twisting together in her lap. "After my mother died nothing was ever completely mine," she muttered. "My father devoted himself to his practice, I spent my life taking care of the house and family. Then my sisters began attracting young men, they were called on and courted, a-and I was always overlooked, and one day I realized my youth was gone—"

Justin laughed, unable to stop himself.

Celia stiffened in outrage. "How dare you laugh. I knew I should not have told you any—"

He reached out and tangled his fingers in the curls at the back of her head, forcing her to look at him. "Your youth is not gone," he said, his eyes gleaming with amusement. His gaze traveled over her small face, and his voice softened. "In some ways you're still a little girl."

She decided he must be jeering at her. And yet she was paralyzed by his nearness, the warmth of his hand. "Do not mock me," she managed to say.

"You would have been courted by anyone you showed the slightest interest in. But you wanted something special." His fingers played lightly in her hair. "Philippe almost understood, didn't he? But he couldn't see into that last part of you, the part you keep hidden from everyone. I know exactly what you wanted from Philippe, *ma petite*, but you would never have had him all to yourself. Philippe was as devoted to his practice as your father was to his. He was not the kind to ignore the needs of his patients just because his wife wanted him at home. You would have had to share, and share generously. And you would have hated it. You never let him know that you felt that way, did you? Philippe married you because he thought you would be the perfect wife for a man of his profession . . . when the truth is you would have resented every moment he spent away from you."

Celia lowered her head in shame, feeling exposed, as if all her sins and faults were there on her face for him to see. She thought of lying and telling him he was wrong, but she knew it would be useless. How had he been able to guess at her most private feelings? Was she that transparent to others or only to him? "That is a terrible thing to accuse me of," she mumbled. "I would not have been so possessive and selfish . . ."

"It's not terrible. Some men dream of being loved that way."

"That girl did not love Philippe selfishly," she said, and his hand dropped from her hair.

"No. She would have been happy with whatever he chose to give her."

"What did she say to you when she thought you were Philippe?"

"That," Justin said dryly, "is between her and Philippe."

The discoveries about Philippe caused endless questions to turn through Celia's mind that evening. She went to bed and fell into a troubled sleep, and the nightmare that sometimes haunted her came back. It was as vivid and terrifying as ever. She was leaning over the ship's wooden rail, staring at corpses in the bloody water. Philippe was still alive, reaching up to her. But she could not help him—she could only watch in horror as he flailed and began to sink underneath the surface. Dominic Legare was behind her, his growling voice promising death, his hands reaching for her throat, choking off her screams. There was no one to help her, no place of safety, no chance of escape.

Celia woke and sat up with a gasp, finding the sheets twisted around her body. Her bedroom was quiet, dappled with shadows and moonlight. Unsteadily she wiped her tear-streaked face and took several long breaths. She tried to reason with herself. Philippe was dead, and she was safe from Dominic Legare. It was ridiculous to be afraid. Why did her own mind torture her with such images? Her wild heartbeat began to slow, and she lay down again, her teeth chattering. She could not help thinking of the first time she'd had the nightmare, and the way Justin had held her afterward. He'd been so strong and soothing . . . *No,* she told herself, *don't think about it.* But the memory returned insistently.

She thought of how he had comforted her, and then had taken her in a fury of passion, possessing her body as if she had been created solely for his pleasure. Blushing with shame and arousal, she thought of his thighs straddling hers, his dark head bent over her breasts. *"Mon Dieu,"* she whispered, and buried her face in the pillow, trying to go back to sleep.

The next day she stayed in the *garçonnière.* She occupied herself with her sketches and watercolors, but her artwork was not as calming as usual. In the middle of the cool, blustery afternoon she took a walk in the garden and encountered Justin, who was exercising his leg.

"I wondered when you'd come out of hiding," he remarked. His blue eyes traveled boldly over her close-fitting gown of gray muslin and ruby velvet. Although the gown was high-necked it displayed the fullness of her breasts, and it clung to her waist and hips as she walked.

"Hiding?" Celia repeated coolly, ignoring his masculine inspection. "I was not hiding."

"Then why did you have breakfast and lunch in the *garçonnière?"*

"Because I wished to be alone."

"You were hiding from me."

"I was avoiding you. I do not happen to find your company enjoyable, much as that may surprise you! But I suppose you do not believe it."

He smiled slowly. "Not entirely."

"I suppose you think that when you leave I'll throw myself into your arms and beg you to take me with you."

"Not at all. You'll stay here and be a *tante* to Lysette's children until you're old and gray. You'll be a model of propriety. They'll find it impossible to believe you were ever young. After a few decades have passed your misadventures with me will be nothing but a distant memory. You'll be quiet and contented, respected by everyone who knows you."

"It doesn't sound like such a dreadful fate."

"For you it would be."

"Oh?" She gave him a haughty stare. "What kind of life do you think would be better for me?"

"I offered it to you once."

He had offered to make her his mistress and take her around the world. He had thought she would jump at his promises of homes and jewels and fine clothes, as if she were nothing but an expensive whore. "Your offer was an insult!"

"You're the only woman I've ever wanted such an arrangement with."

"Are you making the offer again?" she sneered.

"As I recall, I never withdrew it."

"You are mad if you think I would consider—"

"You'll consider it," he said. The amusement left his gaze, and his eyes flashed dark and blue. "Before I leave for good I'll make certain of that."

She froze as he walked toward her with his faulty steps. "No," she whispered. His hands clenched at her waist.

"Little fool. You know there's something between us that no one else would begin to understand. Something you never had with Philippe."

She slapped his face and wrenched herself

away from him, breathing choppily. Her palm was tingling from the force of the blow, and she saw that she had left a red mark on his cheek. She was shocked at her actions, horrified by how easily he had caused her to forget herself. They stared at each other for a moment, and then Justin's intensity faded. He surveyed her with his familiar insolence. "All that fire," he said softly. "That night at the lake you nearly burned me alive."

"After what I've done for you I deserve better than your crude remarks!" She heard him laugh as she whirled and tried to leave, but then he caught her hand.

"Celia, wait—"

"Leave me alone!"

"You're right, you deserve much better than that. Forgive me." Faced with her glare, he enfolded her small hand in both of his. "I won't mention that night again."

"*Bien!* Now leave me in peace a-and take your offer with you!"

His blue eyes were remorseful. "I shouldn't have teased you. I behaved badly."

"You *always* behave badly." But she stopped trying to pull away from him.

He smiled at her, and his gaze fell to their joined hands. When he looked back at her face, there was a new seriousness in his tone. "Let me walk with you."

"*Non,* you should go inside and rest—"

"Please."

Suddenly she was disarmed and flustered. His hands were warm and strong around hers. "Please," he repeated quietly, and she could not resist.

They walked the length of the three-acre garden. Justin exerted himself to be nice, nicer than he ever had been to her before. He entertained her with stories of pranks he and Philippe had pulled, charming her out of her uneasiness and making her laugh. He glanced at her frequently, and in spite of herself she could not stop herself from comparing the way he looked at her to the way Philippe had. Philippe had been quietly confident and very certain of her. But there was a searching quality in Justin's gaze, as if there were a thousand things about her that he had yet to discover. The reference he had made before to the night they had been together had truly distressed her . . . and yet, he was the only man in her life who had ever seemed to consider her a passionate woman. And somehow being thought of in that way was not altogether unpleasant.

"You're beautiful when you laugh," he told her when they were almost back at the main house, and she looked at him in surprise.

"I wonder if it is wrong to laugh, to enjoy anything, when I am mourning Philippe. Sometimes I feel guilty even for smiling when he is not here to share—"

"No," Justin murmured. "Philippe would want you to come to an acceptance of his death and then go on. There are years ahead of you that should be lived, not spent in regret and sorrow. He would want you to be happy."

Celia looked up at him wonderingly. "Why are you being so kind?" she half-whispered.

He took her face in his hands. "I'm not being kind. I'm never kind." He stared into her eyes, and then glanced down at her throat, where a telltale pulse was throbbing violently. Her small hands fluttered up to his wrists, trying to pull them away. "Relax," he said. "I'm not going to kiss you." He grinned mischievously. "Unless you ask me to."

Suddenly she laughed, and shook her head within the frame of his hands. "Let go of me, you buffoon."

He chuckled and dropped a kiss on the top of her head before she could twist away. "There—I can't seem to help myself with you."

Late in the evening Justin made his way to the bank of the bayou. Since he had been able to walk on his own he had gone to wait there for a few minutes each night, suspecting there would soon be some word from Risk.

The bayou was quiet, the moss-draped cypress rustling with the softest of breezes. Snowy egrets and wild geese settled in their camps for the night. Slowly the filtered sunlight dissolved, leaving the surface of the water like onyx. The lemon trees on the plantation sent their citrus fragrance through the air. He heard the distant sound of a Negro woman singing, her crooning low and plaintive. The song was a Creole lullaby he remembered from childhood.

> *Others say it is your happiness*
> *I say it is your sorrow*
> *When we are enchanted by love*
> *Farewell to all happiness . . .*

The sound drifted into silence. Leaning his weight against a tree, Justin stared into the water with narrowed eyes.

Time was running out. He was healing quickly, and the danger for him increased each day that he remained here. No one would continue to believe the story that he was Philippe for much longer—the gossip and suspicion in town were spreading rapidly. Although Max was confident in his own power to protect his son, Justin knew he was not safe—from the authorities, or from Legare. He had to disappear and hide somewhere until he was well enough to go after Legare.

There was nothing keeping him here. Except Celia. A self-mocking smile twisted his lips.

After he vanished from her life she would be safe and content. This was what she was meant for, being surrounded by family, respected by friends, secure in the knowledge that each day would be as well-ordered as the last. She would never want to leave everything that was familiar.

Justin's smile died away. Distractedly he raked his hands through his short hair until it stood on end. His entire being rebelled against the new-found feelings, but he could not seem to get rid of them. The realization was infuriating. His mother had shown him that women could never be trusted. He had always regarded them as entertaining creatures to be used for pleasure and then discarded.

Where Celia was concerned, however, he was driven by something he didn't understand. If it were only physical desire, he could have found someone else to satisfy his need. There were other women more experienced, more seductive, women who affected the senses like the finest liquor. But his hunger for Celia was more than that. It had not begun on Crow's Island or even at the lakeside cabin, but during his illness. He knew he couldn't have survived the fever and wounds without her. For the first time in his life he had relied on someone else, on the fine-tempered strength of a woman half his size. She had fought for him; she had reached into his very dreams to pull him away from death. A link had been forged between them, and now she was part of him, haunting his thoughts, tormenting him. He tried to imagine never seeing her again, living out his life half a world away from her. Silently he damned her and himself.

A quiet splash from the bayou drew his attention. Justin drew back into the shadow of the tree, listening intently. A low, warbling whistle floated to his ears. Justin grinned. He peered at the approaching pirogue and its two passengers, waiting until it had reached the bank. Softly he spoke from the darkness. "A fine thing to dump a helpless man into the laps of the Vallerands."

Risk stepped from the pirogue to the muddy bank, easing his way toward the direction of the voice. " 'Tis a ghost I'm hearin', to be sure."

Justin was heartily glad to see Risk—and Aug, who was tethering the pirogue to the bank. "Hello, Jack." He approached Risk, and the younger man seized him in a rough embrace punctuated by a hearty clap on the back.

"My God, man, the look o' ye!" Risk exclaimed, standing back to survey him. "Scraped clean an' smellin' pretty. An' not long ago ye were totterin' on the brink o' the grave!"

Justin smiled slightly. "You could have left me for dead, Jack." His expression sobered. "Once again I owe you my life."

"An' I won't be lettin' ye forget it."

Aug came to join them, and Justin exchanged greetings with him, clasping hands briefly. "Griffin," Aug said, "once again you have cheated the devil." His teeth showed in a smile. "Even he would not have you, eh?"

Justin smiled ruefully and shook his head, studying the pair of them. He was troubled by what he saw. Even in the worst of times Risk had never lost his roguish air, but it was gone now, replaced by a sharp, hunted look. And there was an unfamiliar tenseness about Aug, for all that he tried to keep his dark face expressionless.

"So they've pieced ye back together again," Risk observed. "Soon ye'll be as fit as before, I'll warrant."

Justin gestured with his cane. "The leg isn't good." He sent a brief grin to Aug. "But for your handiwork I might be balancing on a wooden peg right now." He turned his attention back to Risk. "Tell me what's happened."

"Ye won't like it," Risk said gloomily. "With the navy gunboats crawlin' all over the water, there's been idle time aplenty for Legare an' all his rovers. Legare's claimin' Crow's Island as his own. We've been tryin' to empty the last of our warehouses before he gets his paws on our spoils. I've got goods stashed right an' left—God knows what to do with most of it."

"What about the crew?"

"No one knew if ye were dead or alive. The men have scattered, some o' them layin' low, while others . . ." Risk paused, then continued grimly, "They went to throw their lots in wi' Legare, rotten bastards. Ye've got to take matters in hand, Griffin, an' soon. Our tidy little business has got its guts ripped out, an' all its legs in the air. A bit o' resurrectin' is needed."

Justin contemplated the situation. Shadows from the trees played over his averted face. He was surprised by his own hesitancy. A month ago he would have thrown himself wholeheartedly into preserving his small kingdom of rascals and scavengers. It was all he had ever had, all he'd wanted. Before, he wouldn't have needed to think twice. But now . . .

"Maybe we shouldn't resurrect it," Justin said slowly. "Maybe we should just clean up the remains."

"An' then what?" Risk asked, puzzled. "Start from scratch?"

Justin looked at him then, and grinned recklessly. He felt an unexpected lightness and freedom, as if he were casting off a burden that had been strapped to his back for years. "The *Vagabond* is yours, Jack. Take it with my blessing."

Risk's mouth dropped open, and his one eye squinted in surprise. "Sweet Jesus, man, do ye know what ye're sayin'?"

Justin nodded firmly. "I've tweaked the devil's nose one too many times. I'm not fool enough to think my luck will hold forever. I've enjoyed the hell out of our roving, but it's time for me to stop."

Risk stared at him wildly. "Come to yer senses, man! Ye were born a wanderer, a rover, like the rest of us. What else is there?"

Justin shrugged. "Even if I wanted to continue as before, it wouldn't be possible. My leg will never be what it was."

"Ye can't stay here. Is that what ye're plannin'?"

That provoked a low laugh from Justin. "I'm not a fool. After I even the score with Legare I'm going to disappear." He laughed. "God, I never thought I'd take to the idea of settling somewhere, but suddenly it holds a strange appeal. I'm beginning to want things I've always had contempt for. I can see you don't understand. Well, you will someday—if you live long enough."

Risk stared at him incredulously. "What's happened to ye? Aug, damn yer scaly hide, say something to him!"

"It is finished," Aug said quietly, his ebony eyes fixed on Justin's face.

Justin nodded briefly, knowing that Aug understood the nature of the change inside him. It boiled down to a matter of caring whether he lived or died. Now that he had begun to care about his own life, he would stop taking chances, his instincts would soften, his aggressiveness would be tempered by a concern for safety and self-preservation. The crew would not want to follow such a man. They needed a ruthless leader, one with no vulnerability.

"There's only one thing I have left to do," Justin said. "I'm going to repay Dominic Legare for what he did to my brother."

Aug replied with no hesitation. "I will help you."

Justin looked at Risk questioningly.

Risk swore. "So will I," he said sullenly. "That's three of us against Legare's hundreds."

That brought a smile to Justin's face. "Any other malcontents who'd care to join us?"

"With luck we could gather p'raps a dozen. 'Tis a nasty business Legare runs, but the profits are tidy an' the men follow him like sheep."

Justin nodded matter-of-factly. "Then we'll begin by—" He stopped, his instincts warning him of someone's approach even though there was no sound. His gaze flickered around the area. There was a rustle from the woods behind them. Someone was about to intrude on their gathering. Justin signaled for Risk to creep behind their uninvited guest, while he and Aug slipped back into the shadows. The cautious steps drew closer.

A dim shaft of light fell across Celia's white face and pale hair. "Justin?" she called softly, bewildered, turning in search of him. Suddenly she heard feet trampling the underbrush behind her. "Justin?" There were footsteps all around her, closing in rapidly. She gave a sob of fright. Wildly she ran a few steps, only to stop short at the sight of Aug's threatening visage. Gasping, she backed away, her pulse racing. "Jus—"

"I'm here," his voice interrupted, and she turned toward the sound. Justin was a few feet away, wearing an expression of annoyance. "Right here."

"Oh—" She stumbled to him, seeking the safety of his arms. They closed around her, warm and comforting.

"What the hell are you doing here?" he asked curtly.

"I-I saw you walking away from the house earlier," she stuttered, huddling against his chest. "I did not kn-know that anyone else was here, I . . ." She was breathing so hard she could barely speak.

"Why did you follow me?" Although his tone was harsh, his hand was gentle as it rubbed up and down her back, soothing her shudders.

"I . . . wanted to tell you something . . ."

"If I ever again catch you wandering around the plantation alone, out of sight of the main house, there'll be hell to pay. I'll beat you, *comprends?*" He smoothed her hair and straightened her collar. "It's dangerous for you to venture out here alone, especially down by the bayou. Don't you know what kind of human filth makes its way to and from the river at night? They'd snap up a little treat like you in the blink of an eye. What if you'd come across some of Legare's men? What if—''

"I didn't think," Celia said, her voice muffled against his shoulder.

"Well you should have," Justin scolded gently, and would have continued had he not suddenly become aware of Risk's and Aug's astonished gazes. They had never seen him behave this way with anyone before. He looked at them over Celia's head, his brows lowering in a challenging scowl.

Risk's green eye widened, and he snorted in disgust. "Jesus, now I'm understandin'," he muttered, looking betrayed. " 'Tis all because of a woman. As bloody simple as that."

"There's nothing simple about it," Justin replied, toying with a lock of Celia's shining hair.

"For *this* ye're givin' up everything?" Risk demanded. "She's only a woman—why, there are hundreds like her, thousands, everywhere! Tell him he can't do this, Aug!"

Aug looked at Justin thoughtfully as he answered Risk. "There is a saying . . . you must tie your handkerchief to fit your head."

Risk sputtered in indignation. "What the hell does *that* mean?"

Justin laughed. "It means circumstances change. And so do people." He silenced Risk's grumbling with a warning glance. "Enough, Jack. Go to the pirogue and wait for a minute. Madame Vallerand and I require some privacy."

" 'Tis come to that now, has it?" Risk muttered as Aug dragged him down to the bank of the bayou. "Privacy. Now he wants *privacy* . . ."

Left alone with Justin, Celia stared at him anxiously, rubbing her upper arms as if to ward off a chill. Earlier she had been too frightened to think, and she had run into his arms as if it were the most natural thing in the world. She had come in search of him in order to talk about what he'd said before, to tell him that he was right—she had wanted things of Philippe that he would never have been able to give her. And there *was* something between her and Justin, something she could deny no longer.

"Now," Justin said. "What is it you wanted to tell me?"

Celia shook her head hastily. "Nothing. Nothing important. I am sorry I intruded. I did not intend to."

He studied her in a leisurely way. "Actually your interruption was convenient. I want you to give my father a message."

"What message?"

"Tell him I'll be gone for the next few days. I'll return no later than Friday."

She flinched as if he had struck her. "*Gone* . . . but you cannot, you—"

"I don't have a choice. In my absence my . . . business seems to have fallen apart. There are some things I have to salvage."

"You cannot go," she said frantically. "You are not well enough. This is only the fourth week since you came here! You could not protect yourself. Legare is looking for you. He will find you, and—"

"He won't."

"He did before, and you almost died! Is your greed so great that you must risk your life for the sake of money and property?"

"It's not just that. If I'm going to take revenge on Legare for Philippe's death, I need to find out how many men and supplies are available. I want to assess the situation for myself."

"And then?"

"Then Aug and Risk and I will come up with a plan and set it in motion. It's going to take a little time. I'll return in two, maybe three days."

Celia recoiled from the unpleasant reminder. When Justin had been ill, she had taken care of him with the sole intention of making him well enough to go out and kill Dominic Legare. But even if Justin succeeded, he would probably lose his own life in the endeavor. It was too dangerous. Legare was too powerful and well-protected. And now . . . now she wanted Justin alive more than she wanted Legare dead.

"Killing Legare will not do anything for me, or for anyone else," she said. "It seemed necessary before, but now—"

"It's still necessary."

"You must wait. You must stay here and allow some time to pass before you—"

"There is no time."

Celia felt blind, unreasoning rage sweep over her. It didn't matter that she had no right to demand that he stay. It didn't matter that he had made no promises. All she knew was that he was leaving, and that he might not come back. And he was standing there with that matter-of-fact expression and mocking smile on his lips. "You know you're not well enough!" she cried in passionate fury. "You fool!—You can't even walk well, and you are going out there where you'll be hunted by everyone on both sides of the law. I hope they find you!"

His expression changed. "Celia—"

"If you want to die so badly, I hope they get you and . . . give you what you deserve! I hope you never come back. You don't care about anyone, you're greedy and selfish, and I hate you! I hate you!''

She saw him moving toward her, his stride broken but swift, his face harsh. Thinking he was going to hurt her, she cowered away. He seized her shoulders in his powerful hands, holding her as if she were a rag doll. ''No,'' she whimpered as he bent and kissed her, his mouth hard and punishing. She sobbed angrily as his arms clamped around her back and hips, pulling her tight against him.

''You're going to drive me mad,'' he muttered, staring down at her white face. ''You already have! After that night at the lake I thought I was rid of you, but thoughts of you tormented me day and night. I made plans to come back for you. I thought if I took you one more time I'd discover you were no different from other women. And then I'd be free.'' His arms tightened cruelly as Celia fought his embrace. ''But then I was wounded and you were there. Every touch of yours was heaven and hell. I thought about putting my hands around your neck and throttling the life out of you—anything to stop you from becoming necessary to me. But it's too late now. You're mine, and you have only yourself to blame. You made yourself mine.''

''*Don't*,'' she wept. ''It's not true—I won't listen—''

He crushed her mouth in a greedy kiss. Treacherous excitement engulfed her, and she shuddered violently. This was what she wanted, what she needed, his strength wrapped around her, his mouth on hers. Her lips parted to admit his thrusting tongue, and her arms clutched his broad shoulders.

Suddenly Justin's kiss turned gentle, his lips

twisting over hers, his tongue teasing lightly, then sliding deep into her mouth. Celia had never forgotten the taste of him. She moaned and strained her body against him as his hand slid between her thighs, exploring through the folds of her gown. The bulging hardness of his loins pressed against her belly, and she quivered in pleasure. His dark head lowered as he bit the tip of her chin, and then his mouth glided over her white throat. She tilted her head back, her eyes closed, her mind reeling at the love-words he murmured. He was shaking just as much as she was with a hunger that had no end. Both of them were possessed by a sweet madness. She had thought she would never feel it again.

Impatiently Justin searched through her thin muslin gown, cupping her full breast in his hand, his thumb coaxing the soft nipple into a hard peak. "I'll never get enough of you. Never." He covered her mouth with his, drinking in her sweetness, and she responded feverishly. Her hands slipped down to his buttocks, her fingers digging into the flexed muscles. It was all he could do not to lift up her skirts and sink himself into her soft body.

Raising his mouth with a curse, he dragged her head to his chest and held her shivering form against his. His palm was hot against her cheek, his heartbeat like thunder beneath her ear. Celia clenched handfuls of his shirt in her fists and gasped weakly. It was a long time before the frantic desire faded, leaving an ache in the pit of her stomach. She felt his hand on the side of her face, forcing her to look up at him. His eyes were as blue-black as the sky, and she felt herself drowning in their darkness. "Celia," he said hoarsely, and touched his lips to hers with incredible gentleness. She wrapped her arms around his neck and burrowed her head against his chest. He nuzzled her hair, his lips playing through the soft wisps at her temple. A cool breeze whisked across her skin, causing her to shiver. His arms tightened before he pulled away from her without a word.

Dazed, she watched him pick up his cane and make his way toward the bayou. Never had her arms felt so empty. Her lips trembled, but she did not call after him. She was possessed by a fear greater than any she had ever known. They had not yet begun to know each other, and already he was a part of her. She was terrified that she could not survive losing him.

"How long did he say he would be gone?" Max asked, utterly controlled, his face like granite.

"Two or three days," Celia said unsteadily, sitting next to Lysette. Although Celia had been careful not to reveal any of the details of her encounter with Justin, she thought that Lysette had an inkling of how she felt. Lysette was an intuitive woman, but most people were usually too dazzled by her beauty to pay heed to the sharp intelligence behind her pretty face. At the moment Lysette was looking at her with an odd mixture of sympathy and speculation. She squeezed Celia's hand in a comforting gesture. Celia kept her gaze on Max, wondering if an explosion of anger was forthcoming. "He is in terrible danger, isn't he?"

"Yes, he's in danger," Max said curtly. "The plantation is the only place he is safe. It is known around the Gulf that Legare has offered a fortune to anyone who will bring him Justin's head in a sack. And my son's fate will not be much different if he's caught by the authorities. At the moment I've been pressing Governor Villeré to expend some of his political capital on granting a full pardon to him—a damn difficult thing to do when I can't exactly admit that 'Philippe' is Justin! It does not help that Justin has decided to go gallivanting around as Captain Griffin right in the middle of this ungodly mess!''

"*Vraiment*, do you really think the governor would consider pardoning him?'' Celia asked in astonishment.

"I don't know,'' Max muttered. "It's impossible to predict. If only Claiborne were still in office.''

"At least Villeré is a Creole,'' Lysette said. "That should help our cause, *n'est-ce pas?*''

"Not necessarily,'' Max replied. "At present he seems to have devoted himself to the cause of limiting the immigration of 'undesirable persons' to the state. And my son falls well within *that* category.''

Lysette frowned. "But if you prevail, Max, and the governor does pardon Justin?''

"Then Justin will be safe from the authorities.'' He gave both women a humorless smile. "Until then, however, he'll have to continue masquerading as Philippe. Which means he had better return in time for the Duquesne ball on Saturday.''

Lysette regarded him with a perplexed expression. "Can't we offer some excuse for him, *bien-aimé?*''

Max laughed grimly. "I was just told this evening by the Duquesnes—cousins on my mother's side—that they are turning their ball this weekend into a celebration to welcome Philippe home. He will be the guest of honor. As they described it, all of

New Orleans will attend. And expect him to make an appearance.''

Celia heard Lysette's gasp of horror. She stared at Maximilien, her mouth sagging open. ''But . . . but what if Justin is not back in time?''

''Then,'' Max said darkly, ''we're all finished.''

Late the following evening Justin had managed to assemble a dozen men whom Aug had sworn could be trusted. They met in the lakeside cabin. For various reasons none of them had accepted Legare's invitation to throw their lots in with him. Justin was satisfied as he looked over the gathering. Among them were Duffy, a short but stocky Irishman; Tomas, a handsome mulatto; and Sans-Nez, a disfigured and surly-tempered brawler who had lost a goodly portion of his nose in a knife fight. None of them had been the ablest of the *Vagabond* crew, but they were the most vengeful. They had agreed to take part in the scheme not only for the chance to plunder the island, but also because they each nursed old grudges against Legare and his men.

Sitting on the wooden chest, his long legs crossed at the ankles, Justin formed a plan with Aug while the rest threw in their comments. It was a far more democratic system than Justin usually employed, but this was a riskier venture than any they had undertaken. If he was to lead them into such danger, it was their right to offer suggestions.

''We'll have to destroy Legare from the inside out,'' Justin said, looking at Aug. ''If you could approach him and somehow convince him you've decided to join his lot, you could work behind the scenes to help us.''

Aug nodded. ''I will gain Legare's trust.''

"I don't know what Legare might require of you to prove your loyalty," Justin said. "If you decide to back out—"

"No," Aug interrupted. "What is the rest of the plan?"

"With your help we'll smuggle the men onto the island and launch a surprise attack. The only difficult part will be staying hidden until the right time."

Sans-Nez spoke up, his face twisting with an ugly smile. "I know the underground tunnels as good as anyone. Years ago when I sailed with Legare, he had me locked up down there for weeks for taking a woman André wanted."

Justin nodded. "See if you can remember enough to draw a map for us."

"What about Legare?" Risk asked. "Who's going to take him down?"

Justin arched his brows and smiled mockingly. "Jack, I'm surprised you need to ask. Killing Dominic Legare will be my personal and very great pleasure."

Chapter 10

The three days that followed Justin's departure may as well have been three months. Celia could do nothing but think about Justin. She realized that he was as necessary to her as he had claimed she was to him. He had said she belonged to him . . . well, she had not admitted it out loud but she knew he was hers in the same elemental way. Ever since he had been brought to the plantation he had been hers to tend and take care of, hers to worry over and want.

Theirs was an impossible match. Even so, the separation caused her to ache physically. It wasn't a sharp pain but a dull emptiness in every part of her. She craved the sight and sound of him, his alert interest in her, his arrogant demands for her attention. She had not realized how many of her waking hours had been occupied with him.

Her loneliness was aggravated by the way Max and Lysette relied on each other in times of trouble. They lavished affection on each other and their children, finding occasions for laughter and affection even in the midst of all their worry. One morning the couple was absent from the breakfast table, and the entire household was aware that they had decided to spend the morning alone in

257

their bedroom. When Lysette emerged later, her face was glowing and there was a soft radiance in her hazel eyes. Celia was glad for their happiness, but it made her even more aware of her own solitude.

At suppertime on Friday the conversation was stilted and quiet. Lysette occupied herself with Rafe, who talked to her in happy gurgles. She was trying to start the baby on solid food, but he had more interest in playing with the mashed banana than eating it. Celia forced herself to chew and swallow, but every bite of the pompano and mushrooms sautéed in wine and butter seemed to stick in her throat. Although Max seemed marvelously collected and unconcerned, he checked his watch every fifteen minutes or so, something he never did with such frequency.

"Bien-aimé, what time does the ball begin tomorrow?" Lysette asked Max.

It was at that moment that Justin entered the room, stopping just inside the doorway. He sniffed the air appreciatively. "Mmm . . . I'm starved. I hope you've left enough for me."

Max leaped up from his chair. "Were I not so relieved to see you," he said, "I would probably be inflicting significant damage on you, my foolhardy son."

Justin grinned and put a protective hand over his side. "You'll have to take your turn, Father."

Max pinned him with a searching gaze. "I assume your interests have been secured and there will be no more unexpected disappearances?"

"Aye."

"How is the situation?"

An unpleasant hardness crossed Justin's face. "In the past few weeks Legare has marked Isle au Corneille as his and appropriated everything in sight. Ships, ammunition, property . . . No one dares to cross him.''

''And neither will you,'' Max said. ''Your days as Captain Griffin are over. This little jaunt of yours might have ruined even the slightest possibility of a pardon from the governor.''

''Pardon?'' Justin laughed shortly. ''If you were the closest friend of President Monroe himself you couldn't manage that. In any event, I don't need a pardon. Soon I'll be leaving for good.''

Max scowled and began to argue, but Lysette interrupted adroitly, hoping to prevent a fullblown quarrel. ''Thank God you have arrived in time, Justin.''

''In time for what?''

Max proceeded to explain about the Duquesne ball.

Celia set down her fork, aware that her hand was trembling visibly. She let her gaze travel over Justin hungrily. He was dirty and unshaven, the beginnings of a sunburn crossing his cheekbones and the bridge of his nose. His vital presence affected her senses like an invigorating drug. She wanted to throw herself at him, smooth her hands over his tangled brown-black hair, hug herself to his body. But not once did he look at her. It was as if she were not there.

''. . . there must be some way to avoid it,'' Justin was saying to Max, who shook his head.

''Rumors will fly if you don't appear.''

Justin swore and shook his head. ''So be it. I've already thrown in my lot—no chance of retreat now. I'll go to the ball and play the gentleman. And I'll do it so well no one will dare suggest I'm not Philippe.'' He turned his attention to Lysette. ''*Belle-mère*, would you have Noeline send up some supper for me?'' He plucked at his sweat-stained shirt ruefully. "I believe a bath and a change of clothes are in order."

"Yes, of course," Lysette looked at him in concern. "How is your leg? You have not injured it again, have you?"

"Not at all." Justin smiled slightly. "I'm fine, *Belle-mère.*"

He left without having acknowledged Celia with so much as a flicker of an eye.

Celia felt as if all the breath had been stolen from her body. There was a sickening sensation inside her. Why had Justin ignored her? Perhaps that scene before he had left had been a game to him. Perhaps it had amused him to reduce her to such a state. Confused and miserable, she tried to appear as if nothing were troubling her. She toyed with the food on her plate and even managed to take a bite now and then. After downing an extra glass of wine, she lingered with Max and Lysette in the parlor after supper. Sitting near the fire, she warmed her slipper-clad feet. There had been no sound from Justin upstairs. They surmised he was exhausted after his three-day absence and had gone to bed.

"You seem tired, Celia," Lysette said.

"*Oui,*" Celia murmured, staring moodily into the fire. She was not tired, she was filled with anxiety and hurt. Justin Vallerand was a monster, and she despised him. She had nothing but contempt for a man so facile with lies and empty promises! She bade the Vallerands good-night and trudged out of the main house to the *garçonnière.* Not wanting to face the housemaid, she went through the house by herself and entered her bedroom. The darkness made her skittish and uneasy, and she fumbled with the tiny candle of the veilleuse lamp on the bureau.

She saw the shape of a man in the corner of the room. Catching her breath, she froze in terror. He stepped forward, and the gleam of his eyes became apparent. Her heart beat against her ribs. She stared at him as if hypnotized. "Justin?"

He was freshly shaven, clad in a loose white shirt and dark breeches. His hair was damp and tousled, wet strands clinging to his neck. He didn't move, but she felt crowded by the sheer size of his long, lean body. "I couldn't look at you," he said hoarsely. "I knew if I did I would snatch you up and drag you to the nearest bed."

The shadow-filled room was suddenly unreal, a place that existed only in a dream. Anticipation unfurled in the pit of her stomach. Knowing she did not have the will to turn him away, she managed a shaking whisper. "Justin, please go. Please."

"No."

He took both her hands in his, felt how cold they were, and slipped them inside his shirt to warm them against his chest. His heart pounded heavily against her palms. With infinite care he slid his arms around her back and pulled her trembling body into his.

Celia dropped her forehead to his shoulder. "We cannot. This is wrong, wrong—"

"*Tais-toi, mon coeur,*" he whispered, and pulled out the comb that fastened her hair. The silken blond locks unraveled, falling softly down her back. His hand searched through the fine strands, his fingers curving to her skull, and he tilted her head back. He pressed his mouth to the base of her throat, then slid it up to the hollow underneath her jaw.

The sensation of his lips on her skin sent shivers of delight through her body. Celia made a halfhearted attempt to pull away, but he kept her firmly against him. His mouth brushed over hers with tantalizing lightness. Slowly her hands inched around his neck. He nibbled gently on her lower lip, stroked it with his tongue, teased mercilessly until she was breathing fast and her hands were warm and perspiring.

Sealing his lips over hers, Justin thrust his tongue deep into the warmth of her mouth. A groan of satisfaction came from his throat, and his head moved to change the angle of the kiss, fitting them together more securely. His fingers fumbled at the back of her gown. When the long line of tiny looped buttons proved difficult to unfasten he used both his hands to rip the garment in a swift movement, sending buttons scattering across the floor.

Celia gasped and tried to back away, startled by his sudden roughness as he yanked her clothes down to her waist. But when her body was revealed to him he became gentle again, his lips moving over her forehead, his hand sliding over her naked breast. Lightly he squeezed and stroked the white mound, then toyed with the soft pink nipple until it tautened. She arched her back, pressing herself against his warm hand, her breath catching with pleasure as he touched her other breast. Between her thighs there was a sudden trickle of warmth, the same wetness she remembered from the other time they had been together, and she flushed with mingled shame and excitement. He murmured quietly as if he knew what was happening inside her, and his lips sought hers again. Her mouth opened, accepting him fully, and she made no attempt to stop him as she felt him pushing the rest of her clothes down to the floor.

When she stood naked before him he pulled off his own shirt, revealing the scarred, powerful body she had become so familiar with. Celia reached for him, her arms winding around him, her tender breasts pressing into the thick black hair on his chest. Kissing her fiercely, he took her hand and pulled it down his flat belly to the straining bulge of his breeches. With shaking fingers she undid the metal buttons that constrained him, while his hot breath rushed in her hair and his hand clenched at the back of her neck. The opening of his breeches was spread wide, and his arousal sprang free, hard and silken, startlingly hot.

Timidly she touched him, her curiosity outweighing shyness. Her slim fingers explored the sensitive head, the heavy veined shaft, and he said her name in a guttural voice, his hand closing over hers. Slowly he guided her in a long, rhythmic stroke. Shaken by the intimacy of the moment, she hesitated when his hand fell away, and then she continued to caress him.

Justin tightened his fist in her hair and buried his face in the flowing golden locks. Passion surged through him, and he was helpless under her hands, every nerve quivering tautly. Easing her away from his body, he stripped away the last of his clothes and pulled her to the velvet-draped bed.

Celia leaned back on the crisp sheets and reached her arms out to him. He lowered his body to hers, using his knee to push her thighs apart, and they spread easily for him in welcome. He cupped her breasts in his hands, his mouth delving into the fragrant valley between them. She cried out as he kissed and licked the delicate buds of her nipples, using his teeth in tantalizing bites that excited her beyond bearing.

Lovingly she wound herself around him, entwining him with her silky limbs, kneading his hard-muscled back. Reality was driven away by a sensuality she had not felt since the night at the lake, and once again she was caught in the spell of the lover she had remembered with such fear and desire.

His hand slid over her belly to the downy curls between her thighs, finding her wet, swollen passage. Growling in satisfaction, he fondled her gently.

"Please," she whispered. "Please . . ." His head moved down her body, his tongue sliding into the indentation of her navel. His mouth wandered lower, through the moist thatch of hair, and her heart raced. She tried to sit up, choking out a protest.

His strong hands clamped on her thighs, holding them wide, while his mouth opened her and searched for the tiny nub that ached exquisitely. She sank back against the pillows, her struggles dissolving. The movement of his lips was relentless, nurturing, devouring. Her hips undulated in response to the sleek plunge of his tongue, and her fingers went to the dark head between her legs.

Sensing that her climax could no longer be contained, Justin lowered his body over hers, pulled her leg high over his hip, and penetrated her in a swift, skillful stroke. She groaned and thrust herself at him, and he drove solidly inside her.

"You're mine," he said against her trembling lips. "You'll never escape from me . . . never . . ."

Dazed, she could only stare at him while the

pleasure gathered in rippling waves. He lunged violently as she arched against his hard body and shuddered in fulfillment. And he shared her pleasure, letting it course through him with its vital heat.

He held her close as she wept afterward, her slim body crushed against his. His lips moved over her tear-streaked face, while his hand coasted up and down her back. "Don't," he said, and although he meant it as a command, it sounded like a plea. "Don't, my love, *mon coeur.*"

She sniffled and tried to turn away from him, but he would not let her. "It has happened all over again," she said miserably, glaring at him. "If only you had stayed away. If only I could hate you!"

"You love me." He cradled her head in his hands, wiping at her tears with his thumbs.

"What good is it?" she railed. "You will leave me, and I will lose everything, and I cannot go through it again, I won't!"

"I'm coming back for you after I finish with Legare." Justin knew he should not make such promises, but he couldn't help himself.

"You won't come back. And even if you did, I would not go anywhere with you, you selfish, immoral pirate—"

He kissed her throat, her shoulder, her breast. "I'm not a pirate anymore. I've given the ship to Risk."

"You cannot change your character as if you were discarding one hat in favor of another! Such things do not happen overnight."

"You'll help me to change."

"*Alors* . . . you want to keep me with you. For how long? And what will happen when you tire of me?"

"I want you forever. I couldn't tire of you any more than I could tire of living or breathing." He took her small hand and pressed it against his heart until she could feel his pulse against her palm. His gaze pierced hers. "I couldn't live without you. If you refuse to go with me, I'll stay near you until I'm caught and hanged."

"Do not be foolish," she said unsteadily.

"I'm not being foolish. I didn't choose to feel this way . . . couldn't stop it . . ." He pressed her hand more tightly against his chest. "I'll come back for you. I want a life with you. I want to make you happy, give you things I never thought I could give anyone . . ."

"Then I'm to be an outlaw's mistress?" Celia asked gruffly.

"Aye, that and a companion, partner, wife—"

"Wife?" she repeated in astonishment. "Y-you are asking me to marry you?"

Justin urged her onto her back and braced his arms on either side of her head, his mouth gentle on her kiss-bruised lips. "No. I'm not *asking*."

Celia considered him for a long moment and smiled tremulously. "Then I'm not to be given a choice?"

"I can't afford the possibility of refusal."

"You told me once you were not susceptible to love."

"I wasn't. Not until you."

"You want me as a convenience. To save you the trouble of seeking other women to satisfy your desires."

He rained swift kisses all over her face. "I'll be your convenience. I'll teach you to have an appetite for me, *ma belle*, until you plague me with your constant demands."

"I'm a sudden fancy of yours. It is because I

once belonged to Philippe that you find me attractive—''

Justin clamped his hands on either side of her head, staring down at her with lightning-blue eyes. "I love you, dammit! I love you because you belong to me. I love you for taking care of me. For making me feel as if there is still some good left in me. Philippe was a better man than I'll ever be. God knows he deserved you more than I do. But he's gone now . . . and I need you."

Her gaze was dark and soft. "What do you need me for?"

Ruthlessly he laid his heart before her. "Love me. Help me become worthy of you. Help me find the courage to try. You're the only one who can."

Celia gazed at his face, as stark and beautiful as a marble sculpture. She wanted to take away the haunted look in his eyes, lavish him with all the things he needed from her. Lifting her hand to his forehead, she pushed back a lock of sable hair. "I'll be yours, I'll follow you anywhere, everywhere, if you'll promise me one thing."

"What is it?"

"Give up your revenge on Dominic Legare."

He was still, staring at her through the darkness. "I can't."

"It will not bring Philippe back. You do not owe it to me, or the family, or anyone. Is it not enough that you killed Legare's brother? He had a close attachment to André. Is that not enough of a retribution?"

"André was as worthless a creature as any that ever scuttled over the earth. If you think the exchange of my brother for Legare's was equal—"

"But what if you lose your life?" she asked desperately. "Must I lose you as well as Philippe?"

Even before he spoke, she saw the refusal in his face. "I've already set the plans in motion."

"You could stop it if you wanted to!" Celia turned away from him, scarcely able to contain her churning emotions. She was angry with him, almost as much as she was afraid for him. "If you won't promise me, then leave." Her spine stiffened as she felt his lips brush between her shoulder blades. "I don't want you here in my bed. You can choose me or your revenge, but you cannot have both."

"We won't be safe anywhere until Legare is dead," Justin said flatly. "He'll scour the world until he finds me. The danger will be just as great for you if I take you with me."

"We will go somewhere he can't find us." She pulled his palm to her breast and caressed the back of his hand. "You'll keep me safe, Justin."

Justin could not control the instant response of his body. She moved softly against him, and he found it difficult to think. "Celia, you don't understand. I—"

"You said you wanted to change."

"Yes, but first—"

"All I want is for you to love me."

"I do—"

"Then forget about revenge. For me."

"Damn you," he said thickly, his senses tortured by her nearness. He needed her again, had to feel her tight and hot around him once more. Pushing her thighs apart, he groaned her name and pulled her hips up to his. His hand searched over her stomach, between her legs.

"*Promise me,*" she whispered.

He could not refuse her anything, her love was too precious. "Damn you, all right," he groaned, urging his loins against her buttocks, letting her feel the rigid pressure of his arousal. He feasted on the nape of her neck, her shoulders, his pulse rocketing as he felt her weight settle naturally against his thighs. Searching for the hot, slick entrance to her body, he pushed into her from behind. His hand shook against her stomach, and his head hung over her soft shoulder.

Celia clung to the hard arm wrapped around her waist and arched against his chest. There was a giddy rush of her senses in response to the flex of his body. "Move with me," he entreated, gasping heavily. "Push back . . . *oui, comme ça, ma petite*, just like that . . ."

She moved in a luscious counterpoint to his rhythm, losing awareness of everything but him. He kissed her throat and moved his hand to her breast, sheltering her wild heartbeat in his palm. Her hand covered his, cupping it closer, and then time was suspended as the rapture broke over her. He thrust and thrust again, long, leisurely strokes that drew out her pleasure until she was exhausted. She felt the hot flood of his release within her, and his arm pulled her body tighter into his until she could barely breathe.

They collapsed to their sides, her smaller form tucked into his spoon-fashion. After a while her breathing slowed, and so did his, falling gently in her hair. Celia blinked tiredly. She knew he was falling asleep. She should remind him that he did not belong there. She did not want him to be discovered in her bed.

"Justin, you should not stay," she said groggily.

His voice was a low rumble near her ear. "I'll leave before the sun rises."

"You should go now."

He grasped her closer and burrowed under the

covers obstinately. "I have little enough time with you as it is."

She slept in his arms until the night began to fade, and awakened as she felt him drawing away from her. He bent to take one last kiss, and her warm, clinging lips lured him to take a deeper taste. With a muffled groan he made love to her once more, spreading her limbs wide and sheathing himself in her softness. She quivered and pressed her small fists against his back, straining up to his hard body. He clasped her head to his chest, concentrating on the motion of plunge and withdrawal.

They tried to make it last forever, but all too soon he felt her delicate shudder, and the exquisite tension was released in a searing burst of fire. He lowered his head and kissed her chest, his lips resting on her heart. She stroked his dark head, her eyes prickling with tears. Then the warm, crushing weight of his body lifted, and suddenly he was gone.

Celia was not certain what to expect of Justin when she joined him and the Vallerands in the parlor the next evening. Perhaps he would give her a roguish smile, a mocking comment, something that would betray his new familiarity with her. Instead he looked at her with a seriousness she had never seen before, his face still, his eyes hot and intensely blue.

Lysette was dressed in her sea-green gown, her red hair twisted on top of her head and anchored with diamond combs. She took Celia's gloved hands in hers. "How lovely you look in your ball gown," she exclaimed, and turned a bright smile to her husband. "Doesn't she, Max?"

"She does indeed," Maximilien said automatically, but there was a preoccupied air about him. Celia knew he was troubled about the evening to come. There would be many old friends and acquaintances at the Duquesne plantation. Even if Justin's performance was flawless, their suspicions would not be put entirely to rest. Much of the responsibility of convincing everyone that he was Philippe would rest on Celia's shoulders. If she appeared uncomfortable or at odds, the ruse would most certainly fail.

Celia had dressed in the most resplendent gown she owned, a silver-blue satin with a high waist and a stomacher of white roses and pearls. The scooped bodice was as low as propriety permitted, the short sleeves gathered at the top with loops of pearls, the hem finished with a broad band of pleated white satin. Her hair was curled in light ringlets and caught up in the back with three white roses.

Justin and Max were dressed identically in black breeches, single-breasted waistcoats, snowy white shirts, and starched white cravats. Maximilien was as superbly elegant as always, but Justin was not comfortable in the stiff cravat and confining clothes. Not after years of being accustomed to the uncivilized attire of Captain Griffin. And he hated not being able to carry a weapon. In the crowd tonight he would feel like a cat divested of its claws and set in the middle of a pack of sniffing hounds.

Celia approached him, resting her hand lightly on his arm. As he looked down at her, some of his inner agitation faded. She was so pristinely beautiful with her ice-blond hair and alabaster skin. Her gaze was steady on his. Her gentle strength supported him like an invisible bulwark.

"Where is your cane?" she asked softly. "Aren't you going to carry it tonight?"

"I'll manage without it."

Her lips curved in a smile. *"Oui,* I think you will manage quite well tonight. In those clothes you look exactly like Philippe. To everyone but me, that is."

Justin would have replied, but his attention was caught by a hard, questioning stare from his father. His blue eyes met Maxmilien's piercing golden ones. It was obvious Max either knew or suspected what was going on between them. *Don't make foolish mistakes,* his father's gaze said. Justin smiled slightly, sending his own silent warning: *Don't interfere.*

The Duquesne plantation blazed with light and merriment. It was a typical Creole ball, the women delicately beautiful, the men hot-tempered and dangerous, the music vigorous, and the gaiety infused with volatile energy. For all their apparent frailty, the ladies were known to dance for hours without tiring, sometimes all night. Sometimes the young bucks would provoke each other into duels which would be held outside as they tested their honor and their masculine pride.

The guests had brought their own guests, for this was the time of year when relatives visited family homes and stayed for weeks on end. Strangers—of Creole or French descent—were always welcome. There was nothing Creoles loved more than delving into an unknown's background and asking countless questions about his family and past. Even better was to discover a common ancestor, no matter how obscure. Creoles felt that a person was not quite acceptable unless he was related either to their family or to someone they knew.

The matrons, dressed in satin gowns and elaborate wigs, sat on small silk-upholstered chairs and busily kept each other *en rapport* with the latest gossip, for the details of the newest scandals must be scrutinized. To them, nothing that happened in the world at large was as important or as fascinating as what occurred in New Orleans.

The married men collected in their own groups, discussing politics, hunting, and other such masculine subjects, while the unmarried ones went through the intricacies of courting the favor of strictly chaperoned young women.

A startling hush fell over the gathering as the Vallerands entered the large cream and white colored ballroom. The Duquesnes hurried to greet them, and suddenly there was a multitude of welcoming cries. Celia braced herself as a crowd surrounded them.

"Dr. Vallerand," an elderly woman exclaimed, "to finally see you with my own eyes—*c'est merveilleux!*"

"Philippe! I did not believe it until this moment—"

"They said you were wounded—"

"Is it true about the pirates—"

"It is a miracle, *vraiment*—"

Justin replied gravely to the inquiries and statements, suffering many impetuous embraces and hearty kisses. Creoles were never too abashed to display their feelings. Evidently Justin's appearance was enough to quell any suspicions, for he could detect no signs of hesitancy or censure in any of the faces around him. After a while, the initial torrent began to slow, and his Uncle Alexandre appeared with his Aunt Henriette in tow.

Justin glanced at Maximilien, who had remained by his side. "Does Uncle Alex know who I am?" he asked out of the corner of his mouth.

"He has not asked," Maximilien replied matter-of-factly.

Of course not. Alexandre was Max's younger brother, unquestionably loyal to the family. Whatever story they put forth Alex would support. Unfortunately his wife, Henriette, a lovely but featherbrained woman, was given to gossip. It would be necessary to maintain the pretense in front of her.

"Philippe." Alexandre took his shoulders and embraced him briefly. Like the other Vallerand males, Alex was tall and dark-haired, with a temperament that could be as charming as it was volatile. His eyes met Justin's. He nodded briefly as if he saw what he had expected. "It is good to see you again—though I never expected to."

Justin grinned at him, knowing Alexandre was not deceived. "You always were my favorite uncle, Alex."

Craving attention, Henriette stepped between them and lifted her face pertly. "Shame, shame, Philippe, refusing to see anyone all these weeks! I've had no news to give my friends during Thursday coffees!"

"Forgive me," Justin said, and laughingly placed a kiss on either side of her face. Henriette seemed to believe he really was Philippe. "Truly, there's been nothing of interest to tell. I've done nothing but rest and submit to the expert nursing of my devoted wife." He grinned down at Celia. He would have liked to slide an arm around her waist, but Philippe would not have made such a familiar gesture in public.

"Philippe, when you walked in you seemed to

limp,'' Henriette observed tactlessly. "Is it permanent?''

There was a split-second of silence, and Celia answered before Justin could. "It may be,'' she said, looking pointedly at Henriette. "But it gives him a rather dashing air, don't you think?''

Henriette flushed. "Oh yes, of course.''

Justin smiled at Celia as Alexandre dragged his wife away. "Little heart, I don't need protecting,'' he said softly.

"Empty-headed, gossipy hen,'' Celia grumbled. "She is no credit to the Vallerand family.''

"Neither am I,'' Justin said dryly, pulling her to the side of the room underneath one of the many large columned arches. The Vallerands stood in a small group and watched the dancers negotiate their way through a quadrille, their feet moving airily over the shining maple floor. Lysette smiled and conversed lightly with those who sought her attention while Maximilien became involved in a conversation with their host, George Duquesne.

Innumerable people approached Justin, men who wanted to hear the story of his escape from the pirates, women who made attempts to flirt with him, elderly matrons who asked his advice on how to treat their ailments. Celia was able to help with the latter, explaining that her husband was not yet well enough to resume his practice. Occasionally she hinted at remedies for them to try. There were many things she had learned from being a doctor's daughter, and she was thankful that her memory was excellent when it came to such matters.

Realizing that the evening was progressing smoothly, Celia began to relax. No one seemed to suspect Justin. His imitation of Philippe was perfect, down to the way he stood with his thumbs hooked in his coat pockets, and the way he caught at his lower lip with his teeth just before he smiled. Because of his height, he often inclined his head when talking with people. Philippe had always been like that, approachable, ingratiating, striving to make himself accessible to everyone. It was not like Justin, who usually didn't care if he intimidated others.

Celia found herself studying Justin quizzically, realizing that she preferred him as himself. She missed his free laugh and sardonic comments, and his wont to say and do the unexpected. Philippe would have adored a gathering such as this, while she knew that if Justin had the choice, he would rather be alone with her. Guiltily she banished the disloyal thoughts. Glancing around the room, she found her attention drawn to a figure in the distance, a man standing by a window built into the wall between the ballroom and the dining room.

His face was turned toward her. He was as thin as a blade, and as well-dressed as any of the other gentlemen present, but she found him somehow sinister. The he flashed a jagged smile at her. Cold terror squeezed her heart until it stopped beating.

The room swayed around her. Forgetting herself, she tried to wheeze Justin's name, but sound was impossible. Suddenly Justin was in front of her, his large hands gripping her arms. He stared at her waxen face. "Celia?" he murmured. "Celia, what is it?" He had to bend his head to hear the whisper that came from her shaking lips.

"Legare."

Immediately Justin turned his head and surveyed the room, but he could see nothing. Celia looked as well. The hideous apparition was gone.

She tried to recover herself, but her mind was whirling.

Maximilien joined them, his golden eyes alert. *"Qu'est-ce que c'est?"*

"I don't know," Justin said frankly, holding Celia steady.

"Get her out of here before she attracts any more attention. The French doors lead to the outside gallery. I'll join you in a moment."

Justin complied, clamping his arm around Celia's shoulders as he guided her outside. The night air was cold and tranquil. They were surrounded by darkness as they retreated to the lee of one of the immense columns. He forced her chin up, looking into her terrified eyes.

"I s-saw Dominic Legare," she babbled. "I saw him in there, st-standing, looking at me. He . . . he smiled at me. You must believe me, he . . . he is *here*—"

"You've been thinking about him a great deal lately," Justin said calmly, sliding his hand to the back of her neck. He felt the tremors that shook her entire frame. "Is it possible you saw someone who looks like him?"

"No, it was *him!* He is somewhere nearby, right now, I *know* it was him! Justin, please believe me, you *must*—"

"All right," he said, pulling her body into the shelter of his. He held her protectively. "Breathe deeply, *petite*, and try to calm yourself."

"No, we must—"

"Shhh. Be quiet."

She buried her face in his chest and felt her wild panic fade as his body warmed hers. "I'm here," Justin murmured. "He won't hurt you. No one will hurt you." Her frantic breaths slowed, and Justin's arms loosened.

Maximilien's voice interrupted them. "Explain, Justin."

"Dominic Legare is here," Justin said grimly. "She saw him in the ballroom." Had he not been so worried he would have laughed at the sudden astonishment on his father's face, an expression Max rarely wore.

"Describe him," Max said tersely.

"Lean and of medium height, with reddish-brown hair worn in a queue."

Celia pushed herself away from Justin, adding unsteadily, "A-and a smile like a shark."

Justin gave a short huff of laughter, recalling Legare's pointed teeth. "An apt description."

Max was frowning. "That sounds like Antoine Bayonne. A friend of George Duquesne, a French planter. He also has dealings with some of the richest merchants in the city. On occasion I've talked to him myself. He is an intelligent man with a sharp wit."

"I'm not familiar with the name," Justin said.

"Bayonne first appeared in New Orleans four—no, five years ago. Since then he has established himself with the Duquesnes and a few other Creole families."

Justin regarded him intently. "Have you seen him here tonight?"

"Not yet, but I can inquire of Duquesne . . ." Max paused and asked in a dangerously soft voice, "Do you mean that the man who caused my son's death may be within reach at this moment?"

Before Justin could reply, a young woman's voice called from the French doors. "Dr. Vallerand? Dr. Vallerand, are you outside?"

Justin glanced at Max and Celia, then stepped out from behind the column. "What do you want?'' he asked brusquely, facing the young woman. It was Amalie Duquesne, George's eldest daughter.

"Dr. Vallerand,'' she said tearfully, *"ma mère* sent me to find you. It is my little brother Paul—he has been ill all day and has suddenly become much worse. We have sent for Dr. Dassin, but until he arrives you must do something for Paul. He is upstairs. *Maintenant,* you must see him.''

Justin stared at her, began to say something, but then bit the words off. He raked his hand through his hair. "It would be better to wait for Dassin,'' he said curtly.

The girl shook her head wildly. *"Non, non,* Paul may die! He is coughing until he cannot breathe. Dr. Vallerand, you must come upstairs and do something for him!''

Celia emerged from the darkness and stood by Justin's side. She was pale but controlled. "Have you tried a steam kettle?'' she asked. "Have him inhale the steam until—''

"We have tried that for hours,'' Amalie replied. "It has not helped at all.''

Celia and Justin stared at each other. They would have to do what they could until Dr. Dassin arrived. There was no other choice. *"Bien,* take us upstairs to your brother, Amalie,'' Celia said, forcing thoughts of Legare to the back of her mind.

They proceeded in silence to the sickroom. Celia recognized what was wrong soon after she began to look at the listless boy. He had a hacking cough that sounded like croup, a thready pulse, and a bluish pallor. She had seen these same symptoms years before when the illness had spread among the children of a village near her home. She had gone with her father on many of his rounds. A telltale membrane formed in the back of the throat, in the worst cases sealing it off until the child could not breathe at all.

Paul, a boy of not more than four or five years, seemed unaware of her presence. He coughed weakly and began to choke. Celia realized with dread that they could not wait for Dr. Dassin. She knew what had to be done. She had seen her father perform the procedure, a technique he had learned from a talented surgeon in Paris. But she had not had any medical training, and there was every chance she would hurt more than help.

Paul's breath rattled harshly. Madame Duquesne broke into frightened sobs. "Oh, Dr. Vallerand, you must help my little boy, I beg of you—"

"Madame," Celia said, gathering her courage. Something had to be done or the boy would suffocate before her eyes. "I believe my husband would like you to bring a very sharp knife and a piece of hollow cane, just a short length, perhaps two inches."

Madame Duquesne looked at her with wide eyes and then glanced at Justin. He nodded shortly, and the woman fled to fetch the articles. As soon as she left the room, Justin was at the side of the bed, pushing the child's hair back and staring into the small, sickly face as the boy struggled to breathe.

Carefully Celia poured water from the hot kettle into the wash basin. "They should have sent for the doctor sooner," she said in English. "Perhaps he will arrive before we have to do anything."

"I know Dassin," Justin said, stripping off the foul-smelling poultice the Duquesnes had placed on the boy's chest. He used a handkerchief to wipe it clean. "Cantankerous old man. He delivered Philippe and me. Though I doubt he would count that among his most distinguished achievements."

Celia gave him a despairing glance. "Justin, I . . . don't know if I can do this."

"Then tell me what to do."

Celia hesitated and shook her head. "No, I've seen it done before. If I can just remember how my father . . ." She concentrated, her brow furrowing.

"He's not breathing at all," Justin said tersely, giving the small shoulders a shake. The child was unconscious.

Celia's brain began a swift, methodical ticking. Madame Duquesne burst into the room, and Celia herded her back, taking the knife and snippet of bamboo from her. "Dr. Vallerand requires privacy," she said firmly. "Please, madame, allow him just a minute or two."

"*Oui*, if that is what he wishes, but I would rather stay and—"

"A minute or two," Celia repeated, and gently urged her out of the room, closing the door behind her. She washed her hands, the knife, and the hollow tube, and sat on the bed. Justin tilted the child's head back until his neck was fully exposed. Celia's hand hovered over it with the knife, trembling slightly. She did not want to cut him in the wrong place, perhaps open a vein and be forced to watch as he bled to death.

"Go on," Justin said quietly.

She whispered a prayer, then made an incision near the base of his throat. There was a small spurt of blood, and she worked the cane into the puncture. She bit her lip until it ached. Suddenly there was an indrawn rush of air through the tube. Frozen, Celia watched and listened, assuring herself that the breathing would continue unhindered. "Thank God," she said, and shuddered with relief.

Justin released the breath he had been holding and wiped away the streaks of blood. "What now?" he asked.

"The cane will allow him to breathe until his throat clears. In one or two days it can be removed. It should heal quickly . . . that is, if he survives the rest of the illness."

There was a fluttering knock at the door, and Madame Duquesne's voice. "Dr. Vallerand? Dr. Dassin has arrived."

Dassin strode into the room with his medical bag. He was a small but distinguished man with an intimidating presence. His clothes were old-fashioned: knee breeches, a long floral waistcoat, and a narrow-shouldered frock coat. A gray bob wig was settled on his head. His sharp gray eyes went from Celia to Justin. Justin stared at him without blinking, knowing that Philippe and Dassin had been close friends.

Some glint of hope, anticipation, went out of the doctor's eyes, and he sighed somewhat bitterly. He went to the bed and examined Celia's handiwork, smiling reassuringly as Paul awakened. "Ah . . . *c'est bien* . . . do not try to talk, *mon fils*." He glanced at Celia and Madame Duquesne. "*Il va bien*—all is well for now. It would seem that Dr. Vallerand has the situation well in hand. Perhaps the ladies would leave us for a few moments to discuss the diagnosis?"

Celia looked at the old doctor warily as she washed her hands. Reluctantly she complied with his request, following Madame Duquesne outside the room and closing the door. Dassin opened his medical bag and rifled through it idly. "I was foolish enough to hope that I would indeed find Philippe Vallerand here tonight," he said in his rusty voice. "But I am not like the crowd of fools downstairs who have not seen through your ruse. You and Philippe were born into my hands. I have never had difficulty in telling the two of you apart."

"Congratulations," Justin said sardonically.

"Your brother was a healer. It was his love and calling. You, however—" The doctor broke off and gave a mirthless laugh. "I should have expected that you would outlive him. Bad blood. In your case it came to fruition, eh?"

"Evidently."

"After your mother's death I found it interesting to observe how the years of neglect caused Philippe to strive for better things, while you became nothing but a callous bully. Philippe attempted many times to convince me of your latent virtues, although I was always skeptical."

"Are you going to keep quiet about my identity?" Justin asked impatiently, seeing no reason to dance around the question.

"*Oui*. But only for Philippe's sake. I believe he would have preferred it."

Justin went to the door. "It is fortunate for me that Philippe was well-loved by so many people." With that, he left to find Celia.

She was waiting for him at the top of the stairs. "Does he know?" she asked.

"I'm beginning to wonder who doesn't."

"Will Dassin keep our secret?"

"He said he would. For Philippe's sake." Justin scowled and raked his hands through his hair.

"What is wrong? What did he say to you?"

Justin looked at her with narrowed blue eyes.
"It's not important."

She studied him for a moment. In spite of his
blank façade, she sensed the bleakness he felt, the
guilt and hopelessness. "He reminded you of the
past, didn't he?" she asked softly. "But the past
doesn't matter anymore." She took his arm and
tugged him to a secluded corner. Standing on her
toes, she wrapped her arms around him and
brushed a kiss on his lean cheek. He and Philippe
had been deserted by their mother and then ne-
glected by their embittered father. How could a
child not rebel in such circumstances? Being the
stronger-willed of the two, Justin had been more in
need of discipline and attention than Philippe, and
had suffered more from its absence. "Everything is
different now. Nothing you do will make me stop
loving you or believing in you, nothing—"

He cupped her face in his hands and kissed her,
his mouth urgent. She pressed herself against him
while he caught at her lips with softly biting
kisses. "I love you," he said raggedly, pressing
his forehead against hers. "God, I hate this feeling of having so much to lose. If I could have you
for the rest of my life, I'd never ask for anything
else."

"Justin," she said weakly, and with a groan he
let go of her before his desire for her flared out of
control. They stared at each other with frustrated
love and need.

Justin sighed tautly. "We should go downstairs. By now Father probably has Bayonne held
at swordpoint. God knows, I wouldn't be surprised by anything this night has in store for us."

Reluctantly Celia nodded and took his proffered arm, allowing him to lead her down the

curved walnut stairway. As they reached the central section of the house with its twenty-five-foot ceiling and large chandelier, Celia felt a warning chill that echoed what she had felt in the ballroom. She knew Legare was near, even before she saw him standing at the figured bronze clock which had been placed on a wooden lacquered table. It was a minute or two past midnight. Justin's arm turned to steel beneath Celia's fingertips. He stared at Legare's sharp-featured face.

Legare was the first to speak. "Dr. Vallerand." He drew out the name with cool enjoyment. His uneven teeth showed in a smile. "I have been looking for you."

Chapter 11

Justin stared at Legare without expression. "Antoine Bayonne, isn't it?"

Celia was vaguely aware of people crossing through the hall, music, dancing, and the laughter of the guests. All of them were unaware that the two most wanted buccaneers in the Gulf were holding a casual conversation in their midst. She stared at Legare while images flashed before her . . . the deck of the ship, covered with bodies . . . Philippe's blood-soaked back . . . Andre's bloated face . . .

"Go, Celia," Justin said quietly, prying her hand from his arm. "It's all right. Go to Maximilien."

Her fingers dug into his arm more tightly. She clung to him as if he were a lifeline, and she stared at Legare with dilated brown eyes. She couldn't have moved had she wanted to. Justin gave up trying to coax her away and turned his attention back to Legare. "You've taken a great risk," he said. "I could have you arrested on the spot."

"You would be arrested as well. You would hang as surely as I."

"I wouldn't mind so long as you went first."

"Before you make any decisions, you should

listen to what I have to say. I have a story to tell you, Dr. Vallerand. It begins on the deck of a captured ship overrun with buccaneers. The heroine of this tale is a lovely blond woman"—Legare smiled at Celia—"who attempts to bargain for her own life and her husband's. She alerts us to the possibility that there is a Vallerand aboard. The name, of course, is a familiar one with all its connotations of privilege and power. Her husband is a doctor, a claim which intrigues my men and me. When he is not found among our captives, our curiosity prompts us to fish among the bodies that have been cast off the ship. The elusive Vallerand is found. Lo and behold, he is still alive." Legare paused, observing the effect of his words.

Celia stared at Legare like a frightened rabbit. Justin silently contemplated various means of dismembering the bastard. He did not believe a word Legare was saying. "Go on," he said flatly.

Legare resumed the story with relish. "Having decided he might be of use in the future, I cause him to be brought back to Crow's Island and imprisoned. Being a thoroughbred of hardy stock, the captive survives his wounds. At this point I must confess that my preoccupation with many important matters—most especially finding my brother's murderer—causes me to forget about my caged Vallerand for some months. Until an astonishing report is brought to my attention. I accompany one of my trusted gaolers down to the maze at the bottom of the fort. To my genuine surprise I am facing the image of my bearded nemesis, Captain Griffin! After some persuasion, the prisoner reluctantly admits that he has a twin brother. But then I learn of rumors from New Orleans that Philippe Vallerand has returned to his family from the jaws of death. Knowing that said Vallerand is still enjoying my hospitality, I decide to pay you a visit. Amusing tale, is it not?''

Justin looked at him, his face turning white underneath its tan, his eyes a blaze of fiery blue.

Two great tears rolled down Celia's cheeks. ''Philippe is alive?'' she asked brokenly.

Legare gave her a jagged smile. ''Why so distraught, madame? You seem to do well enough with either brother.''

Justin gripped Celia's face in his hand, forcing her to look at him. ''He's lying,'' he said. ''Philippe is dead.''

Legare smiled. ''Can you be certain?''

''What do you want?'' Justin snapped.

''Most of your men have joined me, Griffin. There is nothing left of your impudent little organization. Being an intelligent man, you are aware that it would be useless to run from me. You can either wait for me to settle matters between us at the time I choose, or you can try to gain something out of it. I would be willing to make an exchange. You for your brother.''

Justin did not even notice the pain of Celia's stabbing nails. ''Even if I believed you had him, what makes you think I'd risk my own life for my brother's?''

''On the island you agreed to fight to the death for his wife,'' Legare observed, not needing to voice the conclusion that if Justin had risked his life for Celia, he would do the same for his own brother.

Justin kept all emotion from his face. ''I want proof that you have Philippe,'' he said. ''After that we'll talk about arrangements.''

''If you're playing for time—''

''Nay.'' Justin gestured to the crowded ballroom nearby, his mouth twisting. ''It should be obvious that time is something I can ill afford. And you won't waste it if you want me in your custody rather than the authorities'."

"You desire proof? Send your man Risk—or anyone else of your choosing—to the island. We'll allow him to see your brother and leave unharmed." Legare looked from Justin's face to Celia's and bowed perfunctorily. "I'll take my leave now. My compliments, madame. *Bon soir.*"

Justin watched Legare stroll casually out the front door. His blue eyes did not swerve from the predatory form until Legare was out of sight. Then he glanced at Celia, whose silent tears had stopped as abruptly as they had started. "He is trying to trick you," she whispered. "Don't let him—"

"Shhh . . ." Justin took her head in his hands, tilting her face up to his. He would have given his life in that moment if it would have taken away the horror in her eyes. He felt all his intense love for her well up from inside him, flowing from his body to hers, forcing out the coldness and the fear. Her eyelids fluttered down, and she gripped his wrists. The unexpected strength of her hold on him was electrifying. He didn't know how long they stood there, didn't care who might see them, only sank deeper into the warm closeness until he was rudely torn away by the sound of Maximilien's grating voice.

"You found Legare, didn't you? What did he say? Where is he?"

"Father." Justin let go of Celia and faced Max. "He's gone," he said in a low voice. He did not hedge. There was no time to be anything but blunt. "He claims that Philippe is still alive. That Philippe is his captive."

"*What?*" The golden eyes widened.

"Don't do anything yet. If the naval or civil authorities become involved, Philippe will pay with his life. I have to find Risk. Celia will explain. Take care of her."

Max swore quietly and tried to stop his son, but Justin left without another word.

Justin went on horseback to the cabin at the lake, where Risk was staying. During the journey a fine mist saturated his hair and his clothes, but he didn't notice the damp or the cold. The cabin was dark. Opening the front door, he walked in heedlessly. The click of a revolver greeted him.

"It's me," he said.

Risk lit a small lamp and regarded him through the yellow-white glow, his one eye filled with a catlike gleam. He set down the revolver. "What's happened?"

"Any word from Aug?" Justin asked brusquely.

"None."

"Legare's taken him into the fold?"

" 'Twould seem so." Frowning, Risk waited for Justin to explain why he was there.

"I saw Legare tonight," Justin said, and smiled grimly as Risk stared at him in astonishment. He proceeded to describe the encounter in detail. When he reached the part about Legare's offer for an exchange, Risk exploded.

"Aye, he'd bloody well like that! He'd like to take ye captive without givin' ye the right to die with a sword in yer hand. An' once Legare has ye at his mercy, ye'll be trussed, gutted, an' carved like a roasted fowl till ye're beggin' for death."

"If Philippe is still alive, I have no choice."

Risk shook his head. "Ye're mad, Griffin. If he has Philippe, it's not likely there's much o' the

poor divvil left! 'Sides, I'd wager a fortune yer
brother is at the bottom o' the sea, not in Legare's
fort. An' what about that pretty little hen waitin'
for ye at the plantation? In all the time I've
knowed ye, I've nivver seen ye want anything
like ye want her."

Justin glowered at him. "Are you suggesting I
should let my brother rot on the island so I can
keep his wife?"

Risk shrugged noncommittally.

Justin's first impulse was to blister Risk's ears
with a few choice words, but he checked himself,
realizing that Risk's perspective was the same as
that of the other men he'd roved with for the past
years. Take what you wanted, no matter what it
did to anyone else. He himself had believed in it
for a long time. But he couldn't live like that anymore. And he couldn't live with himself if he
turned his back on his brother, his twin, even
though it meant losing Celia to Philippe.

"I have to know if my brother is alive," Justin
said. "Will you go to Isle au Corneille?"

"Aye. I'll go to the damn island straightaway.
An' I'll see if there's any truth to Legare's claim.
I'll back ye against Legare, Griffin."

"Good."

"But only if ye promise that afterward ye'll be
takin' yer place at the helm o' the *Vagabond* once
more, an'—"

"No," Justin said quietly. "I told you before.
I'm through with it. I gave you the ship—"

"I don't want the bloody ship!" Risk exploded.
"Don't ye see, the men won't follow me! I'm not
fit to lead 'em, an' I've no wish to be! I can't command. It's either follow *someone* or give up me
rovin' for good!"

Justin stared at him through narrowed eyes. "I

can't do this anymore, Jack. Did you think it
would go on forever?''

"Aye!" Risk burst out angrily.

Justin shook his head. "Don't look so betrayed.
You've profited from our ventures. Why not relax
and enjoy some of the wealth you've gained? You
could have an easy life now—"

" 'Tis not a different life I'm wantin'. I want
the same one. The same as it's always been!''

"That's not possible," Justin said heartlessly.
"We've both changed."

"Nay, I'm the same," Risk muttered. " 'Tis
only you that's changed."

Once Celia's terror subsided she fell into an exhausted sleep, and the dream of Philippe came
back. He was drowning, and she was reaching for
him, and all the while Legare lurked behind her,
his malevolent voice in her ear. She woke with a
start.

What if Philippe were still alive? She couldn't
begin to imagine the suffering he had gone
through. Poor Philippe—what if they had tortured him, starved him? He would need someone
to take care of him and make him well again.

She was frightened, not only for Philippe but
for herself and Justin. Legare had seemed so confident and powerful tonight, so certain that he
would get exactly what he wanted. The thought
of Justin at Legare's mercy was too horrifying to
contemplate. She would do anything to keep that
from happening.

A swarm of worries plagued her. If somehow
Philippe did come back, she would still be his
wife. She would owe him her loyalty and support
for the rest of her life. She would lose Justin. Celia
shied away from the thought. She had cared for

Philippe deeply, but there had been none of the wildness and magic, the tenderness and consuming need that Justin freed in her. *Bon Dieu*, how could she bear loving him and never having him, being kept apart from him forever?

She twisted in the tangled sheets, her fingers plucking fitfully at the soft linen. It was not long before dawn. When would Justin come home? And if Risk returned with the news that Legare's claim was true, what would Justin plan to do?

The sound of uneven footsteps slipped into her awareness. Celia sat bolt upright. Closer the broken tread came, up the stairs, to the door. Her heart thundered wildly. Justin had come back to her. Leaping out of bed, she went to the door and threw herself into his arms just as he reached the threshold. He caught her with a quiet growl, lifting her until her feet left the floor. Her fingers combed through his hair while her lips moved frantically over his throat. Locked in passion and desperation, they relinquished themselves to a desire that left no breath for words.

Justin felt the warmth of Celia's body through her thin nightgown. He pulled the garment up in huge handfuls until her hips and bottom were bare. His hand clasped over the soft roundness, pulling her loins against his. She squirmed against him, searching for a balance she could not find, and kissed his chin, his rough jaw, his mouth. Responding violently, he wedged her lips open, pulling her tongue into his mouth and sucking on it. Through the layer of his breeches she felt the straining length of his arousal fitted tightly against her aching softness.

His hips nudged against hers in a slow rhythm that matched the movements of his tongue. She whimpered in her throat, caught helplessly against his hard body, pleasure rising through her in a burning tide. Realizing what was about to happen, she tried to pull her mouth free, but it was too late; the sweet convulsion had overtaken her. Gasping and shuddering, she clung to him while the maddening rhythm of his hips continued and his lips searched hotly over her neck. When the last spasm had left her body, he let her down and pulled the nightgown over her head, throwing it to the floor.

She helped him with his clothes and slipped her hand in his, leading him to the bed. His dark form towered over her, and he pushed her to the mattress, following her down immediately. She caught her breath at the exquisite agony of his ravaging mouth, the pluck of his teeth on her nipples, the wet swirl of his tongue. His hand moved between her legs, and she opened to him eagerly, welcoming his invading fingers. Bending over her, he crushed her mouth with his, absorbing her moans.

She rubbed her palms over his shoulders, her fingertips brushing over the ridges of scars and the muscled plane of his back. With a soft purr she stroked his lean hips and buttocks, letting her nails scrape until he groaned at the delicate clawing. Pulling her hips underneath his, he mounted her, holding her clasped between his powerful thighs. Trembling, she reached for him and tilted her hips to receive him. "Justin," she gasped, "Take me now . . . *now* . . ."

He caught her wrists in his hands and stretched them far over her head. As she stared at him she thought dizzily that he was still as darkly savage as he had been on Isle au Corneille. His head dropped to her breasts and he kissed and suckled at her sensitive nipples until she cried out in torment. Only then did he press forward, easing into the swollen core of her body.

Breathing harshly, he pulled back a few inches and then sank deeply inside her, his face contorted, his fingers entwining in her hair. She met every lunge with her own feminine strength, gripping his back and digging her heels into the mattress. Her slim arms wrapped around him, and then her legs, and he was so completely held, possessed in her softness, that he could no longer contain the burst of his seed. The fierce excitement dissolved in a rush of fulfillment. Justin clutched her tightly, his breath coming so fast that his lungs ached.

When he had strength enough to move again, he rolled to his back, and she draped herself on top of him. He pushed her silken hair back from her face and stared into her dark eyes, wanting to say a hundred different things, but finding himself speechless. She smiled faintly and brushed a kiss on his lips. His hands slid from her shoulders to her white breasts, stroking with the lightest of touches. She straddled his thighs and leaned back in wanton invitation. Justin felt himself harden again, and he clasped her hips, positioning her over his rigid shaft. She reached down to guide him into her, and both of them stopped breathing as she slid down the full length of him.

Justin muttered her name. Her eyes half-closed as she raised and lowered herself in a compelling rhythm. Drugged by the sensual pleasure, Justin followed her languidly, savoring the movements of her lithe body. His hands roamed from her shoulders to the glinting down between her thighs, teasing and tormenting until she arched above him in a shuddering release. His own climax was not as sharp and deep as before, but longer, slower, seeming to spread from his toes to the top of his head in a fiery glow.

Celia relaxed on top of him and settled her head on his chest. "Justin," she whispered thickly. "What will happen to us?"

"Shhh, little heart . . . we won't talk about it until we know for certain if Philippe's alive."

"But what if he is? What will you—"

His fingers came to her lips, silencing her. She would have asked more, but he hushed her again and began an idle stroking of her neck and back. Tears slid from her eyes and fell to his chest. It felt so natural to be in his arms, but she knew it was wrong. All the other times they had been together, she had believed herself to be a widow. Now, by giving herself to Justin when she knew her husband might still be alive, she had betrayed Philippe.

"I shouldn't love you," she said, spreading tears and kisses across his neck, his shoulders. "I never wanted to love you."

"I know." He held her tightly. "I know."

"My feelings for Philippe were never like this, even though I—"

"No," he murmured. "Don't compare. It's not fair to either of us."

"But I want you to understand. I . . . I could never have loved him like this, never—"

"I understand." He kissed her until she was quiet.

Suddenly she was exhausted, and she closed her eyes. "Don't leave me," she mumbled.

"*Non, petite coeur* . . ." He kissed her forehead and cuddled her until she drifted into sleep.

* * *

The sound of a bell rang through the crisp morning air. The plantation was just beginning to awaken, chores being started, food being cooked, voices calling sleepily. Justin and Max ambled away from the main house down the long plantation drive, oblivious to what was going on around them as they talked. Their long, lazy strides matched perfectly, and their dark heads were bent at precisely the same angle. They walked past the smooth lawn while the wind strew leaves about their feet.

Justin looked at the *garçonnière*. Celia was still sleeping. He had wanted to wake her before he left her bed that morning, but he had seen the lines of strain on her face even as she slept. She would need rest in order to face the next few days.

Max followed his gaze. "You care for her, don't you?"

"And you disapprove."

"No, I do not disapprove," Max replied. "I would have put a stop to any liaison if I thought you were taking advantage of her. But that does not seem to be the case. From the moment you arrived there was . . . an attachment between the two of you that I did not feel I had the right to break." Max paused and added wryly, "I have been surprised by your attraction to Celia."

"She is a beautiful woman," Justin pointed out.

"Yes, but hers is a quiet beauty. And her inner qualities . . . intelligence, kindness, dignity . . . no, she is not the kind I would have expected you to show an interest in."

"It's more than an *interest*," Justin muttered.

"So you may have intentions toward her. But what if Philippe is alive?"

Justin shoved his hands in his pockets and stared at the ground in frustration. "I wouldn't take her away from him. And I think that ultimately she has too much honor to leave him.''

''It is possible that Legare's claim is just a ruse—''

''Possible, but I don't think so. I think Philippe is alive.'' Justin's voice was hard and determined. ''Jack Risk has gone to the island to find out for certain. He'll come here tomorrow night with the news. If they do have Philippe, I swear he'll be brought back safely. I'll stake my life on it.''

''I don't want you to stake your life on anything,'' Max said swiftly, and stopped him. They faced each other. ''We will find another way, *mon fils.*'' The golden eyes were filled with anxiety and love. ''Your life is as precious to me as Philippe's.''

Justin was momentarily taken aback. His father had always been so aloof and self-controlled. The display of emotion made him uncomfortable, elicited a yearning he had not felt since he was a boy. ''There is no other way—'' he began, and Max interrupted, more overwrought than Justin had ever seen him.

''Don't you think I understand? You are like me, Justin, more like me than Philippe. For years you've been driven by anger and guilt, just as I was. You've made the same mistakes. It wasn't your fault that some things were easier for Philippe than you. It wasn't your fault that I didn't give you the guidance you needed. I was so absorbed in my own grief and bitterness that I turned my back on my sons. I'll regret that for the rest of my life.''

''It wasn't your fault that I turned out a blackguard,'' Justin muttered. ''I'm not like you, I'm like . . . her.''

''Your mother?'' Max clarified, his thoughts

turning to that distant time when he had been married to Corinne. "She was selfish and scheming, Justin. But she wasn't evil. Is that what you thought, that you were fated to be a scoundrel because you were her son? You have not one drop more of her blood in you than Philippe did."

"Yes, but he . . ." Justin shifted his weight to his good leg and averted his gaze from Max's. "He was the good one."

"That is nonsense," Max said shortly.

"Is it? All I know is that Philippe was everything I wanted to be but couldn't." Justin felt heat creep up from his collar as he struggled to express what he had never put into words before. How strange, that the compulsion to make his father understand this one thing was almost as strong as the need he'd felt to tell Celia he loved her. He'd always been secretive about his feelings, afraid they would be used against him. Now it seemed confessions were being dragged from him, and he was helpless to stop it. "For a long time I didn't understand why she was gone," he said, "and why you had turned so cold and bitter. I thought that all of it was my fault, that if I had been good, if I had been like Philippe, she wouldn't have been unfaithful to you. She would have cared about her family. She would still be alive and you—"

"No," Max said roughly. "It had nothing to do with you. Look at me!" There was a vibrant note of command in his voice that was impossible to disobey. "No matter what you did, no matter how you behaved, you couldn't have changed anything. It was not your fault. I'll make you believe that if I have to say it a thousand times."

The winter breeze wafted over them gently, filling the air with the rustle of leaves and the scent of cypress. Justin stared at his father without blinking. He felt a curious sensation of relief, and a betraying sting in his nose and eyes. Oh God. Had his self-control become so corroded? He shook off the feeling and summoned a crooked smile. "That won't be necessary," he said. "I believe you."

"Then you know you don't have to redeem yourself by giving your life for Philippe's."

"My motives aren't noble. This is a matter of practicality. I'm the only one who can get Philippe out of this safely. You could comb through the civil authorities and the navy, and you wouldn't find a man who knows one-tenth of what I do about Dominic Legare and the island."

"And if I gain Philippe and lose you?" Max asked.

Suddenly Justin grinned. "You'd give a damn?"

Max scowled and grabbed him by the scruff of the neck, like a wolf with an annoying cub. The gesture coming from a man any less than Max's size would have been ridiculous. "Yes, I'd give a damn! That's what I've been trying to tell you."

Justin continued to smile. "I give a damn about you too, Father."

"I won't lose you," Max said grimly.

"No, not if you keep from interfering."

Max released him reluctantly, remembering Justin's dislike of being touched. They began to walk again, and Max said abruptly. "There is something I didn't intend for you to know until after the matter was resolved. Now I think you should be made aware of it."

"What is it?" Justin asked warily.

"Commander Matthews and Lieutenant Benedict are assembling a combined force of sailors and marines to attack the island. They've been planning it for some time.''

Justin stopped in his tracks. *"What?* How long have you known about this?''

"For weeks, actually.''

"Why the hell didn't you tell me?'' Justin demanded angrily.

"I didn't feel you needed to know.''

"Dammit, when is this little expedition supposed to occur?''

"The day after tomorrow.''

"The day af—'' Justin broke off with a foul oath. "The fools! There'll be heavy loss of life. There are ships in the harbor with long guns and carronades. They'll take out half the force before Matthews gets close enough to fire on the island!''

"Perhaps. But Legare's presence has become too much of a menace. They can't allow it to continue unchallenged any longer. They feel the assistance of the army will give them the necessary strength.''

"Have you told Matthews about Philippe? That he may be a prisoner on the island?''

"Of course not. If I had, the authorities would have come to arrest you immediately.''

"You'll have to go to Matthews and Lieutenant Benedict and tell them everything, Father. About me and Philippe and the whole charade.''

"No,'' Max said decisively. "If you're hoping to rely on their mercy, *mon fils,* you'll quickly discover that there will be none for you. Come morning they'll have you swinging from the gallows.''

"Not if they know I can be of use to them. You must find out *precisely* when they plan to attack, down to the minute. Convince them to wait until after I exchange myself for Philippe. That way Philippe will be safe.''

Max looked unimpressed. "And how will you be of any use to the naval force then?"

"I'll have some of my men on Isle au Corneille to protect me. Aug will smuggle them there. Then I'll lead an attack from within the fort. Tell Matthews that we'll set fire to the munitions warehouses and use the fort's own cannon to take out the defenses in the harbor. We'll weaken them from the inside. Then the naval squadron will be able to take the island without resistance. Matthews will have to agree to that."

Max shook his head. "There are too many opportunities for something to go wrong."

"There always are." Justin glanced at him, surprised by the feeling of companionship he had never experienced with Max before. "We have to do it this way. For Philippe's sake. Make Matthews understand that I can help him."

Max scowled, but he did not argue.

Justin was relieved as he realized that his father would do what he asked. "Father . . . you realize that after this I'll have to disappear for good."

"I'm still attempting to arrange a pardon for you."

"Not even you have that much money or influence. If I'm not caught, I'll leave and hopefully be presumed dead."

"And we'll never see you again," Max said quietly.

Justin hesitated. "No."

"And what of Celia?"

When there was no immediate reply, Max looked at his son. Justin's face was remote and his jaw was tightly clenched. "She'll be better off with Philippe," Justin managed to say. "There's only one kind of life I can offer her, and I've come to realize I . . . don't want that for her.''

After walking back to the main house with Max, Justin kept himself occupied with small tasks for the rest of the day, repairing a few loose boards in the bell tower and joining in the effort to clear a fallen tree that had partially blocked the drive. As he worked alongside the slaves, Justin reflected on the irony that on Isle au Corneille and among most pirate crews, men of color had freedom and authority equal to any white man, whereas here in the civilized world they were reduced to slavery. The value of a man like Aug, intelligent and perceptive, able to organize men and carry out plans with skill and inventiveness, could never be realized here. Here Aug could not sit at a table and partake of a meal with him. Their friendship would be governed by intolerable restraints devised by a hypocritical society. Justin realized that his friendship with Aug and the past few years of living and fighting alongside his crew had changed his beliefs radically.

Although there were many freedmen in New Orleans, and it was common—even encouraged— for white men to take mulatto or octoroon mistresses, a male with any drop of Negro blood would be hanged for having an affair with a white woman. Since Justin had arrived here he had dared to ask Max if he felt there was anything wrong with such a system. To his surprise, Max had admitted uncomfortably that with his own increasing interest in his shipping business, he had recently been considering freeing his slaves. Justin hoped that he would, although he knew that it would cause trouble, even outrage, between the Vallerands and many important Creole families.

While Justin worked on the plantation, Celia

spent the entire day with Noeline in one of the slave cabins, caring for a mother and two children who had fallen ill. Justin was glad of the time spent apart from Celia. He did not want to face her just yet, not with the knowledge that he was going to lose her. Last night he hadn't been able to stay away from her. But the more he loved her, the more important her safety had become, more important than his own life or his own needs. She would be safe with Philippe, and she would come to find contentment with him. That was all that mattered.

Risk strode in solitude from the beach on Crow Island to the fort, illuminated by the red glow of sunset. In less than a minute he was besieged by three men bent on divesting him of his weapons. He held them at bay with his cutlass. "Blast ye, keep yer paws off," he said. "I'm here at the invitation o' Nicky Legare, ye stupid bastards."

Growling insults and warnings, the three of them forced him to surrender his sword, pistol, and knife, then accompanied him toward the fort. Risk adopted a cocky grin, calling out cheerfully as he caught sight of a few men who had formerly sailed with Captain Griffin. "Ahoy, ye slimy traitors!"

Roughly he was ushered inside the fort to Legare's private rooms. He would have guessed that a man with Legare's unimaginable wealth would surround himself with treasure and finery, but instead the rooms were painfully spare. No objects of art, beauty, or luxury adorned the place. Risk had seen prison cells that offered more comfort. It confirmed the opinion Risk had always held that the man wasn't quite human. Legare sat on a low, hard bench, his arms resting on a rectangular table.

"Mr. Risk," Legare said crisply. The lamplight struck a crimson glint off the dark pupils of his eyes. "I've been expecting you."

Risk gave him a mocking bow. "Aye, Griffin delivered yer kind invitation, Cap'n Legare. Now, if ye don't mind, I'd like to see about that other victim of yer hospitality, namely Dr. Vallerand."

"By all means, let us pay him a visit." Legare stood up and walked to him. "And on the way, Mr. Risk, perhaps we can discuss a few things—"

"Aye, the arrangements for the exchange."

"Perhaps first we should talk about your future."

"Talk all ye want," Risk said airily. "I'm hard of hearin', meself."

Legare opened the door, his gaze sharp on Risk's face. "Perhaps not as much as you think. In my view, Griffin has made a poor bargain with you, Mr. Risk. You do something for him, and he repays you with nothing."

" 'Tis called loyalty," Risk muttered.

"An expensive proposition, this loyalty. Expensive for you."

"Ye're wastin' yer breath," Risk said stiffly.

"I'm not finished yet," Legare murmured, leading the way down to the underground prison.

Step by step, Risk followed him.

The next evening Justin went down to the bayou to wait for Risk. He had not seen Celia for twenty-four hours. She had kept a vigil all night and day with the fever-ridden mother and children in the slave cabin. In the meanwhile, Justin was certain that Risk would bring the news he wanted, and their plans would proceed accordingly. It would be a relief to have it confirmed that his brother was alive. He loved Philippe, and would have even if his twin hadn't been the most gentle-spirited and honorable person he'd ever known. Philippe had never been exposed to real violence before. God only knew what five months of imprisonment might have done to him. Oh, he was going to enjoy killing Legare!

Justin's thoughts were interrupted by the awareness that Celia was coming to find him. He knew it even before he heard her footsteps and her soft voice.

"Justin . . . you have been avoiding me."

"What do you want?" he asked, trying to sound brisk.

"To wait with you."

Justin glanced at her. Although the night was cold, Celia wasn't wearing a cloak or shawl. Her long-sleeved dress was blotched on the bodice and under the arms with perspiration. It was clear she was tired from hours of leaning over sickbeds and stirring herbs and syrups in boiling pots. An acrid medicinal scent clung to her, instead of the usual fragrant lavender. Her hair was drawn back in an uneven coiled braid, while several locks straggled over her forehead and cheeks. He wanted to take care of her, to put her in a hot bath and rub the soreness from her back. "You're going to be cold," he said gruffly.

"No, it was stifling in the cabin. I wanted fresh air." But she was already beginning to shiver as the breeze blew against the damp patches on her dress. She protested as he took off his coat and put it around her. "Justin, do not, *vraiment*, I am not cold, and . . . oh . . ." The thick wool was warm from his body, and it held his scent. She snuggled deep into the garment, making him laugh.

"Justin," she asked, her voice muffled, "if Risk brings the news that Philippe is alive, what will we do then?"

He sobered immediately. "We'll discuss that when we know for certain."

"That sounds ominous," she said.

He studied her with his dark blue eyes. "No matter what the outcome of all this is, it won't be easy for anyone. You understand that, don't you?"

She gave him a faltering smile. "I will be happy as long as we are together." When it became clear he wasn't going to reply, her smile vanished. "Justin," she whispered, "please hold me."

He couldn't have refused her even if both their lives had depended on it. His arms were around her before he could even think. Her small form was made bulky by his coat. As her head rested on his shoulder, the warmth of her breath sank through his shirt to the skin beneath. She leaned against him while he gazed at the bayou.

"I kept dreaming about Philippe," she said almost absently. "In all those dreams he was drowning and I kept reaching for him. But I could never save him."

"You'll have him back soon."

"What do you mean—"

"Shhh." Gently he pushed her away from him as a pirogue approached. It was Risk, rowing steadily, his unwashed hair covered by a kerchief. He glanced over his shoulder at both of them and grinned. Justin made his way to the bank to secure the pirogue while Risk climbed from it. His gaze alighted on Celia first.

"Is he alive?" she burst out.

"Aye," Risk said with a chuckle. "Alive, well, an' itchin' for ye, darlin'."

Justin scowled. Celia was too innocent to know that among sailors the word *itch* had a purely sexual connotation.

"Did they mistreat him?" Celia asked.

"He's been held in one o' the cells in the bottom o' the fort," Risk said, looking at Justin. "Ye know the ones. Used when the slave corrals were bustin' at the sides an' they needed more room. By God, he's the spit o' you, Griffin!"

"Did you see Aug while you were there?" Justin asked.

"Nay, I couldn't—"

Celia interrupted in surprise. "Aug is on the island?"

Suddenly there was silence. Justin took her by the shoulders and stared down at her. "Go back to the house," he said.

"But that is not necessary, I will be quiet, I will not say another—"

"Go back to the house," he repeated softly, his eyes piercing. Abashed, she dropped her gaze and left, cursing herself for not having been silent.

Lysette was rocking Rafe to sleep while Evelina was playing with her dolls. Angeline, the younger daughter, was fretful and bored, and Celia decided to coax her to the parlor for storytime. A small fire crackled in the grate, lending a warm glow to the room. Angeline cuddled in her lap as they looked at a drawing in her sketchbook. It was a game they'd begun playing soon after Celia had shared her artwork with Justin, Celia sketching imaginary people and places and scenes, encouraging Angeline to help her make up stories about them. The stories forced her to concentrate on something other than Philippe, and Celia began to relax. It was an enjoyable way to pass the time, and she delighted in the little girl's assertiveness.

How lucky Lysette Vallerand was to have three beautiful children and a husband who loved her, and a large home and a multitude of friends and interests to keep her busy. Celia could have had such a life with Philippe. Perhaps there was still a possibility of it. But it was no longer what she wanted. She was not even certain exactly what kind of life Justin would offer her, and she didn't care. She knew she would be loved as few women were ever loved, and that Justin would take care of her. Undoubtedly her father and family would believe she had gone mad. She had always been so quiet, so moderate and predictable in all things. The thought made her smile ruefully, and she turned her attention back to Angeline.

Justin went to the library and found his father sitting before the fire. The yellow glow turned Max's hard face into a mask of bronze and gold.

"Philippe's alive," Justin said. "Jack confirmed it."

Max inhaled sharply. "Is he all right?"

Justin's gaze was bleak. "Considering that he's been Legare's prisoner all this time, probably not."

"I'll go to Commander Matthews now. God willing, he'll agree to your plan."

"Be persuasive, Father."

"Of course," Max said matter-of-factly, and left the library.

Justin wandered to the parlor where Celia sat with Angeline. He paused at the side of the doorway and watched unnoticed while the little girl pointed her chubby finger at one of Celia's sketches. ". . . the princess went in there," she was saying to Celia, who lifted her blond brows questioningly.

"Into the dragon's cave?"

"*Oui*, to find the king's stolen treasure!"

Celia's pencil moved busily at the side of the page, doing a quick line drawing. "Yes, but then the dragon returned, and he found her in his cave! What did the princess do?"

"She . . ." Angeline frowned thoughtfully. "She made a pet of him!"

"Oh, but he was a very mean dragon."

"*Non*, it is only that he was very *sad*."

Celia smiled and kissed the top of Angeline's head. "Poor dragon," she murmured.

"Yes, poor sad dragon . . ."

A clutching pain began in Justin's chest as they continued the story. He had never seen Celia so tender and maternal. The extent of what he was about to lose was suddenly made clear, and it shook him badly. He wanted to give her children, he wanted a family with her, the kind of life he had never even been able to dream of before.

The story of the sad dragon was concluded, and Celia looked up to find his blue eyes on her. She shifted Angeline from her lap. "Darling," she said to the little girl, and handed her the sketch, "why don't you go see if your *maman* is finished with Rafe now?"

"I want to do another one."

"After dinner, I promise."

Giving Justin a chiding look as if she knew precisely why storytime had ended so abruptly, Angeline left the room with dragging feet.

Celia stared at his unreadable face. She wished he would come sit by her, but he remained stand-

ing, preserving the distance between them. "I
know that you and Maximilien are planning
something," she said. "I saw the two of you
walking together yesterday morning. What are
you going to do?"

"You don't need to know."

"But of course I do, I . . ." Celia paused as she
saw how empty his gaze was. "Justin, why are
you looking at me that way? What is going to
happen?"

"Philippe is coming back. You're his wife. After he's returned here safely I'll be gone."

Her brow wrinkled anxiously. "Yes, and I will
be going with you."

"No."

"*No?* Justin, you don't mean that you would
leave me here—"

"That's exactly what I mean. When Philippe returns he'll need you to be his wife and take care
of him—"

"Yes, I want to help him. But I cannot be his
wife. I am going to give him his freedom. He and
Briony love each other, and I belong with you."

"You're married to him, Celia."

She wanted to go to him, but her knees were
too weak. "After all the things you told me, and
the promises you made, you cannot try to tell me
that you don't—"

"A man will say many things when he wants
to take a woman to bed."

Celia felt as if the breath had been knocked out
of her. "I know that you love me," she said in a
low voice.

"I thought I did. But you were right when you
told me you feared you were merely a . . . passing fancy." The words were said so smoothly that
almost anyone would have believed him. But

nothing could hide the twitching muscle in his clenched jaw and his high color.

Celia was confused and terrified, until understanding crept over her slowly. He was trying so hard to be callous and cool, when it was only last night that he had held her in his arms and loved her as tenderly as a man could love a woman. She realized what he was trying to do now, and his reasons for it. Suddenly she got her breath back, and with it a surge of shaky confidence.

"You are lying to me," she said.

"It's not a lie. I've gotten what I wanted from you. Now I'm finished with you."

Celia stood up and walked to him. Justin seemed to steel himself at her approach, looking like a fierce mastiff afraid of a small kitten. "I don't believe you," she said.

"Then you're a fool. You have a husband coming home to you, and I'm going to deliver him to you gladly. I'm tired of you. I'm tired of this game we've been playing."

"You're doing this for me. You think I'll be safer if you leave me behind. Well, I will be—I'll be protected and safe and *miserable*. Is that for the best? Is that what you want?" She began to slide her arms around him, but he flinched and drew back. "Think of how it will be for you, wondering every night for the rest of your life if I am alone, if I am sleeping in someone else's arms—"

Jealous rage sparked in his eyes. "I'll be glad to be rid of you!"

She rested her hands on his chest. "The night before last you begged me to go with you. You said you couldn't live without me."

"That was before I knew Philippe was alive." Desperately Justin tried to ignore the scent of her, the soft brush of her breasts against him. But his body betrayed him, his heart hammering, his loins filling with heat and an all-too-familiar ache.

She pressed her warm mouth against his, and he inhaled sharply. The tip of her tongue investigated the seam of his closed lips, and her slim arms encircled his neck. His body stiffened. It took all of his concentration to keep from crushing her to him. Damn her, this wasn't happening the way he had intended! "I don't love you," he said, beginning to push her away. "I don't—" She took advantage of his parted lips to fasten her mouth to his, and began a gentle search for his tongue. All his wild emotions reared against their restraints. Suddenly he quivered and clamped his arms around her, his control snapping like a brittle twig. Hungrily he molded her to the rigid bulge of his loins, the expanse of his chest, and his greedy open mouth. And she told him without words that whatever he wanted, she would give him.

Frustrated, agonized, he shoved her away, muttering curses under his breath.

Her dark gaze was gently mocking, and full of triumph. "I suppose next you're going to claim that all you feel for me is lust, not love?"

Justin was silent, his chest moving up and down rapidly. He looked as though he would like to throttle her.

"I am not a child who cannot make decisions for herself," Celia said. "I am a woman, and I have decided to take my chances with you. If you leave me, I will spend the rest of my life searching for you." She tilted her head as she peered at his dumbfounded face. "*Alors*, you might as well tell me what you are planning, or I will find out for myself and—"

He snatched her by the shoulders and shook

her roughly before pulling her face-to-face with him. Her hair tumbled free of its tortoiseshell comb and spread around her shoulders. Her toes dangled six inches from the floor. Justin's snarling visage was so close to hers that their noses almost touched. Shocked into silence, she stared at him with wide eyes.

"Stay at home," Justin said slowly, deliberately. "Don't go anywhere. Stay out of this."

Her face whitened. "You are hurting me!"

His cruel grasp did not slacken. "It's not just your choices and your life I want to protect, it's Philippe's. And my own. Do you want to be responsible for my death?"

"No," she whispered, and gulped painfully, her eyes turning glassy.

Justin groaned. "Damn you, don't start that!"

"I'm afraid."

He set her down and pulled away, although it was agony to let go of her.

"You are going to exchange yourself for him, aren't you?" She sniffled. "Exactly as Legare planned it. When will it be? Soon? Tomorrow night?"

"Yes."

"Where is it going to happen?" As he remained silent, she smiled bitterly. *"Where?* It won't make any difference if you tell me. I wouldn't be foolish enough to think I could stop you. I just want to know. I have the right to know."

He looked away from her, and dragged his fingers through his disheveled hair. "Devil's Pass," he muttered.

By now Celia was familiar enough with the terrain around New Orleans to know the name. It was a narrow stretch of swamp located between

the river and the lake where she had spent the
night with Justin all those months ago. Occasionally the small channel was used by travelers and
had to be cleared of the swamp sand and debris
that threatened to choke it off.

"Is that where Legare wants the exchange to
take place?" she asked.

"Yes."

She wiped away tears of fright. "It's all going
the way he planned, isn't it?"

"I'll make it through this, Celia."

"How will I know? Even if you live, you won't
come back for me, will you?"

Justin didn't answer.

Celia bit her lip to keep back a sob of anguish.
"Why did you tell me now instead of tomorrow?" she whispered. "Why couldn't we have
had one more night?"

"Because . . ." Justin paused and thought of
lying to her, and found that he couldn't any longer. "Because then I wouldn't have a chance in
hell of leaving you," he said hoarsely.

Celia knew she could not stop him from doing
as he wished. She should accept his decision with
dignity, but instead she was reduced to pleading.
"Don't leave me, Justin, you don't have to."

"You'll have Philippe," he said.

Celia was overwhelmed with despair. He was
going to leave her, and he thought he was doing
it for her own good. "No, I won't," she sobbed.
"Don't you understand *anything*?" She was humiliated by her own helpless crying, but she could
not stop it. Brushing by him, she strode rapidly
down the hall, heading out of the main house to
the privacy of the *garçonnière*.

* * *

Max waited patiently in the parlor of the Matthews residence until the commander joined him. Some men would have donned a dressing robe for such a late and informal meeting. Matthews came downstairs wearing his military coat, breeches, and shoes. His short but stalwart form was impeccably turned out. The only thing missing was his wig. He passed his thick, square hand over his balding pate, smoothing the short gray strands back over his head. Then he approached Max with a frown.

"Monsieur Vallerand," he said, "I trust you have good reason to call at such an unconventional hour."

"I do indeed," Max replied, shaking the commander's hand. "Forgive me for disturbing your night's rest, but I had no other choice."

Matthews gestured for him to sit down, and Max complied. Were the commander a Creole, he would have offered a drink or a cigar, but that was not the American way. From his familiarity with Americans, Max knew better than to expect the kind of hospitality that his own culture was renowned for.

The commander had come from a privileged family in Pennsylvania, compiled an exceptional record in the Tripolitan war, and served in the Navy Department in Washington, D.C. Since the recent war with the British, Matthews had been assigned to New Orleans. He had encountered only frustrations and obstacles in his efforts to deal with the Gulf pirates. Unfortunately, he seemed to feel that the local Creoles' lax attitude toward smuggling had been responsible for much of his failure so far.

"Monsieur Vallerand," Matthews said, "I've no doubt that what I'm about to say will sound rude. But it is my experience that Creoles never go directly to the point of a conversation, and I am hoping that will not be the case with you. I am tired, monsieur, and I will be quite busy for the next few days. Therefore I hope you will endeavor to tell me the purpose of your visit as concisely as possible.''

''Certainly,'' Max replied politely. ''I have come to discuss the attack on Isle au Corneille.''

Matthews' face turned white, then purple. ''The attack, the . . . the . . . No one is supposed to know about that! Who . . . How . . .''

''I have my sources,'' Max said modestly.

The commander's eyes bulged and his chin quivered. ''You double-dealing Creoles and your intrigue and your spies. I demand to know the person or persons who gave you information that threatens the security of the government, the navy, the state—''

''Commander Matthews,'' Max said, ''I have lived in New Orleans all of my life. Throughout the years I have made it my business to know what goes on here. And it was obvious you would have to take a stand against the pirate threat sooner or later.''

There was utter silence in the room. Max met the commander's challenging stare with an implacable expression.

''What have you come here for?'' Matthews asked bluntly.

''To ask if you would consider delaying the attack.''

''*Delay* it? Why in the name of all that's holy would I consider that? Good God, man, to hear such a thing from you, after your son was victimized by those devilish bastards—''

"He is still being victimized by them," Max said quietly.

"What do you mean?"

"They still have him. My son Philippe is still on the island."

"What kind of rot is this? If your son is still on Isle au Corneille, then who has been living with you for the past—" Suddenly Matthews' jaw dropped open.

"My other son. Justin. Otherwise known as Captain Griffin."

The commander stared at him in icy fury. "By God, he's going to hang for this! And perhaps you along with him!"

"Before you make any decisions," Max said calmly, "you may want to hear me out. I have an offer for you—"

"Bribery won't work with me!"

"My son has offered to help in the attack on Legare. He claims that before your forces arrive he can dismantle most of the island's defenses."

"I don't believe it. Even if he were able to accomplish such a feat, why would he? Why should I trust him? Or you, for that matter?"

"Because he and I want the same thing," Max said gravely.

"And what is that? To make fools of the navy?"

"To save Philippe. Surely by now you understand the Creole sense of blood and loyalty. I would give my life in exchange for any member of my family. In that respect Justin is no different than me or any other Creole."

Matthews' hard stare relented. "I'll hear you out, Vallerand. I don't promise to agree to anything. But I will hear you out."

"That is all I ask," Max replied with relief.

Chapter 12

C urbing his impatience, Justin hovered at the side of the parlor and averted his eyes as Max said goodbye to Lysette. Three days had passed since the Duquesne ball. Tonight the exchange for Philippe would be made. If everything was going according to plan, by now Aug had smuggled a dozen men onto Isle au Corneille. In a matter of hours Justin would gain Philippe's safety and be taken to the island where he would send Dominic Legare to the devil.

"You had better return in one piece, *bien-aimé*," Lysette warned, smoothing the lapels of Max's coat. She had utter faith in her husband's strength and resourcefulness, but that would not prevent her from worrying about his safety. "It is a great trial to have you as a husband, but I have become rather accustomed to you. And I would prefer to keep you at least a few years more!"

Max grinned and brushed a kiss on her lips. "Just keep the bed warm for me, little one."

"At least you will have Alex along to watch over you," she grumbled, and pulled away. She went to Justin and hugged him quickly. "Be careful, Justin. My only comfort is that you seem to have as many lives as a cat."

"It's Philippe you should be concerned about," Justin said grimly. "God knows what hell he's been through."

"We will take care of him, Celia and I . . ." Lysette looked around as if just becoming aware of Celia's absence. "Where is she?"

"In the *garçonnière*," Justin answered. Neither he nor Celia had wanted a farewell scene of any kind.

Lysette met his eyes with a pitying, questioning glance. "Justin, I do not know what is between the two of you, but—"

"Nothing," Justin said curtly.

Lysette was kept from pursuing the matter by Alexandre's arrival. She went to her husband as he pulled on a heavy black cloak. "Max, when will you come back?"

"First Alex will bring Philippe home," he said, kissing her gently. "I will return later."

"How much later?" Lysette asked suspiciously. Her hazel eyes narrowed. "You are not planning to be with Commander Matthews' expedition when it attacks the island, are you? I will not have it! There is no need for you to do such a thing, your place is here—"

Max gestured for Alex and Justin to leave and then began to back out of the room after them. "I'll be safe aboard a gunboat, *petite*."

"You are not needed in the attack as much as you are needed here. You have three young children to consider, not to mention a wife—"

"And a son in danger," he said, slipping into the entrance hall.

Lysette called after him anxiously. "Maximilien Vallerand, *ecoutes-moi bien*—if you are hurt in any way whatsoever I will never forgive you!" She heard his soft laugh, and she stamped her foot in frustration as he left the house.

Celia knelt by the bed and tried to pray, but her concentration was broken by nagging thoughts. She combed through every recollection of the previous day, everything Justin had said to her.

You have a husband coming home to you . . . Philippe is coming back . . . I'm finished with you . . . After he's returned here safely I'll be gone . . .

She thought of Risk and how strangely buoyant his manner had been, considering the fact that Justin's would soon be in Legare's hands. But then, she had the feeling that Risk did not value human life as others did.

Justin . . . Philippe . . .

"Dear Lord," she whispered through dry lips, "please don't let anything happen to him . . . protect both of them . . . please . . ."

She buried her head in her arms. She remembered Justin's face just before she had left him, the hunger in his gaze, the harsh set of his mouth. No matter what he had said, she knew he wanted her. He wanted a lifetime with her, he wanted to be free to love her. But she would never see him again.

A soft sound broke through her agonized thoughts. She lifted her head and looked around the room. Nothing but the sigh of the breeze against the window. Justin was out there, riding through the night. Minute by minute she was losing him.

"Come back to me." She wasn't certain if she spoke aloud or was merely hearing the echo of her own thoughts. "Come back, come back . . ."

She thought of his blue eyes, and her chest ached. She felt as if she were drowning in ice-

cold water that froze her veins and forced all the
air from her lungs. And then . . . then . . . she
was in the middle of her nightmare again, the ship
and the water, and Philippe drowning before her
eyes. Only this time it wasn't Philippe, but Justin.
Legare was holding her, laughing in triumph
while she reached for Justin. Justin was dying,
slipping away from her, sinking beneath the water . . .

"No!" Celia raised herself from her knees and
stood up, gasping unsteadily. Tears spilled from
her eyes, and she brushed them from her cheeks.

Something terrible was going to happen to Justin.

She felt the danger drawing around him. He
was being led deeper inside a trap. Something
would go wrong with his plan. There was no explaining how she knew, all she could do was trust
the feeling she had inside. She had to warn Justin. Chances were that she wouldn't be able to
find him, but she had to try. Rushing from the
room, she hurried toward the stable.

The meeting point, Devil's Pass, was a section
of swamp between the river and Lake Borgne,
roughly ten miles from the Vallerand plantation.
If trouble arose during the exchange, it would be
easy to disappear into the nearby salt marsh with
its numerous bayous, channels, and coves. From
there it was an easy journey to the archipelago,
the stretch of water studded with islands including Isle au Corneille. The pirate island was a day's
travel away.

During the ride, with the wind rushing against
his ears and the horses' hooves creating a thundering rhythm, something of the old recklessness
came over Justin. He experienced the peculiar

freedom of a condemned man—nothing he said or did mattered now; he was in the hands of fate. In the cold night air, suddenly the past weeks seemed like a dream, the memories blurred. He was almost back where he'd begun. But he was different now. His luck, that invisible aura of protection he'd had ever since he could remember, was gone. He was keenly aware of its absence.

Strangely Justin was not afraid; he was filled with unfocused tension that felt like anger. It was directed toward everyone, even Celia. He was not grateful for the brief taste of happiness she had offered him. Given what was to happen, it would have been better if he'd never known her.

The irregular shoreline was covered with shells, swamp sand, and live oak trees. Risk joined them in the cover of the woods, cocking his head to the side as he surveyed the threesome dismounting from their horses. "A skulk o' Vallerands," he said quietly, his green eye alive with interest and irreverence. Justin knew that to Risk the situation, with all its danger and possible complications, was the highest entertainment.

Justin glanced across the channel, only about a hundred yards wide. "Have you seen them yet?" he asked.

"Aye, but they're keepin' their arses well out o' sight now. Look alive—Legare's had them compass the area round about."

"What about Philippe?"

"Yer brother's with 'em. Looks fair, standin' on 'is own."

Noticing that Risk's inquiring stare was directed toward Alexandre, Justin gestured toward him briefly. "My Uncle Alex."

Risk chuckled. "Damned if I knew ye had an

uncle.'' He met Alex's cool stare with a jaunty smile.

Alex slid a sidewise glance to Justin. ''So this is the kind you've chosen to keep company with for the past years, Justin?''

''Risk is a cut above most of the company I've kept,'' Justin said dryly.

Risk produced a length of rope and approached Justin, his carefree manner evaporating. ''They want yer hands tied. One o' the conditions,'' he muttered. ''I row ye across at the same time they row Philippe.''

Everyone was quiet. Slowly Justin put his arms behind his back. Risk bound his wrists securely. Max watched the procedure closely, his eyes on Risk's averted face. Max spoke then, his voice low and soft. ''Why is it that I don't trust you, John Risk?''

Justin's head snapped up, and he scowled at his father.

Max's stare was unrelenting. ''I'm aware that you consider him a friend, Justin—''

''I'd sooner question *your* loyalty than his,'' Justin growled, fiercely defensive. He would never forget that Risk had lost an eye for him. ''What reason have you to doubt him?'' he asked. ''Your infallible instincts? . . . *Bien*, that's a good enough reason for me to mistrust a man who's saved my life a dozen times, isn't it?''

Max frowned and turned away, contemplating the smooth water.

Celia dismounted from her horse and led it into the woods. She had pushed herself and the horse as hard as she could. The closer she got to Devil's Pass, the stronger her sense of danger grew. Every nerve was prickling with fear. She followed

the deep tracks left in the soft ground by the
horses' hooves until she heard the quiet murmur
of voices. Cautiously she dropped the reins and
drew closer to the water, wary of stumbling into
the middle of a dangerous situation.

She leaned against a sturdy tree trunk and
peered through an opening in the thicket. The
white light of the three-quarter moon filtered
through the curtain of mist that hung over the
swamp. Everything was quiet except for the small
ripples against the shore and the dip of oars into
the water. From her vantage point, Celia could
see everything: the two sides of the channel, Legare's men standing on one shore, Vallerands on
the other. Legare was not visible, but Maximilien
was. He stood with his feet slightly apart and his
hands clenched. The exchange had already begun. Pirogues were being rowed away from the
shallow banks, two figures in each small vessel.

Mesmerized, Celia watched and chewed the inside of her lower lip. Justin sat with his hands tied
behind his back while Risk rowed him across the
water. His head was turned toward the other pirogue. Celia knew he was staring anxiously at
Philippe to ascertain his brother's condition. The
vessels passed within ten yards of each other.
How odd and dreamlike it was, the pirogues gliding across the water, one taking away the man
she loved, the other bringing back a husband she
had thought was dead.

Her nails dug into the tree bark. That shaggy
bearded figure, bound and gagged . . . could it
really be Philippe? He looked exactly as Justin had
five months ago, except that his hair and beard
weren't as long, and his skin appeared eerily pale.
The sight of him sent a chill down her spine. Part

of the past she had thought was gone forever was now returning.

She remembered how she had thought of Philippe as a prince who would sweep her off to some enchanted land. It had been like a fairy tale come true. He was a kind, loving man. It was not his fault that she had discovered needs in herself that only Justin could fulfill. How unfair, how wrong that any of this should have happened to Philippe! Guiltily she thought that now they would seem like strangers to each other. But he was her husband. In the eyes of the church or any moral person, it was her duty to stay with him if that was what he wanted.

Justin moved his gaze from the bank where they were headed, his eyes unfocused. His nostrils flared as he inhaled sharply.

Risk glanced at him, rowing mechanically. "What is it?" he asked in a low voice.

Justin wanted to look behind them, but he didn't dare. For the first time in his life he was so alarmed he had trouble speaking. He felt that Celia was somewhere nearby and he was helpless to do anything about it. "Celia's here," he said.

"Celia?" Risk looked startled. "Have ye seen her? Where?"

"I don't know, back there . . ." Justin felt the blood pumping through his body. "After you hand me over to Legare, go back and find her. Make certain nothing happens to her."

"There's a look about ye . . ." Risk murmured, staring hard at Justin. "I've nivver seen ye afraid before, Griffin." Then he shook his head and spit.

The bow of Philippe's pirogue approached the land, and Max clambered into the knee-deep water. Ignoring the warning from the lout who pulled at the oars, Max reached into the pirogue and lifted his son from it bodily. The craft bobbed violently, and Philippe's legs splashed in the ice-cold water. After helping Philippe up the bank, Max pulled off the gag that had kept him silent while Alexandre cut the rope that had secured his arms. Gasping, Philippe stared at him with bewildered blue eyes.

Only the eyes were recognizable to Max. Every other resemblance to his elegant, impeccably groomed son was obscured by the long hair and beard, and the tattered, roughly made garments that Max would not have tolerated on one of his slaves. His cheekbones stood out like knifeblades and his skin was gray-white.

Max reached for him and held him tightly. "My God, Philippe," he said hoarsely, his arms strong and secure around his son. They were both silent for a moment, and then Philippe pulled away, twisting to see Justin being dragged out of the pirogue on the opposite side of the channel.

Philippe turned back to Max. "Why?" he asked desperately. "Why did you let Justin do it?"

"It's all right," Max said. "We have a plan—"

"No, no, you'll never win against Legare! He'll kill Justin . . . He'll . . ." Philippe's thin, ragged form swayed, and Max braced him up.

"I'll see to your brother, *mon fils*," Max soothed. "Everything will be all right. Alex will take you home now, *d'accord*? Go with him. Lysette is waiting and so is Celia."

"Celia?" Philippe repeated numbly.

"Didn't Risk tell you when he visited the island that she is alive?"

"I didn't believe . . ."

"It is true," Max reassured him quietly. "She is alive and well, Philippe."

Philippe slumped in exhaustion and murmured something incoherent. Max looked at Alexandre. "Get him whatever he wants, Alex. And send for Dr. Dassin."

"What about Risk? Isn't he rowing back here?"

Max's gaze shot to the other bank. "I don't know what that little one-eyed whelp is doing," he muttered.

Justin fell to his knees as he was shoved to the ground. Someone cuffed him on the side of his head, making his vision blur and ears ring. When the sparks cleared away, he saw Legare standing in front of him, his lips drawn back in a saw-toothed smile. "By God, I've dreamed of this," he said, and struck him again.

Justin tasted blood. He kept his head bent, deciding not to entertain Legare any more than necessary. Philippe was all right now. All Justin had to do was just stay alive until Aug reached him on the island and the attack began.

He heard Risk's voice nearby. ". . . I should tell you," Risk was saying.

"What is it?" Legare demanded.

"He claimed the woman might be hiding somewhere nearby. If ye choose, it won't be difficult to sniff her out."

Time seemed to stop. Slowly Justin raised his head and stared at Risk through a mist of hatred, realizing everything all at once. Risk had betrayed him. If he could no longer sail with Justin, he would choose to follow Legare rather than stand on his own legs. He'd tried to tell him before, and Justin hadn't listened. "No," Justin rasped. How

much of the plan had Risk told Legare? Aug . . .
what about Aug . . .

Risk met Justin's eyes without shame. "I would
of followed ye the rest o' me days, Griffin. I would
of fought for ye, died for ye. Ye were the one who
ended it."

Legare smiled in satisfaction. "Find Madame
Vallerand, then, and bring her along," he said
crisply. "Captain Griffin seems to have a taste for
her company."

Before Justin could make a sound, there was a
crashing pain at the back of his head. He fell
heavily to the ground. Dazed, he tried to roll to
his side. It took a second blow to bring him down,
and then everything went dark.

Celia could not see the action on the other side
of the water. She stayed hidden and watched as
Alexandre lifted Philippe onto a horse, swung up
behind him, and rode away from Devil's Pass.
Max remained by the water, staring at the opposite shore. Risk did not return. After a few minutes had passed, Max turned with a curse and
strode to his horse.

Celia thought about approaching Max. Surely
he must be going back to the plantation now.
It would be safer for her if she rode with him. He
would be furious to discover she was there, and
would probably give her a blistering lecture, but
she knew that deep down he would have sympathy for her. Picking her way through the
muddy thicket, she took her horse's reins and began to lead it out of the woods. Max was about
fifty yards ahead. She opened her mouth to call
to him.

Suddenly a hand clapped over her mouth and
pinched her nose shut. She tried to scream. She

struggled against a cruel grasp. Her lungs worked
frantically, but she could draw in no air.

Jack Risk's voice burned into her ear. "Ye've
been his downfall every damn step o' the way."

She felt a moment of sickening dizziness, and
then she fainted, plummeting into an endless
chasm of darkness.

Lysette welcomed Alexandre and Philippe inside the house with a cry of gladness. She was
like a small whirlwind, embracing Philippe
fiercely, asking countless questions without waiting for answers, checking him for injuries, giving
instructions to the housemaids to begin heating
water for a bath. Philippe declined to go upstairs
to rest. "I want some decent food," he said wearily, "and I want to stay awake for as long as
possible, and try to make myself believe I am really here."

Noeline rushed to bring a steaming bowl of
gumbo and thick wedges of bread from the
kitchen. Lysette dragged him to the cushioned
settee in the parlor and hovered over him worriedly. Philippe seemed numb, not fully aware of
what was happening around him. His stepmother
was relieved to see that he had no serious injuries. But it worried her, the scarecrow-thinness of
his limbs and the emptiness in eyes that had always been warm and smiling.

Taking his hands in hers, Lysette examined
them and breathed a prayer of thankfulness that
they were undamaged. It had been a particular
worry of hers that the pirates might have injured
Philippe in a way that would prevent him from
resuming the medical practice he loved. Philippe's long, thin fingers tightened over hers.
There had always been an affinity between them.

In many ways they were very much alike, genial and good-natured, the peacemakers in a family of volatile personalities.

"Where is Celia?" Philippe asked.

It was the question Lysette had dreaded. "She is not here," she said. She had discovered Celia's absence only a short time ago, and she didn't know what to make of it.

"What?" Alexandre braced his hands on the back of the settee and leaned toward her. "Where the hell is she?" Alex demanded.

"I don't know," Lysette said, giving him a frankly worried glance. "She is not in the *garçonnière* and one of the horses is gone. Apparently she left without telling anyone where she was going."

"You don't think she tried to—" Alex began, and stopped as Lysette's eyes flashed a warning. It would not be wise to upset Philippe with speculation.

"I am certain she will return soon," Lysette said evenly.

Alexandre frowned. "I will go for Dr. Dassin," he said. Lysette nodded to him, and he left with a purposeful stride.

Philippe's face was drawn. "Is Celia in trouble?" he asked.

"Of course not . . . you are not to worry about anything, *comprends? Bien*, here is Noeline with some soup, and after you eat you will see Dr. Dassin and have a long rest."

Philippe looked at her with the shadow of his old smile. "You almost make me believe everything will be all right, *Belle-mère*."

"But it will," she said, so reassuringly that she almost believed it herself.

"No. Justin is at Legare's mercy," Philippe said huskily. "He traded his life for mine."

"Justin is very resourceful. And he has lived among men like Legare for many years. He knows how to take care of himself—and how to get what he wants. *Mon Dieu,* he managed to rescue Celia from the pirate island and bring her here safely." She handed him the spoon. "Try some of the gumbo," she urged, and he began to eat slowly. The spoon shook in his hand. Lysette wanted to take the utensil and feed him as if he were a child, but she did not offer, knowing he would rather do it himself.

"Alex said that Justin has been masquerading as me," he said after the first few mouthfuls.

"Yes. We thought you were dead. When Justin was brought here wounded, we thought it was the best way to protect him."

"Badly wounded?"

"*Oui.* At first we thought he might die. But Celia . . ." Lysette hesitated, wondering how much he should be told. "Celia nursed him back to health."

Philippe put down his spoon. "And while he took my place she has been posing as his wife," he said quietly.

Lysette nodded.

"He did not try to take advantage of her? Celia is an innocent. She would not understand someone like him, his dark side—"

"No, I believe she . . . understands him very well," Lysette said uncomfortably.

"Really." He rubbed his forehead and looked at Lysette in a puzzled way. "I would have thought someone like Celia would hate him, be frightened by him."

"No, that was not the case. Your brother . . . relied on her."

"Relied on her for what? Justin has always had contempt for soft, gentle creatures of her kind."

"Justin has changed, Philippe. He has made peace with your father. I believe has has come to value many of the things he once discarded so lightly. His cavalier attitude and wildness seem to have been replaced by a new caring . . . and Celia has been—" She stopped and looked at him helplessly.

All at once Philippe understood. His blue eyes held a stricken look as he read her thoughts. "My God. You're trying to tell me there is something between Justin and my wife. That is why she is gone now, isn't it?" He closed his eyes. "No, don't answer. Don't tell me any more. Not right now."

He seemed utterly lost and alone. Lysette wanted to comfort him, but she knew it was beyond her ability. "Philippe," she said hesitantly, touching his sleeve, "shall I send for Briony?"

The name seemed to pierce through his numbness. "Briony," he repeated gloomily. "She wouldn't come if you did send for her. Aside from you, she's the one person in the world I've never had to fear being hurt by. I should have worshipped the ground beneath her feet. And instead I hurt her."

"Philippe, Briony understood why you had to choose someone else—"

"Yes, Briony understood," he said bitterly. "In my vanity and self-importance I felt she wasn't good enough for me. She wasn't educated or refined, she wasn't born a lady." He focused on a distant memory, his lips suddenly touched with a smile. "She'll never be able to speak a word of

French. I tried to teach her, and it was hopeless. If I had married her, everyone in New Orleans would have laughed and gossiped."

"Perhaps for a little while," Lysette conceded. "Would that have mattered?"

"I thought it would." Philippe shook his head listlessly. "What I did to her was unforgivable. Now it is too late."

"Is it?"

"There is no reparation I can offer her, nothing but shallow, useless apologies that she'll only throw back in my—"

"Shall I send for her?" Lysette interrupted gently.

Philippe gripped her hand and stared into her hazel eyes. He took a deep breath. "Yes."

Justin was awakened by the shock of cold water thrown on his face. Groaning faintly, he lifted his chin from his chest. His arms were fastened high above his head—it was useless to even try to tug at them. Gradually consciousness came to him. He had been beaten on the journey to Crow's Island. He was fairly certain one of his newly-mended ribs had been refractured. His entire body ached.

"Open your eyes, Captain Griffin." Dominic Legare stood in front of him with a feral smile. He smoked a thin cigar, exhaling through his narrow nostrils.

Justin discovered that his hands were fastened with iron manacles and attached to a hook on the ceiling. The chains had been pulled tight so that his heels just grazed the earthen floor. His shirt hung off him in tatters. He was somewhere underneath the fort on the island in a large cell that was sometimes used to hold unruly slaves. The room was one of many flanking a wide corridor that gave access to other passageways and rooms in an underground labyrinth of wood, stone, and shell-studded caves.

A considerable crowd of Legare's crew was packed inside the cell. They were lounging on crates, smoking, drinking, their expressions avid with enjoyment. Risk was there also, regarding Justin without emotion. Justin was filled with hatred and self-disgust. He'd been a naive fool. He'd never have believed Risk was capable of watching him be tortured. He wondered when Risk had decided to betray him. It must have been yesterday, when Risk had come to the island to find out if Philippe was alive. Legare would have used the opportunity to talk to him, promise him security and wealth, whatever had been necessary to make Risk change his allegiance.

Noticing the direction of Justin's gaze, Legare seemed to read his thoughts. "It was quite easy to convince him to join me, Griffin. You disappoint me—I assumed you were more intelligent than to place your trust in a parasite. The world is full of little bloodsuckers like him. I fully expect that he'll try to turn on me when I stop being of use to him. But unlike you, I'll cut his legs out from under him before he has the chance." He smiled at Risk as if anticipating that day.

Risk stared back at him and shifted uncomfortably, for once having no cocky replies.

Legare walked around Justin. "In spite of your surprising streak of naiveté, Griffin, I still must admit to admiring you. You've been a challenge. Few men can claim such a distinction. On the other hand, you killed André, the one man on earth I cared for. I'll make you suffer unmercifully for that."

"Your brother," Justin said, "wasn't worth a stinking heap of fish offal. And you—"

Legare sank his hard fist into the healed-over wound in his side and then backhanded him across the mouth, causing Justin to grunt and cough. "Enough about André," Legare said coolly. "Let's discuss a bit of information that Risk was not able to supply. Apparently you were wise enough not to confide everything to him."

Justin had always found that Risk was most effective when given simple, straightforward tasks rather than being told the entire plan. It distracted Risk to have to worry about too many things at once. Now Justin was thankful he hadn't told Risk about the naval force that was coming to attack the island. But there were ships in the harbor that were always ready to defend the island against the approach of hostile vessels. If they weren't taken care of before the expedition arrived—

"I know about Aug and the brace of men he brought onto the island," Legare continued. "Tell me when and how he smuggled them here."

The implications of the question struck Justin like lightning. They hadn't caught Aug and the men yet. Aug was still loose somewhere. He gave Legare a bloody-lipped jeer. "Still looking for them?" he asked. "How long have they evaded you? One day . . . two? They couldn't have done that alone. They must have had help from someone. Maybe from some of your own men."

Suddenly the chuckling and murmuring among the assemblage was silenced.

Legare looked at Justin contemplatively. He reached out and crushed the lit cigar against his chest. Justin's body arched, and he hissed through his clenched teeth as the pain blazed through his skin and needled every part of him. Sweat broke on his face, and the smell of his own scorched skin and hair was rank in his nostrils.

"Next it will be your eye," Legare said calmly.

"Go to hell," Justin gasped.

"But perhaps I'll allow you to keep your eyes for a few minutes more. There is something I would like you to see." He gestured toward Risk. "Mr. Risk, why don't you go and fetch our lovely guest?"

Justin froze. He couldn't mean Celia. Celia was safe at home, taking care of Philippe. They were bluffing. He watched Risk leave the cell. Then he was no longer aware of the others, even Legare. His whole being was suspended in anticipation, as if he were falling from a great height and waiting for the moment when he hit the ground.

An enormous roar of approval echoed throughout the cell as Risk brought in Celia's writhing form. She struggled against Risk's restraining arms and cried out as he twisted a handful of her hair in his fist and yanked roughly. The pirates pressed forward, a multitude of hands reaching out to her dress, her hair, but Legare gestured for them to fall back. They obeyed him quickly, grumbling and hooting. Celia's glittering dark eyes met Justin's, and she went still, although her slim body was trembling visibly.

"Now tell me about Aug," Legare said softly.

Justin forced his gaze to Legare's face. She has nothing to do with any of this. She's my brother's wife—"

"Ah, but Mr. Risk claims you're quite fond of her."

"Aye," Risk spoke up. "Made him into a soft-headed cully, she has."

Justin looked at him with murderous fury. "I'll

kill you," he snarled, his hands twisting violently
in their shackles until his chains rattled. The pain
of his ribs was forgotten. The cheering of the men
in the cell approached a fever pitch, for in his
growing rage Justin resembled a rabid wolf.

Legare took Celia's chin in one hand and struck
her soft cheek with the other. She reeled back
against Risk, and stared at Legare with hatred.

Justin exploded, yanking at his chains in a
frenzy. "Damn you! I'll kill you . . . *I swear it!*"

"She's just a woman," Risk said coolly. "No
different from a thousand others, Griffin."

"Tell me about Aug," Legare said, and produced a knife with a long, wicked blade. "Shall I
carve your name across her pretty face?"

"*No!*" Justin breathed in ragged gulps. "Don't
touch her!"

Legare grinned, and with the flat of the knife
traced an invisible V from Celia's temples to her
chin. It did not leave a mark, but the gesture dem-
onstrated his intentions perfectly. "How did Aug
bring the men here?" he asked.

"Don't tell him, Justin," Celia said unsteadily.
"It will not make a difference, he will do it any-
way."

"Not necessarily," Legare informed her. "If he
is cooperative, I may allow you to live. I am acquainted with several merchants in Africa who
could sell you at a handsome price on the slave
market. Skin as fair as yours is highly prized
there." He glanced at Justin. "Well, Griffin?"

Justin's gaze did not leave the knife, which
weaved back and forth in front of Celia's waxen
face. "He smuggled them here in barrels. Your
men thought it was a shipment of wine taken
from a prize ship."

Legare raised his reddish brows in surprise.

"Where have they been hiding? In the village? It couldn't be the fort. We've searched every inch of it."

"I don't know."

The knife hovered under Celia's jaw. "Come now, Captain Griffin."

"Damn you, I don't know!"

Legare turned his back on Justin and caressed Celia's taut throat. "We must convince him to be more talkative, *n'est-ce pas?* I believe I'll allow my men to amuse themselves with you. Not all at once, of course—you might cause them to quarrel." His low voice cut underneath Justin's bellowing rage as he addressed two of the men. "Boles, Luc, take her to the next cell. My reward to both of you. And make certain there is something entertaining for Griffin to hear."

Eagerly the pair tore Celia from Risk's possession and dragged her from the room. She screamed shrilly, clawing and biting as if she were possessed.

Justin lifted his legs, and smashed his booted feet into Legare's head. In spite of the men's fear of Legare, they all shouted with laughter as they saw that he had been taken unaware and knocked to the floor. Astonished, Legare struggled up and regarded him with disbelieving fury. But in a part of his mind, Justin noticed something else—that he could no longer hear Celia's screams. He was wondering what that meant when Legare raised his knife high and strode toward Justin purposefully.

As Celia was dragged down the corridor by Legare's men, a dark figure leaped from nowhere. A gleaming knife slashed through the air. The brutal hands holding her became loose and

slipped away. Celia's screams died abruptly. She
was paralyzed. Suddenly Aug's hawkish features
and lustrous black eyes were before her, and he
took her arm. She stared at him in bewilderment
and let him pull her away from the two fallen
bodies.

"Aug?" she managed to whisper, coming to
her senses. "Aug, Justin is back there, *Justin*—"
She tried to stop their forward progress, but he
continued to pull her inexorably.

"Quickly, quickly, they will be coming," he
said.

"Yes, but Justin—"

"Do not worry about him."

Just then a thunderous blast came from the direction of the cell, causing her to gasp and stum-
ble. The floor and walls shook around them.
"What was that?"

The moment Legare reached Justin, the wooden
wall to Justin's left exploded, sending splinters
and burning ash flying everywhere. The force of
the explosion sent the men closest to the wall flying backward. Dazed, Justin hung limply by the
chains. There was a ringing in his ears that
drowned out all other sound. Time passed with
disjointed slowness.

For a few seconds he blacked out, and then he
was vaguely aware of men scrambling, fleeing,
falling to the floor. "Celia," he mumbled. He began to stir, raising his head groggily. A few familiar faces swam before him . . . He was lifted
from the hook, and burly arms supported him as
he staggered a few steps, the chains dragging on
the floor.

The world steadied itself, and a small crowd of
his own crew poured through the demolished

wall. Among them, the faces of Sans-Nez and Duffy appeared directly in front of him.

"The woman—" Justin said.

"She's all right, Aug's got her."

His gaze darted around the room. Legare had disappeared. Once released, Justin limped to the prone bodies on the floor and crouched by one of them, ignoring the ache of his bad leg. "*Jack . . .*" It was Risk. He had been caught in the blast. His green eye was open and staring, and the patch had been dislodged from the ruined one. Justin searched for a pulse, and realized that Risk was dead.

Justin was surprised that after the worst of betrayals he could still feel such grief. He wanted to howl in denial and outrage and sadness. Gently he pulled the patch over the disfigured eye socket and closed Risk's good eye. He stood up and stared at the lax features in a kind of trance. He understood why Risk had turned against him. After all they had been through together, Risk had felt as if Justin had deserted him. He had felt there was no other choice than to follow Legare.

Justin would have stayed there longer, but he was aware that the others were watching him. He turned back to them and held out his wrists. "Get these off me," he said. "Legare will organize his men quickly—we don't have much time." Busily they set to work on the shackles with iron implements, smashing the bolts that had held the manacles around his arms. "You blew a hole through the wall . . ." Justin shook his head to clear his brain. "Dammit, how did you know I wasn't strung up against that wall?"

They grinned. "We hoped you warn't," Sans-Nez said.

The irons dropped from his bruised wrists. "You're certain Aug has the woman?" he asked. "Aye."

They were all looking at him expectantly. Justin assumed command automatically, snapping out instructions to the men. As he spoke, his mind raced with options. Risk was dead, Celia was in danger, and Aug was doing God knew what. The plans Justin had made would have to be carried out, but with a few alterations. Before he did anything else, he had to find Celia and make certain she was safe.

"A naval squadron of eight or more ships will be approaching," he said rapidly. "Get to the cannon on the two main batteries of the fort and fire on any pirate vessels in the harbor that aren't dismantled. Legare's men will be trying to assume battle stations. Don't turn the guns on anything flying an American flag. Set fire to the tavern and the munitions warehouses." He paused before adding gruffly, "I'll find Legare."

"Look sharp, Griffin," Duffy advised him. "We set the spring guns in the places ye wanted, and aimed 'em high. Trip over one of them wires and ye'll be shot in the belly."

Justin glanced down at his already battered body and the cigar burn on his chest. "I'm not sure I'd notice," he muttered, and gestured for them to split up. Duffy handed him a knife and a rapier. Justin sheathed the knife in his boot and examined the sword. It was a simple and well-balanced weapon, the hilt constructed of a short grip and a guard that was little more than a rimmed saucer of steel.

Justin moved toward the corridor, and they all scattered to their tasks. He was aware that Duffy lingered behind, watching him. Justin swiveled to face him. His limp, nearly undetectable most of the time, was sharply pronounced. "What is it?" he growled.

"I'll go after Legare with ye, Griffin."

Justin stared at him with penetrating blue eyes, half his face lit in torchlight, the other half in shadow. "Nay, I'll do it alone. The devil himself couldn't stop me."

Duffy turned away, evidently satisfied with what he saw in Justin's face.

Requiring no urging to keep pace with Aug, Celia scampered after him down a dim, sloping passageway. He stopped, causing her to slam into him with a muffled sound. With exaggerated care he pointed out a strange contraption mounted in the center of the floor. It looked like part of a gun. Glinting wires were stretched outward from the wooden casing, blocking off the passageway. Aug stepped over the wire and beckoned for her to do the same. Hitching up her skirts to her knees, she followed suit.

The passage went ever deeper into the ground, and ended in a honeycomb of caves. As Aug led her into one of them, it took a minute or so for her eyes to adjust to the semi-darkness. The cave was filled with empty crates and barrel staves. There was a gaping hole in the floor, about two feet wide. Aug pushed her toward it. "Down there," he said. "It leads away from the fort. Go to the end, and hurry."

Celia stared at him blankly. He wanted her to crawl into that dark hole in the ground? "I can't do that," she said.

"It is safe. Quickly, now."

Her stomach twisted sickly. "There must be an-

other way, somewhere I could hide until . . .''
She fell silent as Aug reached his hand to her.

"Take hold."

Miserably she clasped his proffered hand, dangled her feet over the edge of the opening, and allowed him to lower her down. Her feet encountered smooth stones and a steeply graded incline. She stared up at the dim outline of Aug's head. "Take care of Justin," she said desperately.

"Yes."

Then he disappeared. Surrounded by darkness, Celia sat on the slope and gave a few hysterical sobs. The thought occurred to her that if Risk had betrayed Justin, perhaps Aug had also. Perhaps Aug was not on their side. She reached up toward the opening, but her body only began to slide deeper into the pit, stones and sand cascading all around her.

Screaming, she tried to stop the downward plunge, and finally came to the bottom. She stood up clumsily and explored her surroundings. The sound of her breathing created a hollow echo.

Somewhere ahead, a few thin shafts of daylight broke through the ceiling, dimly illuminating her surroundings. She was in a cool, dank cave that was more than large enough for her to stand in. The floor was covered with an inch of seawater. Walking forward with outstretched arms, she encountered a wall and tested the rough surface with her fingertips.

She was still, listening to the muffled clamor from up above. Perhaps she should stay here and wait. The noise of another explosion rumbled through the walls, causing her to flinch. Pebbles scattered around her. She could not wait alone in the darkness or she would go mad. Biting her lip in concentration, she walked alongside the wall, trailing the flat of her hand against it. She was terrified, but she was even more frightened for Justin.

Remembering the sight of him hanging from the chains, she began to cry. How badly had they hurt him? And the explosion—had he been caught in it? She clung to a thread of hope. Justin was strong and tenacious, he had survived much danger. But she was afraid that even if he had been rescued from the cell, his worry for her would distract him from watching out for his own safety. Step by step she splashed forward through the tunnel.

Justin knew that Legare would be quick to gather his own men and devise a strategy for dealing with the small battery of vandals wreaking havoc within the fort. But he anticipated that many of Legare's own men would seize the opportunity to loot and pillage the storerooms and supplies, contributing to the chaos. With luck, Commander Matthews' force would attack soon, which would force Legare to confront the threat from the harbor as well as the one from within.

Justin began to hear explosions and cannon blasts from the direction of the harbor, rolling like an irregular drumbeat. Hoarse cries and shouts reverberated through the passageways, and alarm erupted over the island. A haze of smoke began to drift in from somewhere. Calculating various places Aug might have taken Celia, Justin made his way toward the stone steps that led to the main level of the fort. Before he reached the first step, someone leaped out at him with a harsh shout, knocking him to the floor. Justin gripped the rapier hilt and rolled, coming to his feet quickly.

''Ned!'' the assailant cried loudly, calling for help, and Justin found himself faced with two pirates, both smaller than he was but eager for battle. They were armed with short, heavy cutlasses, weapons usually carried by those who'd never been tutored by a fencing master. Such men found their limited skills enhanced by fighting at close range. They rushed at him together.

Leaping to the side, Justin parried and thrust at one of them, the rapier finding its mark easily. The man collapsed to the ground with a spreading patch of blood on his midriff. The other pirate swung at him in wide, arcing slashes. Justin had to compensate for his bad leg as he fought. He backstepped and lunged, then dove aside to avoid a downward swing that he couldn't have parried without snapping his rapier.

Groaning at the pain in his ribs, Justin forced himself to roll to his feet once more. Before the man could raise a defense, Justin lunged and sank the sword into the man's bulky shoulder. Dropping the cutlass, the pirate clutched at the wound and staggered back against the wall, sliding to the floor. He regarded Justin through slitted eyes, looking like an animal in a trap. Although the wound was not fatal, he had every expectation that Justin would finish him off. Not long ago Justin would have, without a second thought. Now he couldn't find it in himself. God, what had happened to him?

Breathing fast from exertion, Justin turned away from the pirate. He wiped his sweat-beaded forehead with the remains of his sleeve. Catching a glimpse of a shadow flitting across the floor, he spun around with his rapier poised.

It was Aug, carrying a knife in one hand and a Spanish sword in the other. He looked at Justin in disappointment and shook his head slowly. "You should finish him. You have lost your guts."

Justin gave him an eloquent look. Yes, once he had been callous and unfeeling, it seemed to say, and it hadn't mattered if he hurt someone or someone hurt him. Life had seemed much safer that way. "Where is Celia?" he demanded roughly.

"In a tunnel leading from the underground storerooms to the inland edge of the fort."

"It wasn't on Sans-Nez's map."

"The island whores revealed it to me. They found it underneath the brothel. Legare does not know of its existence."

"Don't tell me you and the others have been—" Justin was cut off by a deafening roar that seemed to billow up from the depths of the earth. The walls trembled and the wooden beams overhead cracked. He looked at Aug. "One of the munitions warehouses?" he said, and Aug nodded.

Suddenly they heard wild shouts. Men came rushing up the stairs, trampling each other in their haste. The air was thick with fear. Justin flattened himself against the wall of a side corridor and gestured for Aug to do the same. When the desperate rush was over, he and Aug emerged from the passageway. "Don't tell me that ever since Risk's betrayal you and the others have been hidden by the whores? In the brothel?"

"Part of the time," Aug admitted. "The whores wanted to get even with Legare. He takes too much of their money and does not provide them with enough protection from his own men. Sometimes the men refuse to pay, and hurt them."

"Not surprising." Justin turned to go back the way he'd come. "I'm going to find Celia."

"But Legare—"

"Aye, I'll see to him. After I find Celia." As he saw the stubborn objection in Aug's gaze, Justin raised his brows mockingly. "If you don't like it, go after Legare yourself," he invited. They both knew that Aug's swordsmanship was not equal to the task.

Aug cursed him in frustration and gestured toward the stairs. "It will be faster to go above ground and find her at the end of the tunnel."

Cautiously they went up the steps, through an empty central hall and a gaping doorway, into the night air. Dawn was just breaking. Fires were blazing around the fort, and they saw that flames were leaping from the bow and figurehead of the tavern, a converted brig.

"This way," Aug said. Justin started to follow him, when there came an unmistakable discharge from the harbor and a screeching whistle overhead. They dove to the sand and covered their heads. Shells rained down on them. One hit the ground perilously close by, exploding with a deafening boom. They were showered with sand and metal debris. Coughing, Justin lifted his head and stared at Aug. "I think," he said, "the navy has arrived."

Chapter 13

$\mathcal{C}$elia's progress had been slow and uncertain, for she could see nothing in the tunnel and the ground was not level. Gradually the thunder-claps from above became less muffled, leading her to believe the tunnel was climbing to the surface. She continued stumbling and feeling her way through the passage, but as the minutes went by her frustration and fear were nearly overwhelming. It seemed as if the tunnel would never end, and she would be caught forever in this darkness. She began to tire, but she was afraid to stop and rest.

Her fingers, rubbed raw by the constant scraping against the rough limestone, suddenly encountered empty air. The wall had ended. Confused, she groped for the edge of it and felt a deep corner. The shape of the tunnel had changed. Breathing fast in anxiety, she explored her surroundings and found that the path split in two. Aug had not told her this would happen—she didn't know which direction to choose. Her sore hands clenched into fists.

"Which *way?*" she said out loud. Her voice resounded in the cave. Leaning against the wall, she began to cry and said all the foulest words

349

she had ever heard Justin utter. She was startled
by a teeth-jarring detonation that sounded as if it
came from right overhead. A few pebbles shook
loose from the ceiling.

Galvanized into action, Celia decided to follow
the path on her left. The tunnel twisted sharply.
She sensed a difference in the air, a tinge of
smoke. She heard a muted scream that was too
high-pitched to belong to a man. Drawing closer
to the noise, Celia discovered a sharp upward rise
in the floor and an opening overhead that glowed
red-orange. She heard the dull roar of fire. Hesi-
tating, she stared at the gaping hole. There was
another scream.

Rushing forward, she clambered up the incline
and pulled herself through the opening into the
burning shambles of a room. There were dislodged planks beneath her feet, planks that must
have concealed the entrance to the underground
tunnel until someone had pulled them loose to
escape. Two of the walls were ablaze, and yellow-
white tongues of fire streaked along the partially
collapsed ceiling. Two women crouched a few feet
away, frantically clawing at a timber that had
fallen over the leg of a mulatto girl. As she glanced
at her surroundings, Celia realized she was in the
island brothel.

The two prostitutes were squawking, swearing,
and coughing. They were free to escape on their
own, but they had stayed to help the injured girl.
Impulsively Celia darted forward and seized the
trapped girl under the shoulders and arms. The
others looked at her in surprise. ''Lift the timber,'' she shouted, tears sliding from her eyes as
a puff of smoke wafted into her face. Gasping and
choking, they strained to raise the heavy wooden
beam the necessary inches, and Celia pulled at

the mulatto girl's shoulders with wrenching tugs. The girl stared up at Celia in terror and struggled to pull her leg from beneath the timber. One of the burning walls swayed, dangerously close to collapsing. Frantically Celia dragged the injured girl free.

Together they all carried the girl to the opening in the floor. Celia clambered through it first and held out her arms while they pushed the mulatto girl toward her. All four of them skidded down the short incline. One of the prostitutes, a plump brunette with a dirt-smudged face, grasped Celia's arm. "Thank you," the woman gasped hoarsely. "Thank you."

"Do you know the way out of here?" Celia asked, and coughed harshly. Even the brief exposure to the smoke had made her lungs feel as if they were filled with soot.

The prostitute gave a wheezing laugh. "If you was aiming to go above ground, precious, you took the wrong turn. Aye, I know the way out. It's not far at—"

The ear-splitting blast of a shell came from overhead, and the tunnel collapsed with a fulminating crash. They screamed and huddled together as the earth crumbled around them. In a split-second Celia knew she was going to die. Her mind emptied of all thought. Her ears were filled with a roaring noise, and then she was submerged in an abrupt quietness. Everything around her was still and cool and gray.

In a while she stirred a little, half-dreaming, half-awake. Her eyes and nose and lungs were stinging. The air was warm and pungent. Coughing, she managed to sit up and wipe her eyes. The brunette woman was gingerly touching a bruise on her own head and swearing, while the

mulatto girl was crying. "What happened?" Celia
asked huskily.

"Cave-in," the brunette said curtly, pointing to
the tunnel, which was completely blocked by rubble. "Now we can't . . . get out that way." She
gave a hacking cough. "And since the blasted
jack-tars above have set the stinking island on fire,
we're trapped here. Cozy little oven . . . won't be
long till we're done like f-four roasted pigeons."

"No," Celia said, crawling slowly to the pile of
debris. She pulled a chunk of limestone from the
top. "The heat and smoke will rise, it won't collect down here. We'll be safe for a while . . . but
still, we have to . . ." She paused as a spasm of
coughing shook her body. ". . . dig ourselves
out," she finished. None of them moved to help
her. She clawed at the rocks with her bare hands.

Then the brunette dragged herself up beside
her. "Plucky little pincase, ain't you?" She
grasped the side of a rock and helped Celia dis-
lodge it.

The tavern was an awe-inspiring sight as it
burned, giving off heat and light that rivaled the
rising sun. Crawling through the flurry of shot
from the navy schooners, Justin and Aug made
their way to the partial shelter offered by one of
the fort's two large parapets. A lone, bloody figure staggered out from the doorway. Justin
tensed, recognizing the man. "Duffy!" He stood
and caught the wounded man as he stumbled,
bearing him gently to the ground.

Duffy held his hands against a stab wound in
the center of his torso, blood flowing through his
fingers. He looked up at Justin with glassy eyes.
"Legare," he gasped. "I fought 'im, but I
couldn't . . . I tried . . ."

"It's all right, don't talk," Justin murmured, throwing Aug a bleak glance. Duffy was a gallant, foolhardy man—no match for someone as cunning and skilled as Legare. Tearing off the tatters that had once been his shirt, Justin wadded up the shredded cloth and pressed it over the gushing wound. It was a useless effort, but he had to do something. Duffy shuddered and gasped, his head falling to the side.

"Griffin."

Looking up from Duffy's still face, Justin saw Dominic Legare's lean, wiry form in the doorway. Legare clasped a bloody sword in his hand. There were no mocking smiles on his sharp-featured face, nothing but deadly purpose in his eyes. He looked clean and unmarked, and invincible. Two other men came up behind Legare. Justin wondered if it had been the three of them against Duffy, if the other two had tormented and cornered him, then allowed Legare to deliver the death-thrust.

Aug leaped up, and Justin followed suit more slowly. His heartbeat was thrumming in his ears and he was swamped with a savage elation that was as pure an emotion as he'd ever felt. He wanted to kill, to spill Legare's blood and dance in it. The roar of hatred drowned out the sound of the fire and the shell bursts. He felt capable of anything, any cruelty . . . He felt almost inhuman.

He saw it all reflected back at him from Legare's eyes. *My God*, he thought, suddenly cold with panic, *what's the difference between us?* The scarlet fog cleared away. He remembered Celia telling him she believed in him, clasping him in her arms and making him believe in the part of himself he thought had been lost long ago. It was because of

her that he was not like Legare, and never could
be. The thought of her steadied him.

As the torrent of desperate energy began to
fade, he became aware of all the things he'd tem-
porarily forgotten—his aching leg, the stabbing
pain of his rib, and all the battered places on his
body. It was good to remember. He had to fight
within his limits instead of trying to push. His
usual extension would be curtailed and he
wouldn't gamble on having much endurance left.

"Aug," he said, gesturing to the pair behind
Legare. "Keep those two outside. No one is to
interfere. If they try anything—"

"Aye."

Legare nodded to the two pirates, who moved
aside. Justin guessed that they would try to rush
Aug as soon as they had the chance. He didn't
think Aug would have trouble dealing with them.

Stepping into the main chamber of the fortifi-
cation, Legare waited for Justin to follow. The
space was small and enclosed, lit by torches and
the weak sunlight that wavered through the doorway. From outside there came sudden battle cries
and the clanging of swords. Legare kept his eyes
on Justin. "It seems my men have decided to test
Aug's fighting skill," he said.

Justin shrugged casually. 'They'll keep him entertained for a while." Before he finished the sentence, he lunged at Legare without warning.
Legare parried easily and returned with a swift
counterattack. Justin fought with grim concentration, finding that he could only accomplish his
usually smooth riposte with an awkward hop on
his bad leg. His rhythm was off.

Legare laughed contemptuously. "You pathetic
fool. You've lost whatever ability you once had."

He disengaged with a sneer, as if the fight was not worth his effort.

Justin followed readily, attacking and then redoubling, putting Legare on the defensive. He made a feint and then sank the tip of the rapier into Legare's shoulder. Legare leaped back, but there was a smear of blood on his shirt. Enraged, Legare pressed forward with forceful strokes. Justin held his ground, knowing his leg was not strong enough to support him under a long drive backward.

The blades crashed and slid together until the hilts nearly met. The men gritted their teeth and pushed in a pure test of strength. Justin threw Legare back with a mighty shove. Legare returned quickly. Suddenly they were in the midst of a long, unendurable exchange, parrying and lunging, each seeking to gain an advantage. It was too rapid for either of them to think; instinct alone guided the flashing swords. Somehow Justin broke through Legare's guard. This time the wound he inflicted was a shallow jab in the side.

The expression on Legare's face became demonic. He advanced with purposeful lunges, forcing Justin to hop back. Justin's breath hissed through his teeth as he defended himself against the attack, and then he saw with a tingling shock that Legare's face registered victory. At the same time he felt empty space underneath his heels. He was poised on the edge of a stairwell. Striving for balance, Justin slid down the first two or three steps and raised his sword just in time to parry a thrust.

They were startled by a deafening explosion as a shell hit the parapet and shook the entire structure. Thrown off balance, Justin tumbled backward down the stairs, rolling over and over until he hit bottom. The rapier clattered down a few steps and came to rest halfway down the stairwell, hopelessly out of his reach. Justin lay in the semi-darkness for a few seconds, looking dizzily up at the place he had fallen from. His mind registered the shape of Legare walking down the steps, closing the distance between them.

Justin forced himself to move, dragging himself up, crawling and stumbling into a shadowy passageway. He fell again. A mere two inches from his nose he saw a wire wrapped around a peg. He blinked and stared at the object. Panting, spitting the copper taste of blood from his mouth, he raised himself up and carefully avoided the wire, staggering deeper into the passage. He slid to the floor and leaned his back against the wall, waiting, gulping for breath, and cradling his arm against the knifelike pain in his side.

Legare paused in the entrance, staring into the concealing depths of the passage. There was no sound except for Justin's broken gasps. "Captain Griffin," Legare said scornfully. "What a fraud. To think I once considered you a threat. Killing you will be cheap sport indeed."

Legare lifted his sword and walked into the passage. His boot struck the wire, and the spring gun swiveled.

A shot cracked in the narrow hall, making Justin's ears ring.

Legare hesitated and then continued to move. The sickening thought that he hadn't been hit raced across Justin's brain. Then Legare began to fall forward, clumsily aiming the point of his sword. Justin jerked to the side, the rapier slicing through the air and narrowly missing him.

Legare let out a howl of fury that congealed his blood. *"Damn you, Griffin!"*

Then all was quiet. As Justin's eyes adapted to the darkness and daylight crept timidly into the shattered parapet, he saw Legare's face frozen in a death mask, eyes staring blankly and lips curled back in a grimace. He had been fatally wounded in the stomach. The spring gun had done its work.

Justin stood up and braced himself against the wall, looking down at the twisted form. Dazedly he wondered why everything was so quiet and still, why the noise and explosions had stopped. The naval siege had ended. Soon military officers would be swarming over the island.

"Griffin," he heard Aug's voice from above.

Laboriously Justin left the passage and mounted the steps. He picked up his rapier as he ascended. Aug was at the top, regarding him without surprise. Justin frowned at him. "How did you know Legare wasn't the one left standing?"

"I have known you too long to doubt you," Aug said simply.

Another body was crumpled right outside the entrance, one of the two men who had challenged Aug. Justin glanced at Aug questioningly. "Where's the other one?"

Aug shrugged. "He ran away."

Justin smiled slightly, and then thought about Celia. "Get me to the entrance of the tunnel." They set off to the edge of the fort. Aug grabbed a burning torch that had been stuck in the sand. Flames and black smoke leaped toward the sky from the palmetto-thatched village, the tavern, and the brothel. The burning island was a vision of hell.

A copse of twisted oak guarded the entrance to the tunnel. The opening in the ground was nearly concealed by shrubs, fern, and moss. "She should be out here by now." Aug said, searching the edge of the thicket.

"Celia!" Justin called hoarsely, then took the torch from Aug. "Something's wrong," he said, knowing instinctively that searching above ground was a waste of time. He crouched low as he entered the tunnel. Gradually the space widened, but not enough for him to stand up. He was aware of Aug following him. "Celia!" he called. All he could hear was the mocking echo of her name. They forged ahead about one hundred feet and then the course branched off in two directions. Justin paused. "Which way did she come from?" he asked.

Aug pointed straight ahead. "There."

Justin glanced at the sharp turn to his right. "Where does that lead?"

"The brothel."

"We'll try that way first."

"It is not likely she would have—"

"It's damn likely she did," Justin said grimly, taking the path to the right. "I know her. She has a talent, a *gift*, for being in the wrong place at the wrong time."

They made their way along the twisting course. Justin smelled smoke, and he frowned as they continued. He stopped short as he was confronted by the collapsed tunnel, heavy rock, dust, and debris blocking their way. Near the top of the pile was a fissure through which small hands were prying. Smothered cries reached his ears.

He dropped the torch and the rapier, his mind going blank. In a frenzy he hurled himself toward the opening, grasping a large hunk of rock and struggling to pull it away. Cursing, straining, he sent the boulder tumbling down the pile. Aug worked beside him, both of them pawing and tearing at the rock wall.

Justin forced his head, shoulder, and arm through the opening they had widened. Blindly he reached out, grabbed hold of a slim arm, and began to pull. Aug helped him drag a buxom woman with brown hair through the hole, and she collapsed in a heap at the bottom of the pile, coughing weakly.

Desperately Justin reached in again. His wrist was grasped by another pair of female hands. A second woman was pulled through the wall of rubble, and a third, and Justin saw that Celia wasn't among them. Shaking, he threw himself at the opening. *"Celia!"* His eyes blurred with sweat and tears. "Celia—"

He felt a hand grip his, and he clenched it hard enough to make the delicate bones compress beneath his fingers. He pulled her arm through the hole, reached in and grasped the back of her dress, and hauled her out. Celia lay against him, her body trembling. Justin cradled her in his lap, terrified that it had been too much for her, that she might die. With a low animal groan he rubbed his cheek against her singed hair. "My God . . . Celia . . . "

Her arms clenched around his neck. "I'm all right," she whispered against his ear. "I'm all right."

After a minute her swollen eyes slitted open. She heard the rough choking of his breath in her hair and realized with astonishment that he was crying. She twisted to sit up in his lap, staring at him. "Justin . . ." Her voice was hoarse. She wiped his tearstained cheek with her fingers, leaving streaks of black across his face. As he stared at her and felt her reassuring touch, some of the torment left his gaze. "It wasn't that bad . . . I haven't been hurt. Now . . . get me *out.*"

She began to push herself off his lap, and his arms tightened. He didn't want to let go of her.

"I can walk," Celia insisted hoarsely, and looked toward Aug, who had picked up the mulatto girl. The brunette prostitute had the torch and was leading the way.

Lunging to his feet, Justin helped Celia up and kept close behind her as they advanced to the end of the tunnel. She found that she couldn't regain her breath. Her lungs and throat felt as if they had been scoured and set on fire. But she didn't have any serious burns, and very little smoke had filtered into the cavity beneath the brothel floor.

They reached daylight, and she crawled out of the tunnel with a cry of gladness. The prostitutes flopped onto the ground underneath the shade of the trees. Wearily Celia sat down, relishing the feeling of having the sky overhead. She inhaled deeply, coughed, and forced herself to take in more shallow breaths. The cool breeze blew around her, and she lifted her face to it. Never in her life would she go underground again, no matter what the reason.

Justin leaned over her, his eyes shot with red, his face haggard and drawn with torment. Without a word Celia put her arms around his neck and kissed him, pressing her smoke-tinged lips to his. *C'est bien,*" she said, and stroked the back of his neck. He shuddered and held her, closing his eyes. "Are you all right?" she asked.

"Am *I* . . . ?" Justin laughed shakily against her hair. "I didn't know where you were. I thought you might be dead. No, I'll never be all right again." He grasped the back of her head and turned her face up to his. "How could you do that to me?'' he whispered angrily, and kissed her. The pressure of his lips was hard and hurtful. He lifted his head and glared at her. ''I told you to stay at the plantation where it was safe! I should beat you for following me!'' Before she could answer he crushed her mouth with another punishing kiss.

''Vallerand.'' Aug's voice interrupted them.

Justin looked up at him. Aug was holding the mulatto girl at his side, supporting her. The girl's leg was burned, but she was fully conscious and clinging to Aug as if he were a lifeline. The other two prostitutes were with him.

''We must leave the island,'' Aug said. ''A schooner is moored on the other side. There is still time to reach it.''

''You're taking them?'' Justin asked, gesturing to the women.

Aug nodded. ''They wish to go. And the men will welcome them.''

''There's no question of that,'' Justin said dryly.

''Come, we must hurry.''

Justin was quiet.

Celia tightened her arms around his neck and hid her face against him, afraid he was thinking of leaving her here alone. ''Justin . . . take me with you,'' she begged. ''Please don't leave me, let me go with you—''

''Shhh, quiet,'' he said, smoothing her hair. ''*Doucement*. I'm not going anywhere.'' He glanced at Aug and smiled. ''Goodbye, *mon ami*. And good luck.''

''They will hang you,'' Aug said quietly.

''We're staying here,'' Justin replied with finality. His blue eyes locked with Aug's black ones. Suddenly he grinned. ''You called me Vallerand.''

"Aye." Aug touched his forehead in a brief salute, smiled at him, and left with the women.

Feeling the tremors running through Celia's body, Justin soothed her gently. "It's all right, *mon coeur*, I'm not going to leave you. You're safe in my arms, and it's all over now."

"Legare is dead?" she faltered.

"Yes."

"And Risk—"

"He's dead." Justin eased her head back and kissed her forehead. His bloodshot eyes stared into hers. "Celia . . . did Risk or any of the others . . . hurt you?"

"No, no."

He seemed to relax a little, stroking her hair.

"You could have escaped with Aug and your men," Celia said. "Why didn't you? I would have gone with you. You know I would have—"

"No. There's still a bounty on my head. I couldn't live with the possibility of you being in danger ever again." Justin took her scraped hands in his, regarding them broodingly. His dark head bent, and he kissed her rough palms.

"It would not matter—"

"Oh yes, it would," he said. "And I'm tired of being a fugitive. I'd rather face a hangman's noose than run any longer."

"*No*," she cried, and wrapped her arms around him.

He winced. "Careful of the ribs," he said through his teeth, and released a taut sigh as her grip loosened.

"What will happen next?" she asked miserably.

Justin stared off into the distance, scanning the smoke-obscured horizon. "A certain Lieutenant Benedict is probably landing his men and combing the island for me. No doubt my father will be at his heels.''

"A-and you . . . you intend for us to just sit and wait for them? Justin . . . how can I sit and wait when . . . when this might be the last time you'll ever hold me, and—why are you *smiling?*"

He bent his head over hers, his teeth startlingly white in his sooty face. "We have a little time together. I'd choose spending a few minutes with you and dying tomorrow over having a lifetime without you"

"*Bien,* that is fine for you," she choked, "but I will not be satisfied with a few paltry minutes!"

He laughed. "Well, there's still reason to hope. My father isn't finished with Governor Villeré yet. And he's accomplished the impossible before." His lips nudged at hers. "Kiss me," he murmured, but her lips were pressed tightly together as she tried not to cry. "Tell me you love me," he said against her cheek, her chin. He caught at her lower lip with his teeth. His warm breath fanned over her skin. "That's all I care about. Tell me."

"I love you," she whispered, and slowly her lips parted beneath his. In the back of her mind she wondered how he could kiss her like this when they were about to lose everything. He caressed her throat with his hand, and her breath caught. Suddenly she had to pull away with a gasping cough. "I'm sorry," she said hoarsely. "I'm sorry—"

He hushed her with a low murmur and kissed her neck, and then his lips returned to hers. In consternation she thought she should convince him to go after Aug. They could escape some-where—that was the only way for them to be to-gether. But his arm was tight around her, his mouth gently ruthless against hers, and she could not think anymore. She let his arm support her, her head drop back, and her mouth open to his lazy exploration. There was no way of knowing how much time passed . . . he made her forget everything but the warm lips against hers and the stroking hand that kindled her nerves to aching delight.

She gave a muffled protest as he pulled away from her. Justin kept his hand at the back of her neck and watched as a six-man detail of sailors and marines approached them. He was faced with an assortment of bayoneted muskets. Holding his arm over his ribs, he stood up slowly and reached down to assist Celia.

Lieutenant Benedict arrived, looking determined and excited. It was not difficult to see that his pride had been wounded at having been taken in by Justin's charade. "Captain Griffin," he said. "It would be wise of you not to offer resistance."

"I don't intend to," Justin said.

Benedict looked at Celia. "Step away from the prisoner, Madame Vallerand."

She did not move. Justin ducked his head and touched his lips to her ear. "I love you, *vas-y*," he whispered, and gave her a little push. She walked away from him with a sob. As the men moved around Justin and secured his wrists, Celia saw a tall, black-cloaked man in front of her. The rising sun was behind him, partially blinding her.

She recognized Maximilien Vallerand's deep, authoritative voice at once. "Celia, you willful little fool . . . " She went to him in relief, and he placed his cloak around her, steadying her with a fatherly arm across her shoulders. He asked if she had been hurt, and she murmured something in reply, but her attention was focused on Justin.

She flinched as she saw the men tug at his bruised wrists.

"Lieutenant Benedict," Max said coldly, "you seem to need reminding that my son provided the means for you to capture this damn island."

After that, their handling of Justin was slightly more gentle as they marched him away. He would be taken to New Orleans and imprisoned in the Cabildo, a government building with massive stuccoed arches and well-guarded prison rooms. Celia watched them with tear-blurred eyes and then turned to her father-in-law. "Max, you must help him—"

"I *cannot* believe you are here," Maximilien interrupted, taking it upon himself to upbraid her. His voice was quiet and chilling. "It is beyond the scope of my imagination. You have placed yourself in danger, caused trouble for Justin, and abandoned Philippe when he needed you. I suspect my home is in an uproar and Lysette is half-mad." It was clear that of all these concerns, the last was the most significant to Max. To him nothing was as bad as causing Lysette distress.

"It was wrong to me to leave the plantation," Celia admitted, her voice hoarse and scratchy. "I followed you, and I shouldn't have, and . . . oh, does any of that matter now? A thousand apologies from me are not going to help anyone, least of all Justin!"

Max looked at her impatient, tear-ravaged face, and sighed. "*Petite bru,* one way or another I will help to extricate my son from this unholy mess," he said. "On that point you may rest assured."

She desperately wanted to believe him. "What are you going to—"

"Your concern, Celia, would be better directed toward another problem."

"Another problem?" she echoed. All else paled in comparison to the sight of Justin being led away.

"It seems to me that you are forgetting something. Philippe is waiting at home for you, and there is much you will have to explain to him. You are his wife, not Justin's. You must question whether the feelings you have for Justin are worth sacrificing the kind of life you have known until now. As much as Justin may care for you, he will never be able to offer you a conventional life."

"I love him."

"Perhaps you do. But it is not always easy to distinguish love from . . . sensuality." Briefly Max's gaze flickered away from hers, for the comment was decidedly personal. Celia knew that Maximilien would not have undertaken such a discussion had he not felt it was absolutely necessary. "To a woman who has lived as quietly as you for most of your life," he continued, "a man like Justin—a black sheep, someone exciting and forbidden—must be very attractive. But that attraction may not wear well over time."

Celia stood her ground, her brown eyes unwavering. "Of course I find Justin attractive," she said. "But I love him for many more reasons than that. I have so much to give to him, things that he needs desperately and Philippe does not."

Max's face softened, and a curious smile touched his lips. "Oh? And what does Justin have to offer you?"

"Everything," she said without hesitation. "I've always considered myself a very ordinary woman, but when I'm with him . . ." Celia paused, staring at a distant point on the horizon. Justin made her feel cherished and beautiful, and so uninhibited that she was free to share everything with him, her heart, mind, and body. And he gave her all of himself just as freely. As long as she had that, she would not care about a conventional life.

"All right, *petite bru*," Maximilien said. He had been watching her closely, and seemed to have made up his mind. "I cannot take one son's part against the other, and therefore I cannot be your ally in this. But neither will I stand in your way. However, I warn you, I do not anticipate that Philippe will be amenable."

Celia had not expected to be so nervous at the prospect of seeing Philippe again. She didn't know what she would feel when she looked into his eyes or embraced him. In the past several months she had changed; her life had gone on while Philippe had been imprisoned. For him time had stopped. He was asleep in his room when she and Maximilien arrived at the plantation, something for which Celia was boundlessly grateful.

Lysette scolded and comforted her at the same time, clearly shocked by Celia's appearance. At first she insisted that Dr. Dassin must be called back to attend to her, but Celia begged her not to. "All I need is a bath and a few bandages," she said. "Noeline can take care of me."

"But your poor hands," Lysette exclaimed, surveying Celia's burned palms, scraped fingers, and broken nails.

"They'll heal. Dr. Dassin could not do any more for me than Noeline can."

"The doctor will be returning tomorrow to see Philippe," Lysette said. "I insist that you allow him to look at you then."

"All right," Celia said reluctantly. She proceeded to ask many questions about Philippe's condition and his emotional welfare, but Lysette was not able to supply much information.

"Philippe is tired and very thin," Lysette said matter-of-factly, "but he has been resting, and Berté has prepared all of his favorite foods. I do not think it will be long before he looks like his former self. He seems somewhat dispirited, but Dr. Dassin says that is normal and will fade. All we can do is keep him surrounded by people who care for him."

"I should have been here to welcome him home," Celia said.

Lysette frowned, looking just as guilty as Celia felt. "There is something I must tell you, Celia. Soon after Philippe was brought here I . . . sent for Briony Doyle. I-I did not know what else to do. He needed someone, and you were not here, and . . . I hope you will not be too angry with me."

"No, no I . . ." Celia fell silent, surprised by a twinge of jealousy. She remembered the sight of Briony in the garden with Justin. So Briony had welcomed Philippe home, had kissed and comforted him. *I am glad she was able to,* Celia thought, feeling terrible for that brief moment of jealousy. Briony had given Philippe her love and her innocence. Somehow Celia felt it was wrong to begrudge the Irish girl a single moment with him. "Did she . . . help him?" Celia asked.

"Yes, I believe so," Lysette said. "She was able to comfort him."

Celia sensed that Lysette would say nothing else on the subject. "Why don't you rest for a few hours before seeing Philippe?" Lysette suggested.

Although she was exhausted, Celia shook her head. "No, I will bathe and change in the *garçonnière* and return in a little while. I want to see him as soon as possible.''

After taking a soothing bath, Celia sent for Noeline, who exclaimed over her with dismay and applied herbal salves on her eyes, her hands, and all her cuts and bruises. She produced a bad-tasting but soothing tisane for her throat and made certain Celia swallowed every drop. Celia wondered who was taking care of Justin. Surely Maximilien would make certain that a doctor was brought to the Cabildo to attend to his son. When she tried to interrupt Noeline's handiwork, determined to find Max and ask him about the doctor, Noeline sat her firmly in a chair.

''Monsieur Vallerand always take care of everyt'ing,'' Noeline said firmly. ''Now *sit*.''

She trimmed several inches of Celia's singed blond hair, cutting it in a straight line across the middle of her back. They pulled it back with a blue ribbon at the nape of her neck. ''I still look dreadful,'' Celia said ruefully, surveying her red, swollen face in a hand mirror.

''Monsieur Philippe ain' gonna pay no mind to dat.''

With Noeline's help Celia dressed in a cream and pale blue gown, long-sleeved and modestly high at the neck, with an overlapping pelerine collar. Deciding there was nothing more that could be done, Celia walked over to the main house and found Lysette in the parlor occupied with some needlework. ''Is Philippe awake?'' she asked.

Lysette shook her head. ''He should be soon. Why don't you go up to him?''

Quietly Celia went to Philippe's room and sat in a chair by his bed, watching him sleep. She had thought she was drained of tears by now, but her eyes moistened at the sight of him. He was dressed in a clean white nightshirt, his dark hair ruffled, his black lashes lying in thick crescents on his cheeks. She remembered how Philippe had smiled at her the first time he'd had dinner at her family's home. She remembered, too, the first time he had kissed her. How overwhelming he had been in his handsomeness and gentleness.

Philippe had been her first love . . . but she understood now that she had cared for him as a beloved friend. There had been an element of restraint between them that no amount of time or affection would have erased. She would always care for Philippe, but she would never be able to love him as she did Justin.

His face was relaxed in slumber, a softer, less chiseled version of Justin's. Unable to help herself, she leaned over and touched his cheek with her fingertips. "Philippe," she whispered, and his eyes opened. The depths of blue were soft and warm, not the shockingly vibrant shade to which she had become accustomed.

Philippe inhaled sleepily, blinking as he looked at her. Seeming to realize that she was not part of a dream, he sat up and stared. "Celia?"

She smiled at him, thinking he might reach for her, but instead he continued to stare. Awkwardly she leaned foward and hugged him, and his arms went around her. "All these months I thought you were dead," he said unsteadily, and she put her head on his shoulder and wept.

Chapter 14

After Celia's tears had dried, she felt more at ease with Philippe, but not for long. The outburst of emotion had not cleared the air at all, and the conversation was guarded and strained. Celia felt that her husband was relieved to see her, but that did not change the fact that there were many obstacles between them.

Sitting on the edge of the four-poster bed, she tried to explain why she had not been there to greet him and tell him everything that had occurred. "What of Justin?" he asked.

"He killed Dominic Legare—"

"Good," Philippe said in a low, savage voice.

"And I think he is well enough, except for a few minor injuries. But they took him away to prison. I . . . I am afraid of what may befall him next. They'll want to punish him. He may be executed—"

"No. Father won't let that happen."

Celia looked into Philippe's clear blue eyes, and she could not help but believe him. Once, a long time ago, she had told him he had the eyes of an angel. How, after all he had gone through, could he still have such a gentle gaze?

Lysette had shaved his beard and cut his hair,

revealing the clean lines of his face. It was unnerving to look at him and see shades of Justin. Most people would claim that Philippe was the more handsome of the two. His face was like a perfect work of art, elegant and kind and open. She could not imagine his lips quirking with Justin's sardonic sneers, his eyes hot with malice, passion, or wild excitement. Justin, on the other hand, would always have the air of a loner, and he possessed an untamable quality that was an integral part of his character.

"Philippe," Celia said softly, "could you try to tell me about the past few months?"

She was compelled to ask. Perhaps if Philippe showed signs of needing her, if he would share the pain he felt with her and let her help him, it might reawaken the old feelings.

But Philippe shook his head. "I can't," he said huskily. "I don't want to talk about it." He diverted her by asking what it had been like for her in New Orleans since their forced separation. Celia began to describe the emotions she had felt in the months following his supposed death, but then she saw the gathering bleakness on his face. Searching for more lighthearted subjects, she managed to amuse him with a few tales of her encounters with his family and friends.

Suddenly there came an awkward silence. Celia realized with dismay that she could think of nothing to say.

She looked at him uncomfortably and wondered what they had found to talk about in France, and in all those letters they had written. Conversations had not been this difficult with him before, had they? She realized she was perched on the chair . . . when had she retreated to it from the edge of the bed? Taking his hand in hers, she pressed it gently, and Philippe grimaced as he felt the traces of salve Noeline had put on her palms.

"Ugh," he said with a laugh, pulling his hand away from hers, "why are your hands slippery?"

Celia flushed slightly. "I am sorry," she apologized. "I scraped them while I was . . . It is just medicine Noeline put on them."

"Don't smear it on the sheets."

Justin would not have worried about a little salve, or the sheets. Justin would have made her laugh by reacting as if she were grieviously wounded, and then he would have showered her with kisses . . . She shoved the traitorous thoughts from her mind.

Philippe settled back against the pillows, his smile dissolving. "I am tired," he murmured.

"I will let you rest, then. Perhaps you will have more strength for talking tomorrow."

Philippe looked at her gravely. "Yes. There are things we have to settle."

"Tomorrow." Celia stood up and leaned over him, kissing his cheek. "*Bonne nuit*, Philippe."

Distraught, Celia went downstairs and left the main house without saying good-night to any of the Vallerands. She needed to be by herself and think. She did not believe Philippe had been deliberately cool to her. He did not know how to talk to her any more than she knew how to talk to him. She fervently wished she had been able to detect some sign of his real feelings for her. It would be so much easier to sort things out if she knew what he wanted and expected!

Celia walked along the path to the *garçonnière* at an unhurried pace, lost in thought. Even if she could never have Justin, she wanted an annulment. She did not think Philippe would want to stay married to her, especially not when Briony was available to him. It would be wrong to attempt a marriage with Philippe, who would forever remind her of his brother. But she did not want Philippe to feel as if she were deserting him. He would have to be satisfied that severing their marital ties would bring them both happiness.

Nightfall was coming quickly, and Celia took a detour through the garden. Every part of her body ached with weariness, but she was too restless to retire for the evening. Sitting on a cold stone bench, she surveyed the thickly planted greenery around her. She shivered as a chilling breeze swept over her. She was no longer so afraid of the dark . . . the only thing she really feared was losing Justin.

She sat there for a long time, contemplating the cloudless black sky pierced with stars. A sleepy yawn overtook her, and she stood up to go to the *garçonnière*. A soft sound came from somewhere nearby. Curiously she crept around a hedge to investigate. She drew back hastily when she saw that it was Philippe. But what was he doing out here? Her eyebrows drew together, and she frowned indignantly. Philippe was fully dressed, and he was clasping a small cloaked figure in his arms . . . Why, he had come outside into the cold for a clandestine meeting with Briony! And he had been too tired to talk with her earlier!

Peeking through a space in the hedge, Celia watched as he pulled the hood from Briony's hair and bent his head to kiss her—a long, openmouthed kiss, unlike any he had ever given Celia. Briony said something to him, and he laughed quietly and hugged her. Celia was affronted by the way he talked to the girl, so eagerly and naturally, as if he had too many things to tell her and not enough time. *I could barely drag a word out of him,* Celia reflected with a scowl. She folded her arms across her chest and watched them, feeling rather like a betrayed wife. It was tempting, the idea of leaping out of the shrubbery and announcing that she had caught them, their secret was out. On the other hand . . .

Philippe's face was clearly visible in the starlight. Celia was amazed at the change in him. The haunted, dispirited look had gone, and his eyes sparkled as he looked at the girl. Briony reached up to touch his face, and he turned his lips into her palm. The tenderness between the two moved Celia in spite of herself.

Suddenly she smiled. Oh, this made everything simple! Philippe was different with Briony because he was in love with her. He would want an annulment without a doubt. He would probably talk to her about it tomorrow, and she would assure him that she thought it was the wisest decision for both of them. She let out a quiet sigh of relief, and stole away before the pair discovered they had been observed.

In the morning Maximilien went to visit the jail, and Celia passed the time in the parlor with Lysette and her children. Her nerves were tightly stretched as she wondered what Justin might be suffering. Once she had been driven by the Cabildo when a particularly hated prisoner had been lodged there. Many of the townspeople had gathered at the courtyard beside the prison rooms, shouting obscenities and throwing refuse at him. The news that the notorious pirate Griffin had been arrested would spread rapidly. What if at this very moment they were visiting the same cruel treatment on Justin?

Evelina and Angeline played with their dolls at

a safe distance from the fireplace while Lysette sat
with a basket of mending. Since there were few
tasks to which Celia could turn her scraped and
burned hands, she sat on the settee with Rafe
cuddled on her chest and read an English-
language newspaper. Occasionally she would say
a few words aloud to check the meaning of a
phrase, and Lysette would translate. The wood
and gilt bracket clock on the mantel ticked with
torturous slowness.

At last Maximilien arrived, bringing with him
the scent of the cold outdoor air as he strode into
the cozy parlor. *"Bien-aimé,"* Lysette exclaimed,
jumping up from her mending. Max took her in
his arms and kissed her briefly.

Celia was prevented from moving by the weight
of the sleeping baby on her shoulder, but her eyes
were fixed on him.

"Max, do tell us your news at once," Lysette
said, removing his coat and tugging him to a
chair.

Maximilien stretched out his long legs comfortably, looking more than a little smug. "I will meet
with Governor Villeré this evening. The word I
have received is that the assistance Justin rendered in the attack on the pirate island has caused
Villeré to consider the matter of his pardon with
new lenience."

Celia leaped up, clutching the baby so tightly
that he woke and began to squall. *"Mon Dieu,* I
am afraid to let myself hope," she said breathlessly.

Lysette smothered Max with kisses and lavish
praise. Evelina and Angeline rushed to him, gig-
gling and sharing in the excitement although they
did not understand the reason for it. For a mo-

ment Max was hardly visible in the swarm of red heads around him.

Rudely awakened from his slumber, Rafe refused to quiet until Lysette took him. Snuffling irritably, the baby laid his head on her shoulder and chewed on his fist. Celia forced herself to sit down again. "What of Justin's condition?" she demanded, leaning forward.

"He is in good health. The doctor has seen to him and none of his ribs appear to be broken. At my insistence Justin has been allowed hot water, soap, and fresh clothes." Max smiled wryly. "In truth, I rather wish he were not being made so much of."

"Made much of?" Celia echoed in bewilderment.

Max shook his head ruefully. "*Bien sûr*, I have been astonished by the reaction of the public to Justin's capture."

"What do you mean?" Lysette asked.

"Apparently throughout New Orleans Justin is being depicted as a dashing pirate. A romantic figure. Stories about his exploits, real and imagined, are being exchanged in the coffee houses and the town square. Ridiculous as it is, the town is agog over him."

"What is this 'agog'?" Celia asked suspiciously.

"It means that there is an admiring crowd encamped outside the Cabildo. He is allowed no visitors—except me, of course—but many women of the town have displayed an untoward concern over his welfare. They have brought foodstuffs and bottles of wine to the building, most of which Justin has passed out to his jailers and fellow cagelings."

"But this is absurd!" Celia exclaimed.

''More so by the hour. I have been told this
morning about three different women who were
supposedly seduced by him at the Duquesne
ball.''

Evelina looked at him curiously. ''Papa, what
is 'seduced'?''

Lysette frowned at Max reprovingly. ''Hush,
Evie, that is not a nice word for little girls to say.''

''*Absurd,*'' Celia repeated, turning pink with
consternation. Justin was *hers*, not some object of
adoration for foolish women who imagined themselves in love with a fearsome pirate! She could
picture Justin's enjoyment of the attention he was
receiving. He was having a high time while she
was here pining for him! ''Did he ask after me?''
she blurted out.

Max's ironic smile faded into a more serious expression. ''In truth,'' he said quietly, ''he wanted
to talk of nothing but you.''

Celia's outrage died away, and she looked
down at her lap, suffused with longing. ''What
did he say?'' she asked.

''Most of it I am certain he will repeat to you in
private. He does seem to expect that while he is
incarcerated you are resolving matters of your
own here.''

''Oh, does he?'' Celia glowered at no one in
particular. ''I suppose he thinks it will be easy. I
suppose he expects that after five months of separation I will simply march up to Philippe and tell
him—''

She stopped with a gasp as she saw Philippe in
the doorway. He was clad in a full-length dressing robe, his dark hair neatly brushed and his blue
eyes steady on her.

''Tell me what?'' Philippe asked gravely.

Celia felt her tongue freeze in her mouth. The

blood rushed to her face, and she was aware that the room had become absolutely quiet. Everyone was staring at her.

Lysette was the one to break the dreadful silence. "Philippe," she suggested softly, "why don't you take Celia to the morning room? Neither of you have eaten. I will send Noeline up with brioches and *café*. You will be able to talk there without interruption."

Celia sipped sweet black coffee out of a delicate porcelain cup, while Philippe broke open a brioche roll and buttered it. She stared at him warily, waiting for him to say something until finally she could stand the silence no longer.

Her cup clattered against the saucer as she set it down. "Philippe, we must begin to think about . . . about our marriage, and the situation we find ourselves in."

A series of emotions crossed Philippe's sensitive face—surprise at her straightforwardness, perturbation, and then determination. "I have been thinking about it," he said. "It has not been easy."

"No, of course not," Celia said. "It is hardly a simple matter."

"In some ways it is."

Celia frowned uncertainly. "Philippe, I know you do not want to talk about what has happened, I know it is painful for you . . . but there are some things I must tell you."

"About Justin?" he asked bitterly.

"About *me*. Philippe, please . . ." Celia reached out to take his hand. "For all those months I thought you were dead, I may as well have been locked in that cell with you. I did not suffer physically, but I felt such terrible grief that I wished I might die.''

Philippe stared at her compassionately. He held her hand in a strong grasp. ''Celia—''

''I knew I would never take pleasure in anything again,'' she continued. ''I would never laugh or be happy. I was certain I would always be alone and I would never love again. And then . . . I reached an acceptance of your death, Philippe.''

Philippe's expression turned cold. ''I wasn't dead,'' he said tightly. Leaning across the table, his hands closed over her forearms.

''But I didn't know that! And then Justin was brought here, so badly wounded that we all thought he might not make it through the first night. He was so different from you . . . so disillusioned and rough, so hot-tempered. At first I hated him. But as I helped to take care of him, it became more and more important that he live, and suddenly . . .'' Celia paused and looked helplessly at him. His hands were uncomfortably tight on her arms. ''Suddenly I wanted to be with him every minute of the day. When we were together I felt more alive than I ever had before. I suppose I knew he was falling in love with me. I could tell from the way he looked at me and spoke to me . . . a-and I knew he was fighting against it just as I was, but . . .'' She drew a trembling breath. ''. . . neither of us could stop it from happening.''

Philippe let go of her and stood up violently, jarring the table so that the coffee sloshed over the rim of the cups. ''Did you let him . . .''

Celia bit her lip, wondering if it was his right to know, if it was even his right to ask. Legally Philippe was her husband. She had been unfaithful to him. But she hadn't known he was alive . . .

Reading the answer in her confused silence, Philippe struggled to contain his feelings of rage and betrayal.

Celia sat rigidly in the chair, not looking at him.

"I should have expected it," Philippe finally said. "By the time Justin was sixteen he had already become an expert at seduction. He must have found an innocent like you easy prey."

Stung by his condescension, she stood and faced him. "I was entirely willing. I wanted to be with him because I love him."

"No," he said with conviction. "You are too inexperienced to know the difference between love and passion."

"And was Briony Doyle as well?"

Philippe looked as if she had struck him. "What?"

Sorry for her impetuous remark, Celia spoke more softly. "I am aware of the relationship you have with Briony. I know that it began before you came to France to marry me, and that you chose me over her because you considered me more suitable."

"That is not—"

"I saw you with her last night in the garden." She watched as the color crept across his cheekbones and the bridge of his nose. "You love her, Philippe. You could find such happiness with her, a happiness beyond anything we could ever find together."

Philippe strode to the window and stared out at the cloud-misted sky. He gripped the windowsill. "I chose between the two of you once," he said. 'I wanted *you*, Celia. For many reasons. One of the most important was that I loved you. I still love you."

"But you love her too."

"In a different way."

In spite of her tension, Celia smiled wryly. "Perhaps you could explain to me which way you love me and which way you love her." She did not intend to sound sarcastic, but that was how Philippe heard it.

"You never spoke like that before," he said flatly. "Justin's influence, I suppose." He turned and leaned against the window frame, hooking his thumbs in his pockets and resting his weight on one leg. "Come here," he said quietly.

She complied, standing a foot or two away from him. He did not reach out to her, merely stared at her intently.

"One of the many differences between my brother and me," he said, "is the way we view duties and obligations."

"Are you saying you consider me a duty? An oblig—"

"Let me speak," he said firmly. "We are married, Celia. Nothing has changed that. You're still legally my wife. Haven't you considered that we have an obligation to honor the vows we took? For better or worse? Circumstances have altered the course of our lives, but the original reasons for marrying each other still exist. We are alike in many ways. We will be able to find contentment with each other." He paused and added emotionlessly, "And so . . . I am willing to forgive your . . . indiscretion. I want you to be my wife."

Celia regarded him with amazement. This was not proceeding at all as she had expected. "But don't you want more than mere contentment?" she demanded. "*I* do!"

"You think that this wild, passionate kind of love will last forever. But it burns out quicky, Celia. What you feel for my brother will not endure . . . It will seem magical, wondrous, for only a short time, and then it will dwindle to nothing."

"How do you know that?"

Philippe's face hardened, reminding her momentarily of Justin. "My father married my mother because she was an exciting woman he felt great passion for. But when the embers faded, there was no real foundation for their marriage . . . and the situation ended in adultery and tragedy. Justin and I both suffered the consequences of it for years."

"But . . . that is not the same as this at all!"

"To me it is exactly the same. I love my brother, but I know exactly what he is, Celia. He's never had a long-lasting relationship in his life."

Celia did not try to argue with him on that point—he was convinced he was right. But she believed in Justin and knew how desperately he loved her. She tried to turn away from Philippe. He caught her hands and kept her there, wanting her to face him. "Philippe," she said warily, "you are brothers. It is only natural that you might feel some sense of competition with him—"

"This isn't about that," he snapped. "This is about the fact that I care for you!"

"And I care for you, Philippe." She bent a determined stare on him. "But that is not an adequate reason to keep me as your wife! The truth is that you are madly in love with Briony Doyle, and you are too stubborn to admit it."

"I am trying to do what is best for all of us—"

"Don't!" Celia stared at him pleadingly. "Philippe, I know how important duties and obligations are to you. But what if there weren't any to consider? What would you choose if you could have whatever you wanted?''

''I've told you what I want.''

''Choose for yourself only, Philippe. For once in your life be selfish. Pretend there are no rules, no responsibilities. Pretend there is no marriage between us. You are free to have your heart's desire. What do you choose? *Whom* do you choose?''

Philippe was silent, his face blank.

''Why did you arrange to meet with Briony in the garden last night?'' Celia asked. ''Because you couldn't help yourself. You long for her, you *love* her . . . and in your heart you want to believe it will last.''

As it became clear that he was not going to answer, she pulled away from him. She would have to be patient. ''I don't think you are being honest with yourself,'' she said softly. ''I think the truth is that we both want the same thing, Philippe. So much has happened . . . neither of us can go back.''

''No,'' he replied. ''But we could begin again.''

Faced with his obstinacy, she shook her head helplessly and asked if they could continue the conversation later. They both needed time to think.

Celia did not see Philippe for the rest of the day, although she stayed in the main house in case he wished to talk with her further. Surely persistence would wear him down. But he took his lunch in his room, and did not venture downstairs. He was either resting or thinking—she hoped it was the latter.

Evening came and there was no word from Max, who must have met with the governor by now. Dejected, Celia curled up on the window seat in the library with Vesta. The orange cat settled in her lap with a loud purr, pawing the soft violet silk of Celia's gown. Celia liked the elegant masculine atmosphere of the library, the heavy mahogany furniture and the rich yellows, scarlets, and blues of the wall coverings and upholstery.

The cat licked a paw delicately and began to preen herself. "Tell me something, *ma belle*," she murmured, smoothing Vesta's fur over and over. "I have noticed your habit of going from one yowling tom to another, heartlessly discarding each suitor when you tire of him. How can your conscience bear it?"

"Of all animals," Philippe said from the doorway, "cats are the least likely to have a conscience."

Celia started at the sound of his voice. "Philippe," she said, with a breathless laugh, "I do not remember your habit of sneaking up on me from before."

He caught at his lower lip with his teeth in his old, thoughtful expression, then smiled at her. "May I come in?" he asked, and she nodded, her gaze flickering over him. His dark hair was neatly brushed, and he was dressed in a navy coat, cinnamon-colored breeches, and buckled shoes. A starched linen cravat gleamed white against his jaw. He looked as if a burden had been lifted from his shoulders.

"Please sit down," Celia invited, gesturing to the space beside her on the window seat. Annoyed at the presence of an intruder, Vesta leaped off her lap and wandered out of the room.

"I apologize for my overbearing attitude this

morning," Philippe said. "You were nothing but honest with me. I realize it was not easy for you."

"No, it was not," she said quietly.

He looked at her steadily, and there was an openness in his gaze that had not been there before. "I felt . . . still feel . . . that something precious has been taken away from me. I don't blame you, or Justin. All I know is that before I was captured by Legare and his men, you were mine and we had a future together. And I believe we would have been content, Celia."

"So do I," she said sincerely. "But Philippe—"

"*Non*," he murmured, "let me speak my piece. Now I realize that not only have you changed, but so have I. The future I once envisioned is no longer possible." He took her hand, and their fingers laced together tightly. She began to sniffle, and he searched in his pocket for a handkerchief, giving it to her with a wry smile. "Since that day we were separated," he said, "I've been trapped in a nightmare. I have lived for so many months without hope, without any feeling . . . nothing is quite real to me anymore. But when I'm with Briony, the nightmare disappears and I begin to feel things intensely, and I can't help but find it alarming. I'm not certain I want to feel anything yet—I just want safety and peace."

"I understand that, after what you have been through," Celia said. "But you *will* be safe with Briony. I saw how happy you were with her."

Philippe looked down at their entwined hands. "I do love her," he said.

"I know that. And she loves you. Why must a husband and wife be exactly alike to find contentment with each other? *Vraiment*, I think the differences make life very interesting." Her fingers tightened on his. "Go to Briony."

He glanced at her with his slow, charming smile. "So you're giving orders now."

"Yes."

"And what should I tell her, madame?"

"Tell her that you adore her, and that you are going to marry her as soon as you obtain an annulment."

His expression turned serious. "Celia, this is what you want?"

"Oh, yes."

"But if you need my help, if you ever need me to take care of you, I will always—"

"No, *mon cher*." She laughed softly. "You are still concerned for my welfare, aren't you? Do not worry about me, Philippe . . . I will not be abandoned or mistreated. Your brother will not tire of me for at least fifty years."

"You are sure about that," he said rather than asked.

"As sure as fate," she whispered, giving him a brilliant smile that he could not help but return.

His lashes lowered. On impulse he pressed a kiss on her lips. It was a dry, affectionate kiss, one a brother might bestow on a sister.

Suddenly Celia felt a hot chill on the back of her neck, and she knew it had not been caused by Philippe but by another presence in the room. She looked up, and her heart stopped as she saw Justin standing there. He was clad in a loose white shirt that was open at the throat, narrow black trousers, and black shoes. He looked so virile and commanding that Celia caught her breath.

She had never seen the twins in the same room together. It was overwhelming. She found it hard to believe that one could ever be mistaken for the other. Although their features were identical, it was easy to see which was the doctor and which was the reformed pirate. One was the kind of man all mothers would wish their daughters to marry, while the other was the kind mothers would beg their daughters to stay away from.

Philippe let go of Celia's hand and stood up. "So you've been pardoned, *mon frère*," he said.

Justin took his hard gaze from Celia and looked at his brother with a slight smile. "Yes. After all of this I'm afraid father's political influence has been severely depleted. He hasn't a single favor left to call in."

"Justin, what you did for me—" Philippe began, and stopped as if at a loss for words. He stepped forward and clasped Justin in a rough embrace. They held fast, and then Justin released him with a laugh.

"The worst part of it was pretending to be you," Justin said. "It wasn't easy, affecting such gentility and kindness. And having to listen politely to accounts of all the maladies plaguing the elderly matrons of New Orleans."

Philippe chuckled. "I must admit, I can't imagine you listening politely to *anyone*."

Justin surveyed his brother appraisingly. "You look well, Philippe. No one is more glad than I to have you alive, and back here safely."

"Thank you," Philippe said. "It is all because of you." Blue eyes met blue as the twins exchanged a glance of understanding. They had been separated for a long time, but nothing would ever break the bond between them.

"When I heard you were dead," Justin muttered, "I felt as if half of me were missing."

"I wanted to kill you myself when I realized you were exchanging yourself for me."

"I never thought twice about it," Justin said simply. "I only wish I could make Legare pay ten times over for what he did to you."

"There are things I need to talk to you about, Justin."

"I know," Justin said quietly. "Whenever you want, *mon frère*."

Celia stood up and took a step toward them. "Justin, I—"

"I see that you have been reunited with your wife," Justin said to Philippe, ignoring her. His voice turned cool and courteous, as if he were complimenting his brother on winning a card game. "My congratulations."

"Actually—"

"Obviously I've interrupted a private moment," Justin said. "I'll leave the two of you to your . . . celebration. We'll talk later, Philippe." Before either of them could reply, he turned and strode from the library.

"Justin!" Celia called after him, but there was no response. Wildly she spun around to Philippe. "H-he misinterpreted the kiss," she said in a panic. "He does not understand—"

"If I don't miss my guess," Philippe said thoughtfully, "Justin expects you to follow after him. It might be wise to do so immediately. And in the meanwhile . . ." He smiled, suddenly looking as eager as a boy. "I plan to pay a visit to Miss Briony Doyle."

"Good luck," she said breathlessly.

"Good luck to *you*."

Rushing down the hallway, Celia caught up to Justin just as he reached the octagonal entrance hall. "Justin, *wait*." She touched his arm. He spun around to face her, towering over her. In contrast to his icy control of a few moments before, he was breathing fast and his blue eyes were simmering with fury. "Justin, Philippe and I were talking, and—"

"Legare was right about one thing," he said tersely. "You seem to do equally well with either one of the Vallerand brothers."

"What?" She gazed at him in astonishment. "Let me explain—"

"Don't bother. It doesn't interest me."

"You are the most unreasonable, thick-headed—"

"I don't blame you for wanting to keep Philippe on the line," Justin sneered. "He's safe, respectable—an exemplary husband. And when you find he doesn't satisfy you in bed, you can always come visit me for a good hard—"

She slapped his face. The crack of her hand echoed in the entrance hall. "After all I've endured, I will not be insulted by you!"

"Oh, I'm not insulting you—"

"You jealous—"

"I quite admire your adroitness in getting what you want."

"I am trying to tell you that Philippe and I have decided on an annulment!"

Maximilien's deep voice boomed out from behind them in annoyance. "What is this uproar about?" He was standing with Lysette at the bottom of the staircase. "Is all this noise and commotion really necessary? I urge the two of you to settle your differences in a more circumspect manner."

Glaring at the two of them, Justin dragged Celia into the nearby parlor and slammed the door.

Max began to chuckle. Lysette glanced at him bemusedly. "*Bien-aimé*, why are you smiling like that?"

Max lifted her up the first two steps so that they were standing nose to nose. "I am thinking of the settee you had upholstered in that slick blue damask," he said, drawing her arms around his neck. "And wondering if they will have more success with it than we did."

She turned pink, and then her hazel eyes widened. "Max, you don't think they're going to . . ."

Max glanced over his shoulder at the closed door, and his amused gaze returned to hers. "It has become very quiet all of a sudden, hasn't it?"

Lysette gave him a mock frown. "Maximilien Vallerand," she said, "your sons are turning out to be nearly as impossible as you are!"

Max grinned arrogantly. "Little one, you would not have me any other way."

As soon as the door slammed shut, Justin turned Celia in his arms and fastened his mouth over hers. She fought him halfheartedly, still incensed by how quickly he had jumped to conclusions. He held her more tightly, his mouth devouring hers until she shivered and relented. She arched against him, pulling at the white shirt until it came free of the doeskin breeches. Her hands slipped underneath the shirt, gripping his hard, broad back.

"Don't ever let me see you kiss another man again," Justin muttered against her throat. "Not even a doddering old grandfather. I can't bear it."

"Jealous . . . irrational . . . oaf," she accused in fitful gasps.

"Yes." He pulled her into the shelter of his body, urging her against the taut length of his arousal. "I love you," he said roughly. Burying his face in her neck, he yanked at the buttons on her high-collared gown. He pulled the comb from her hair, and it fell down her back in a pale river of silk. "You're beautiful, so beautiful . . ."

Flushed and dizzy, she stroked the back of his head and kissed his ear. "Not here," she whispered. "Someone might interrupt—"

"I don't care. I need you." Seeking her mouth again, he explored the silky inner edge of her lips with the tip of his tongue. A soft whimper came from her throat, and he sealed his mouth over hers, his tongue reaching into her sweet warmth.

Celia tugged helplessly at his shirt until he let go of her long enough to remove it. Her fingers sank into the hair on his chest, digging into the thick wiry curls. "You did not spare me a thought," she gasped, "with all those women bringing things to you . . . bottles of wine . . ."

"I had everyone in the Cabildo drinking toasts to your beauty."

She gave a muffled laugh against his shoulder. "Are you truly free now? No charges, no more bounties . . ."

"I'm all yours." He kissed her blond brows, her fragile eyelids. "It's no bargain. Most people will tell you I'm a dangerous gamble."

"And how should I answer them?"

He wrapped his arms around her, hugging her close. "Tell them I can't live without you."

He lowered her to the settee and took her slippers off, then removed his own shoes. His heart began to drum heavily and he gripped her silk-stockinged legs in his hands, squeezing her ankles, calves and knees. Celia wrapped herself around him sinuously, sliding her mouth over the warm skin of his neck and shoulder, devouring his scent and taste. He pushed her to her back and eased the unfastened bodice of her gown to her waist until her arms were trapped within the long sleeves.

Crouching over her, he tugged the top of her chemise down with his teeth. Drawing her nipple into his mouth, he aroused it gently until she gasped and strained to pull her arms free. His head moved over her chest, and he murmured for her to be still. Slowly her impatience melted into languid pleasure, and she relaxed beneath him.

He stripped the gown off her, and her long-legged drawers with it, and tore the front of her chemise straight down the middle, spreading it open carefully. She unfastened the buttons of his breeches, freed his swollen arousal, and caressed him with dizzying sureness. He felt heat gather in his loins, chest, the vulnerable parts of his neck, until he had to pull her small hand away, his self-control crumbling. "Stop," he muttered. "Too fast . . . wait . . ."

Celia lifted her silky perfumed body to his, her fingers trailing down his back in tenderly inquisitive touches. Groaning, he spread his hands over her thighs. He was more than ready to take her. He knew she could draw him inside easily, but he wanted to prolong the moment. Her kiss-reddened lips parted, and her arm curled around his neck, exerting pressure to bring his head down to hers.

Their lips blended, and suddenly he could not bear it any longer; he pushed her legs wide and entered her. The thrust drove her body several inches along the sleek surface of the cushioned settee. Gripping her more firmly, he moved again, and his knee slipped, and they both nearly slid onto the floor. Justin grasped for purchase on the slick upholstery, could find none, and cursed in a guttural tone. A small tasseled pillow was dislodged and fell onto Celia's face. She began to choke with laughter.

"I'm so glad," he said, picking up the pillow and flinging it viciously across the room, "that you find this entertaining."

"*Oui*, very entertaining." Celia wrapped her arms around his waist. "What should I do?" she whispered.

In spite of his frustration Justin grinned at her. "Hold on to me, *mon coeur*. We'll find a way." He pulled her body beneath his, braced one foot on the floor, and reached past her head to grasp the arm of the settee. The position afforded him the leverage he needed, and the rhythm began, slow and deep. Her eyes half-closed, she held him more tightly.

His mouth descended on her breasts, her shoulders, her throat. Celia gasped as he moved between her thighs, as she felt herself gathering around him, and pleasure flooded through her until she couldn't breathe. Shuddering in his arms, she sank into the flowing warmth of release. He pushed deeper and held himself there, his eyes closed, burying his deep cry in her mouth.

Afterward, tangled together, they lay there comfortably. Justin drew her long hair over his chest, toying with the golden locks. Idly Celia's fingertip circled his flat nipple. "The annulment will take some time," she said drowsily. "The marriage documents will have to be retrieved from France, and the Church must be approached—"

"It doesn't matter how long it takes, as long as the thing is done properly."

"It will be difficult in the meantime, all of us staying here together."

Justin shook his head with a slight frown. "No, my love. I'll be staying at a hotel in town."

"Oh, but—"

"I can't live under the same roof as Philippe," he said firmly. "Or the rest of the Vallerands. They would all be watching us. The constant scrutiny would drive me mad."

"But when will I be able to see you?" she asked in dismay.

He smiled and stroked her slender back. "Don't worry. I'll come courting. I'll see you every day. We'll make discreet arrangements to be with each other. Perhaps you'll even find it romantic . . ."

"No, I will find it tiresome, skulking about, making arrangements for clandestine meetings . . ." She pouted and laid her head on his chest. "I want to be with you all the time."

"Soon." His soft laugh resounded against her ear. "*Petite coeur*, just try and stop it from happening."

Epilogue

<hr>

Marseilles

Celia walked across the sand alone, luxuriating in the balmy breeze and the gentle sunshine. Far ahead of her stretched the turquoise waters of the Mediterranean. In back of her was the villa with a small, palm-shaded courtyard that Justin had leased two months ago. Since there was no possibility of being observed on the private beach, she lifted the skirt of her thin white cotton dress and waded into the water, enjoying the feel of it surging around her ankles. Seagulls nearby quarreled over a small fish, squawking noisily.

Marseilles was the most enchanting place in France, she reflected, far better than Paris or even the lush chateau country in Touraine. The prosperous and busy port of Marseilles contained all the best features of a city but also provided the charm of the several fishing villages that surrounded it.

Sitting on the warm sand and dropping back on her elbows, Celia stared at the vivid water. She felt she could never tire of Marseilles. She hoped Justin would not want to leave for another few months. But it didn't matter, she would be sinfully happy wherever they lived.

They had married as soon as the annulment had been procured, and at Justin's insistence had left New Orleans with equal haste. He had fretted and chafed and made no secret of his impatience to be away. Although he was now reconciled with his family, the plantation itself would always remind him of old regrets and unpleasant memories. He had wanted to make a new beginning. Philippe's marriage to Briony Doyle took place only a few days after their departure, and Celia was disappointed to have missed it, but in a way she agreed with Justin that there had been something vaguely disquieting about having Philippe present at their wedding. It would be better for Briony not to be faced with any vestiges of Philippe and Celia's ill-fated marriage at her wedding ceremony.

Parting with the Vallerands had been difficult. They had said their goodbyes at the plantation. Celia and Lysette had both been tearful, while Max was unashamedly reluctant to let them go. There had been an awkward moment when Justin and Philippe had not embraced in the Creole tradition but instead clasped hands in the more impersonal American style. The fact that Celia now belonged to Justin would always be a source of tension between the two of them, but she hoped that the passage of time would soften it.

Philippe had taken Celia carefully into his arms and hugged her, and when he drew back to look at her with a bittersweet smile, she had given him an answering one. They were each happy with the course they had chosen, but they would never forget the private moments they had shared in the past, or that they had once meant something to each other. Celia noted with inward amusement that although Justin had made a great effort to suppress a jealous scowl during the exchange, he could not help clamping a possessive arm around her afterward.

In the months since their wedding Justin had changed in subtle ways, losing much of the cynicism and wariness that had been so much a part of him. He was freer to laugh and tease. At first he had hovered over her with jealous greed, as if she were a treasure that might be wrested away from him at any moment. Now he was more relaxed and assured of her love, and there was new trust between them.

The first test of their marriage had come early, during the journey to France. On the first night of the crossing Justin had come below to their stateroom after touring the deck with the ship's captain, to find Celia gray-faced and cowering in the corner of their bunk. Alarmed, he gathered her in his arms, and she burrowed against his chest like a terrified animal seeking to hide from an unseen predator.

"*Chérie*, what is it?" he asked urgently against her hair. "Are you ill? Did something happen?" After a few minutes she managed to explain that some noises from the deck had brought back all the horror of Legare's attack. She knew that it was not likely the same thing would happen again, but she could not subdue her sense of impending disaster.

Rocking her gently, Justin proceeded to explain why her fears were unfounded. "*Ma petite*, this frigate wouldn't tempt a pirate at all. I should know. It is not loaded with the quantity of goods and expensive cargo that the *Golden Star* was. It has a lighter draft and that makes it faster and less appealing to sea bandits. And the dead-works—that's the part above the water—are built narrow, so that no one could board it easily. And it's armed with carronades, and twenty-eight pound guns, and . . .''

As he continued, Celia stopped listening to his actual words and concentrated on the soothing sound of his voice. She didn't care about all the reasons that there was no danger. She just couldn't help remembering the *last* time she had sailed across the ocean with a new husband! Philippe had assured her with just as much conviction that it would be safe. Her anxiety lessened but did not entirely disappear. There were times when the creaking of the ship or some unexpected noise would cause her heart to throb with terror.

She heartily disliked being at sea, but she tried to conceal it from Justin, for he loved it. He loved the waves and the wind, even the storms. The strain of keeping her fear inside made her irritable and sharp-tongued.

Patiently Justin coaxed her on deck and stood with her at the rail, his arms braced around her until she stopped flinching with each crash of the waves against the hull. He took her around the ship and explained how everything worked, from the chain pumps to the spindle that turned the capstans. After that she still couldn't profess any great enjoyment of the journey, but at least it was tolerable.

Once they had reached Le Havre and traveled to Paris, everything became wonderful. It was summer and France was lovely, the sky clear and luminous. Celia was excited to see her father, brothers, and sisters again. She had written letters to prepare them for the fact that although

Philippe was indeed alive, she was now married
to his brother. She had received a torrent of
shocked, disapproving, and disbelieving replies.

Now that she had introduced Justin to the Verités, she was amused by their reactions. Her bois-
terous family actually seemed to find him
intimidating. She had to admit that even dressed
in the most elegant and conservative clothes, Justin still looked vaguely . . . well, piratical. The
Verités were a pragmatic family who did not like
mysteries and unanswered questions. Usually
they could dissect a stranger inside a quarter of
an hour. But Justin's eyes, bluer than sea or sky,
seemed to mock their indelicate prying.

By the time they left Paris, Celia's sisters were
making calf-eyes at Justin, and her brothers were
repeating tales of his adventures to their friends.
Her father was not so easily convinced of her new
husband's merits, but after conducting a long
conversation with Justin in private, he treated him
with coolness rather than open disapproval. Ruefully Celia reflected that nothing would ever
please her father quite like having a doctor for a
son-in-law, especially one he himself had introduced to his daughter.

When Justin expressed a desire to visit the shipyards and port in Marseilles, they set out from
Paris at once. Now they had been in the port city
for eight weeks, each one more blissful than the
last. For the past few days Justin had spent the
mornings in town, answering Celia's questions
evasively. She knew he was planning something,
and she speculated idly on what it could be.

A shadow blocked the sun on her closed eyelids, and she looked up with a smile. Justin was
there in trousers and bare feet, and a half-open
shirt. The breeze stirred his dark hair. Lowering

his long body beside her, he swept his gaze over her appreciatively.

"You look like a little brioche," he murmured, "warm and golden, and very tasty. I think I'll take a bite out of you."

He leaned over and nipped at her sun-warmed throat, making her fall back and giggle. Disregarding propriety, she had ventured out many times without long sleeves, gloves, bonnets, and frilly parasols, and her milk-white skin had turned a creamy golden color. Her hair, already pale, had lightened to the most brilliant shade of sunlight. Fashionable society decreed that women should shield themselves from the sun, but Celia did not care. There was only Justin to please.

The effect of her glittering hair and golden skin was striking. When Justin took her to the outdoor cafés in the center of town, men literally came off the streets to approach their table, even under Justin's repressive glare. Frenchman appreciated women as much as they did wine, and considered themselves connoisseurs of both.

Celia protested breathlessly as his hand slipped inside her bodice, "Don't, someone will see—"

"The beach is deserted," he returned, kissing her throat. "And if someone does happen along, he'll be French and turn a blind eye to us. The French forgive lovers anything."

"We are not lovers, we are married, and . . ." She sighed in pleasure as his fingers curved over her naked breast. "Justin . . ." she said weakly.

"All right, I'll defer to your modesty, *chérie*. For now." He sat up, pulling her between his thighs so that they both sat facing the water.

She settled her back against his chest with a contented wriggle. "Do not let your hands stray," she warned.

"I'll try. *Pauvre chérie*, a forbearing wife married to a lecherous wolf—"

"Recently an abandoned wife," she said.

"Ah. I wondered how many days would pass before you remarked on my absences. Almost a week. You've been most tolerant."

"Well?"

Justin smiled and watched the ebb and flow of the waves, the silvery sheets of water that spread almost to their feet. He sidestepped her question with one of his own. "You like Marseilles, don't you?"

"*Naturellement.* It is a lovely place, and the people are charming."

"I've been considering . . ." He paused and looked down at the top of her head. "Do you like it enough to stay for a while?"

That caught Celia by surprise. Yes, she would dearly love to stay. However, she had made up her mind that she would never become an encumbrance to him, anchoring him in one place when he longed to be moving. Perhaps this was why he had been gone the past few mornings . . . Yes, he must be restless, he must want to leave. But he was asking how she felt because he would force himself to stay if that was what she desired.

"Well, it would be . . . er, interesting and . . . stimulating to go somewhere new," she said.

"Oh." Justin sounded perturbed. "I thought it might be interesting to settle here for a while."

"*Settle?*" Celia turned around and knelt before him, peering into his face. "*Mon amour*, in your entire life you have never wanted to do such a thing. I know why you suggested it—you think that I require it. But truly my home is wherever you are, and so there is no need—"

His surprised stare turned into a grin. "I've

never wanted to settle somewhere before because I never had someone to settle *with*. If you don't like it well enough here, we'll find somewhere else.''

"But . . . will you not become discontented, staying in one place?''

"Actually, I've taken an interest in the activities at the shipyards. That is where I've been the past mornings. I've decided I would like to build a schooner. I have a particular design in mind, fine-lined, with a sharp bow that would dive through the waves and make her fly.'' His blue eyes gleamed with enthusiasm. "It could be a great folly, of course. But there are men able and ready to work on it here in Marseilles. And I have a yen to spend some of my ill-gotten fortune.''

"A schooner,'' she said, slightly dazed. "But what about all the exotic places you wanted to visit?''

Justin put his hands at her hips and held her there, staring at her seriously. "They'll be waiting for us whenever we wish to see them. But for now I am ready for a home, Celia. I want to belong somewhere with you and . . .'' He glanced down her slim body and back up to her face. "And I want a family,'' he said softly. "Our own family.''

"So do I.'' Celia gave a trembling laugh, her chest suddenly aching with love. "But I am afraid too much domesticity all at once may choke you, monsieur.''

"I know what I want.'' He arched one dark brow while the hint of a dimple appeared in his cheek. "Don't you trust me, little heart?''

"Oh yes,'' she said fervently, and threw her arms around his neck.

Justin laughed in delight and rolled over with

her, pressing her back into the warm, pillowing sand. "Then you agree to stay?"

"I agree to everything."

He pressed a vigorous kiss on her lips. "Intrepid little wife . . . I'll make you glad you took a chance on me."

"You have," she whispered, stroking his brown-black hair from his forehead. "You already have."

Photo by Sigrid Estrada

Lisa Kleypas

is the author of seventeen historical romance novels that have
been published in twelve languages. In 1985, she was named
Miss Massachusetts and competed in the Miss America pageant in
Atlantic City. After graduating from Wellesley College with a
political science degree, she published her first novel at age
twenty-one. Her books have appeared on bestseller lists such as
the *New York Times*, *USA Today*, and *Publishers Weekly*. Lisa is
married and has two children.

"ONE OF TODAY'S LEADING LIGHTS IN ROMANTIC FICTION."
Seattle Times

A breathtaking tale of danger and passion from the phenomenal <u>New York Times</u> bestselling author

LISA KLEYPAS
ONLY WITH YOUR LOVE

Celia Vallerand fears for her life as she stares into the deep, arresting eyes of the dashing man who purchased her from the brigands who had abducted her. But it soon becomes clear that it's her virtue, not her life, that's in danger. The rugged, powerful renegade known only as "Griffin" arouses desires in Celia as dangerous as they are forbidden. And though she knows she must resist him, she fears she may be unable to do so.

But the magnificent adventurer is a man trapped in a perilous deception. And the shocking secrets he guards could deny him the love of the fair captive lady who has enslaved his reckless heart.

ISBN 0-380-76151-3

76151>

0 71001 00750 3